BIZARD
THE BEAR
WIZARD

CHRISSIE KREBS

MARGARET FERGUSON BOOKS
HOLIDAY HOUSE · NEW YORK

Margaret Ferguson Books

HOLIDAY HOUSE is registered in the U.S. Patent and Trademark Office.
Printed and bound in February 2023 at C&C Offset, Shenzhen, China.
The artwork was created digitally using Artstudio Pro program.
www.holidayhouse.com
First Edition
1 3 5 7 9 10 8 6 4 2

Library of Congress Cataloging-in-Publication Data

Names: Krebs, Chrissie, author.
Title: Bizard the Bear Wizard / by Chrissie Krebs.
Description: First edition. | New York : Holiday House, [2023] | Audience:
Ages 9–12 . | Audience: Grades 4–6. | Summary: A bear reluctantly
becomes a wizard when a magic wand crashes into his head, and he uses
his powers to protect the forest animals from an evil wolf.
Identifiers: LCCN 2022013185 | ISBN 9780823451456 (hardcover)
Subjects: CYAC: Graphic novels. | Bears—Fiction. | Forest
animals—Fiction. | Magic—Fiction. | Wishes—Fiction. | LCGFT: Animal
fiction. | Graphic novels.
Classification: LCC PZ7.7.K716 Bi 2023 | DDC 741.5/994—dc23/eng/20220707
LC record available at https://lccn.loc.gov/2022013185

ISBN: 978-0-8234-5145-6 (hardcover)
ISBN: 978-0-8234-5487-7 (paperback)

FOR JEROME

CONTENTS

CHAPTER 1

A DAY IN THE LIFE OF A BEAR

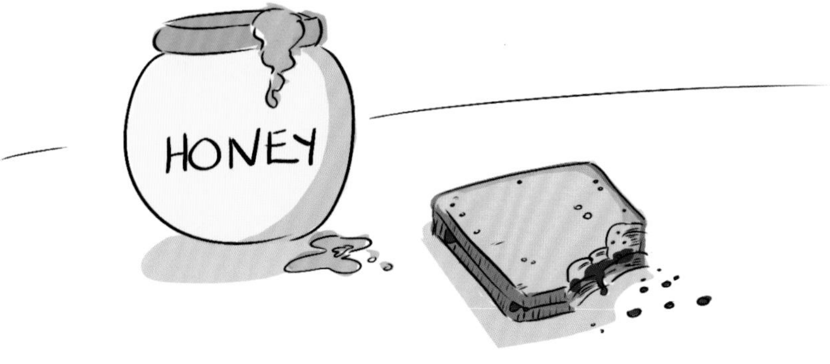
HONEY

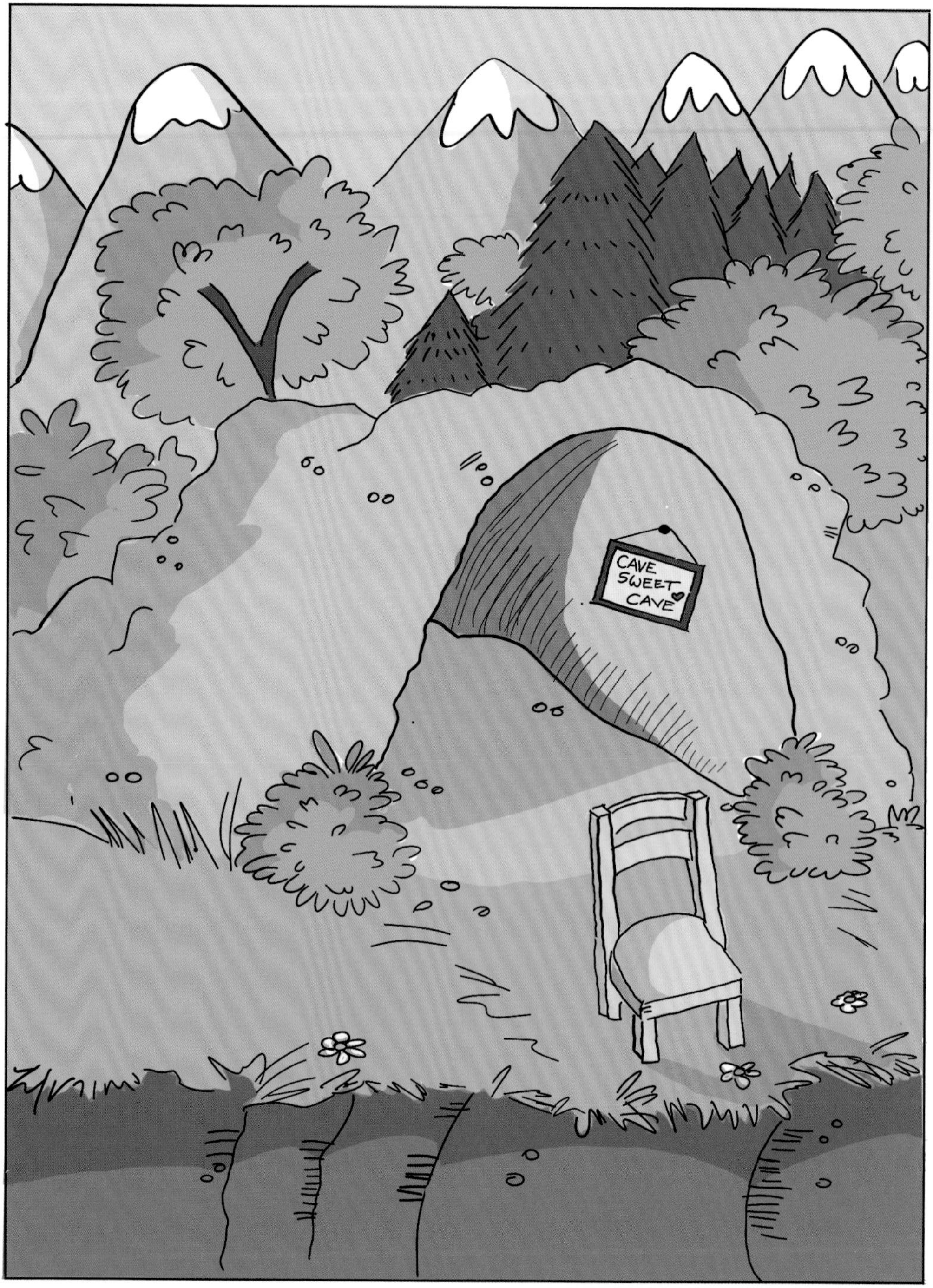
CAVE SWEET CAVE

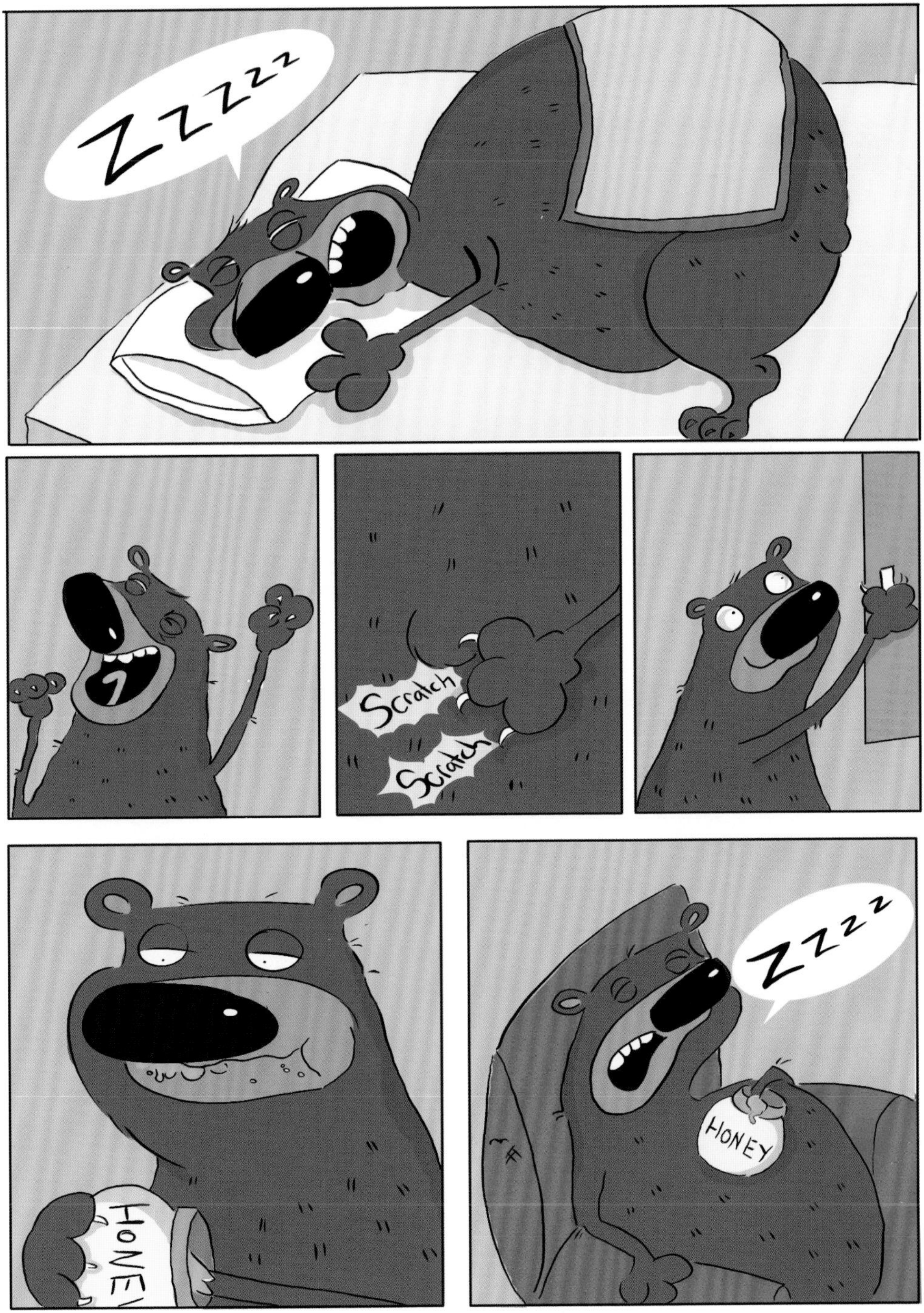
Zzzzzz
Scratch
Scratch
HONEY
Zzzz
HONEY

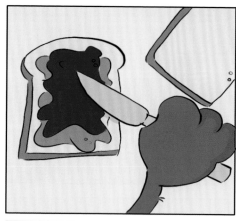

Can't wait to do this all again tomorrow!

CHAPTER 2
THAT WINDY DAY

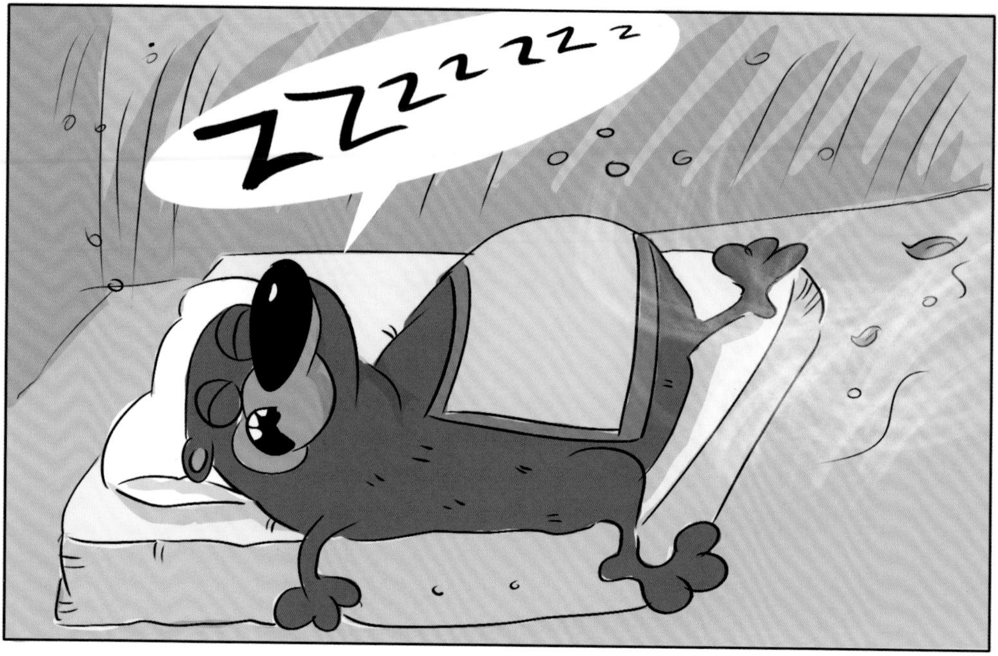
ZZZZZZZZZ

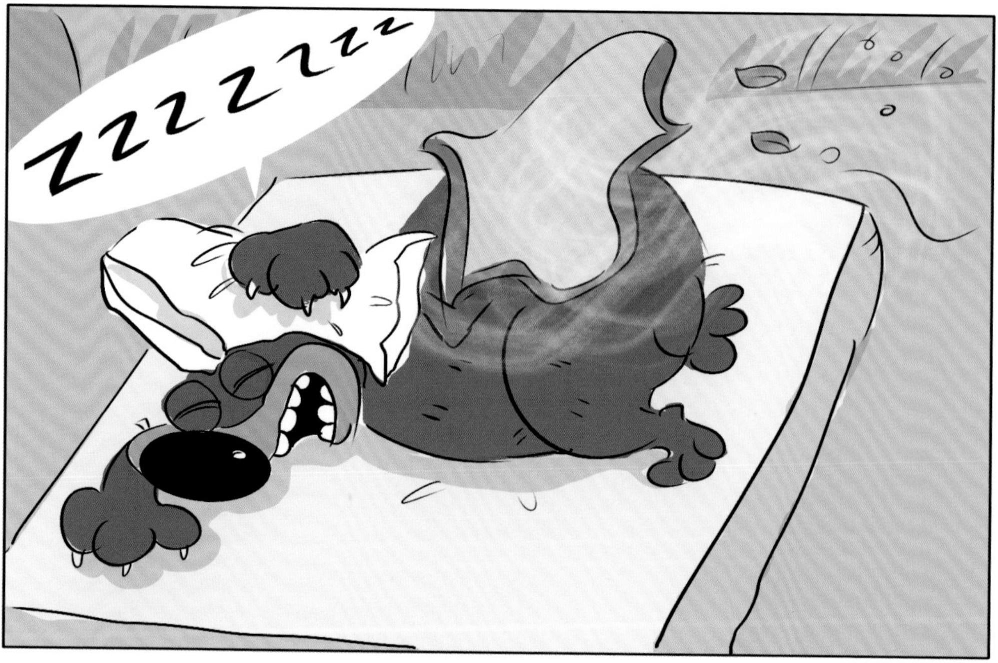
ZZZZZZZZ

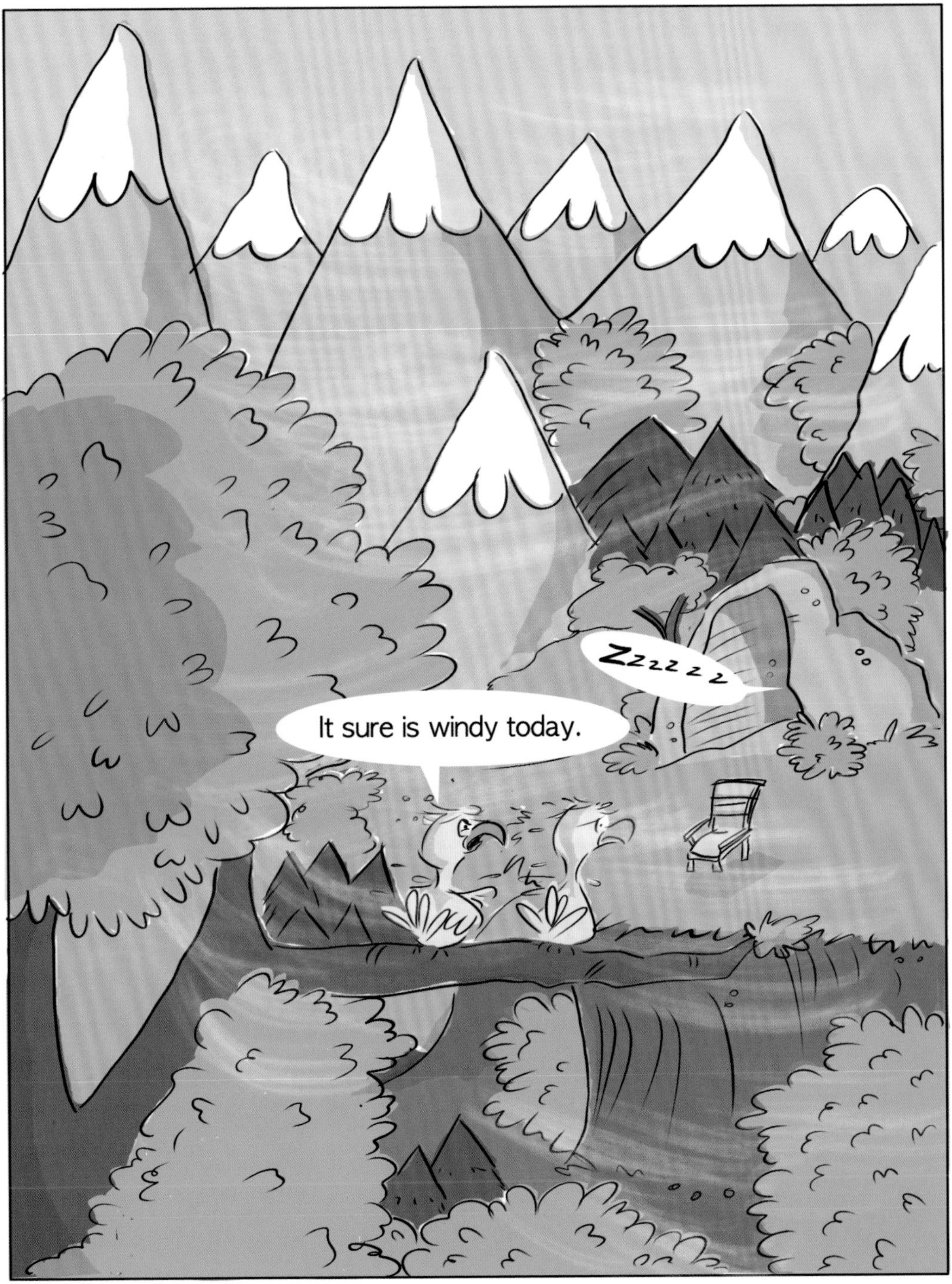
Zzzzzz
It sure is windy today.

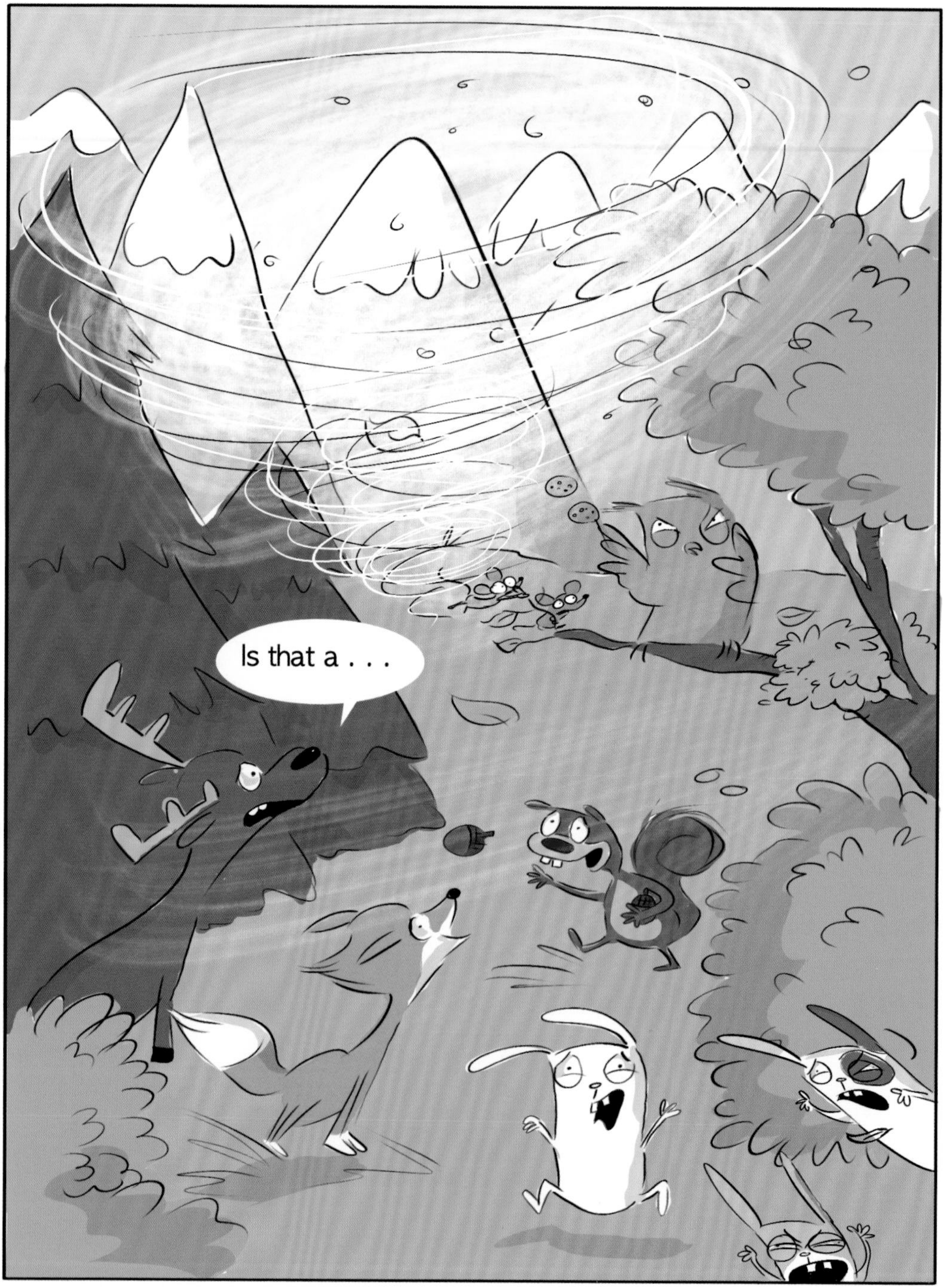
Is that a . . .

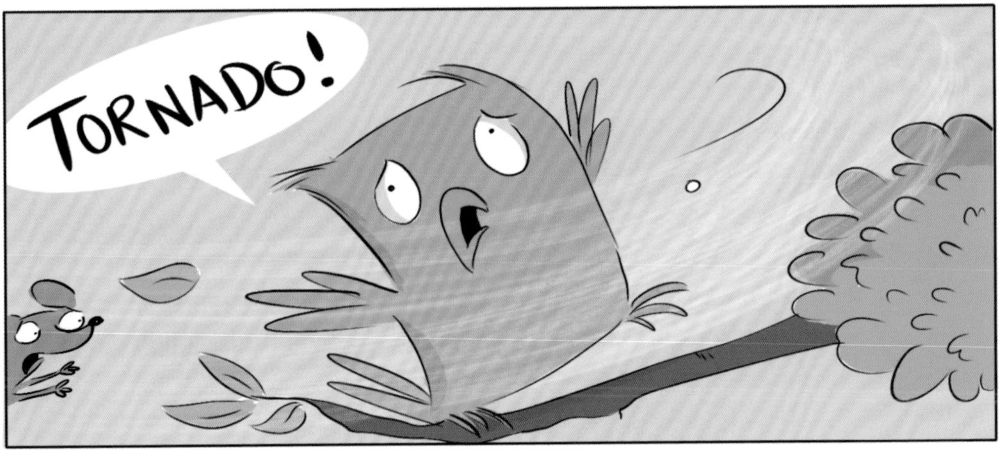
TORNADO!

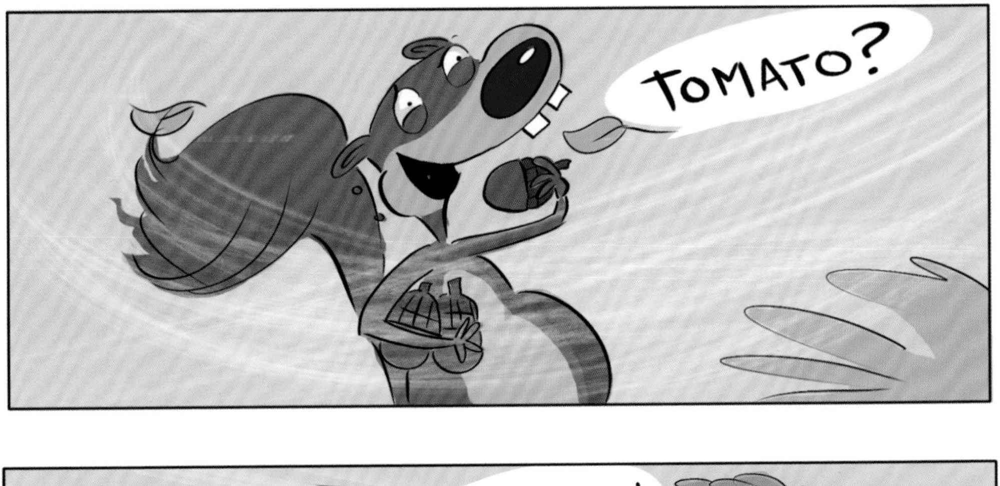
TOMATO?

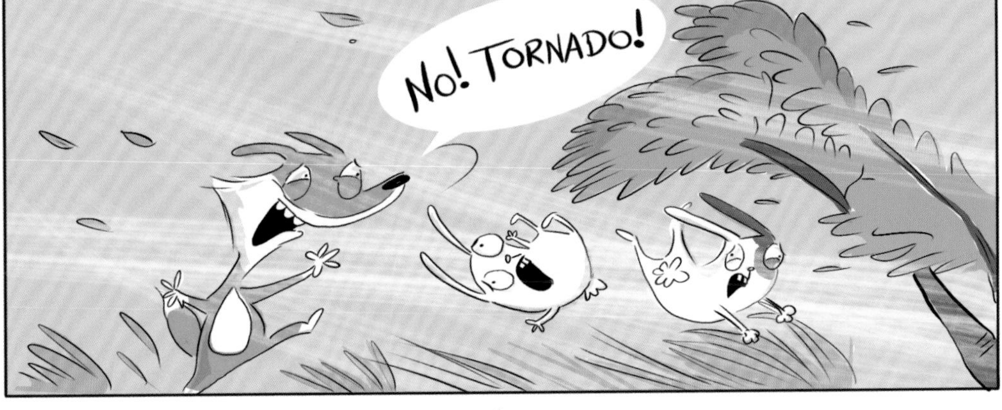
NO! TORNADO!

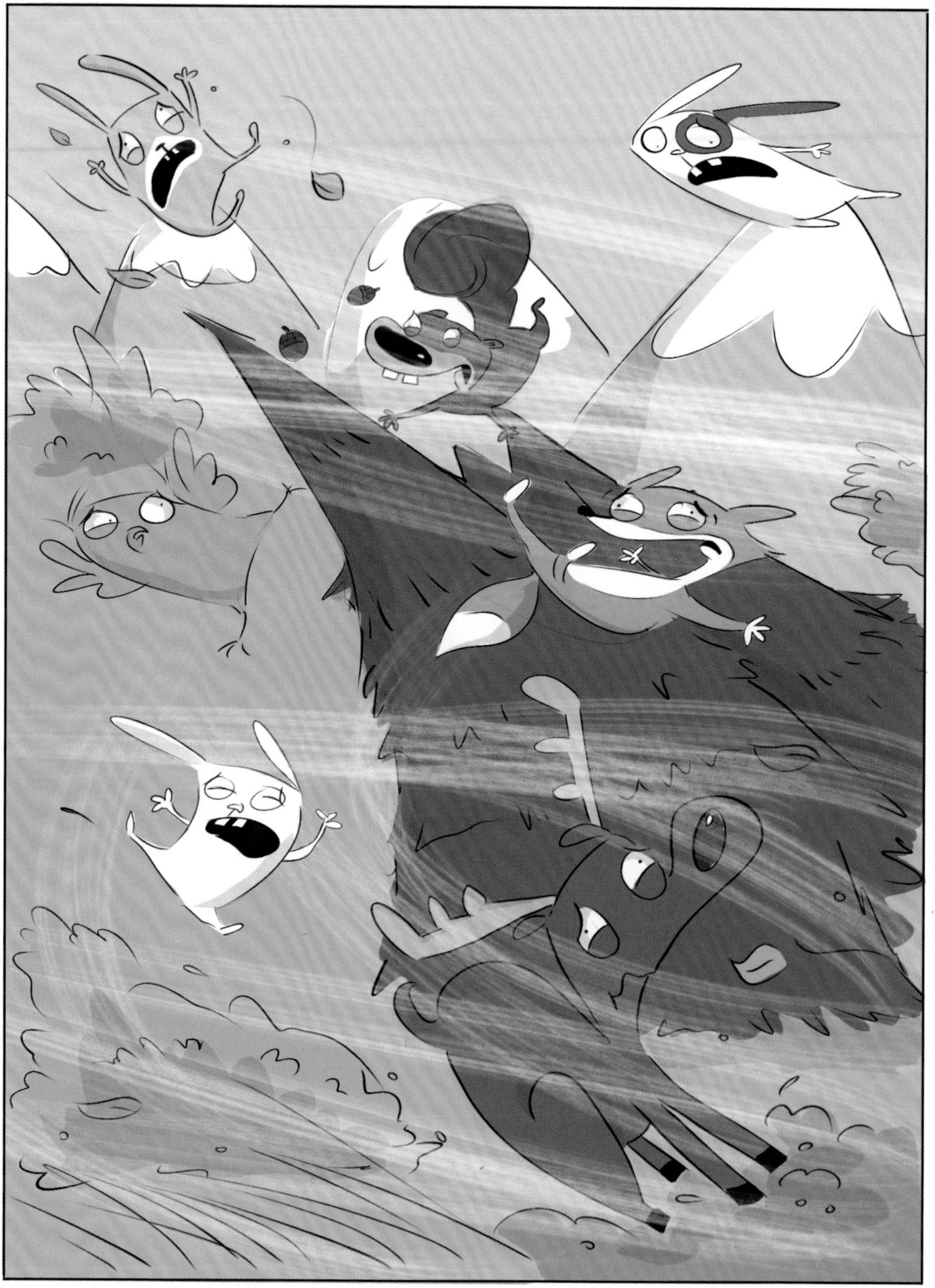

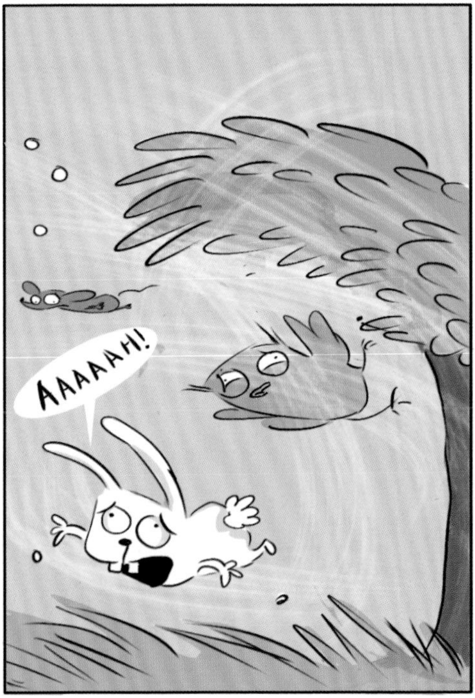
AAAAAH!

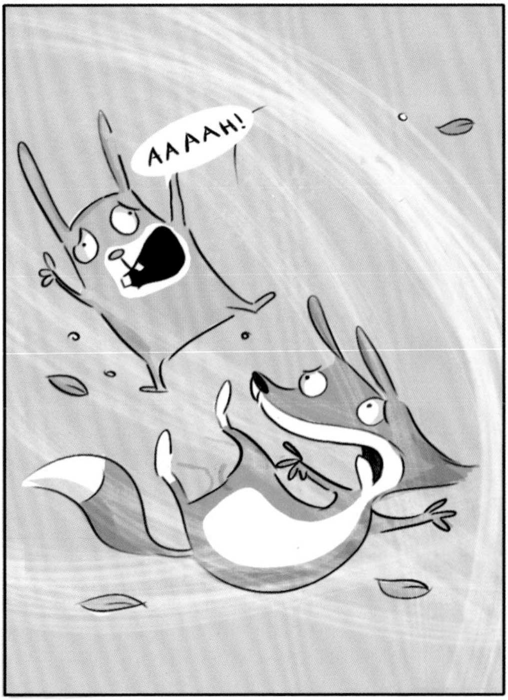
AAAAH!

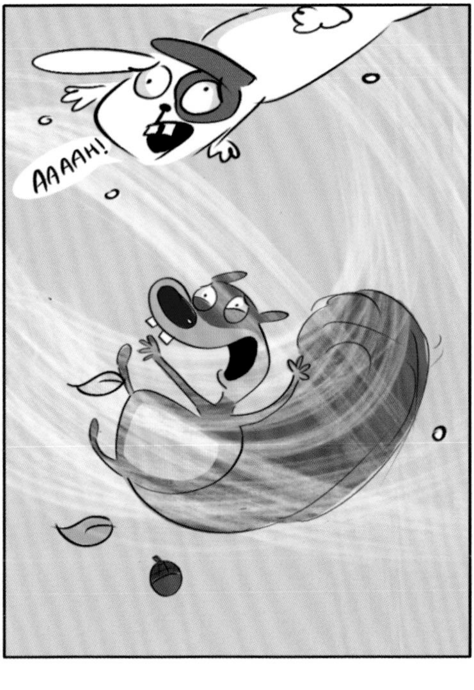
AAAAH!

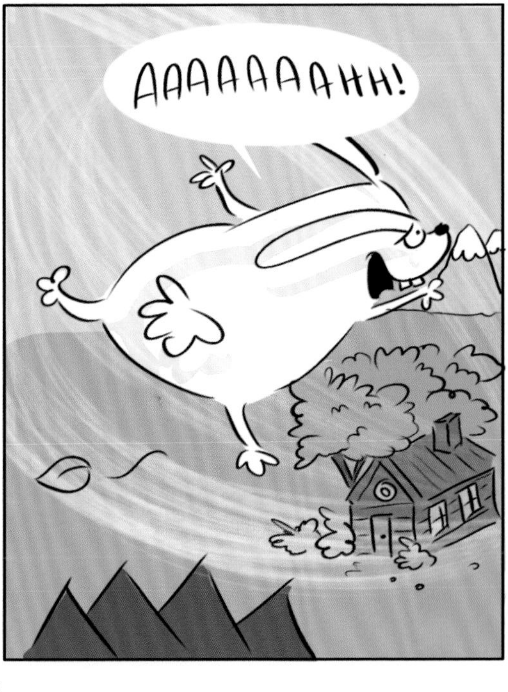
AAAAAAAHH!

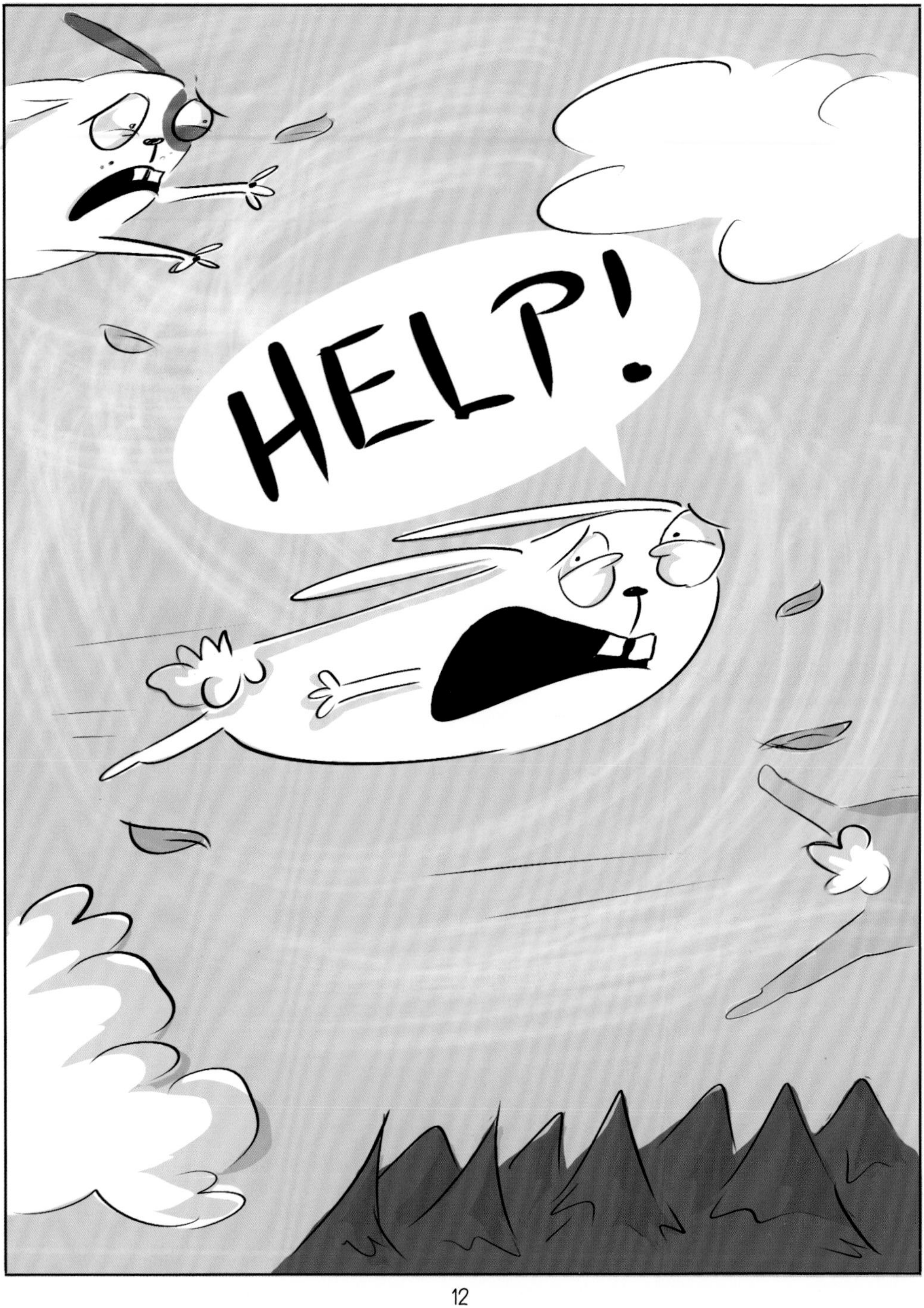
HELP!

CHAPTER 3

THE WIZARD AND THE WAND

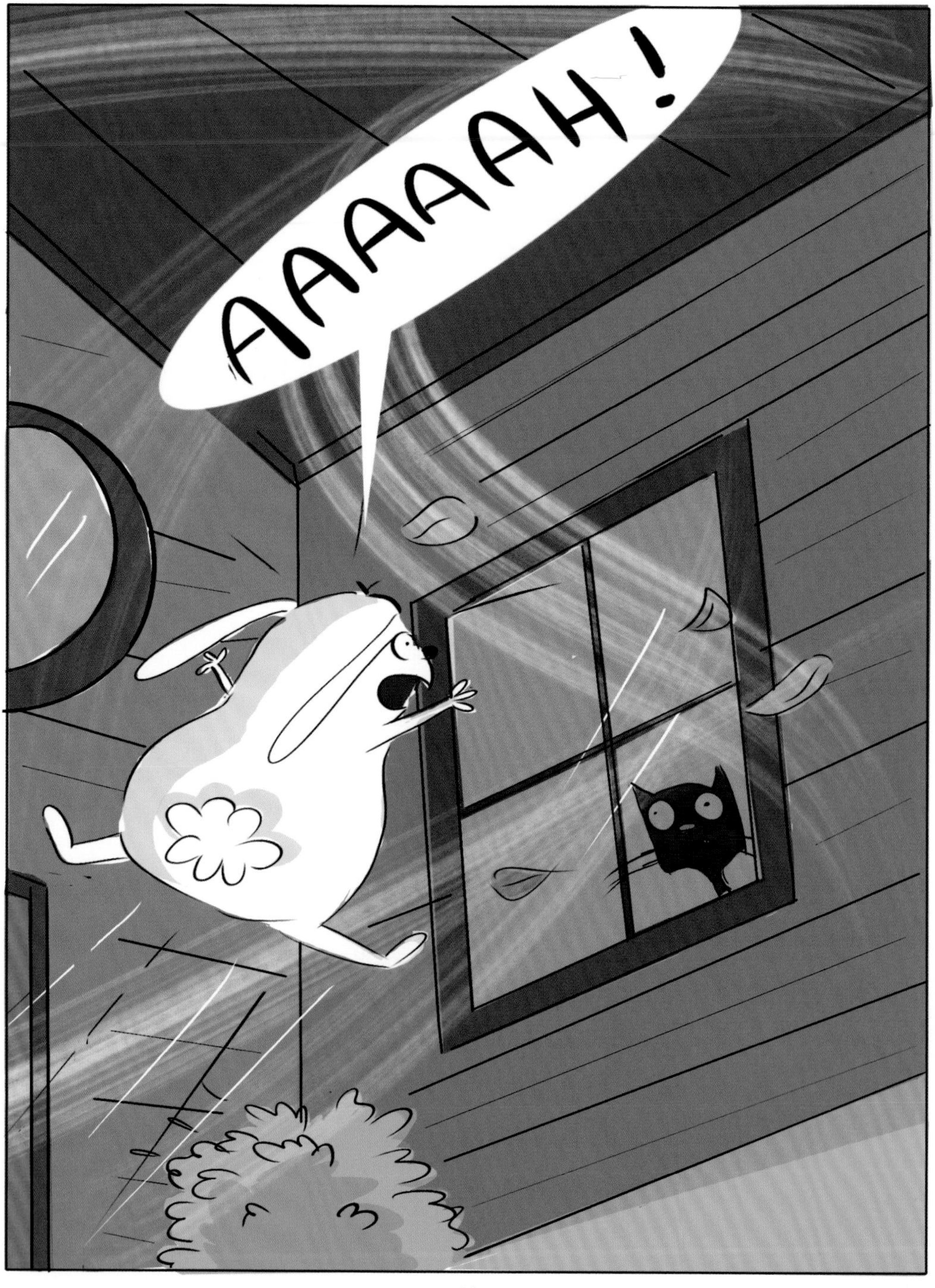
AAAAAH!

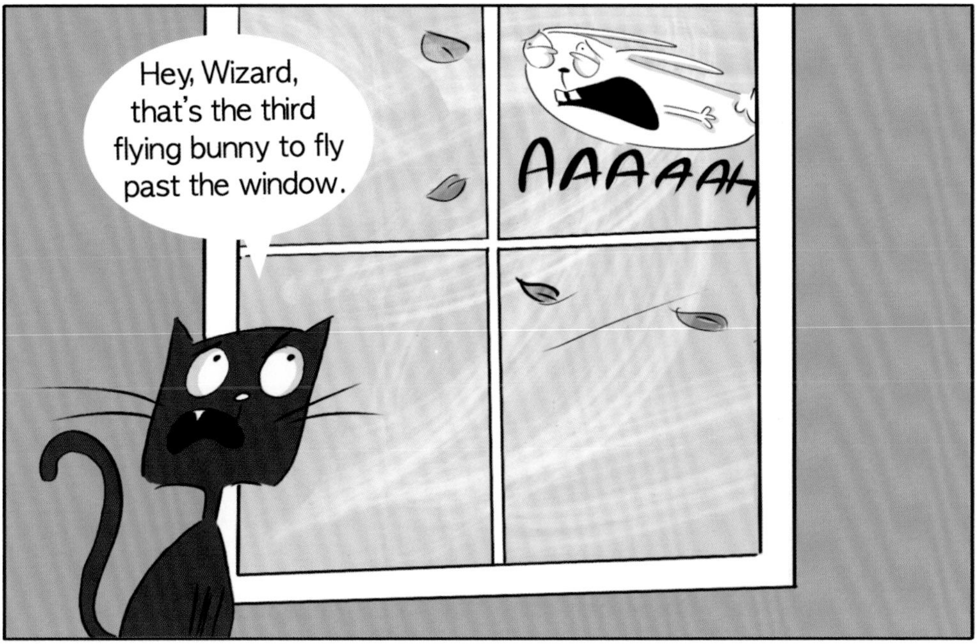
Hey, Wizard, that's the third flying bunny to fly past the window.
AAAAAH

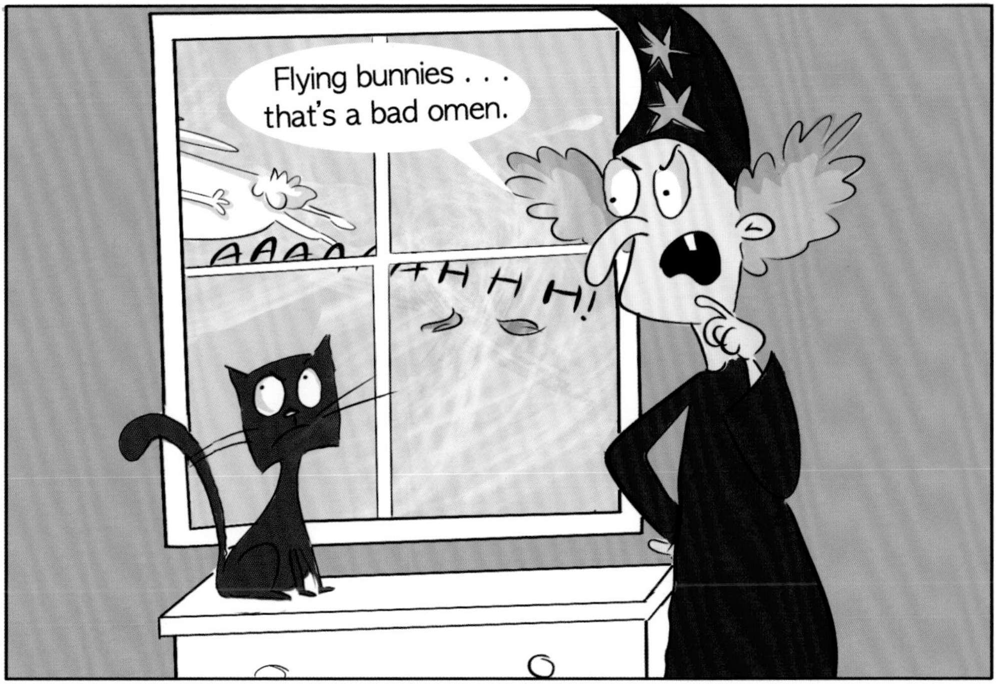
Flying bunnies . . . that's a bad omen.

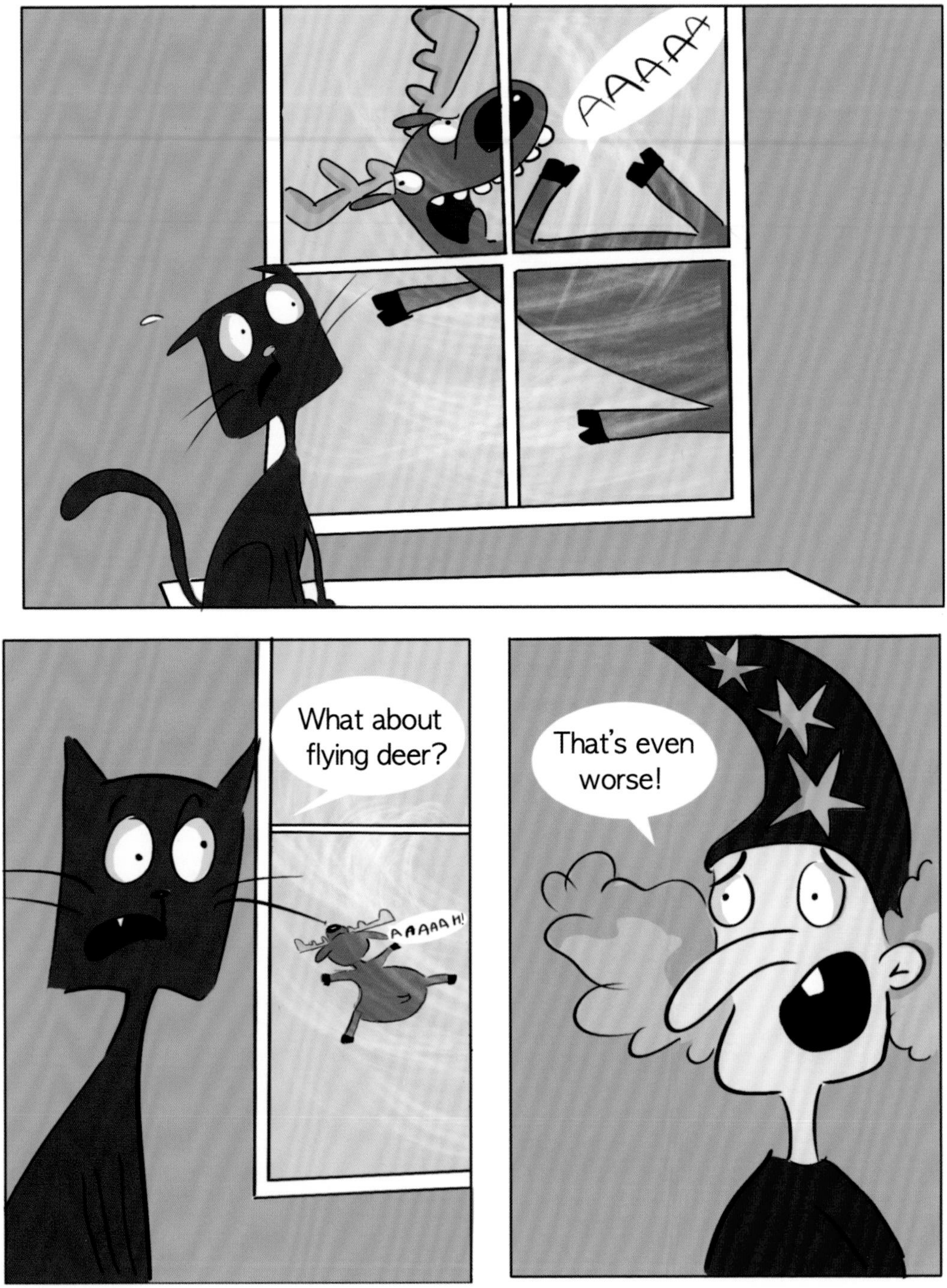
AAAAA
What about flying deer?
AAAAAH!
That's even worse!

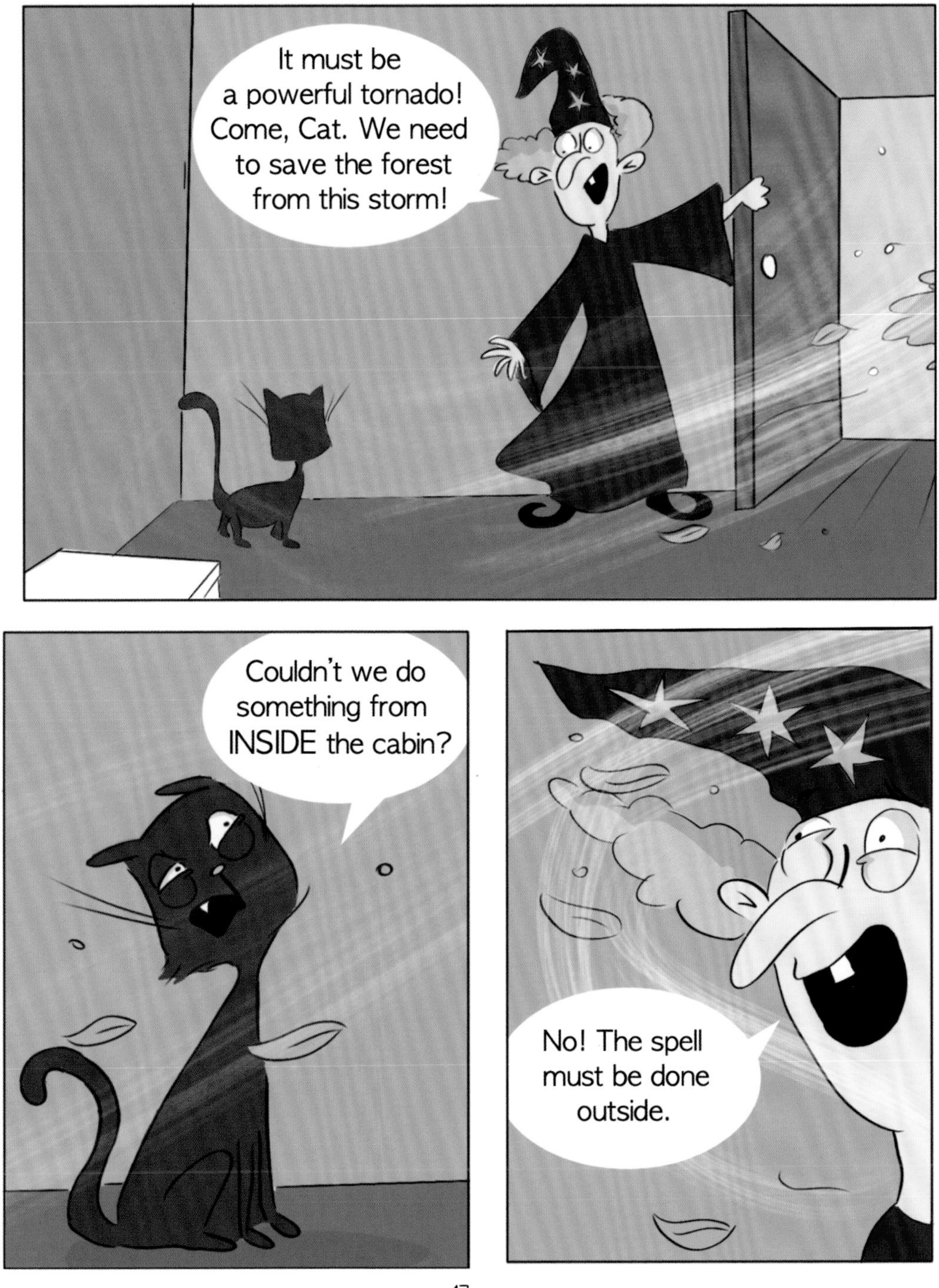
It must be a powerful tornado! Come, Cat. We need to save the forest from this storm!
Couldn't we do something from INSIDE the cabin?
No! The spell must be done outside.

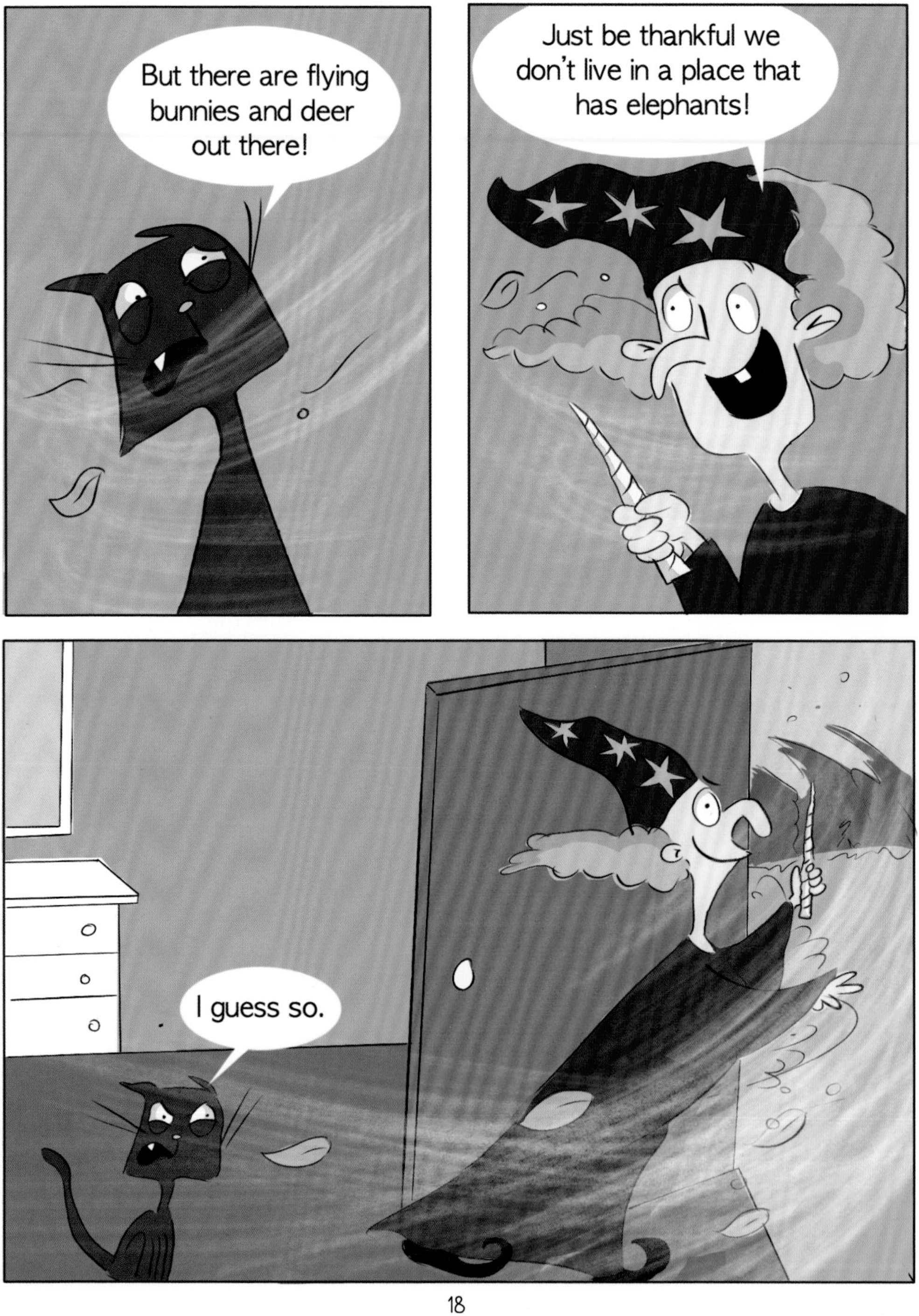
But there are flying bunnies and deer out there!
Just be thankful we don't live in a place that has elephants!
I guess so.

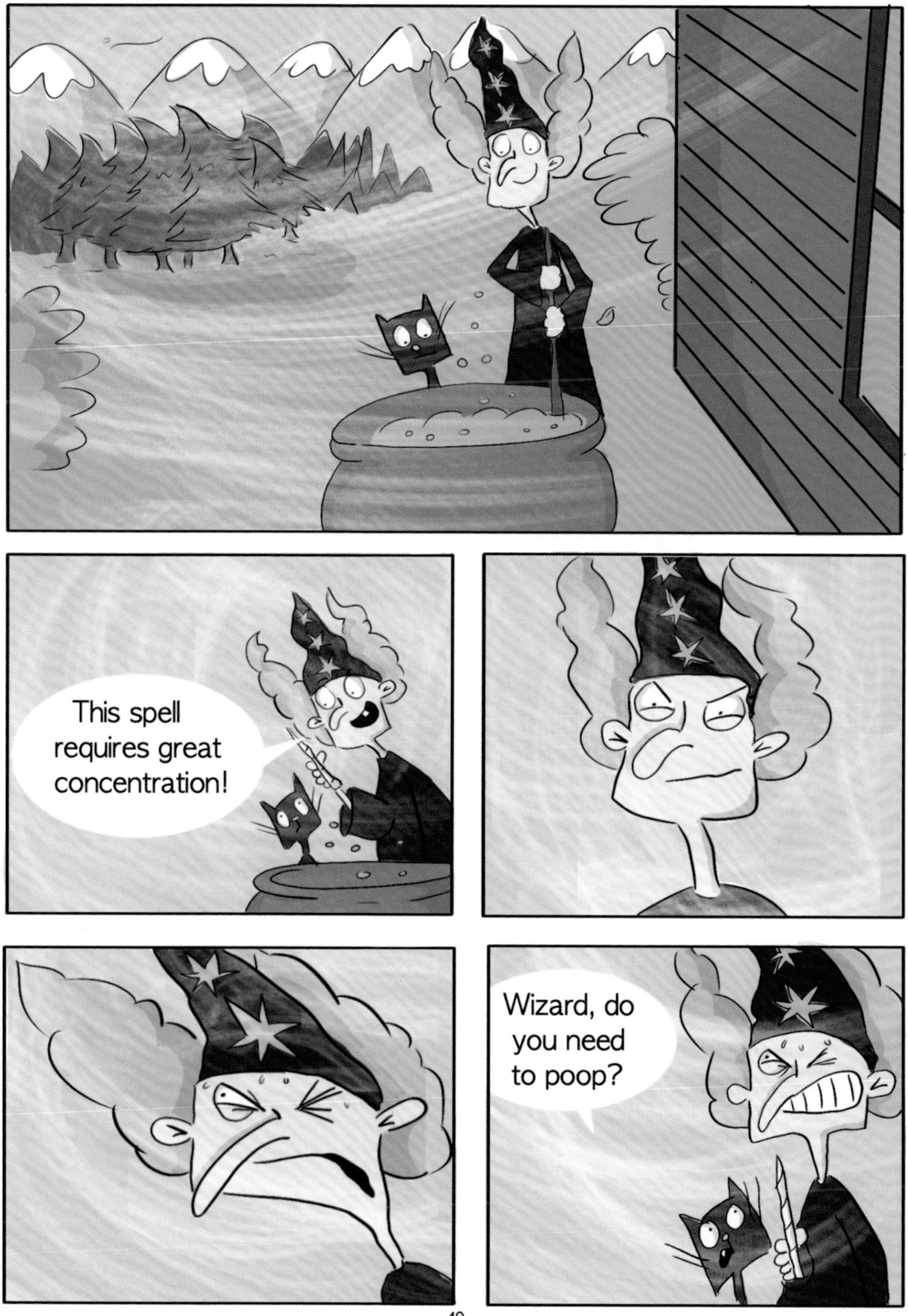
This spell requires great concentration!
Wizard, do you need to poop?

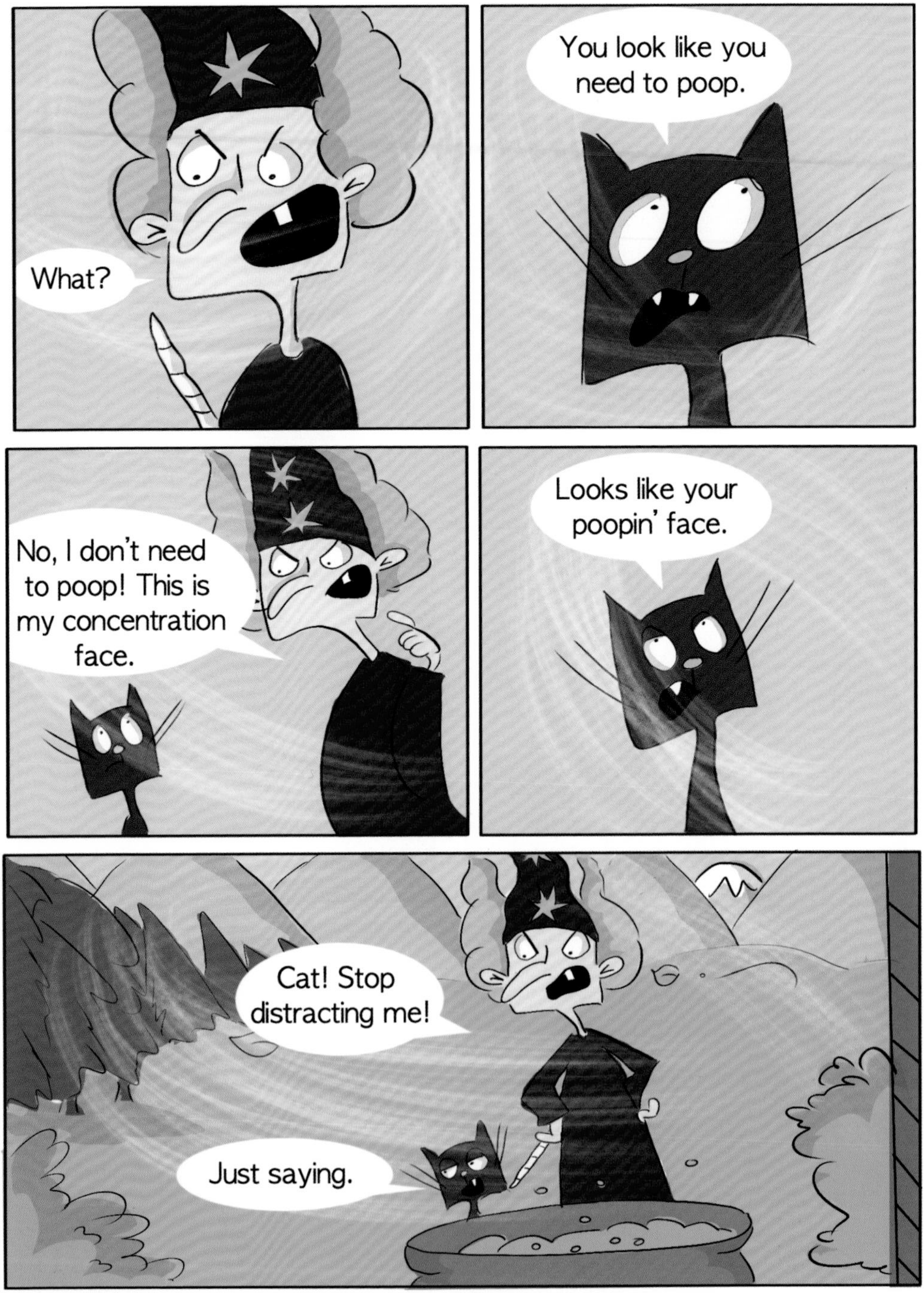
What?
You look like you need to poop.
No, I don't need to poop! This is my concentration face.
Looks like your poopin' face.
Cat! Stop distracting me!
Just saying.

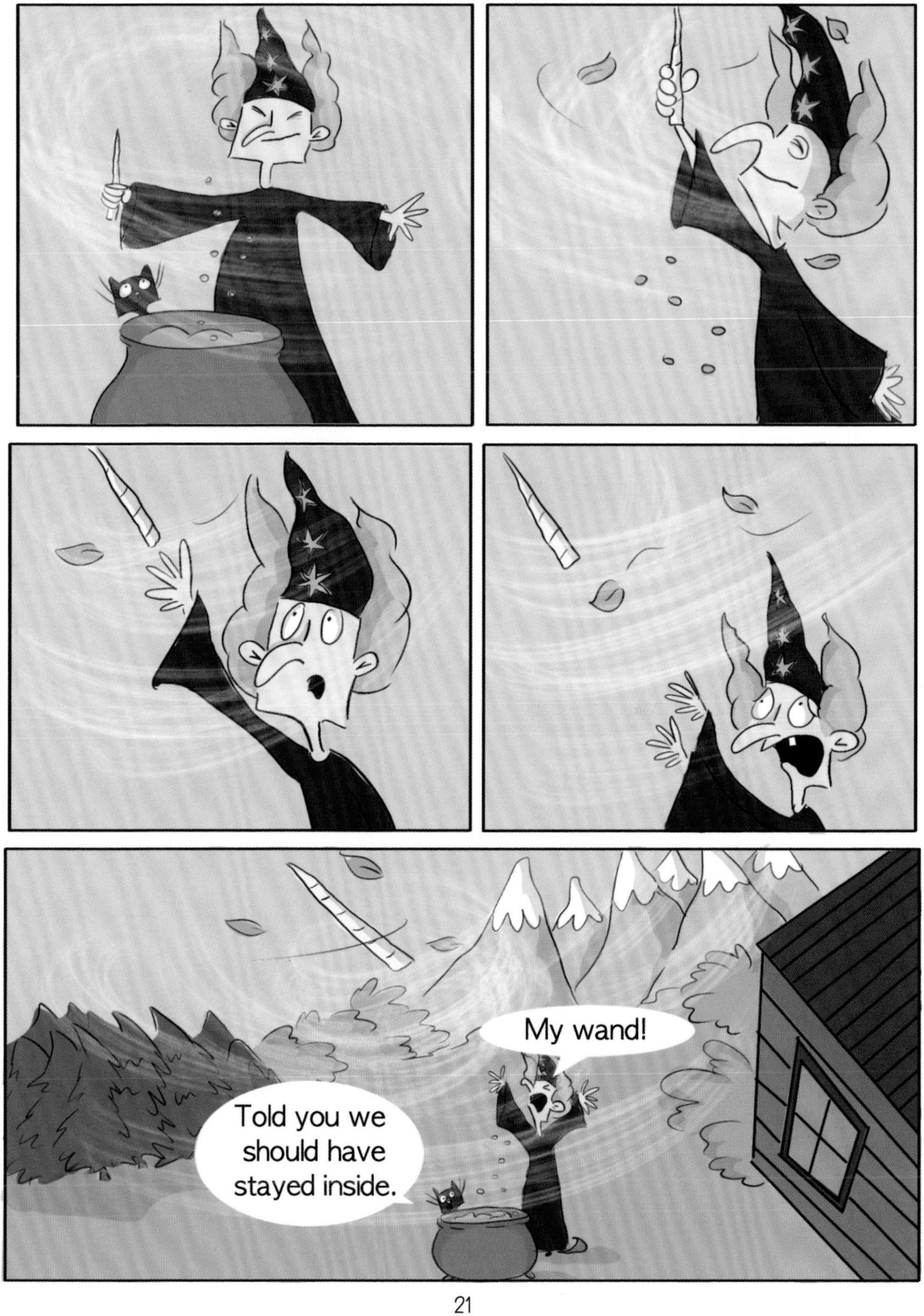
My wand!
Told you we should have stayed inside.

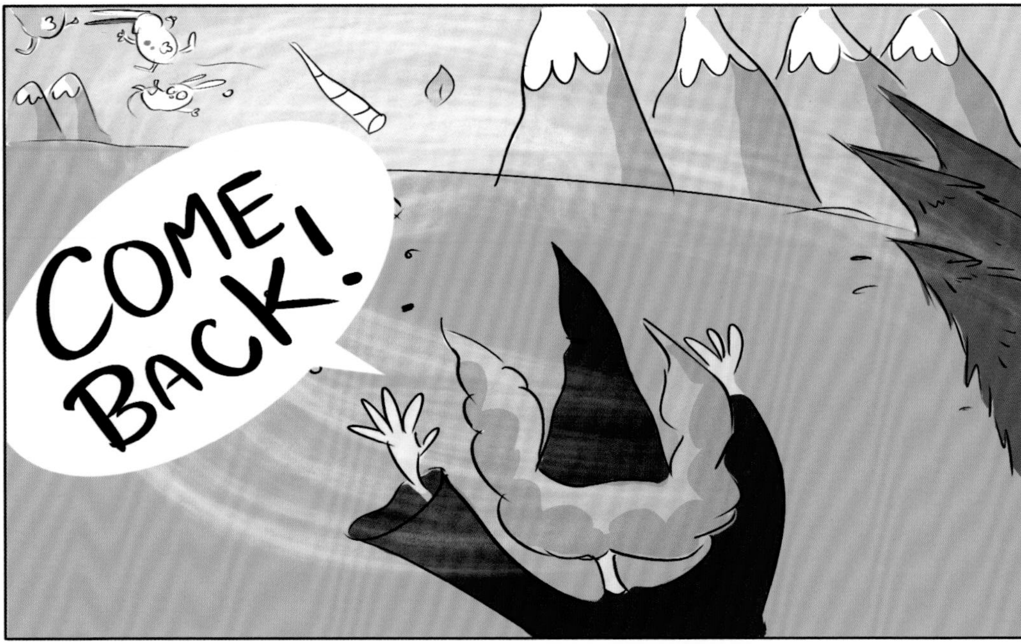
COME BACK!

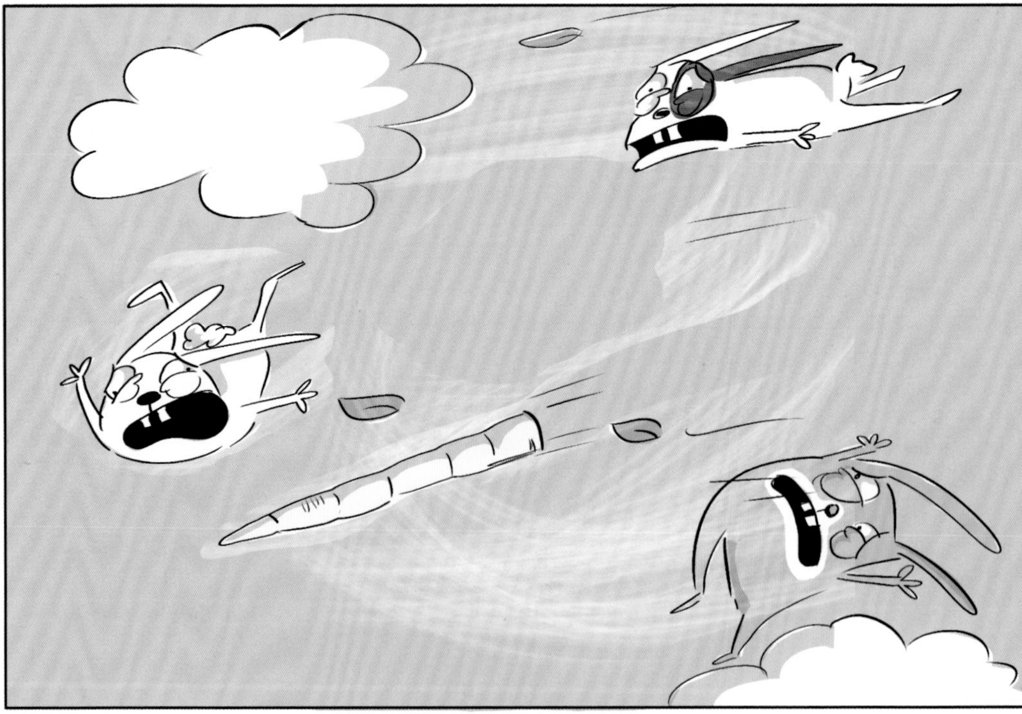

CHAPTER 4
THE
MAGIC HEAD STICK

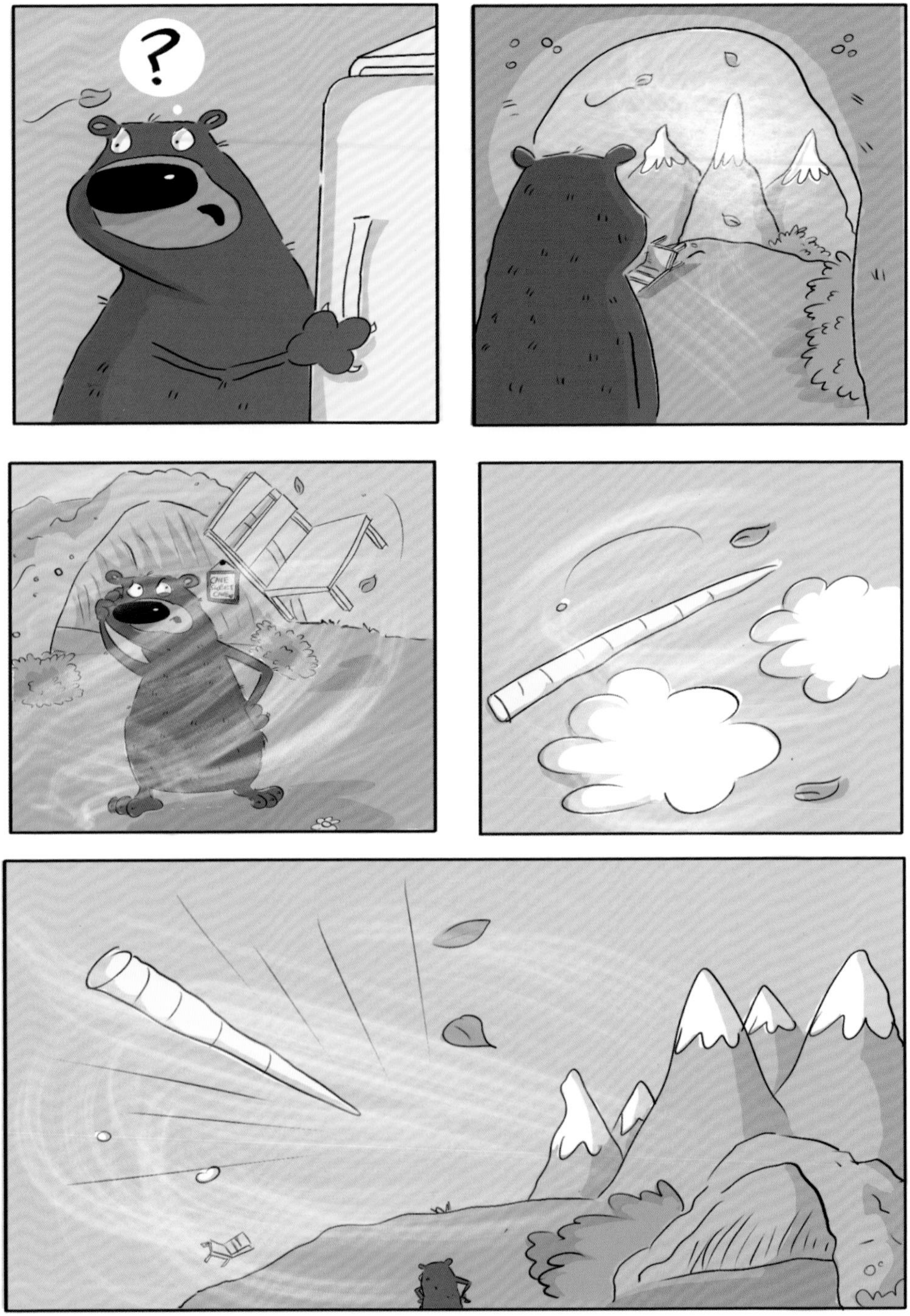
?

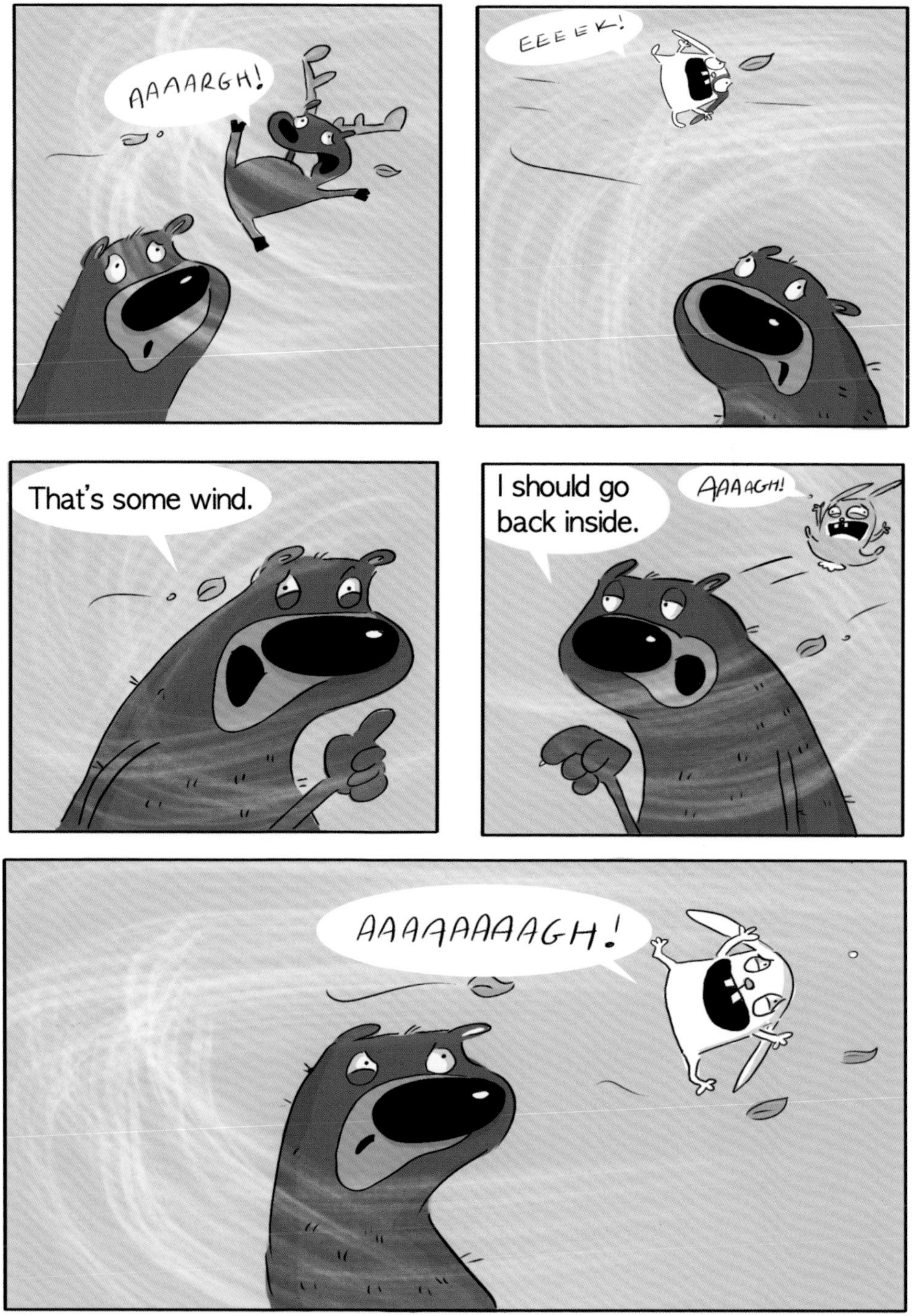
AAAARGH!
EEEEK!
That's some wind.
I should go back inside.
AAAAGH!
AAAAAAAAGH!

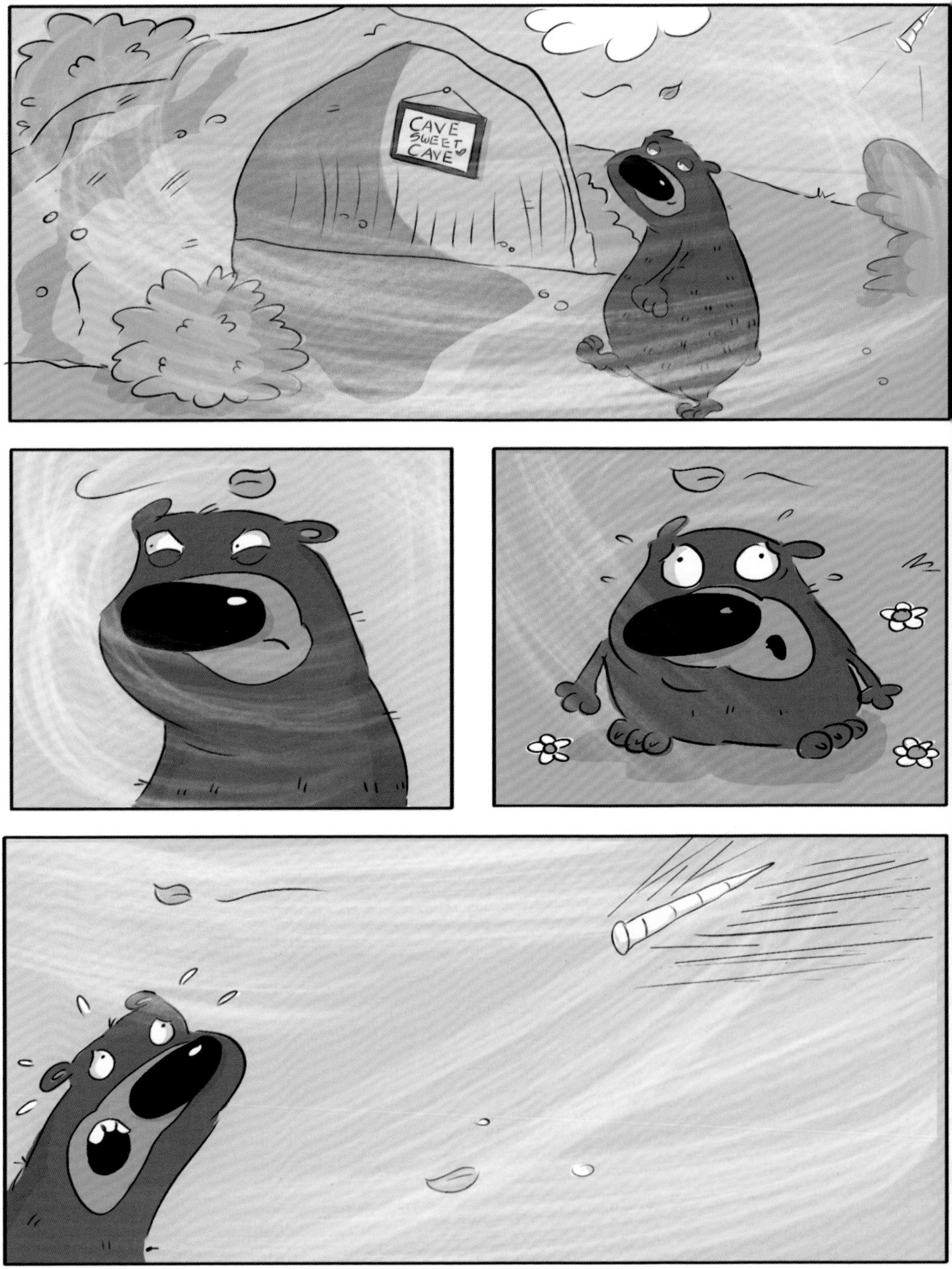
CAVE SWEET CAVE

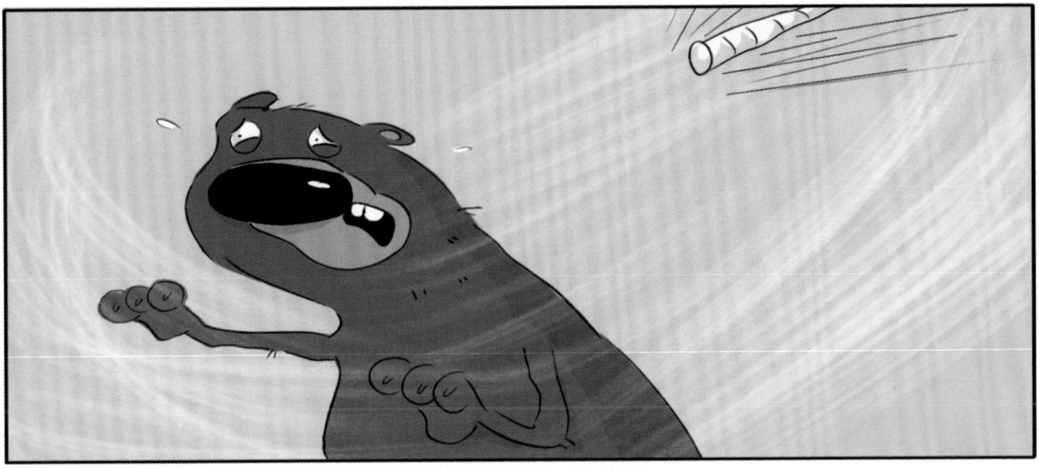

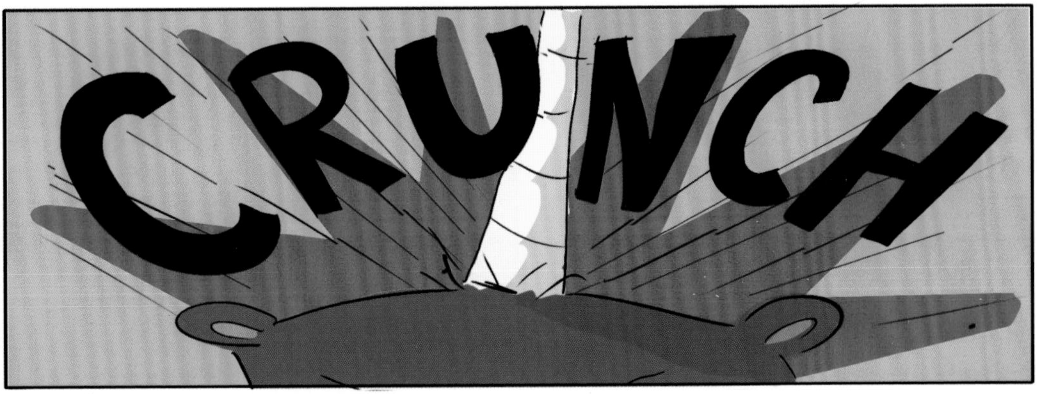
CRUNCH

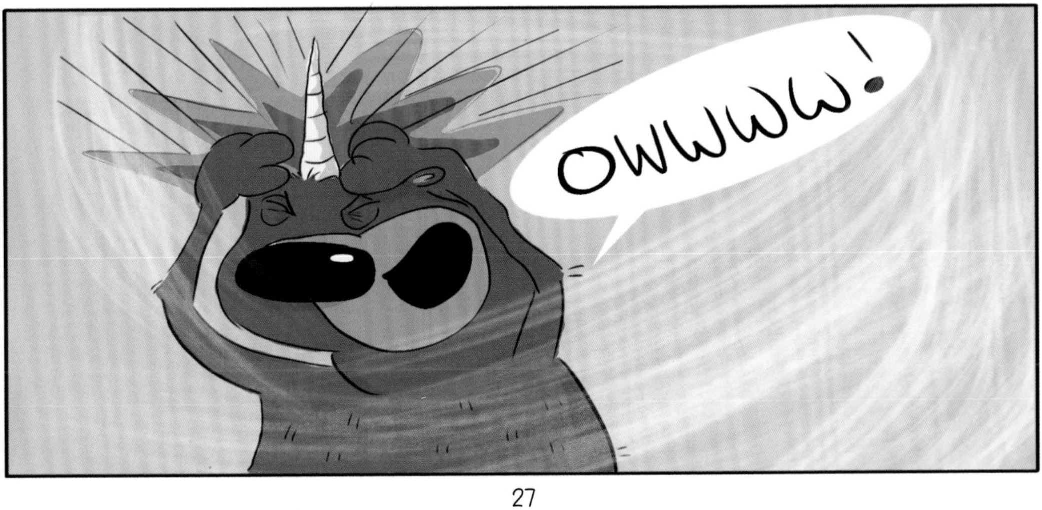
OWWWW!

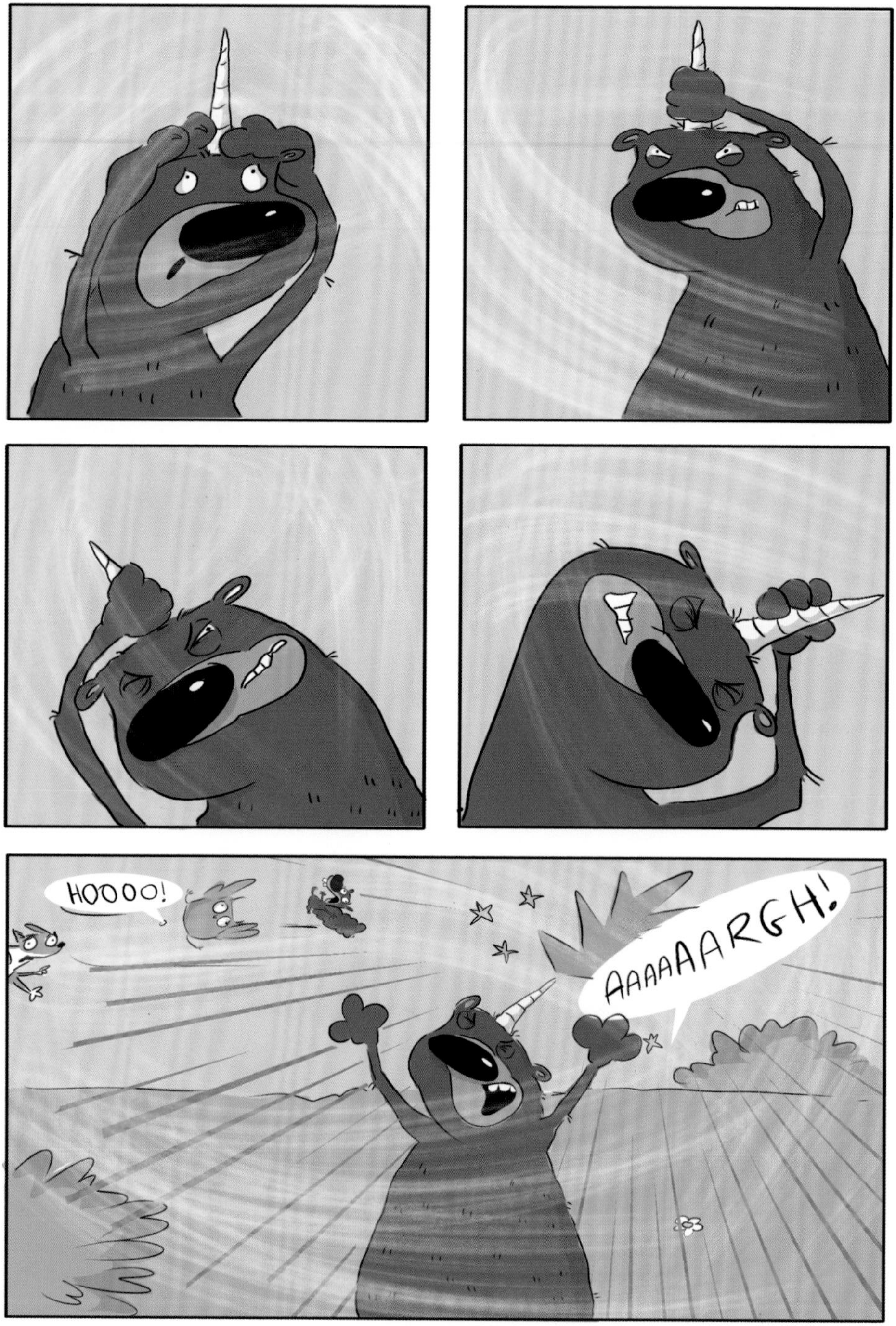
HOOOO!
AAAAAARGH!

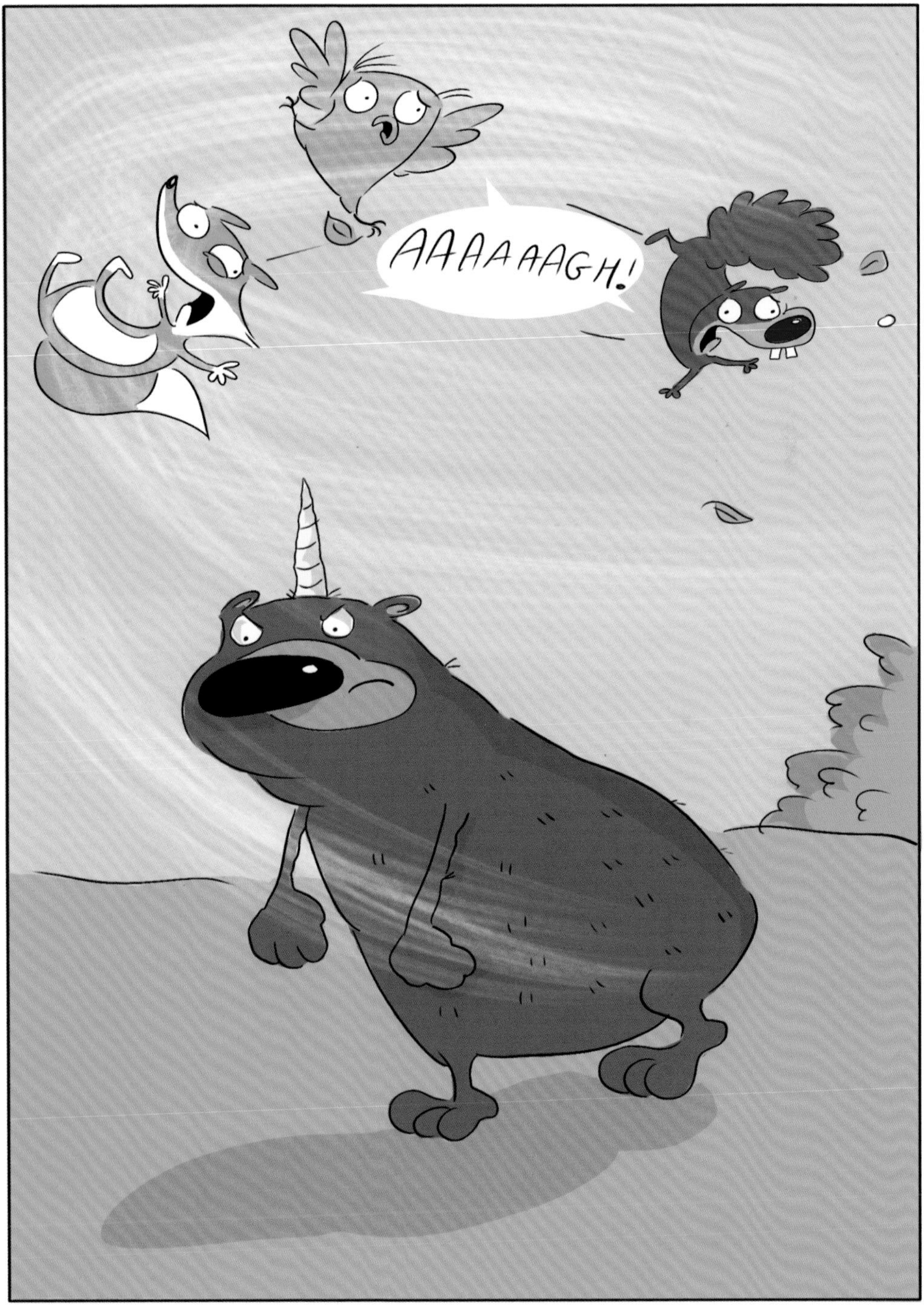
AAAAAAGH!

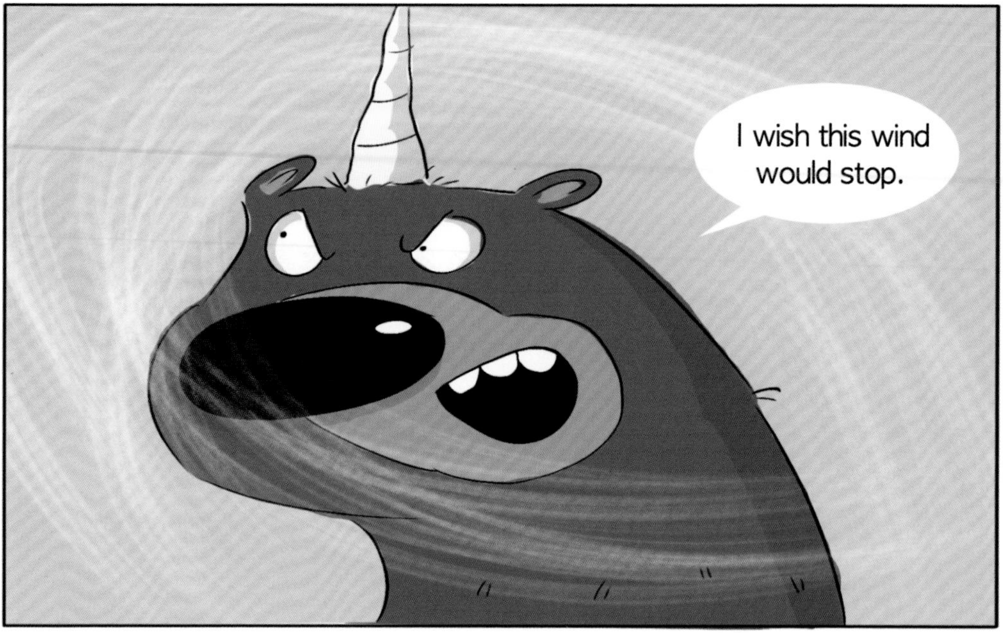
I wish this wind
would stop.

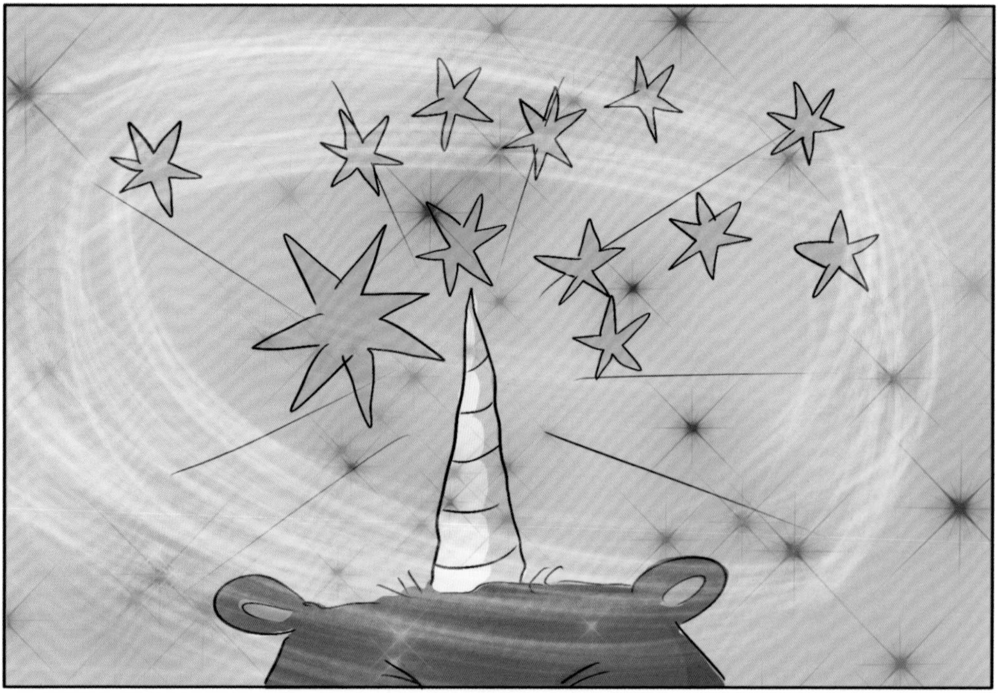

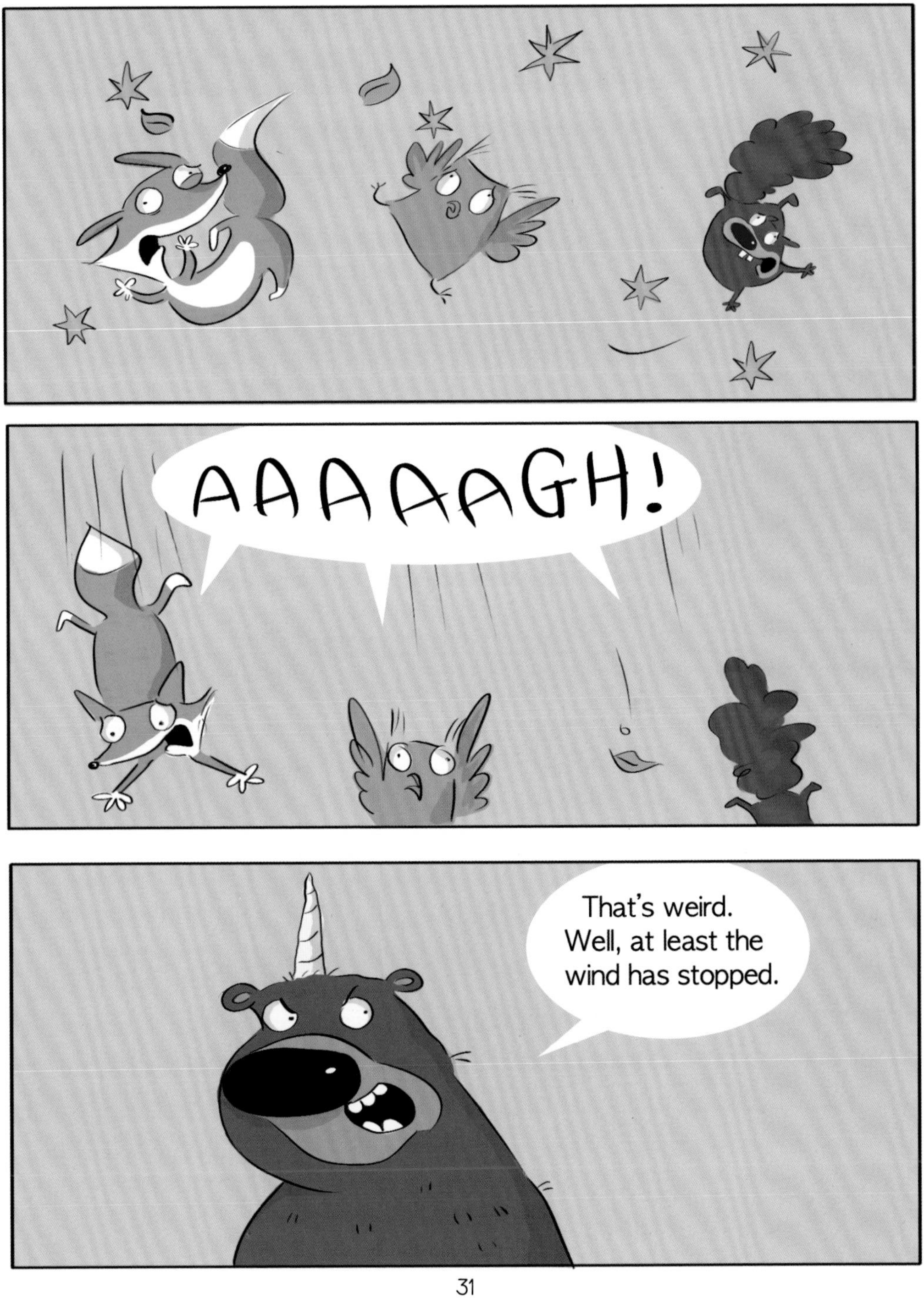
AAAAAGH!
That's weird. Well, at least the wind has stopped.

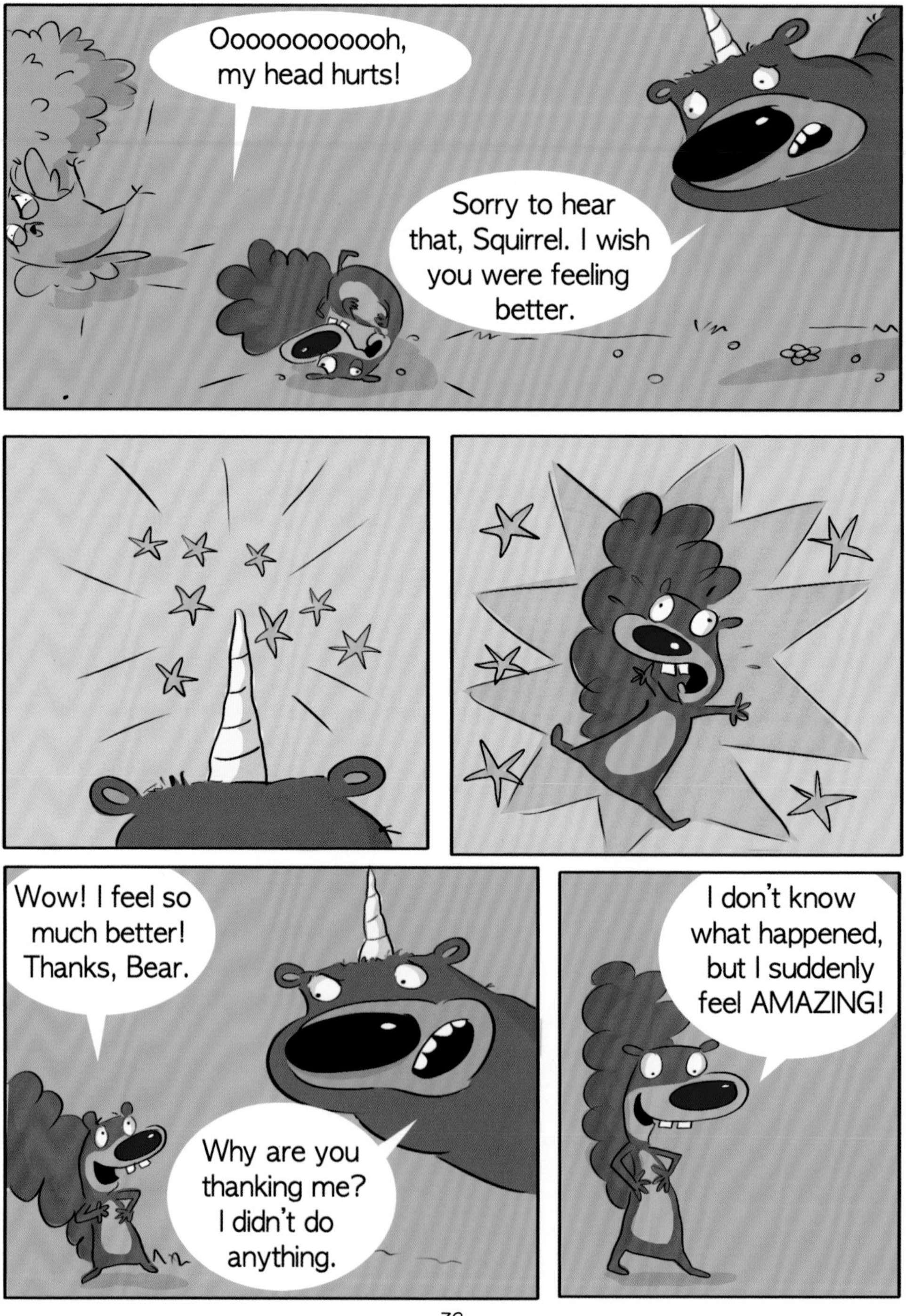
Oooooooooooh, my head hurts!
Sorry to hear that, Squirrel. I wish you were feeling better.
Wow! I feel so much better! Thanks, Bear.
Why are you thanking me? I didn't do anything.
I don't know what happened, but I suddenly feel AMAZING!

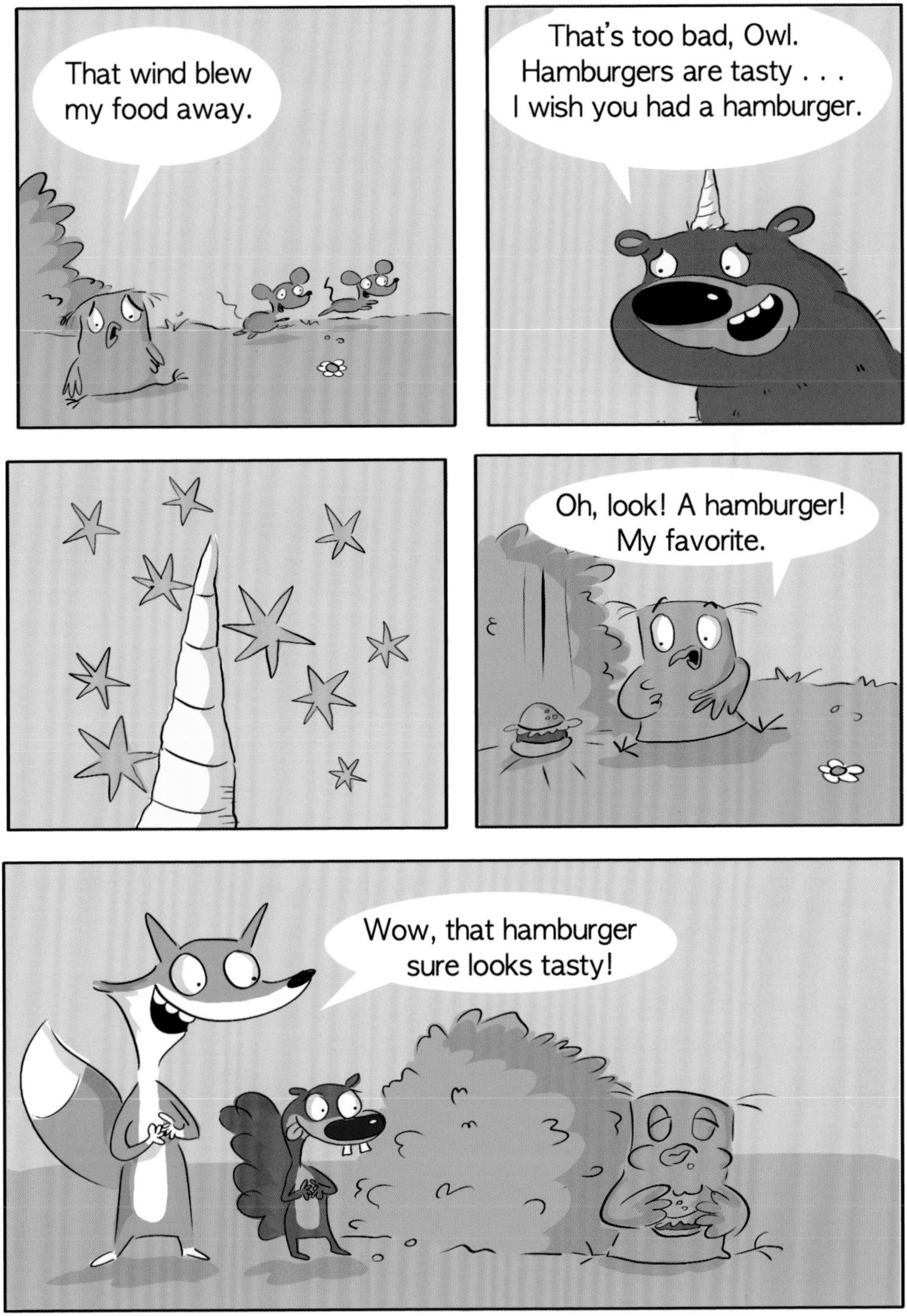
That wind blew my food away.
That's too bad, Owl. Hamburgers are tasty . . . I wish you had a hamburger.
Oh, look! A hamburger! My favorite.
Wow, that hamburger sure looks tasty!

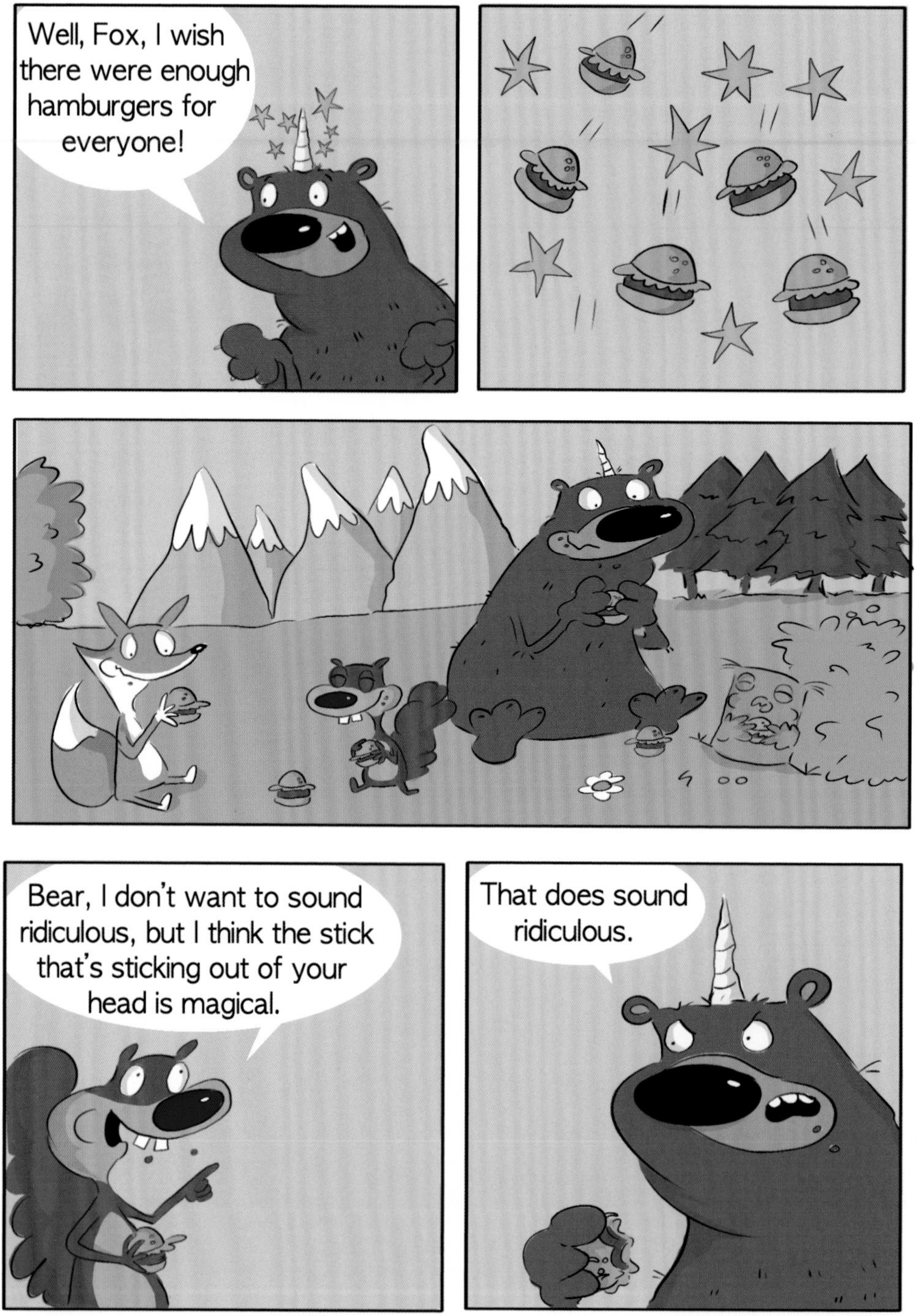
Well, Fox, I wish there were enough hamburgers for everyone!
Bear, I don't want to sound ridiculous, but I think the stick that's sticking out of your head is magical.
That does sound ridiculous.

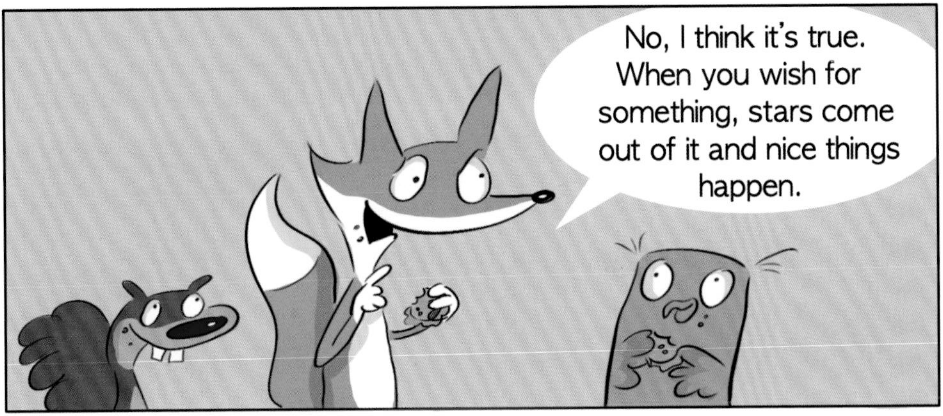
No, I think it's true. When you wish for something, stars come out of it and nice things happen.

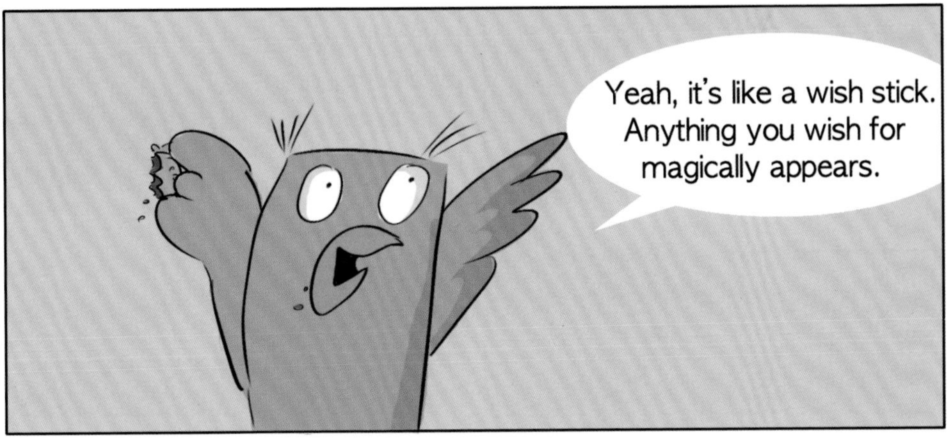
Yeah, it's like a wish stick. Anything you wish for magically appears.

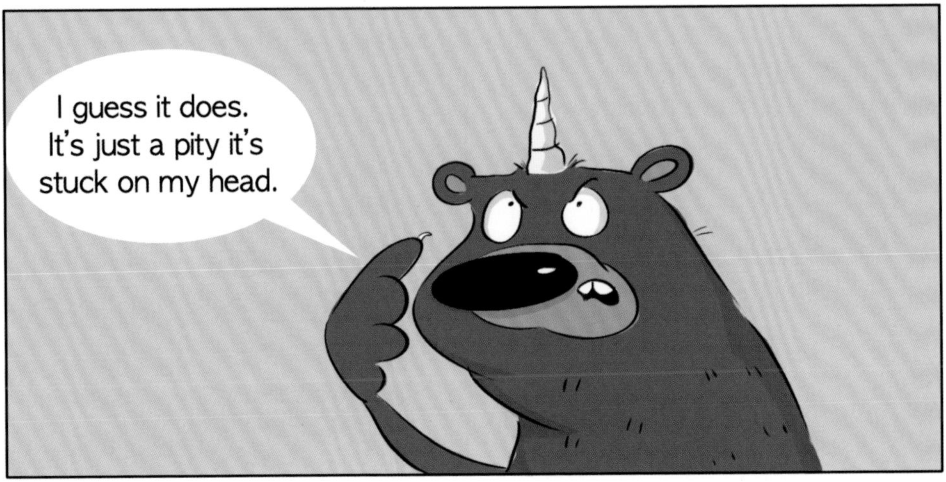
I guess it does. It's just a pity it's stuck on my head.

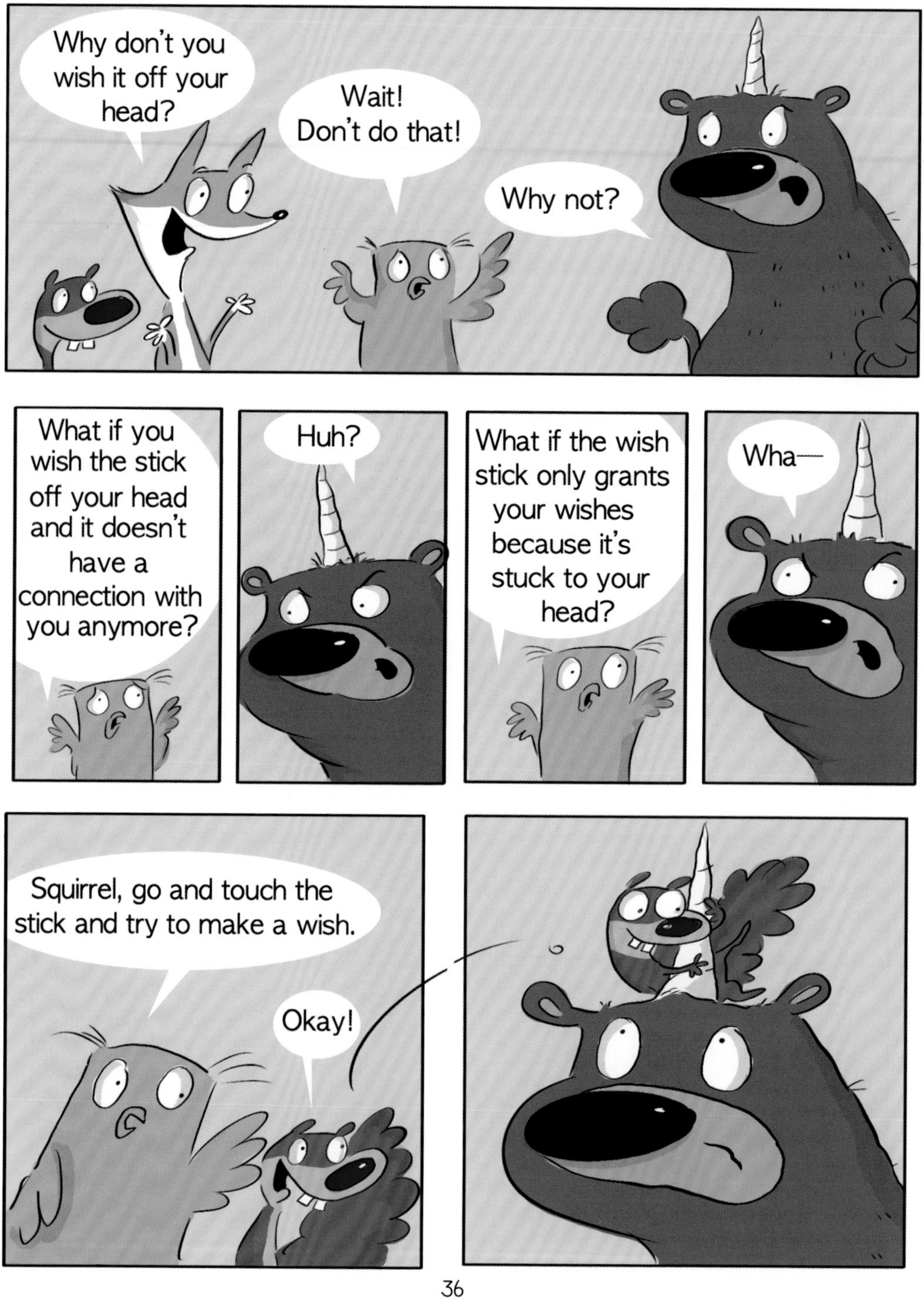
Why don't you wish it off your head?
Wait! Don't do that!
Why not?
What if you wish the stick off your head and it doesn't have a connection with you anymore?
Huh?
What if the wish stick only grants your wishes because it's stuck to your head?
Wha—
Squirrel, go and touch the stick and try to make a wish.
Okay!

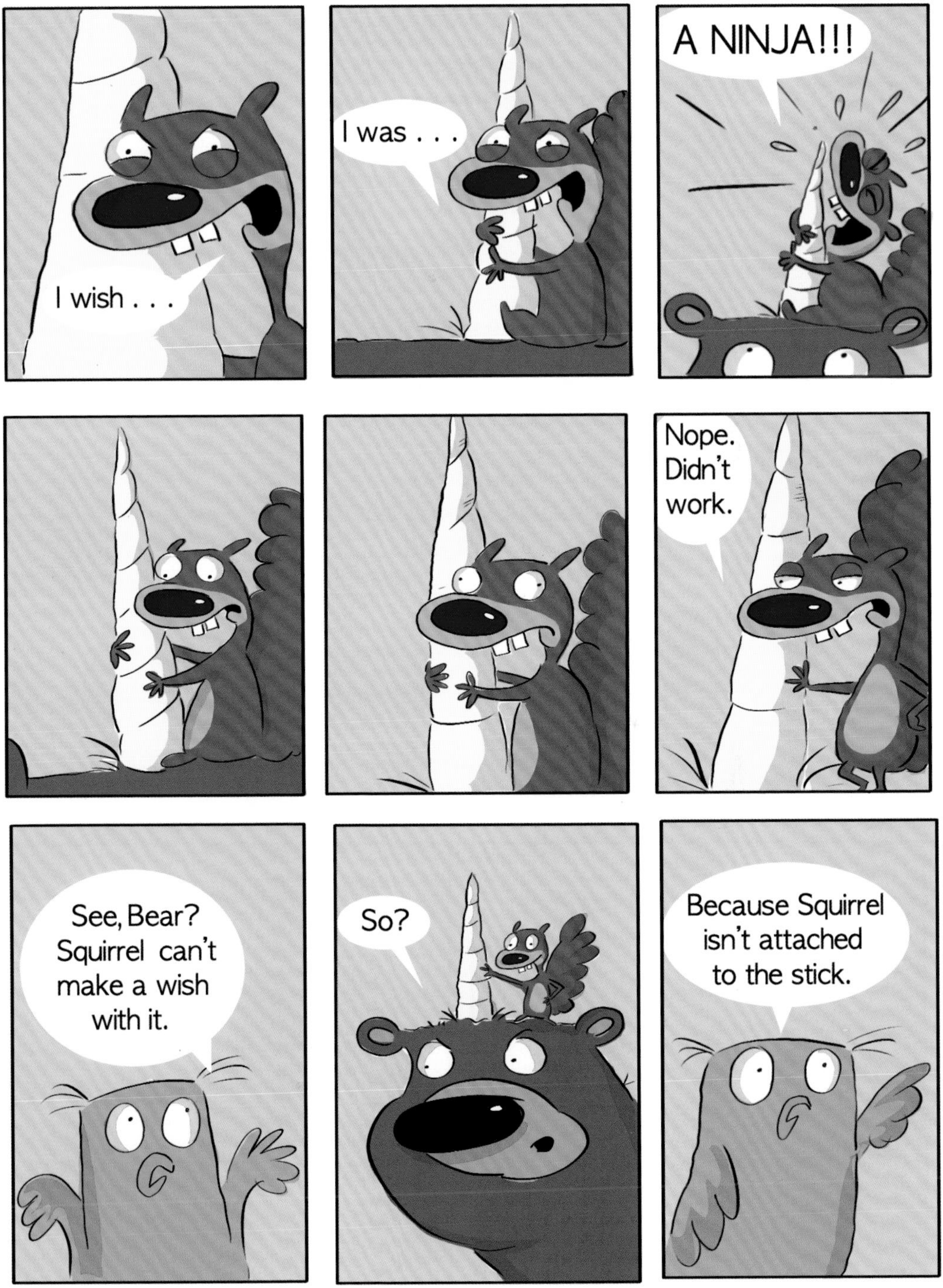
I wish . . .
I was . . .
A NINJA!!!
Nope. Didn't work.
See, Bear? Squirrel can't make a wish with it.
So?
Because Squirrel isn't attached to the stick.

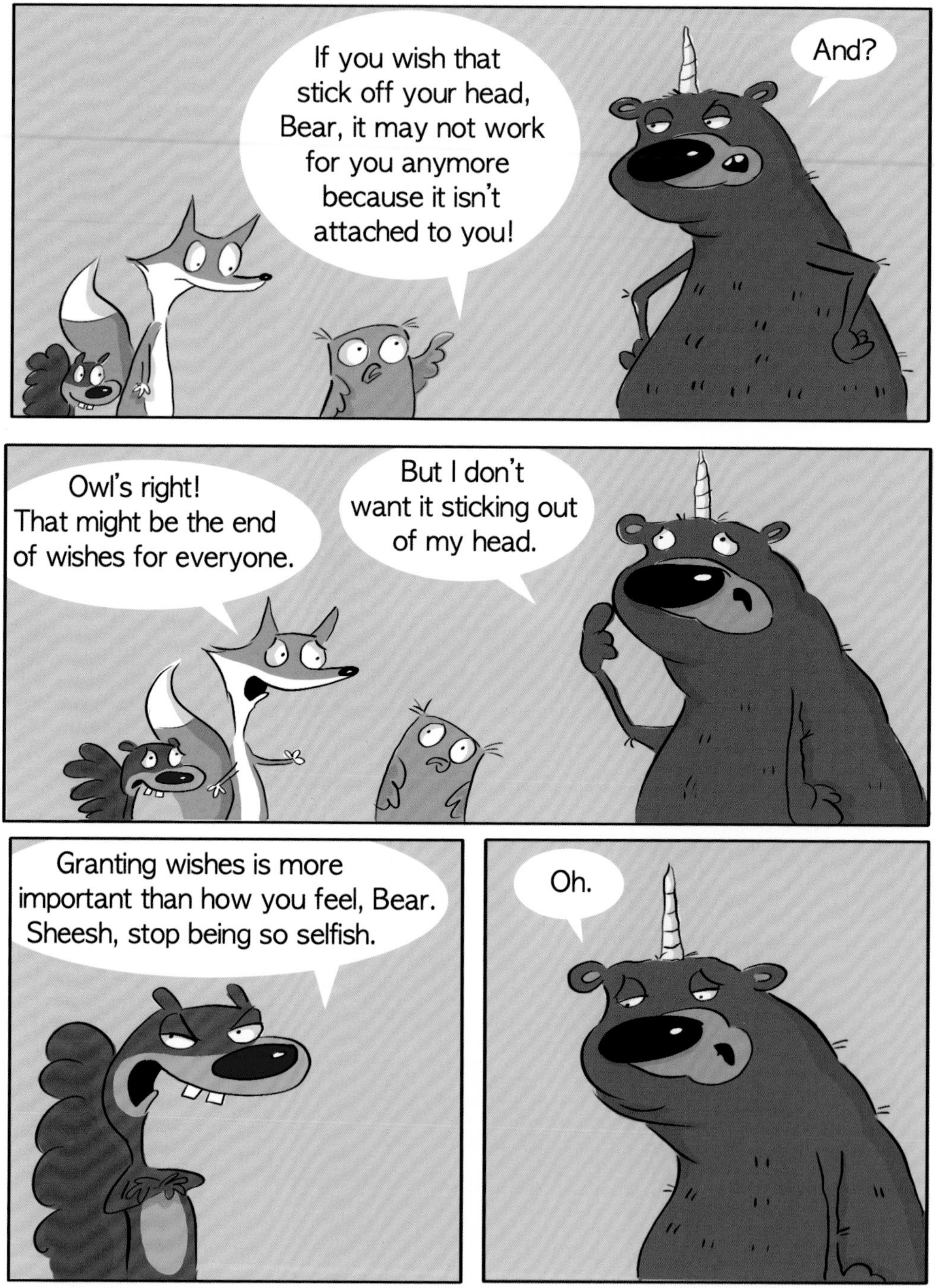
If you wish that stick off your head, Bear, it may not work for you anymore because it isn't attached to you!
And?
Owl's right! That might be the end of wishes for everyone.
But I don't want it sticking out of my head.
Granting wishes is more important than how you feel, Bear. Sheesh, stop being so selfish.
Oh.

CHAPTER 5

THE BIRTH OF A BIZARD

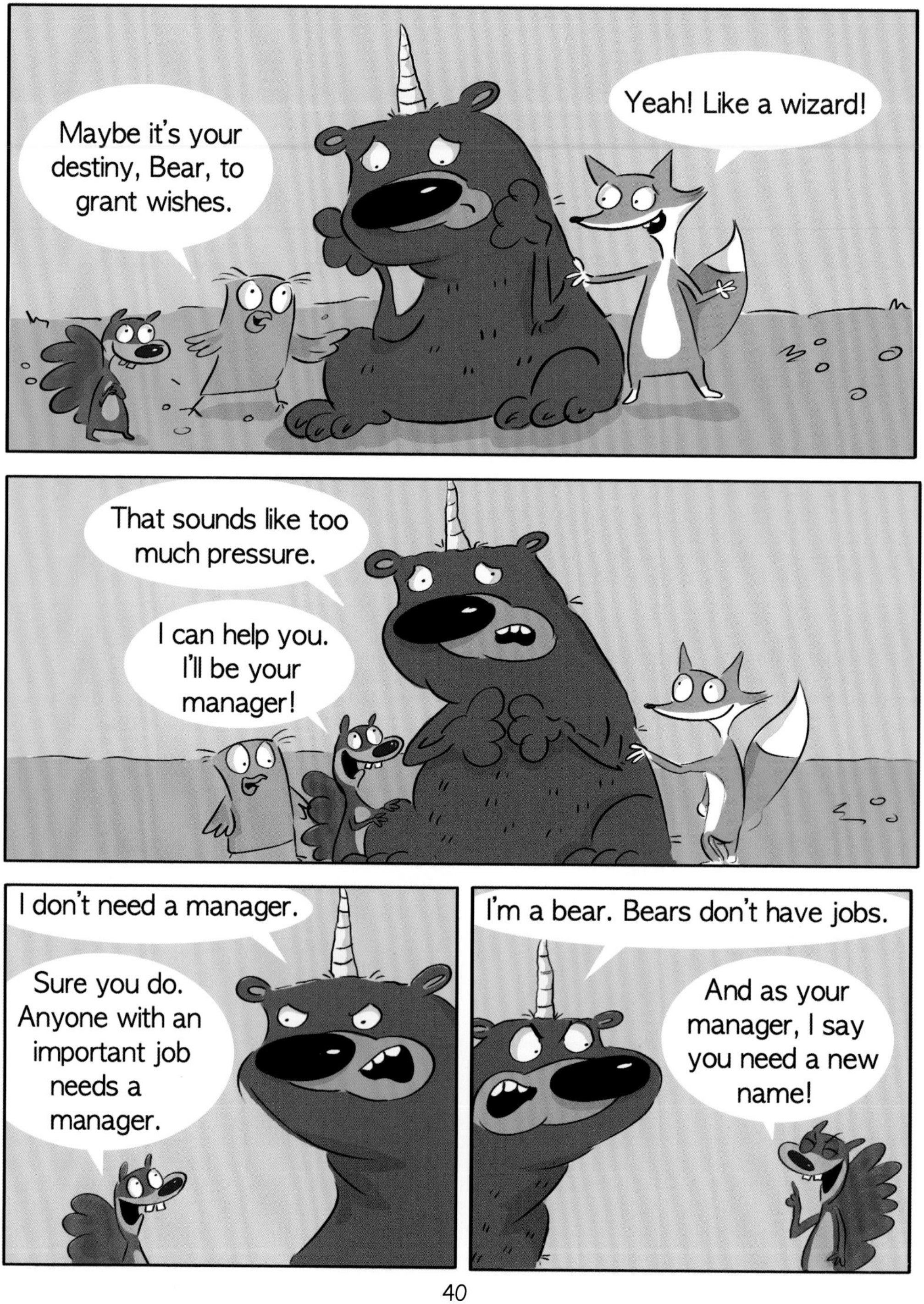
Maybe it's your destiny, Bear, to grant wishes.
Yeah! Like a wizard!
That sounds like too much pressure.
I can help you. I'll be your manager!
I don't need a manager.
Sure you do. Anyone with an important job needs a manager.
I'm a bear. Bears don't have jobs.
And as your manager, I say you need a new name!

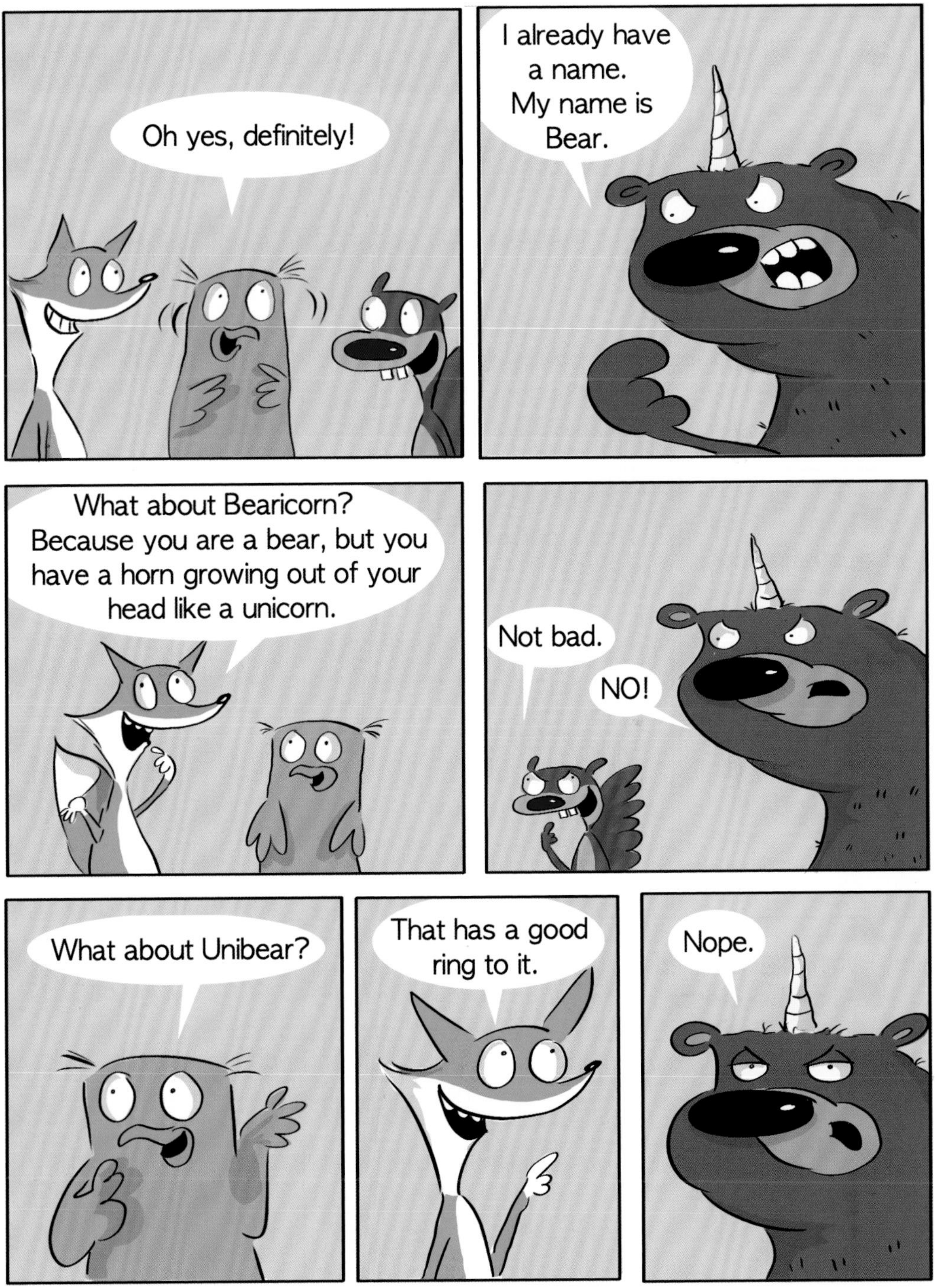
Oh yes, definitely!
I already have a name. My name is Bear.
What about Bearicorn? Because you are a bear, but you have a horn growing out of your head like a unicorn.
Not bad.
NO!
What about Unibear?
That has a good ring to it.
Nope.

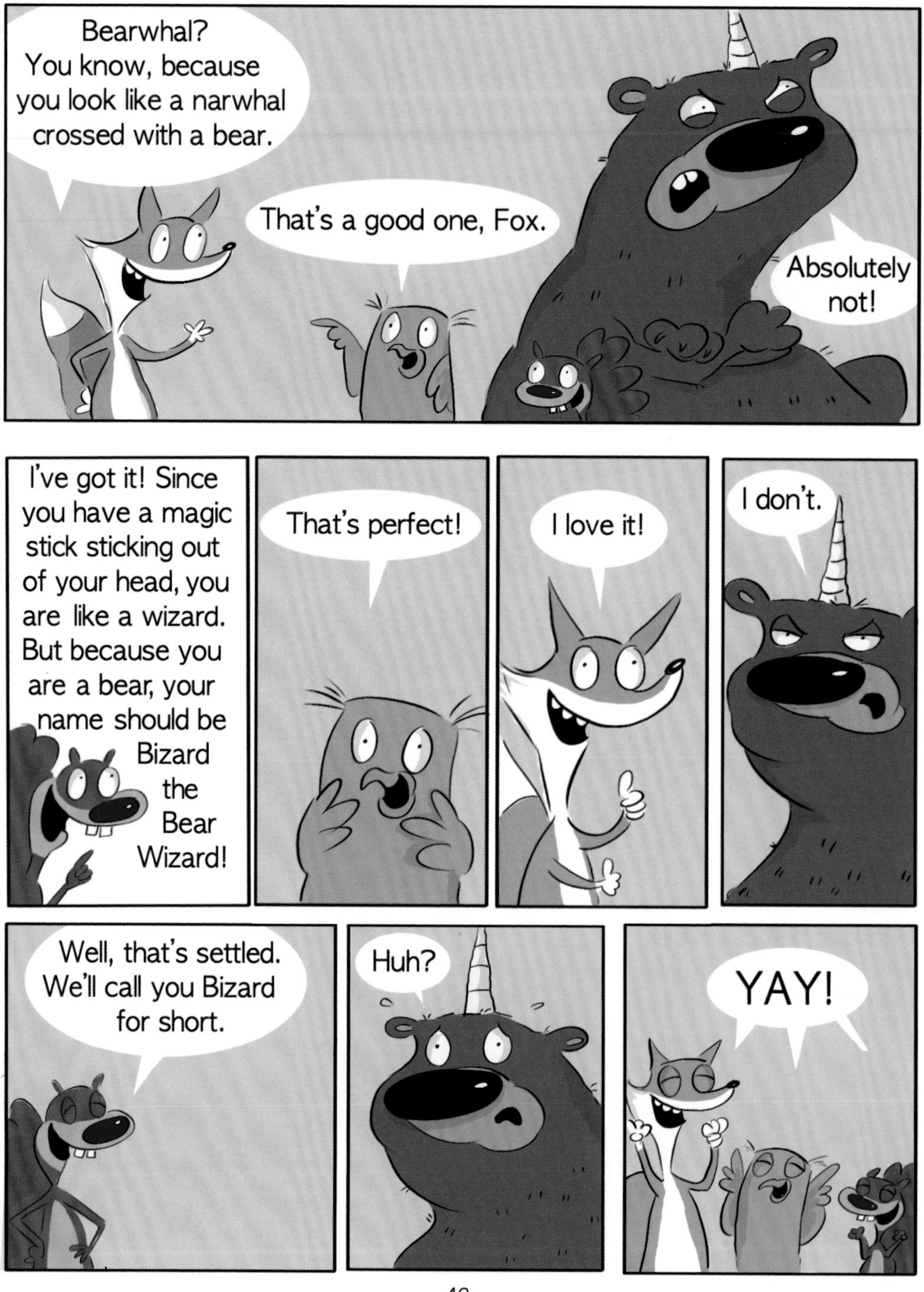
Bearwhal? You know, because you look like a narwhal crossed with a bear.
That's a good one, Fox.
Absolutely not!
I've got it! Since you have a magic stick sticking out of your head, you are like a wizard. But because you are a bear, your name should be Bizard the Bear Wizard!
That's perfect!
I love it!
I don't.
Well, that's settled. We'll call you Bizard for short.
Huh?
YAY!

CHAPTER 6

BIZARD THE WISH GIVER

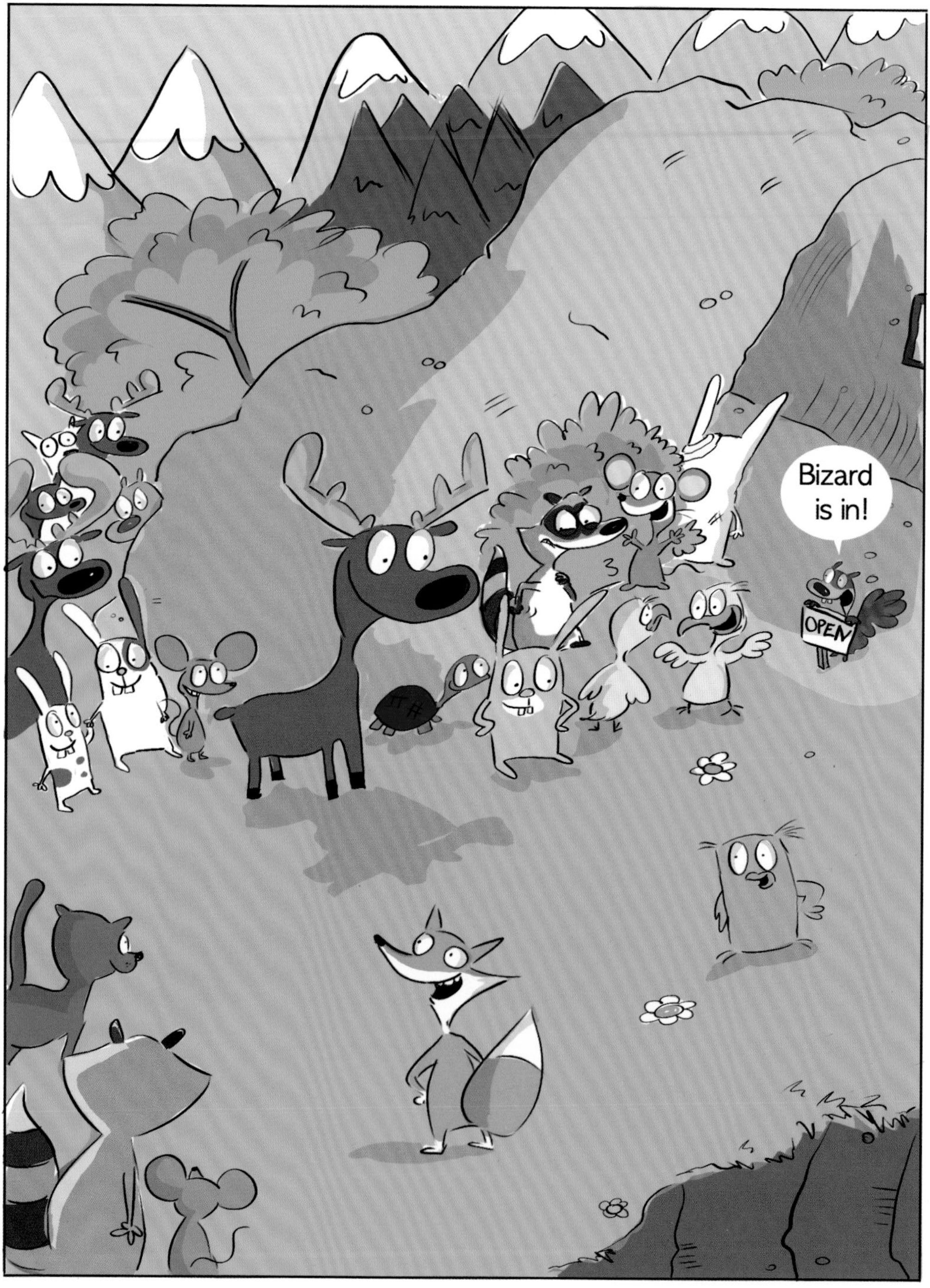
Bizard is in!
OPEN

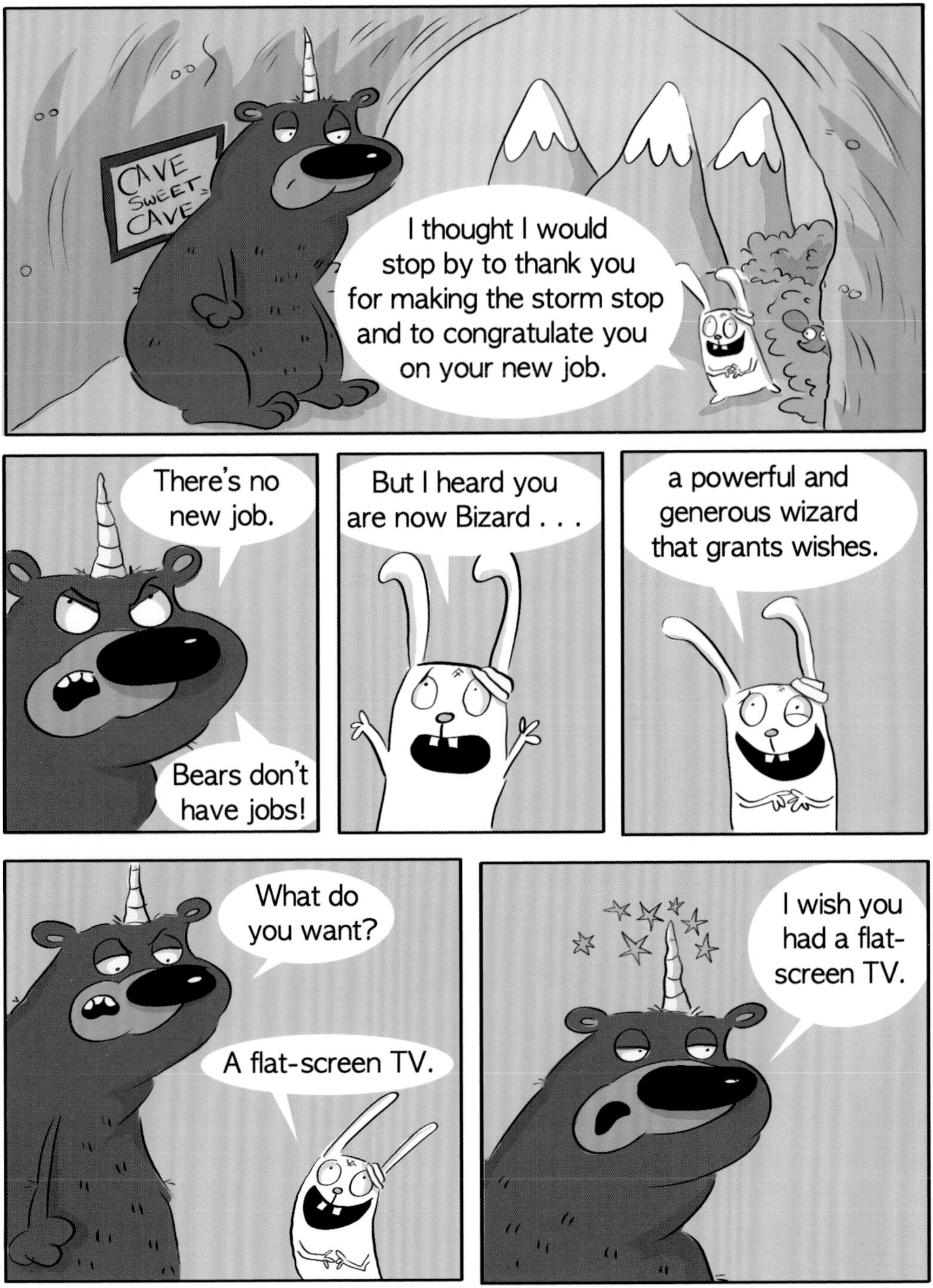
CAVE SWEET CAVE
I thought I would stop by to thank you for making the storm stop and to congratulate you on your new job.
There's no new job.
Bears don't have jobs!
But I heard you are now Bizard . . .
a powerful and generous wizard that grants wishes.
What do you want?
A flat-screen TV.
I wish you had a flat-screen TV.

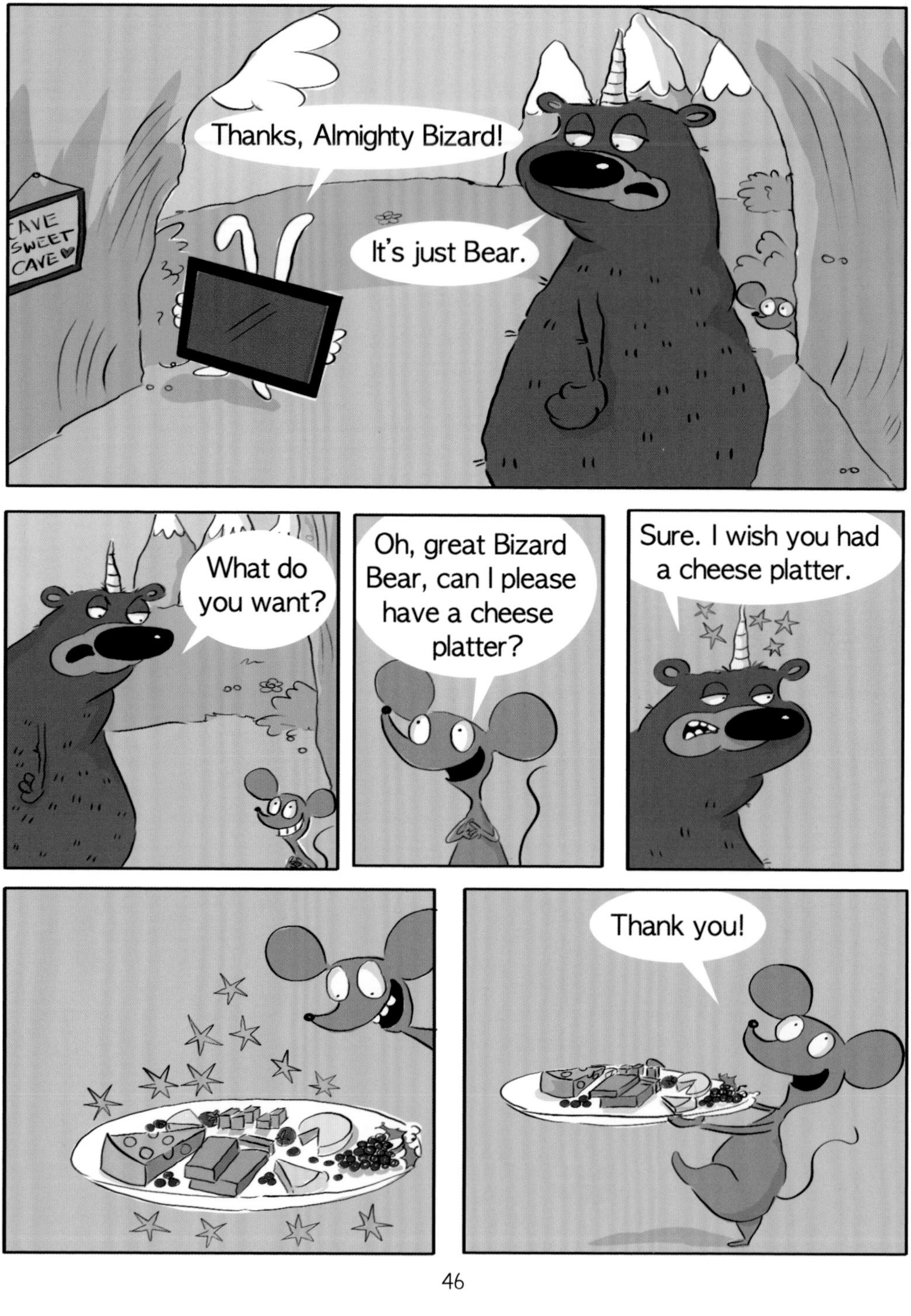
CAVE SWEET CAVE
Thanks, Almighty Bizard!
It's just Bear.
What do you want?
Oh, great Bizard Bear, can I please have a cheese platter?
Sure. I wish you had a cheese platter.
Thank you!

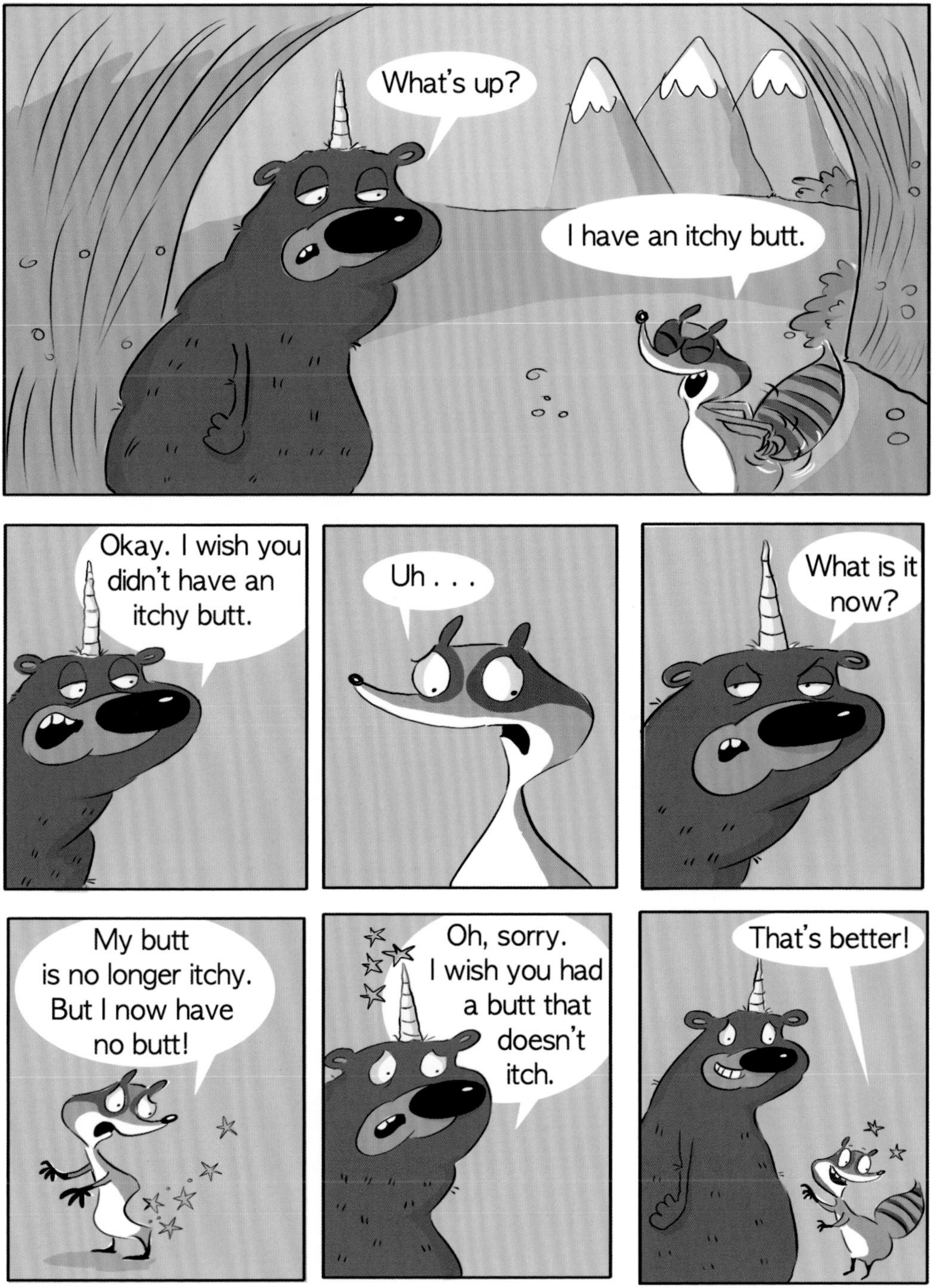
What's up?
I have an itchy butt.
Okay. I wish you didn't have an itchy butt.
Uh . . .
What is it now?
My butt is no longer itchy. But I now have no butt!
Oh, sorry. I wish you had a butt that doesn't itch.
That's better!

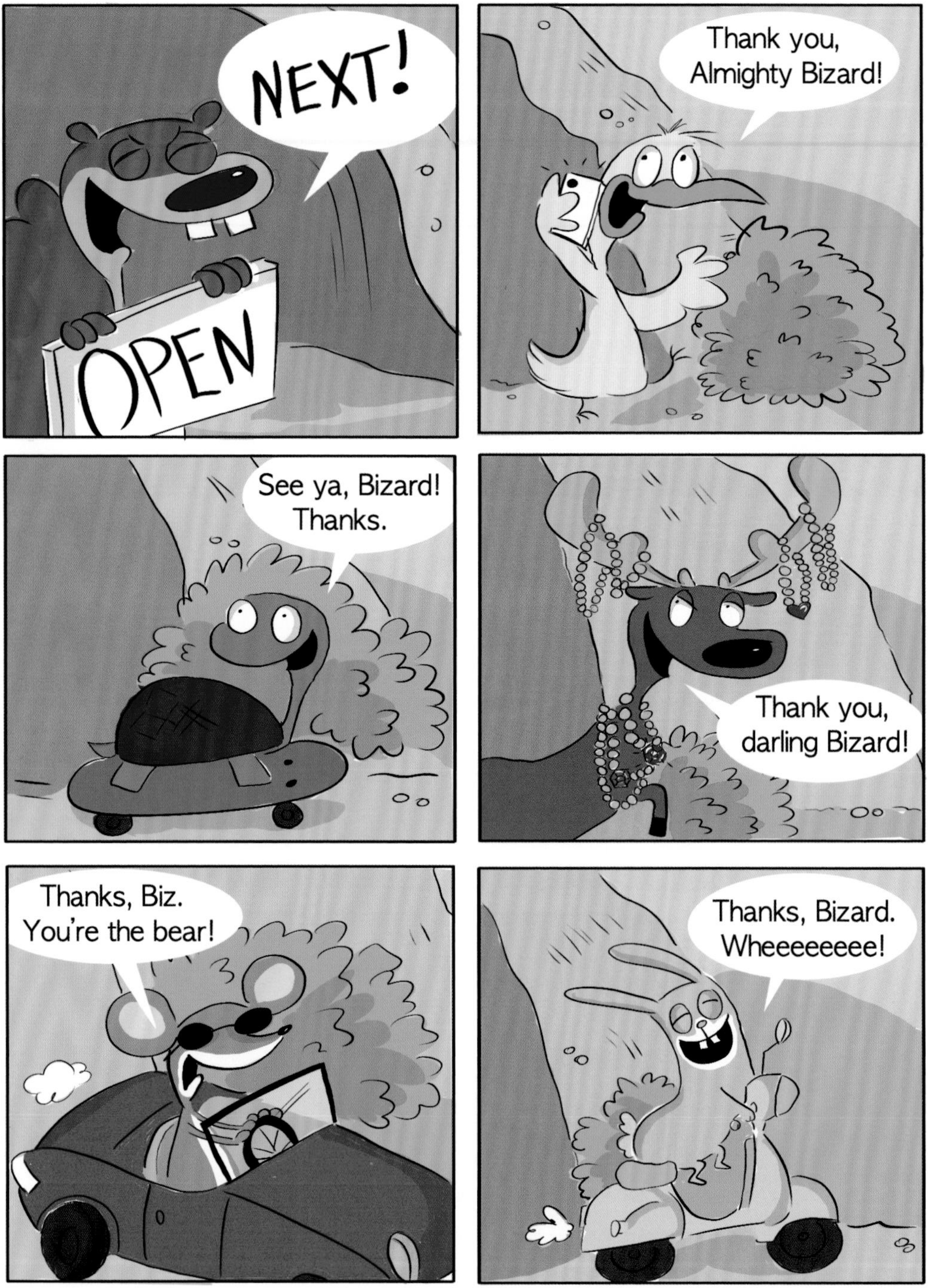
NEXT!
OPEN
Thank you, Almighty Bizard!
See ya, Bizard! Thanks.
Thank you, darling Bizard!
Thanks, Biz. You're the bear!
Thanks, Bizard. Wheeeeeeee!

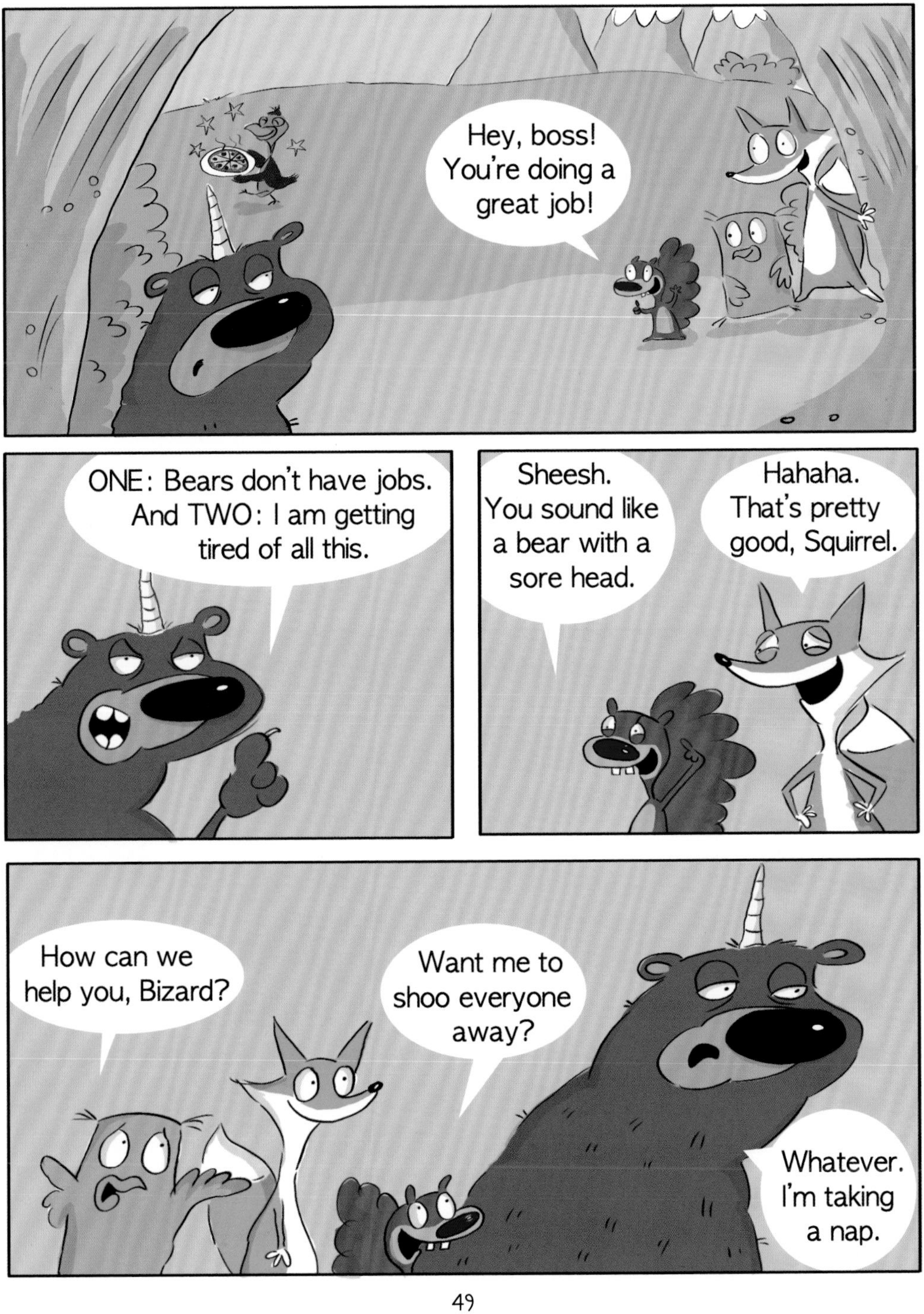
Hey, boss! You're doing a great job!
ONE: Bears don't have jobs. And TWO: I am getting tired of all this.
Sheesh. You sound like a bear with a sore head.
Hahaha. That's pretty good, Squirrel.
How can we help you, Bizard?
Want me to shoo everyone away?
Whatever. I'm taking a nap.

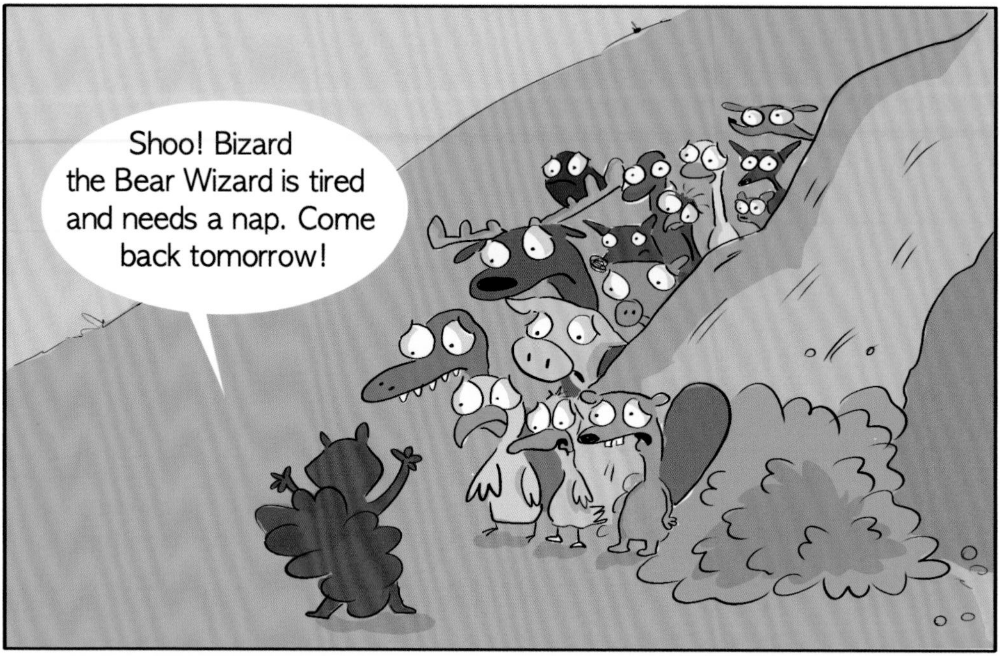
Shoo! Bizard the Bear Wizard is tired and needs a nap. Come back tomorrow!

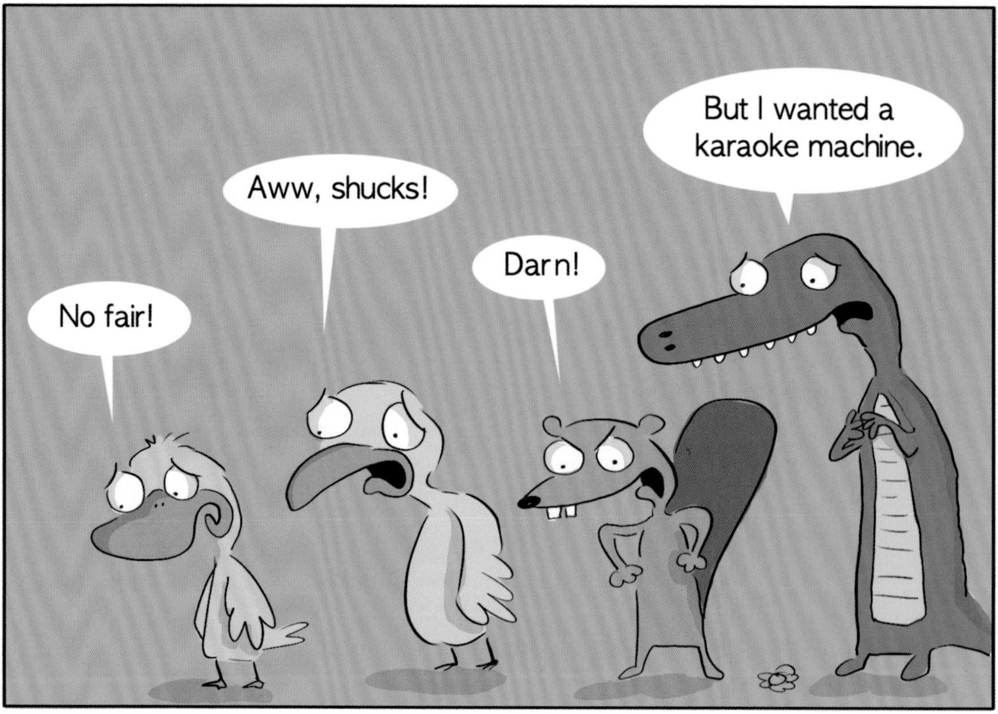
No fair!
Aww, shucks!
Darn!
But I wanted a karaoke machine.

CHAPTER 7

THE POWERFUL WIZARD PAYS A VISIT

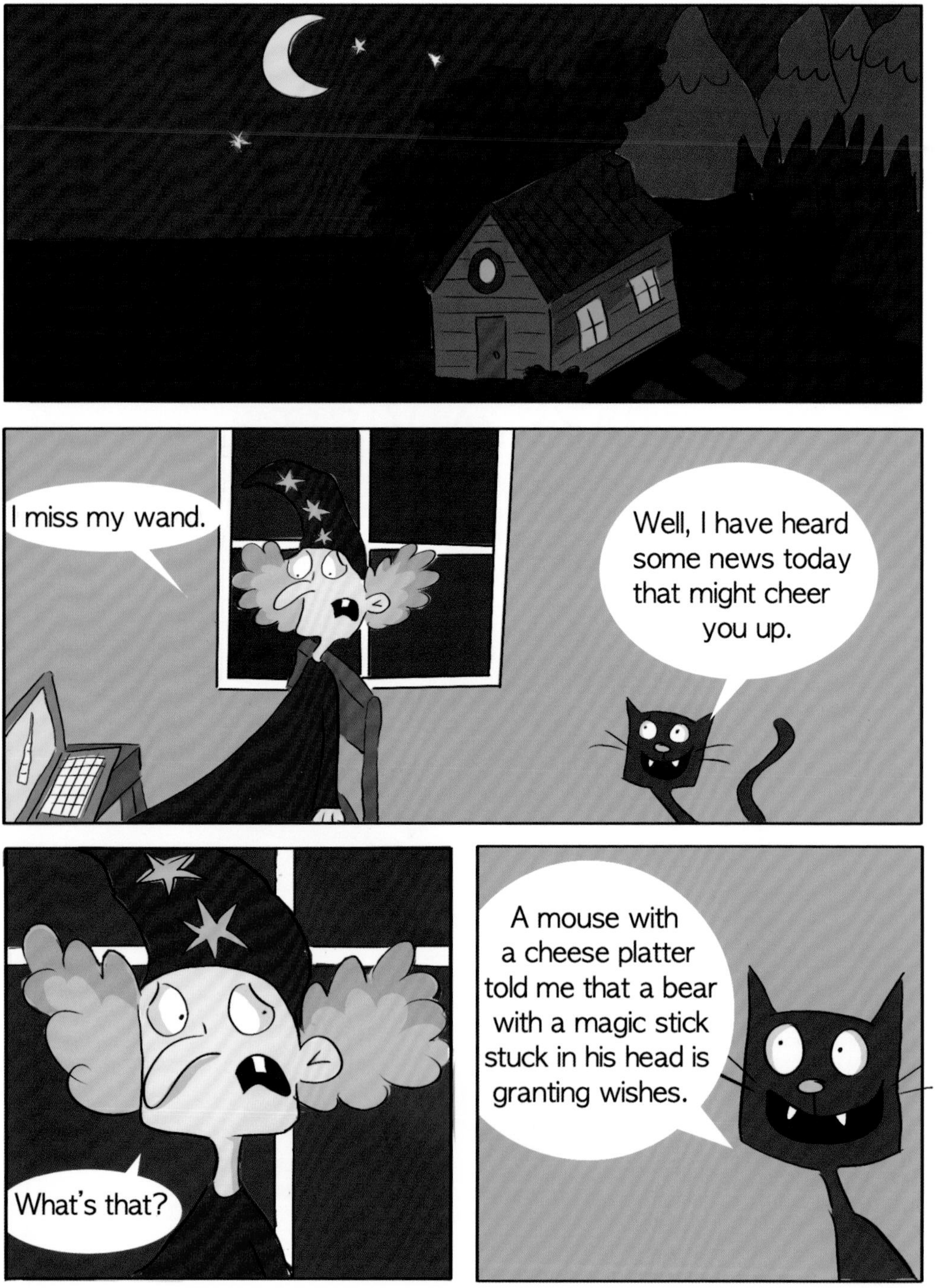
I miss my wand.
Well, I have heard some news today that might cheer you up.
What's that?
A mouse with a cheese platter told me that a bear with a magic stick stuck in his head is granting wishes.

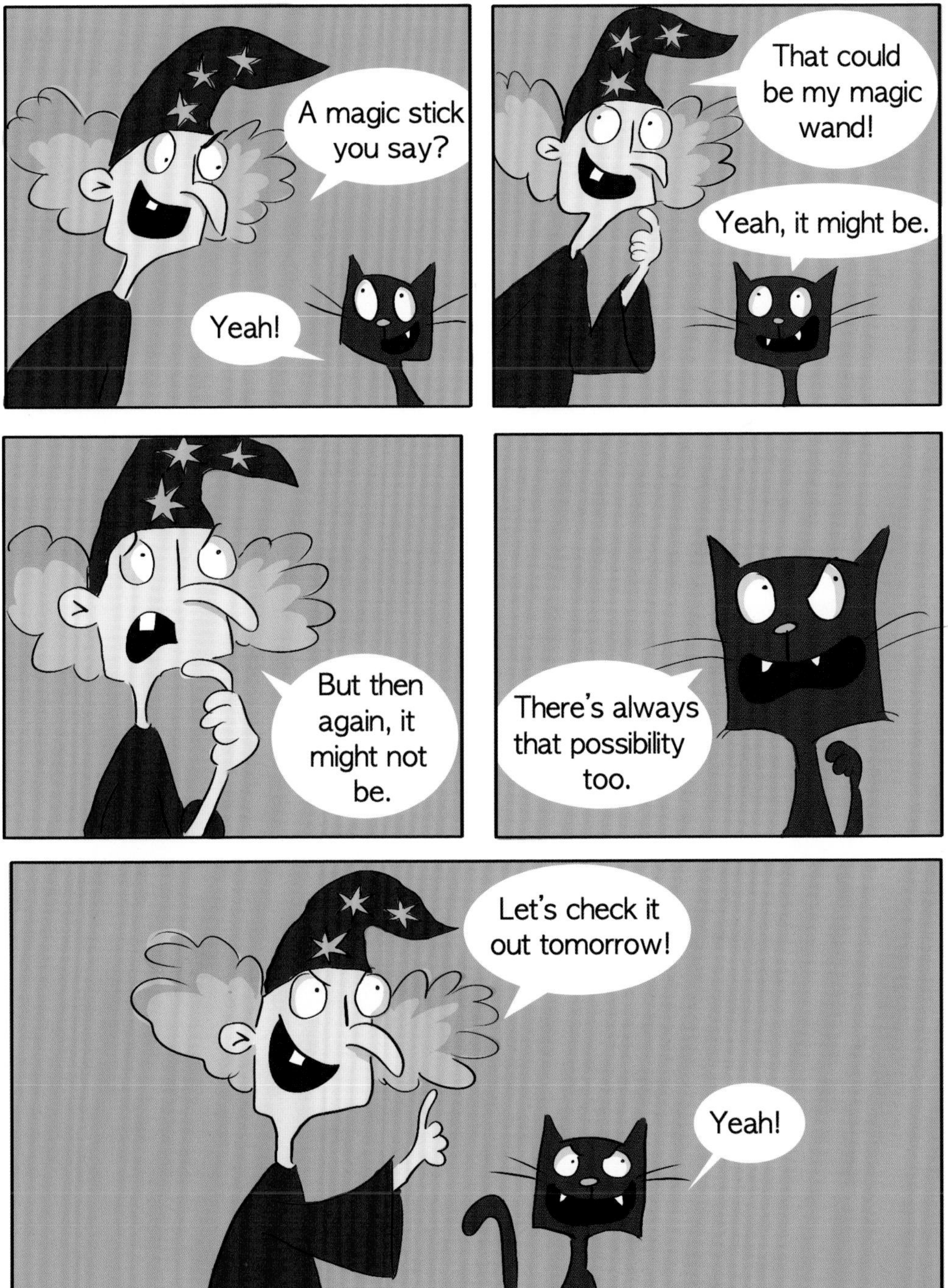
A magic stick you say?
Yeah!
That could be my magic wand!
Yeah, it might be.
But then again, it might not be.
There's always that possibility too.
Let's check it out tomorrow!
Yeah!

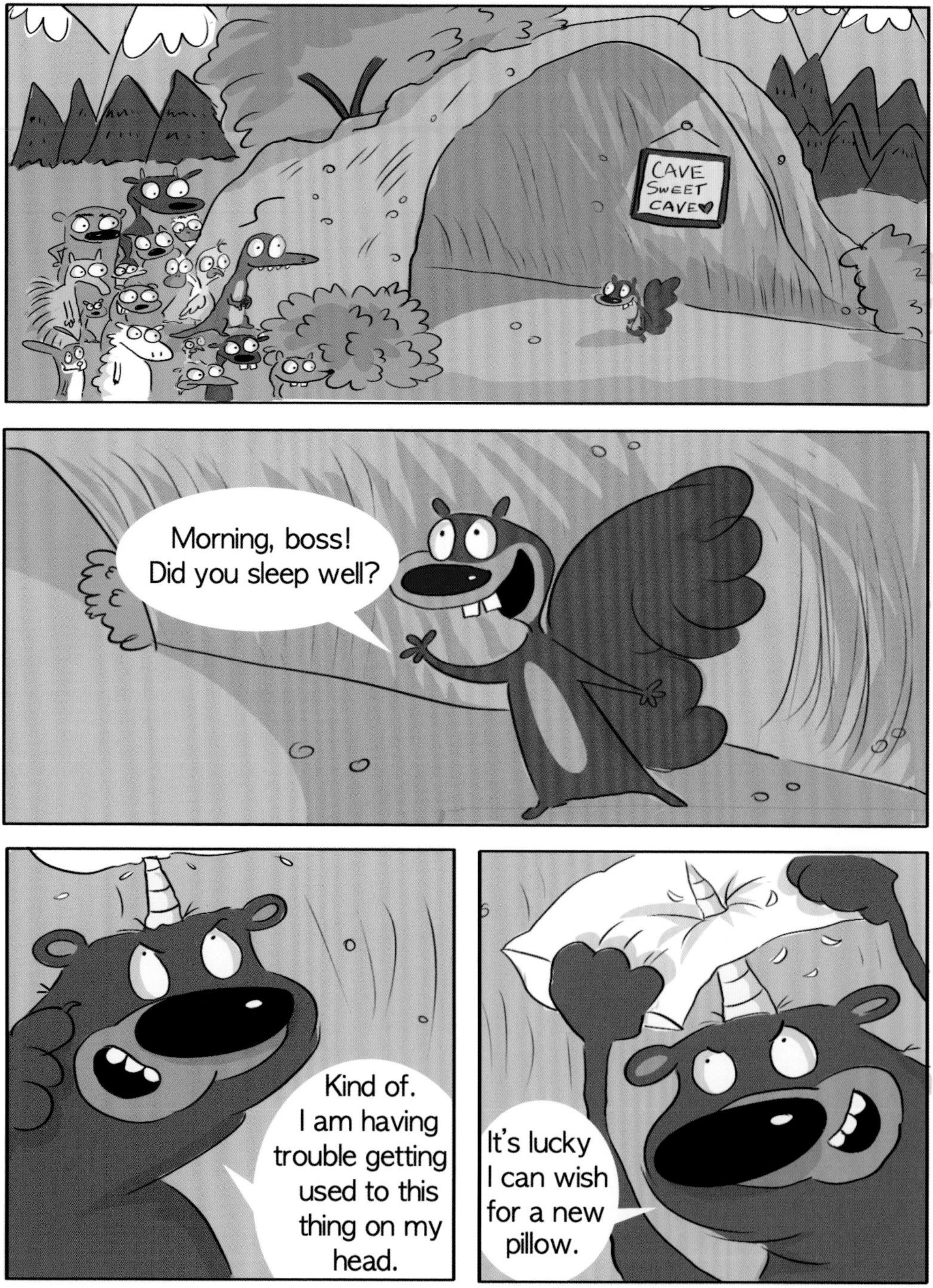
CAVE SWEET CAVE
Morning, boss! Did you sleep well?
Kind of. I am having trouble getting used to this thing on my head.
It's lucky I can wish for a new pillow.

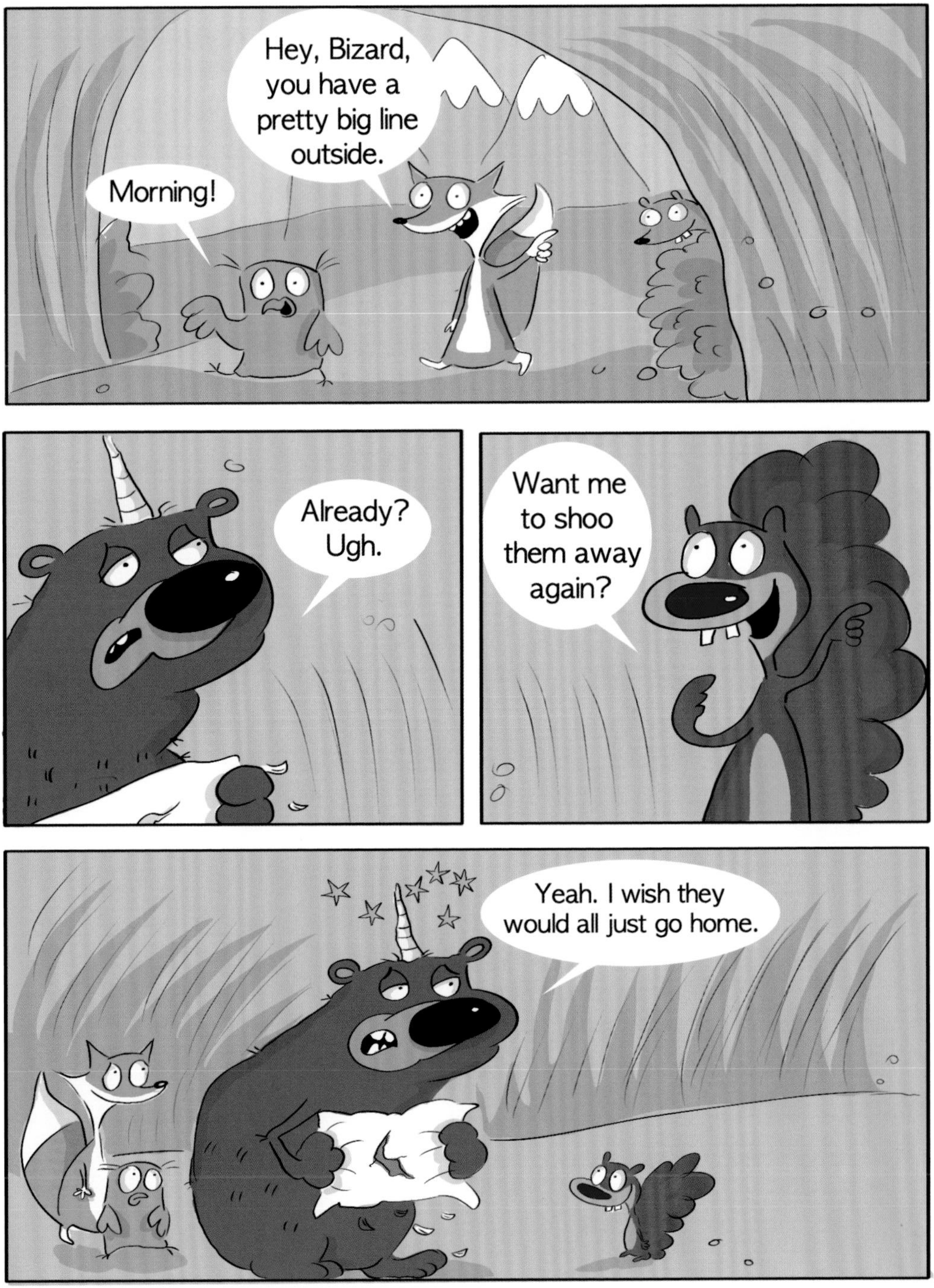
Morning!
Hey, Bizard, you have a pretty big line outside.
Already? Ugh.
Want me to shoo them away again?
Yeah. I wish they would all just go home.

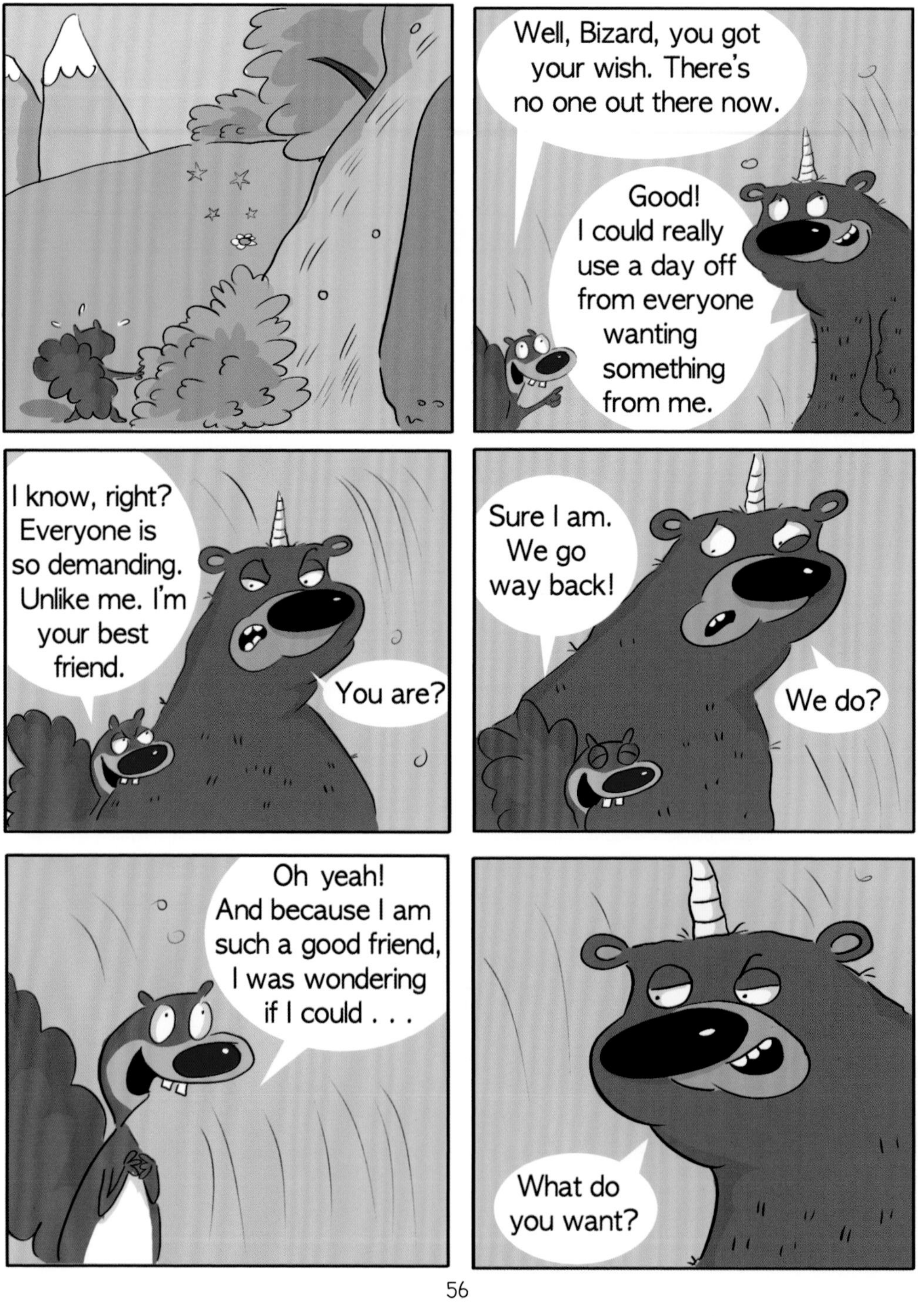
Well, Bizard, you got your wish. There's no one out there now.
Good! I could really use a day off from everyone wanting something from me.
I know, right? Everyone is so demanding. Unlike me. I'm your best friend.
You are?
Sure I am. We go way back!
We do?
Oh yeah! And because I am such a good friend, I was wondering if I could . . .
What do you want?

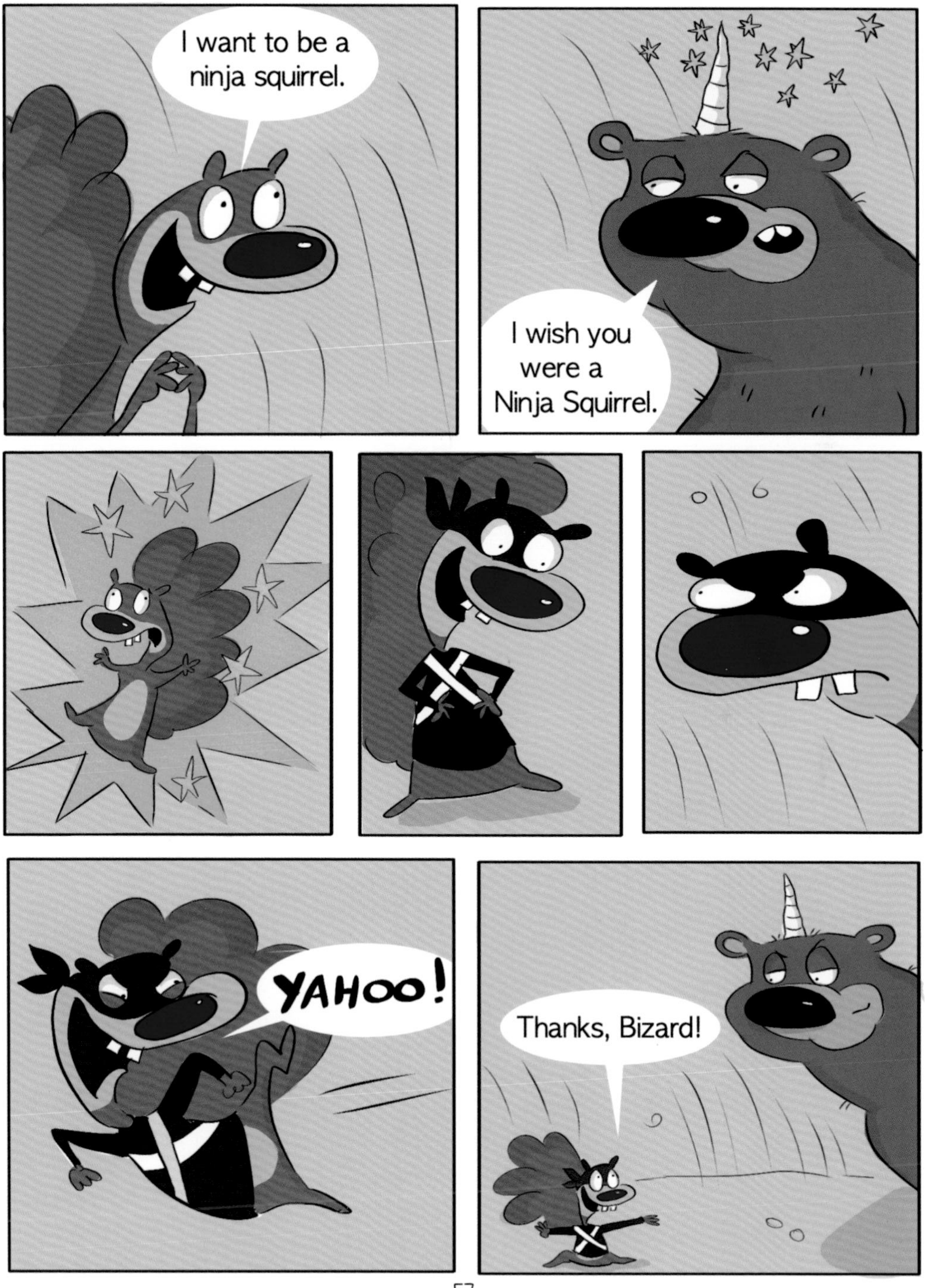
I want to be a ninja squirrel.
I wish you were a Ninja Squirrel.
YAHOO!
Thanks, Bizard!

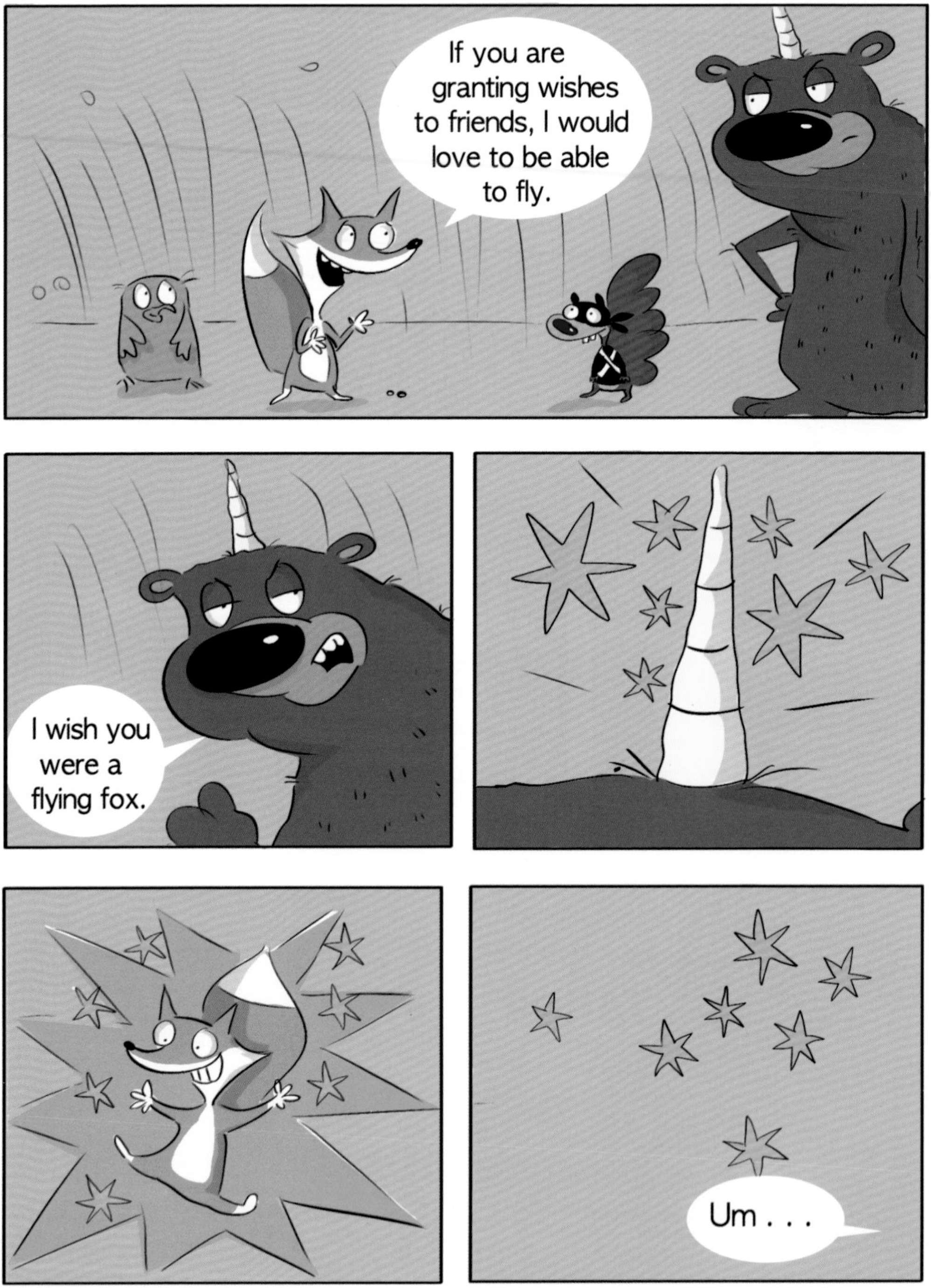
If you are granting wishes to friends, I would love to be able to fly.
I wish you were a flying fox.
Um . . .

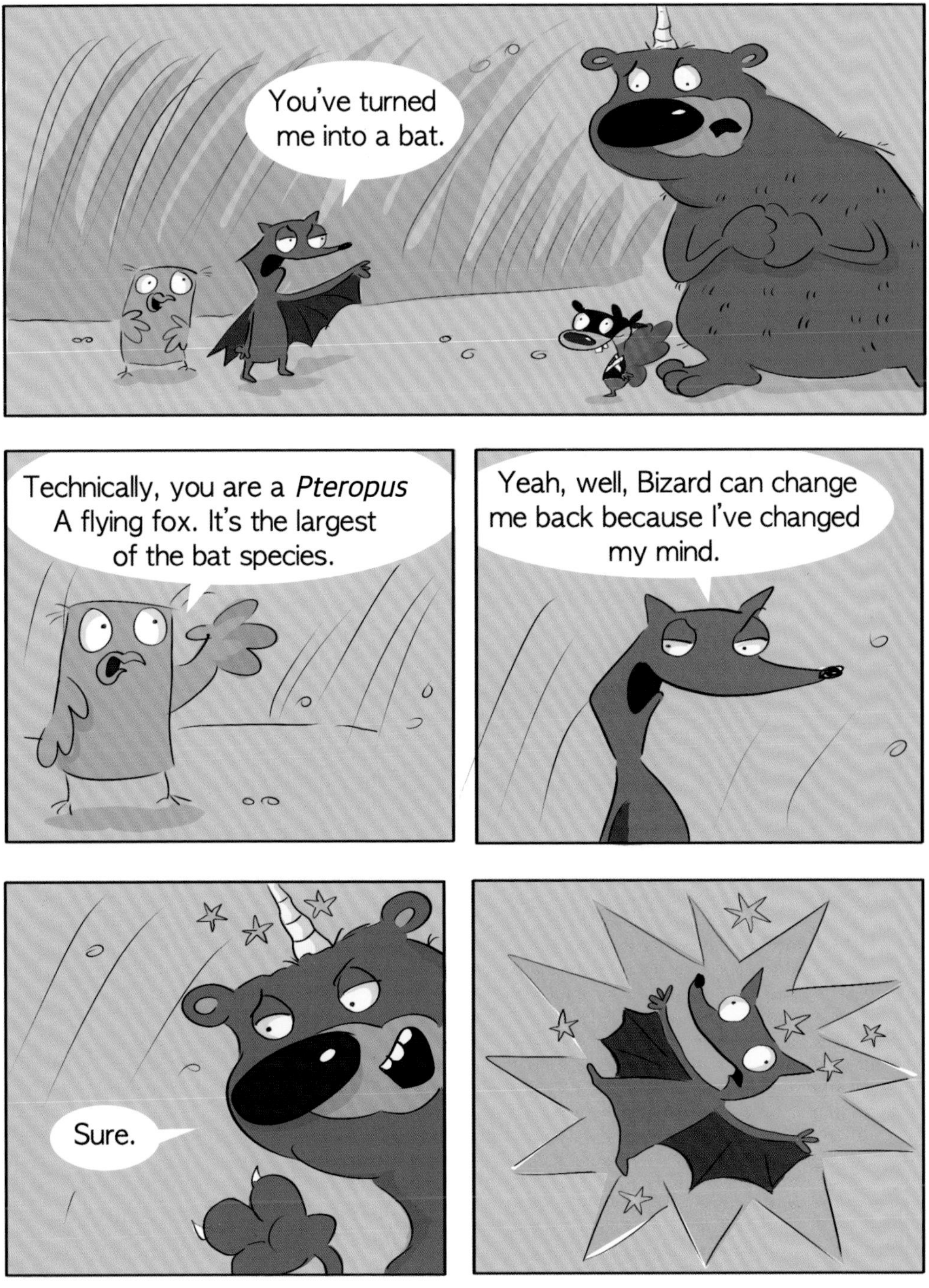
You've turned me into a bat.
Technically, you are a *Pteropus* A flying fox. It's the largest of the bat species.
Yeah, well, Bizard can change me back because I've changed my mind.
Sure.

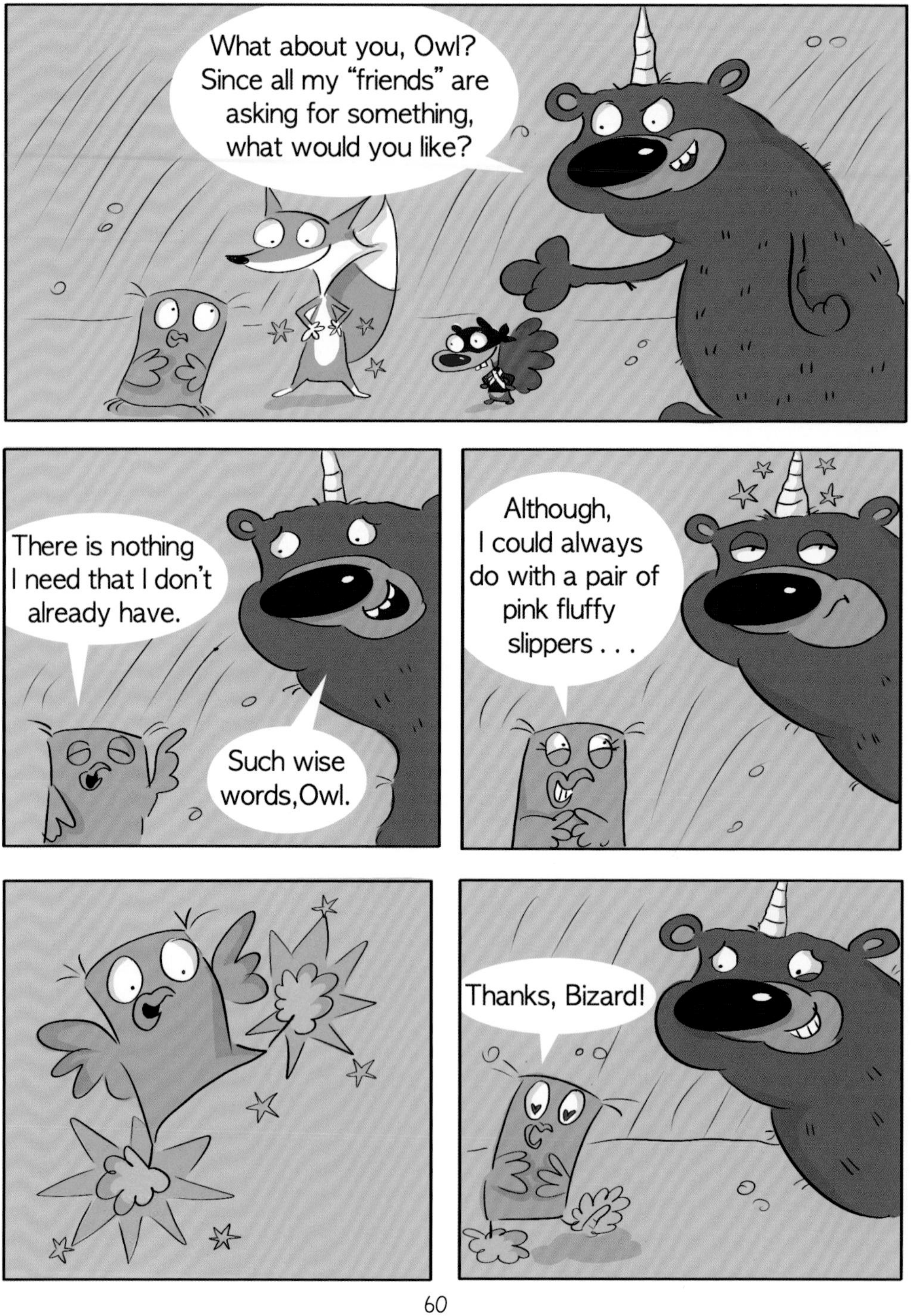
What about you, Owl? Since all my "friends" are asking for something, what would you like?
There is nothing I need that I don't already have.
Such wise words,Owl.
Although, I could always do with a pair of pink fluffy slippers . . .
Thanks, Bizard!

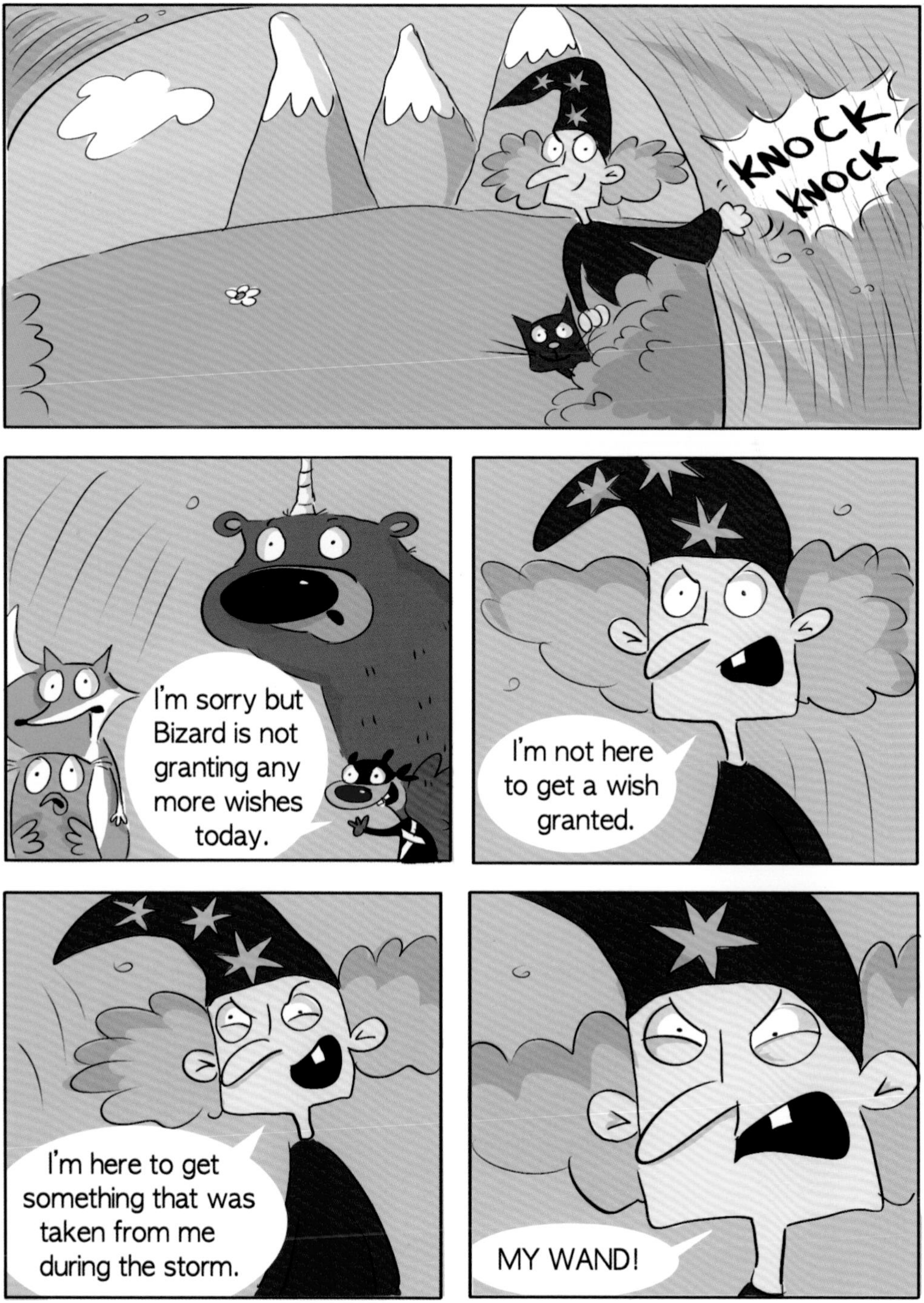
KNOCK KNOCK
I'm sorry but Bizard is not granting any more wishes today.
I'm not here to get a wish granted.
I'm here to get something that was taken from me during the storm.
MY WAND!

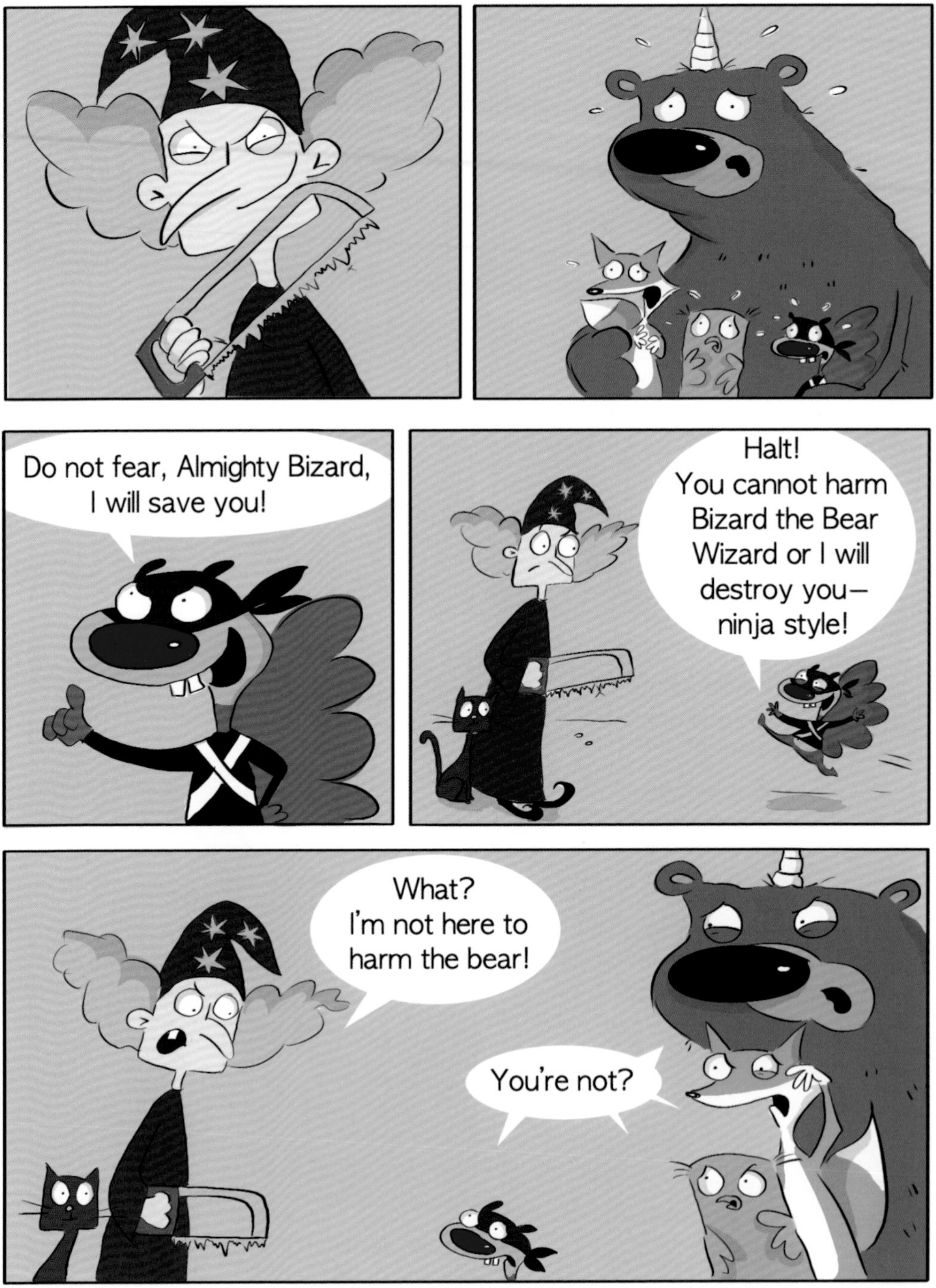
Do not fear, Almighty Bizard, I will save you!
Halt! You cannot harm Bizard the Bear Wizard or I will destroy you—ninja style!
What? I'm not here to harm the bear!
You're not?

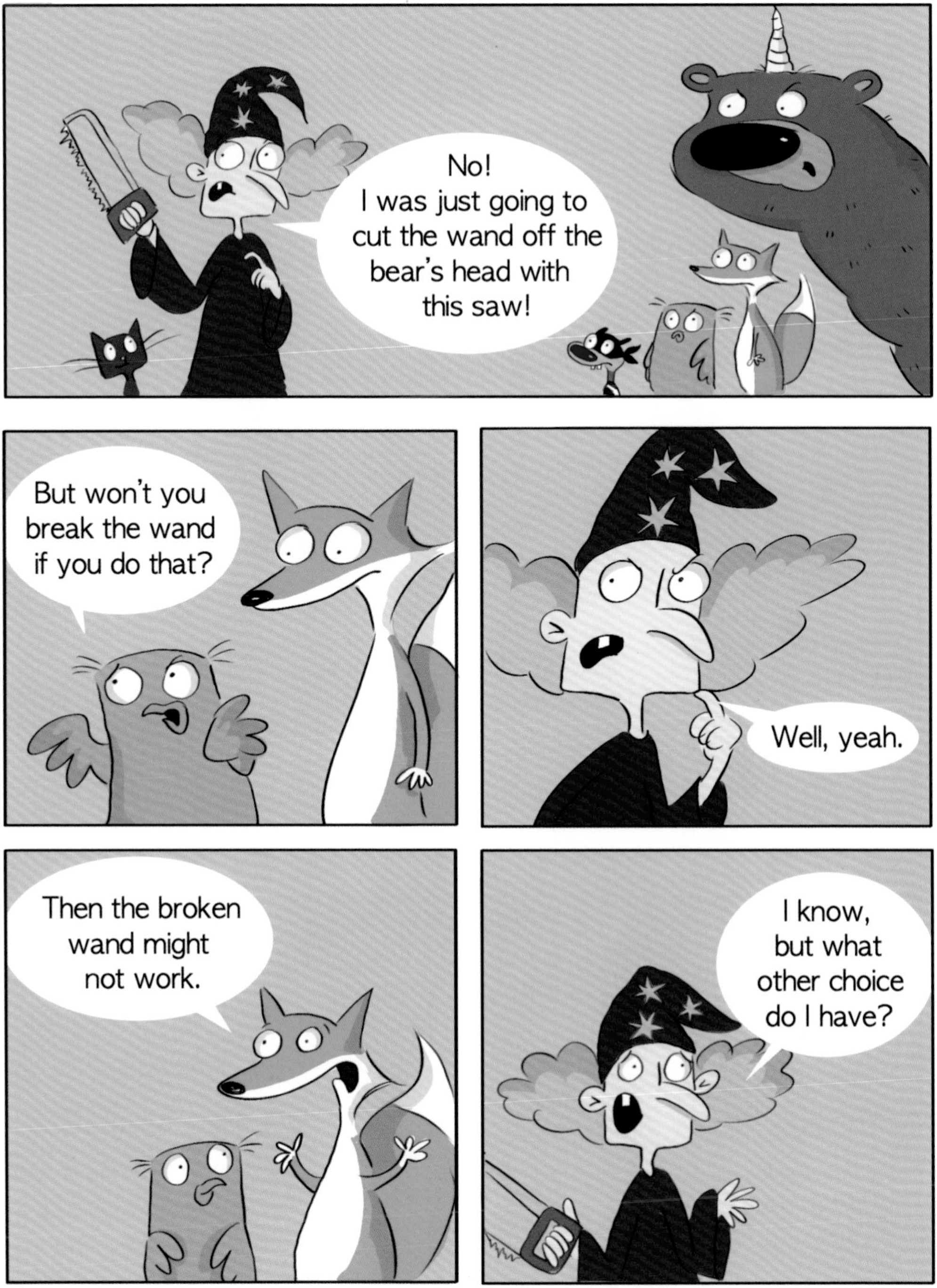
No! I was just going to cut the wand off the bear's head with this saw!
But won't you break the wand if you do that?
Well, yeah.
Then the broken wand might not work.
I know, but what other choice do I have?

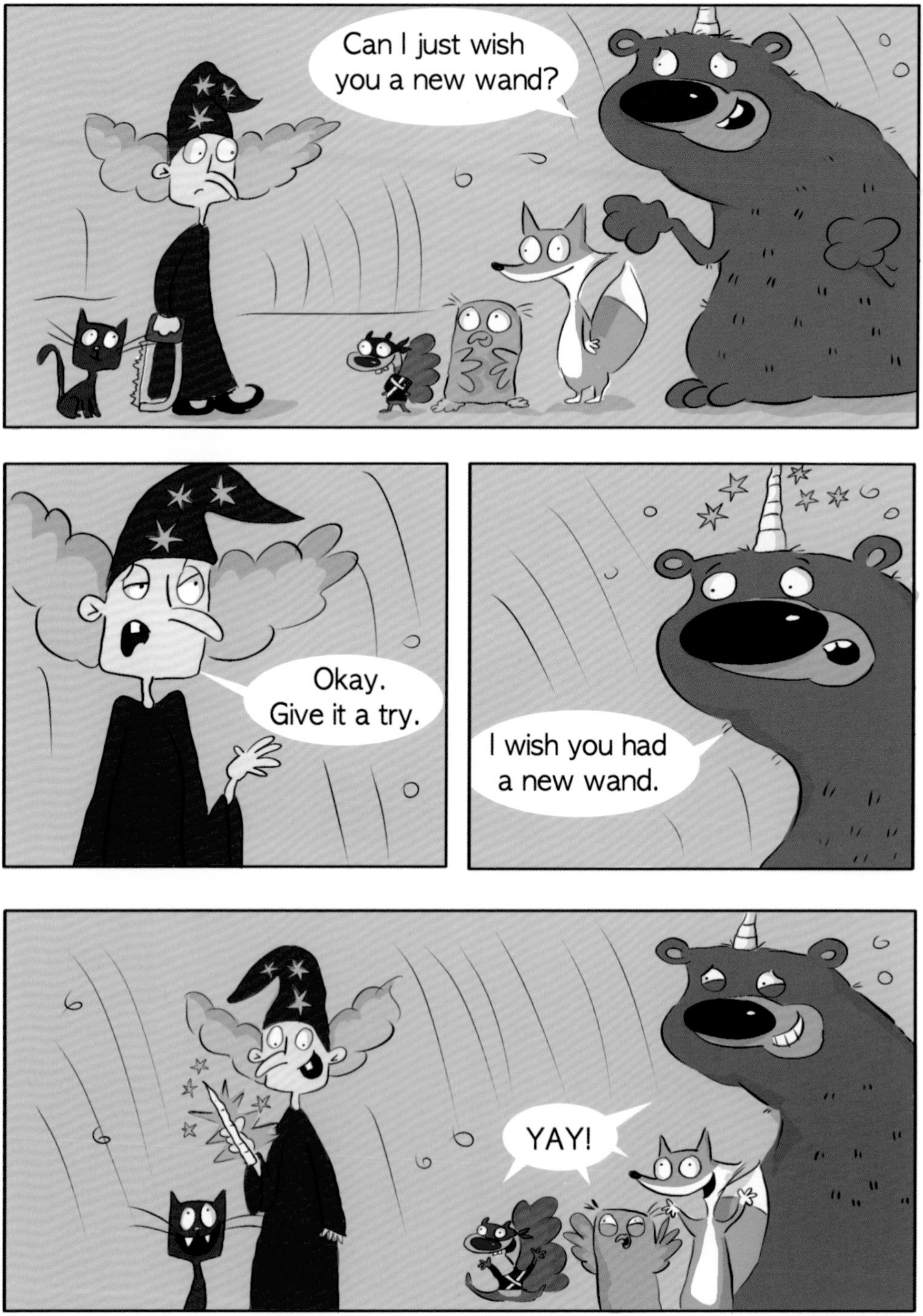
Can I just wish you a new wand?
Okay. Give it a try.
I wish you had a new wand.
YAY!

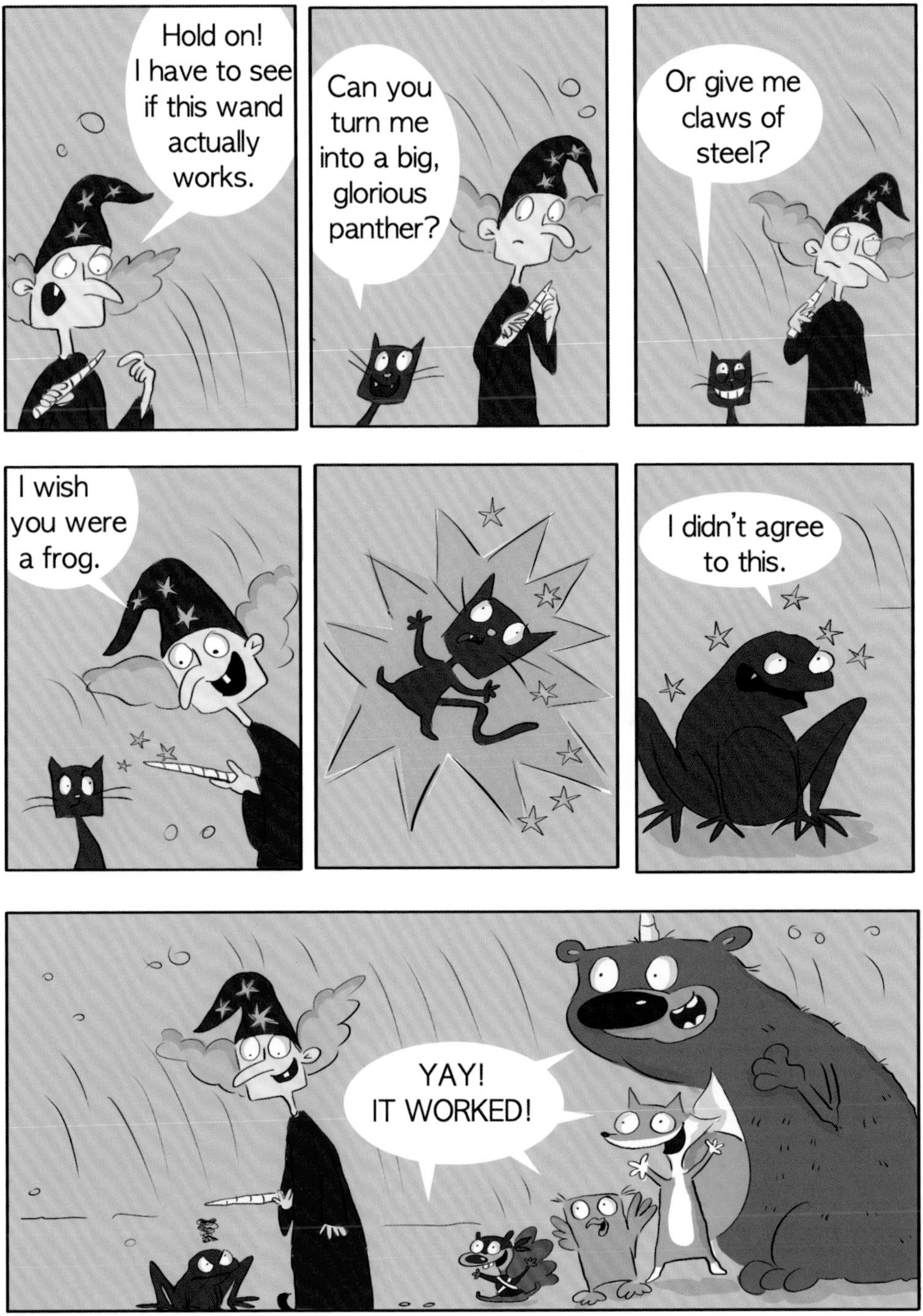
Hold on! I have to see if this wand actually works.
Can you turn me into a big, glorious panther?
Or give me claws of steel?
I wish you were a frog.
I didn't agree to this.
YAY! IT WORKED!

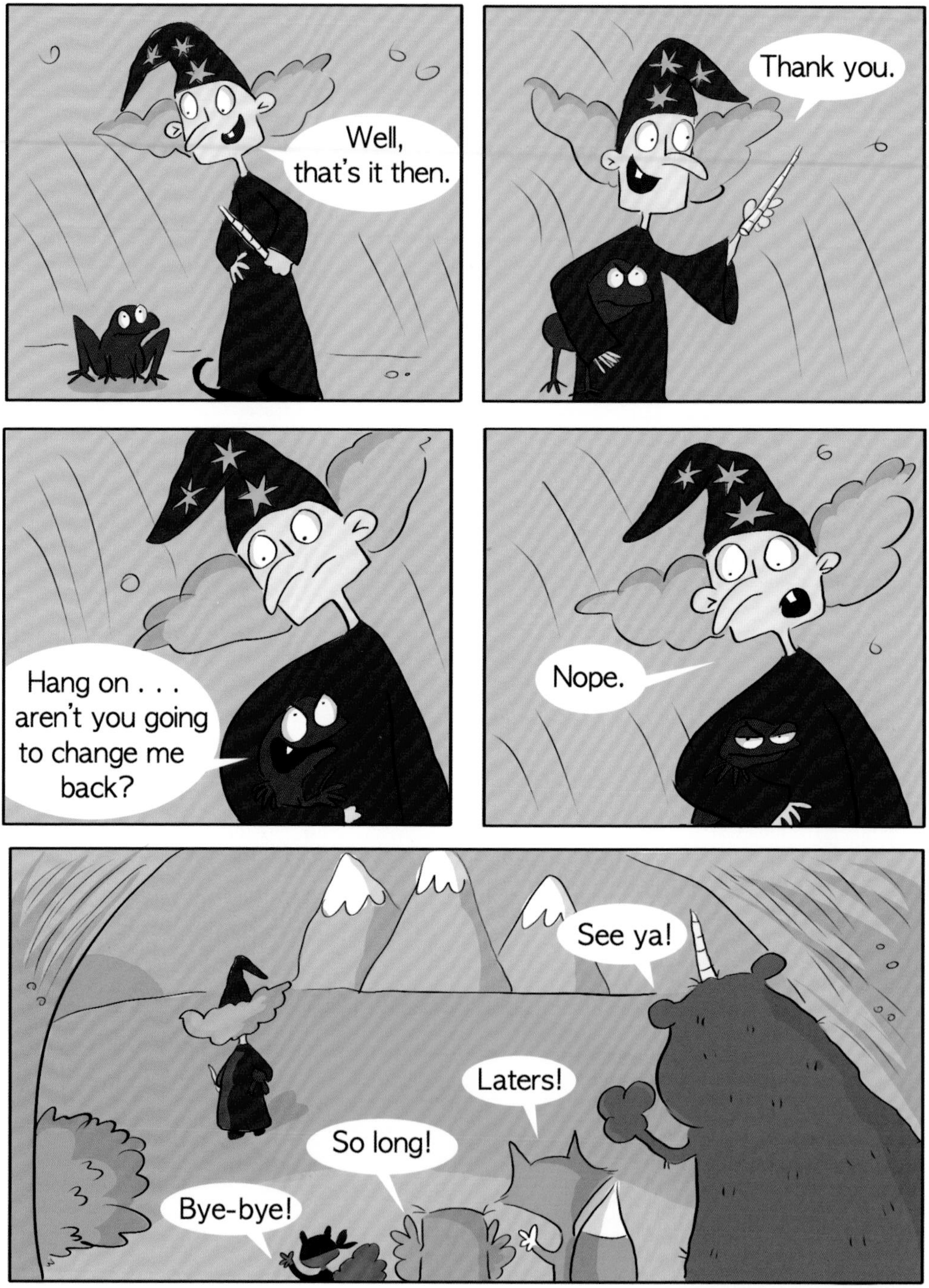
Well, that's it then.
Thank you.
Hang on . . . aren't you going to change me back?
Nope.
See ya!
Laters!
So long!
Bye-bye!

CHAPTER 8

THE BIG BAD GUYS

WOLF →

CROW
↓

Snake
↓

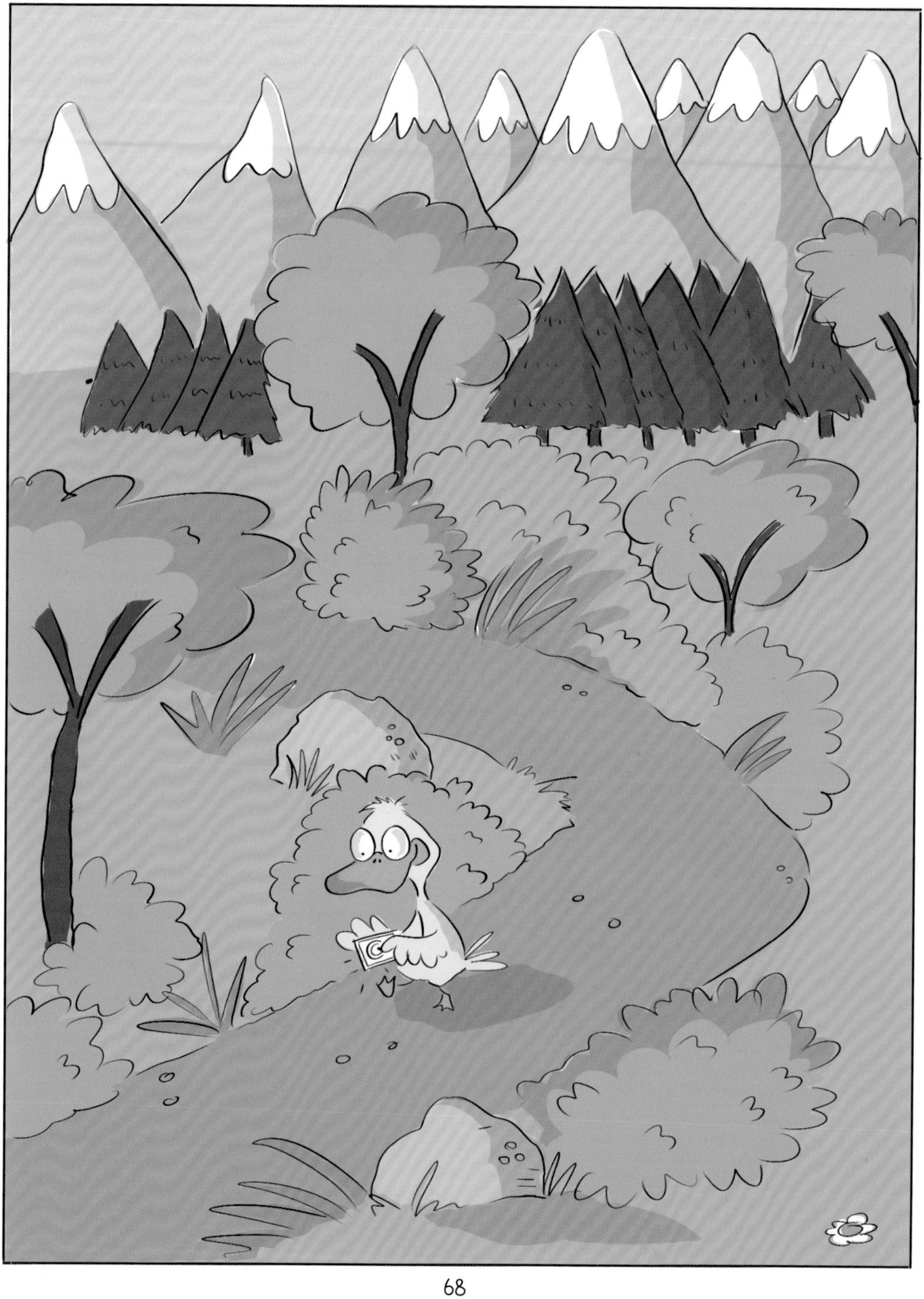

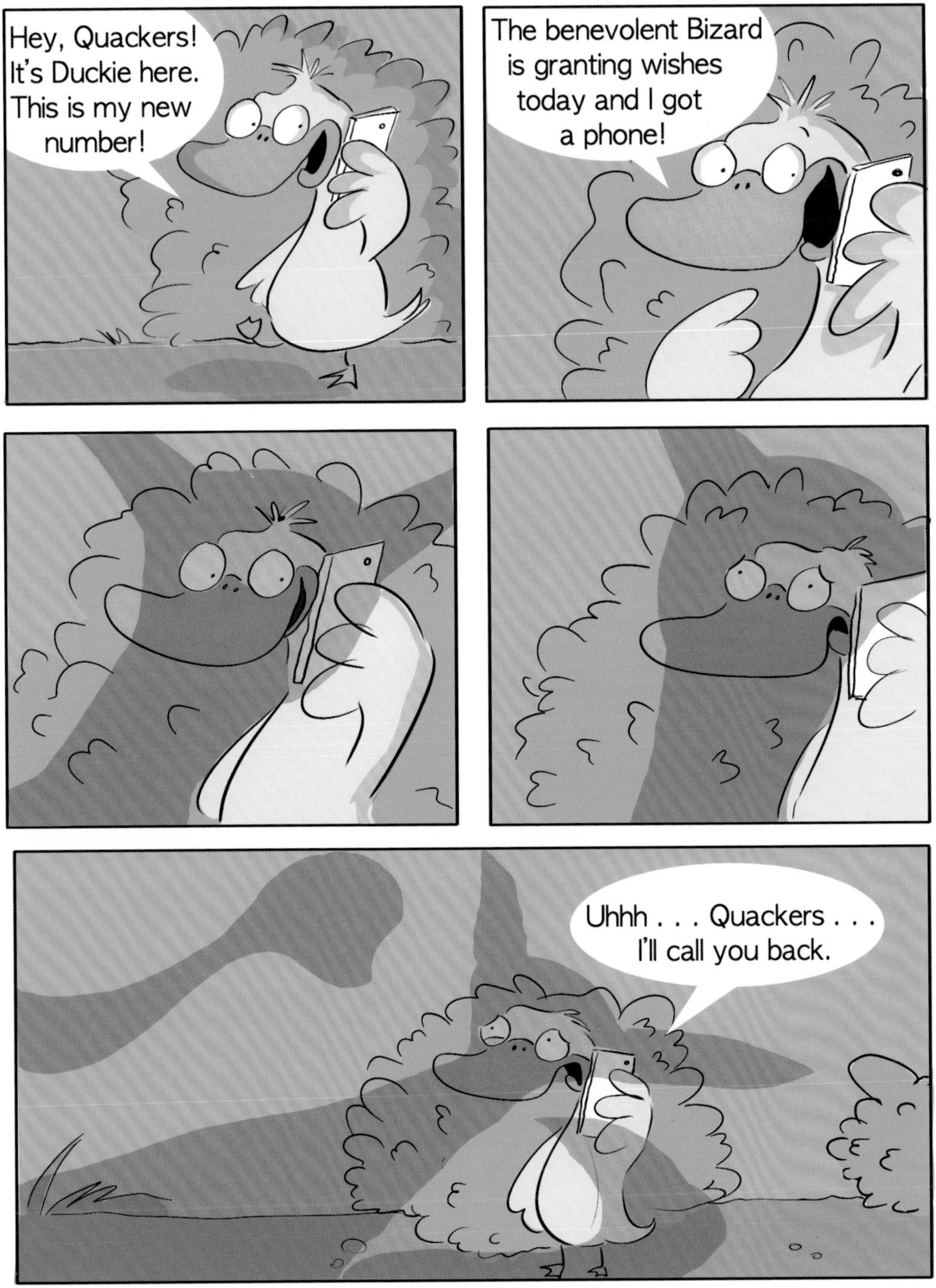
Hey, Quackers! It's Duckie here. This is my new number!
The benevolent Bizard is granting wishes today and I got a phone!
Uhhh . . . Quackers . . . I'll call you back.

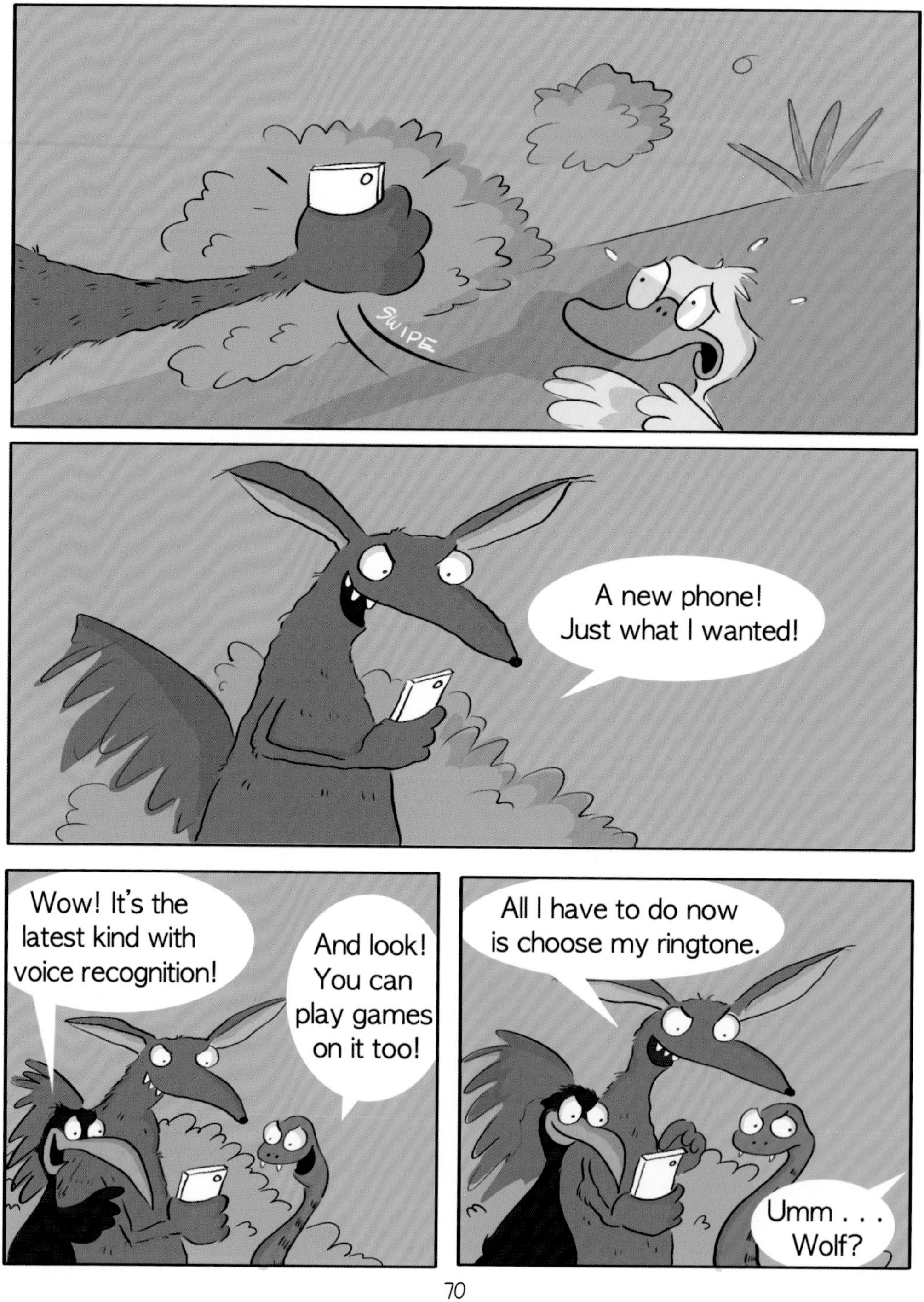
SWIPE
A new phone! Just what I wanted!
Wow! It's the latest kind with voice recognition!
And look! You can play games on it too!
All I have to do now is choose my ringtone.
Umm . . . Wolf?

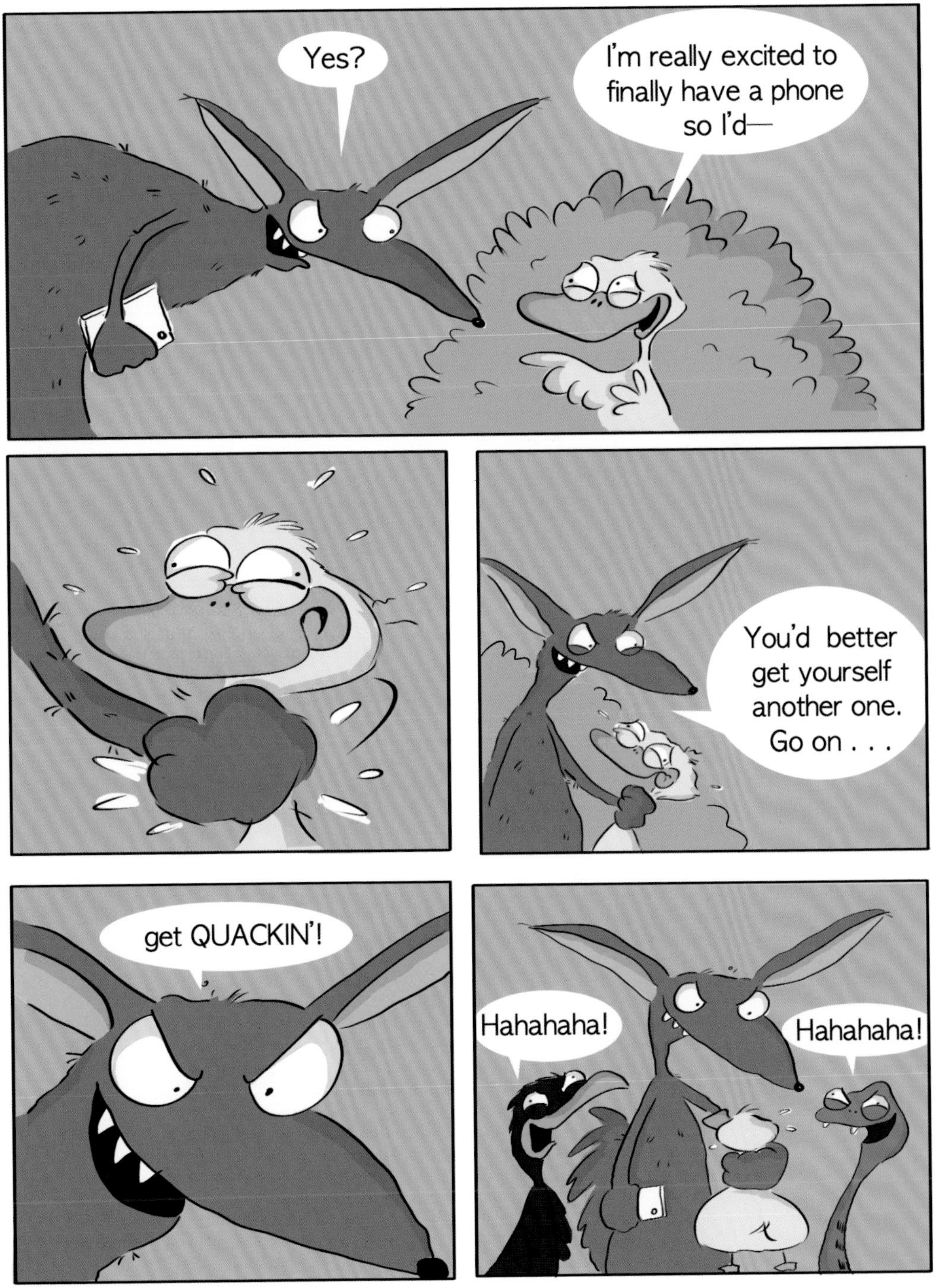
Yes?
I'm really excited to finally have a phone so I'd—
You'd better get yourself another one. Go on . . .
get QUACKIN'!
Hahahaha!
Hahahaha!

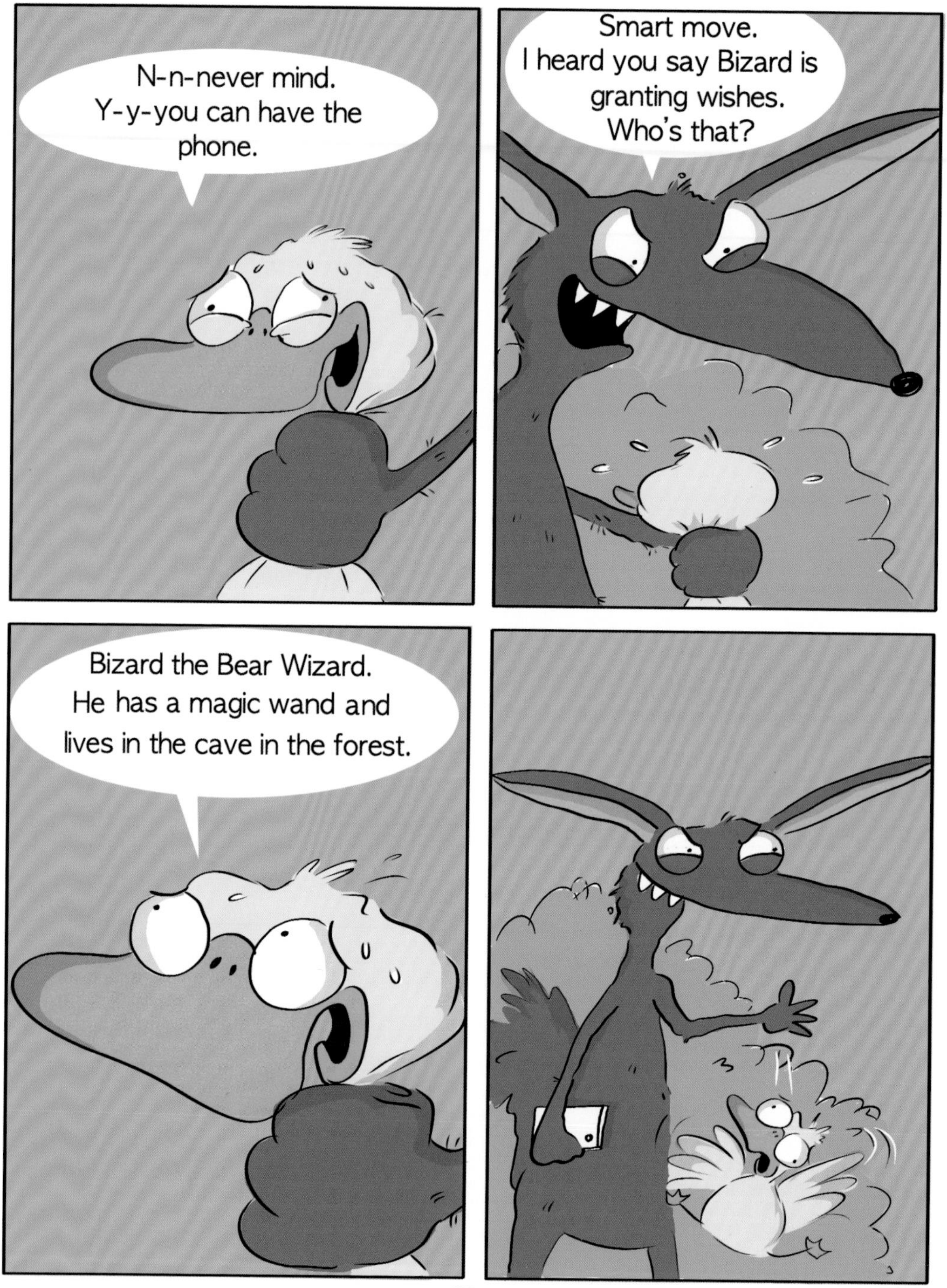
N-n-never mind. Y-y-you can have the phone.
Smart move. I heard you say Bizard is granting wishes. Who's that?
Bizard the Bear Wizard. He has a magic wand and lives in the cave in the forest.

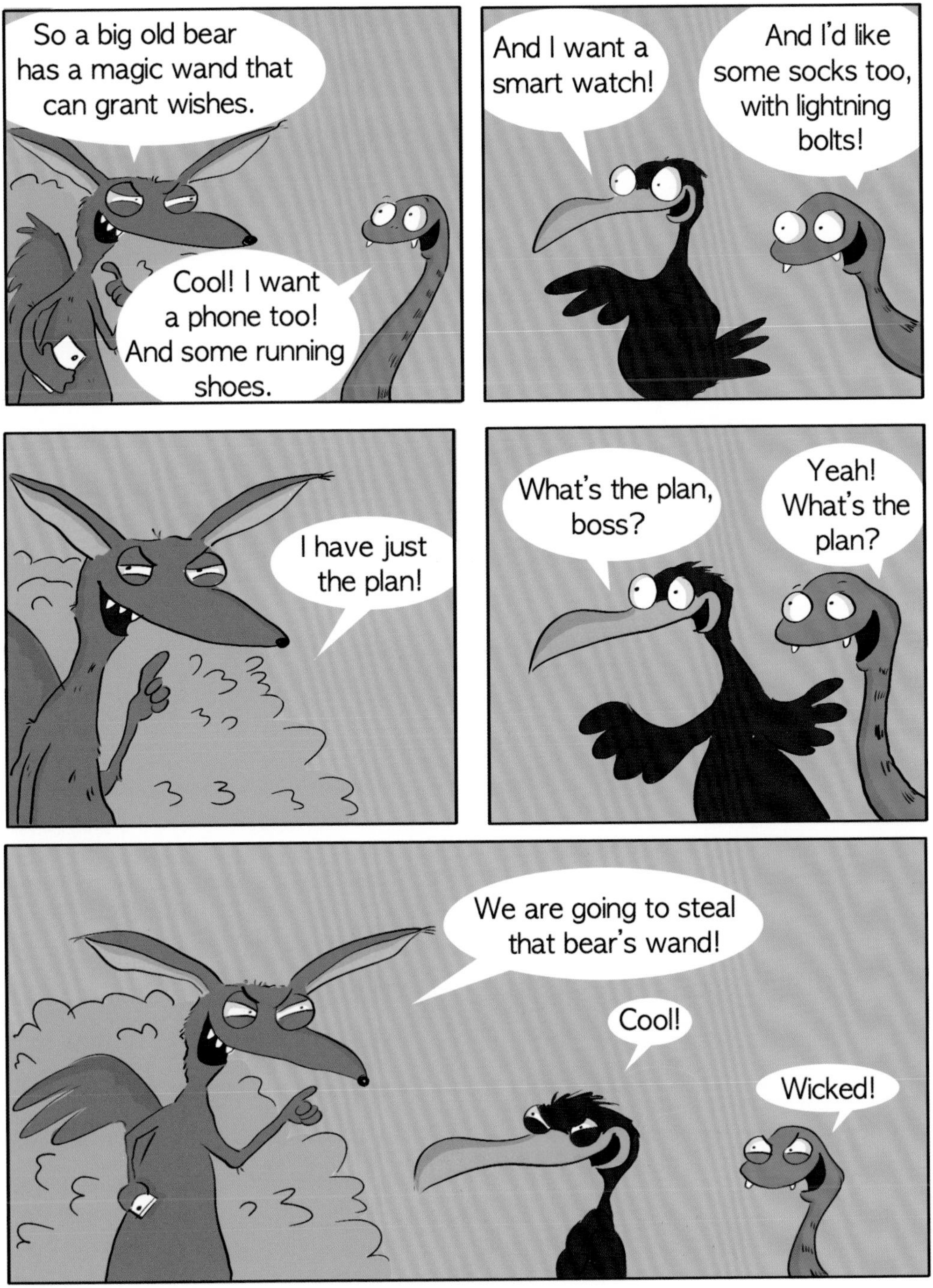
So a big old bear has a magic wand that can grant wishes.
Cool! I want a phone too! And some running shoes.
And I want a smart watch!
And I'd like some socks too, with lightning bolts!
I have just the plan!
What's the plan, boss?
Yeah! What's the plan?
We are going to steal that bear's wand!
Cool!
Wicked!

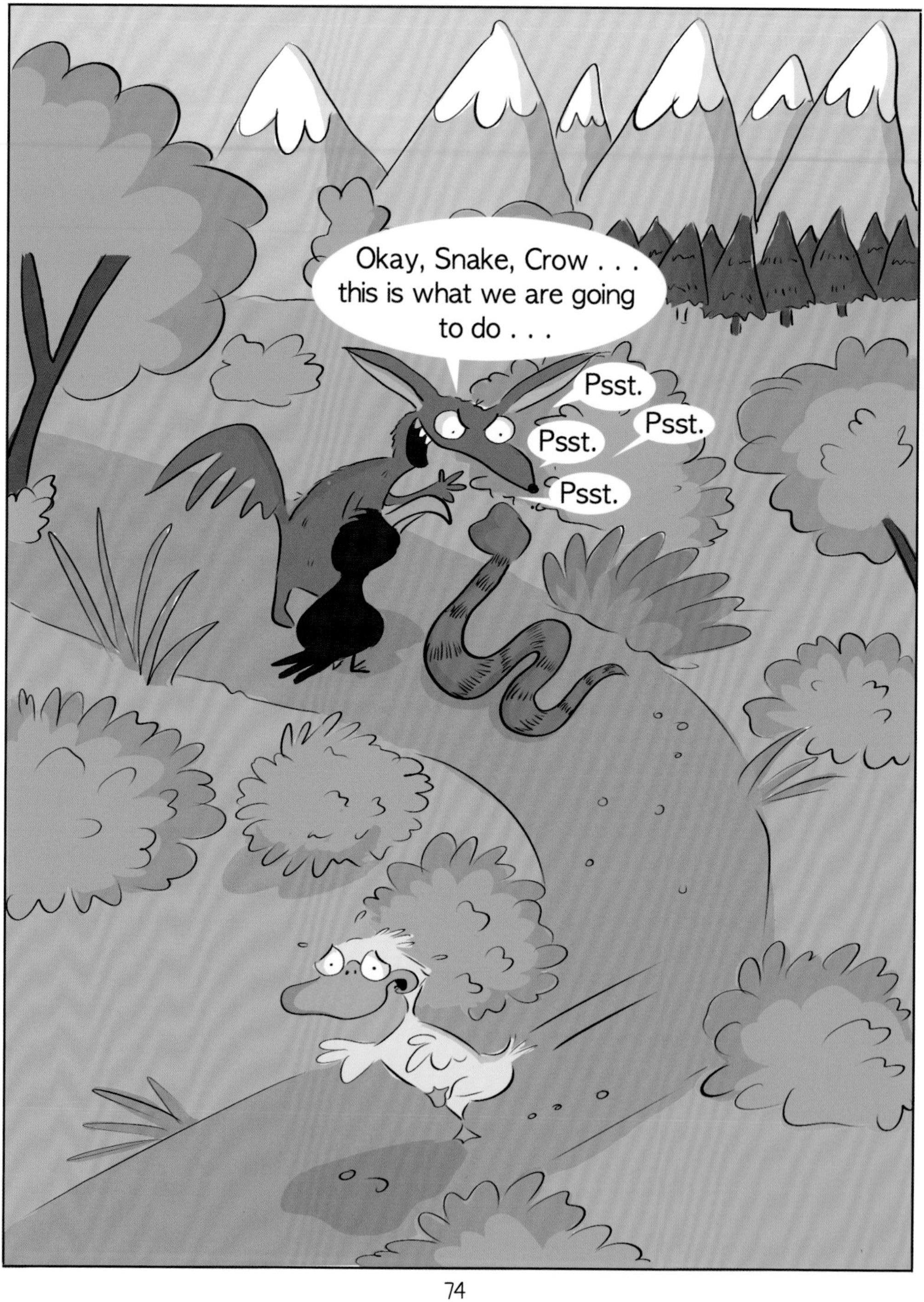

Okay, Snake, Crow . . . this is what we are going to do . . .
Psst.
Psst.
Psst.
Psst.

CHAPTER 9

WOLF'S WICKED WISH

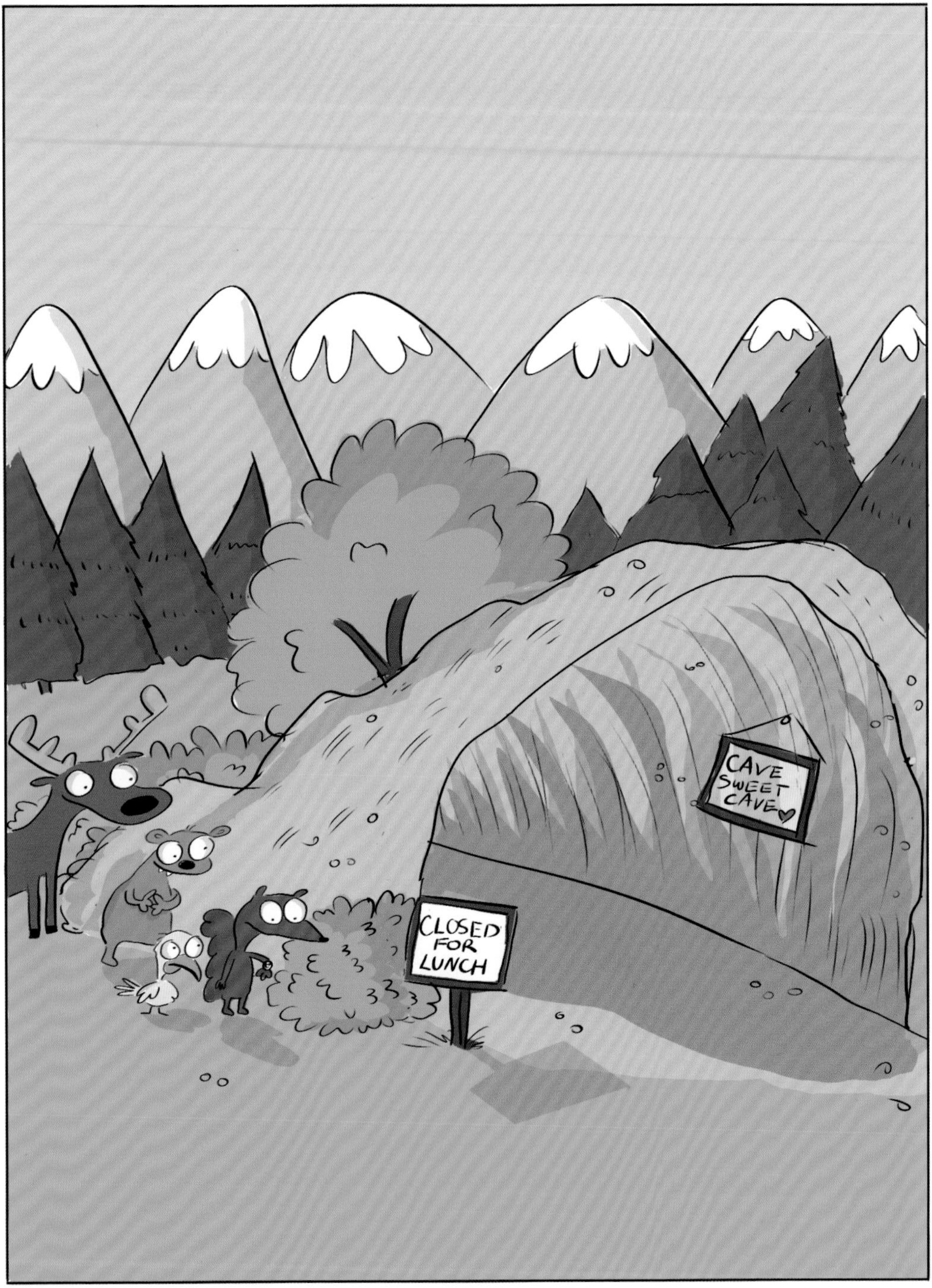
CAVE SWEET CAVE
CLOSED FOR LUNCH

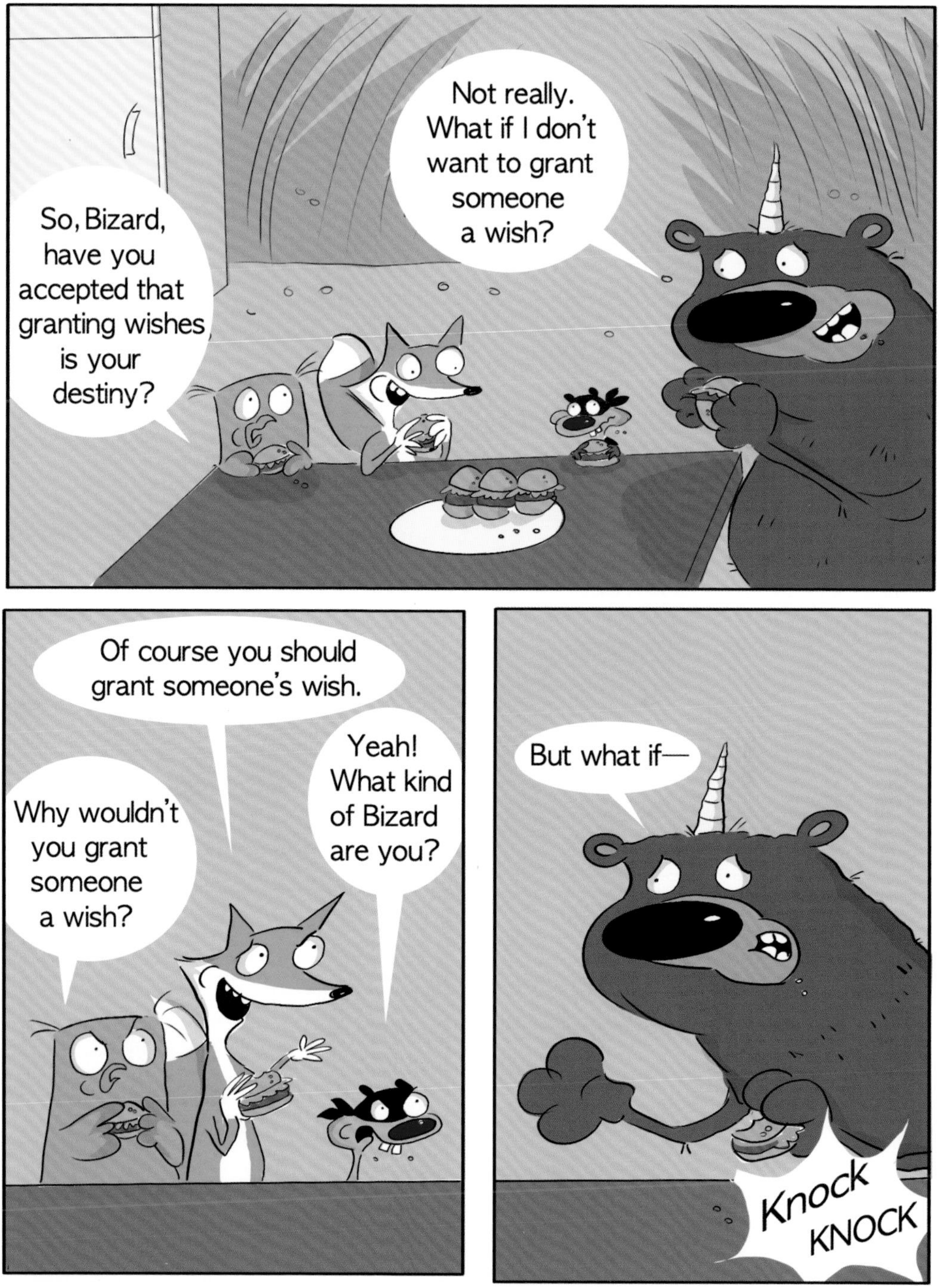
So, Bizard, have you accepted that granting wishes is your destiny?
Not really. What if I don't want to grant someone a wish?
Of course you should grant someone's wish.
Why wouldn't you grant someone a wish?
Yeah! What kind of Bizard are you?
But what if—
Knock KNOCK

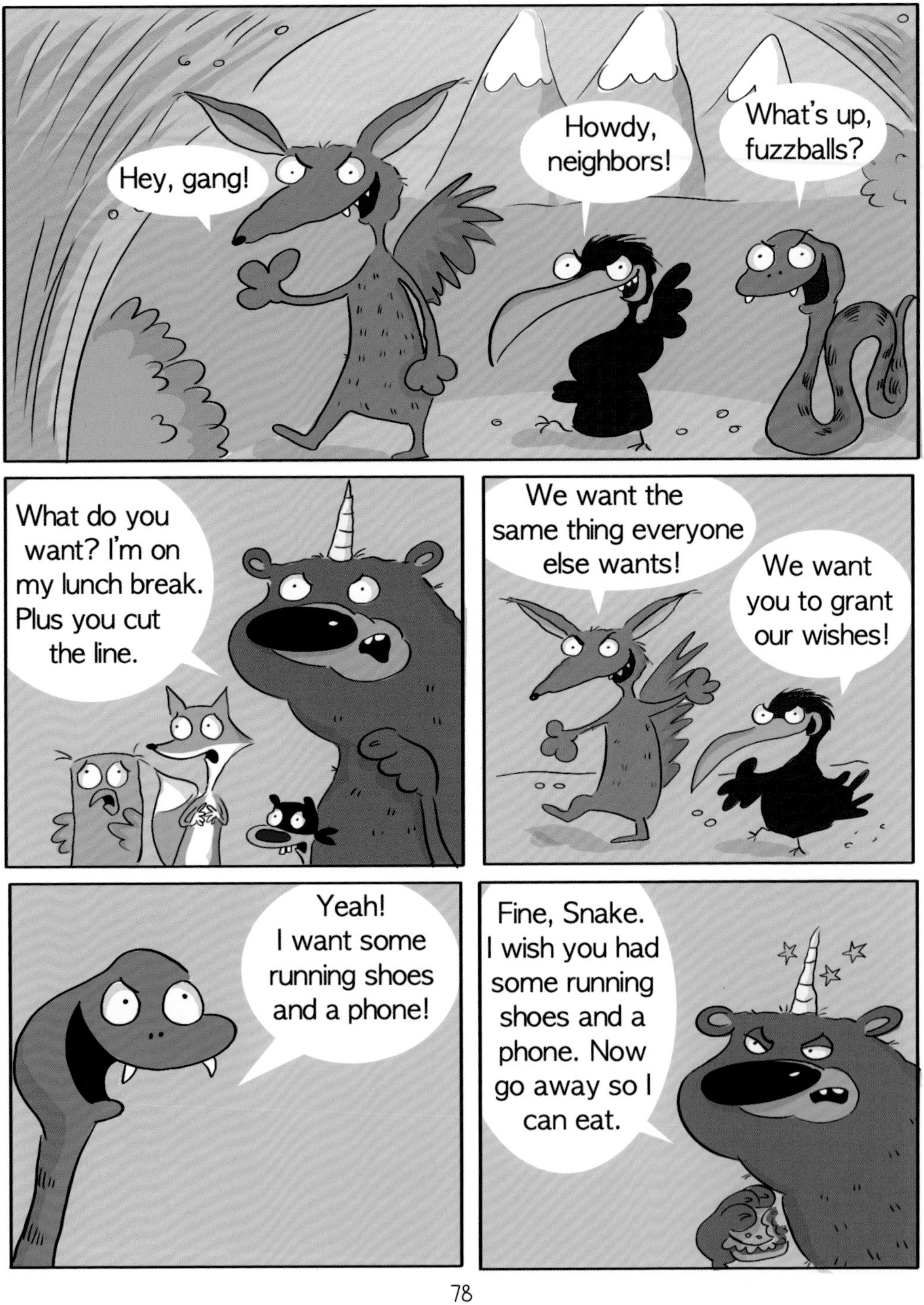
Hey, gang!
Howdy, neighbors!
What's up, fuzzballs?
What do you want? I'm on my lunch break. Plus you cut the line.
We want the same thing everyone else wants!
We want you to grant our wishes!
Yeah! I want some running shoes and a phone!
Fine, Snake. I wish you had some running shoes and a phone. Now go away so I can eat.

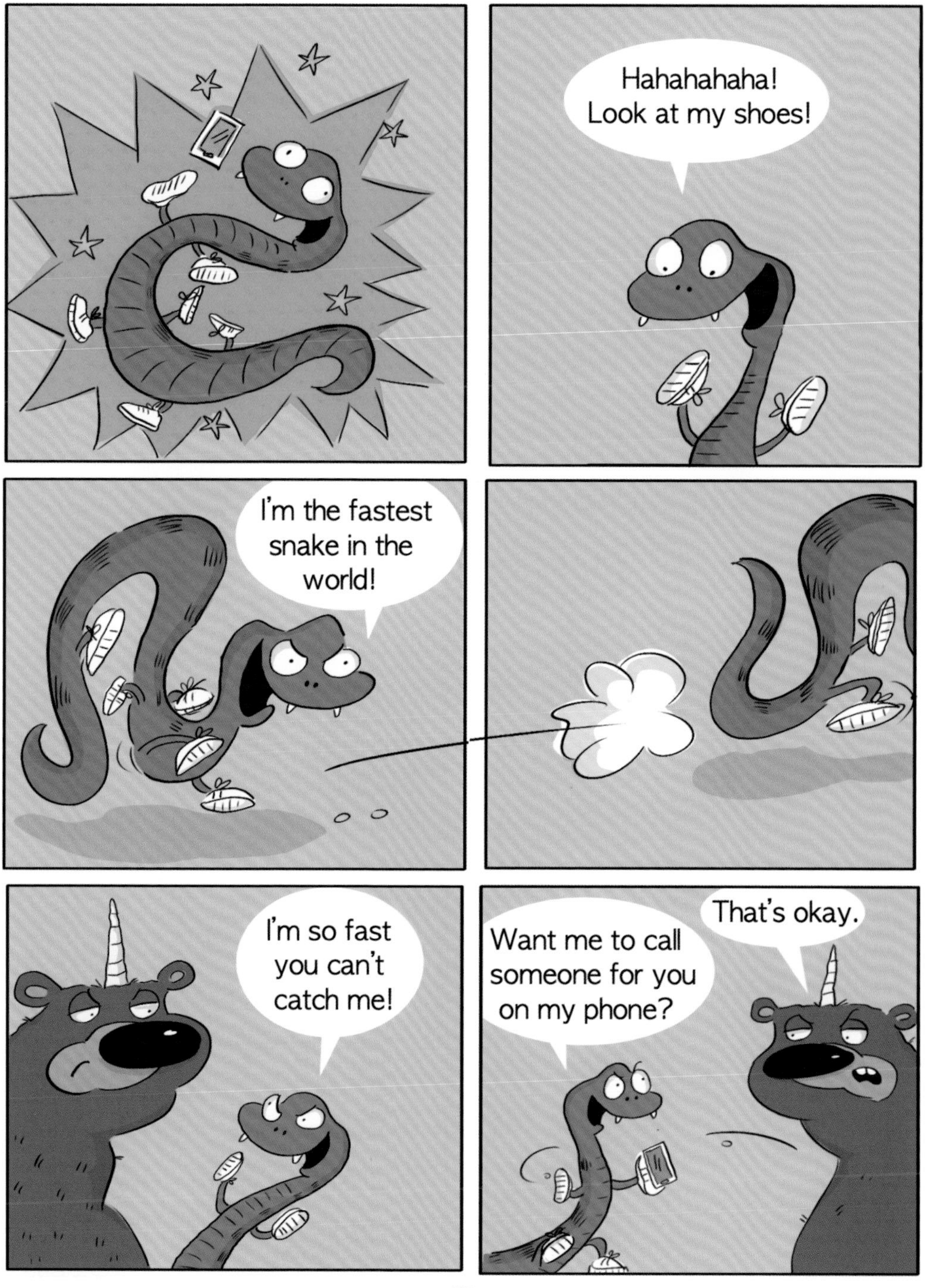
Hahahahaha! Look at my shoes!
I'm the fastest snake in the world!
I'm so fast you can't catch me!
Want me to call someone for you on my phone?
That's okay.

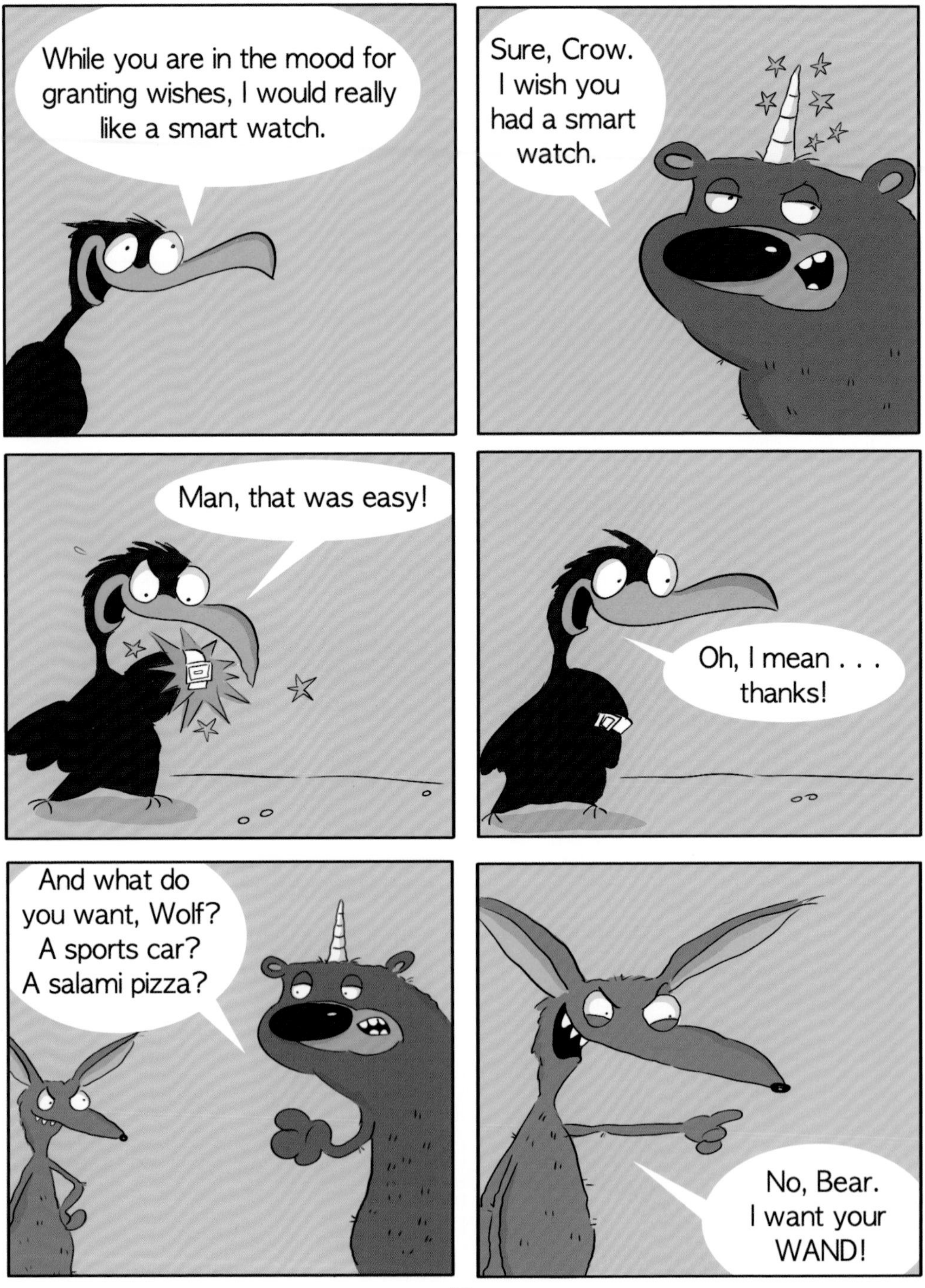
While you are in the mood for granting wishes, I would really like a smart watch.
Sure, Crow. I wish you had a smart watch.
Man, that was easy!
Oh, I mean . . . thanks!
And what do you want, Wolf? A sports car? A salami pizza?
No, Bear. I want your WAND!

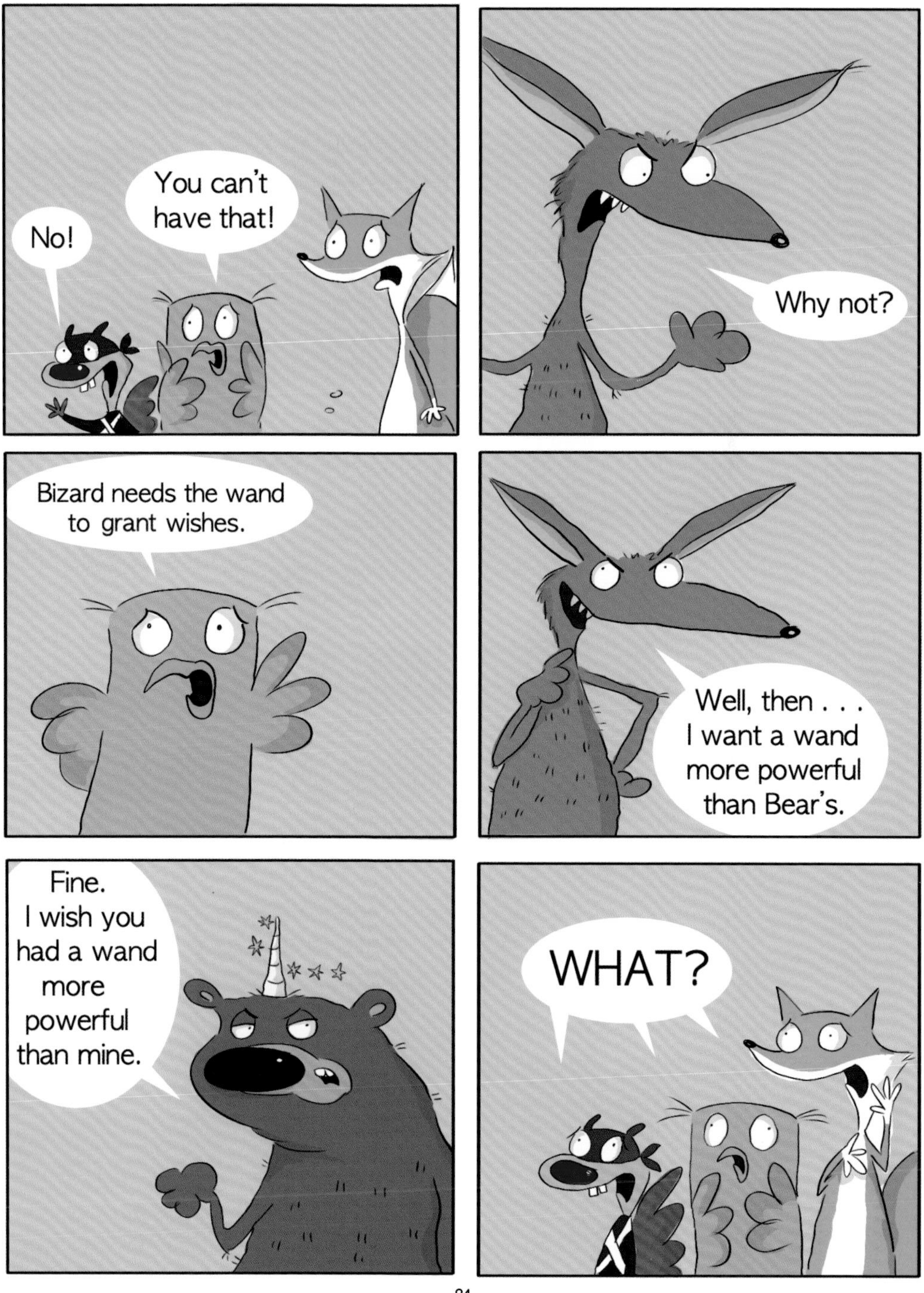
No!
You can't have that!
Why not?
Bizard needs the wand to grant wishes.
Well, then . . . I want a wand more powerful than Bear's.
Fine. I wish you had a wand more powerful than mine.
WHAT?

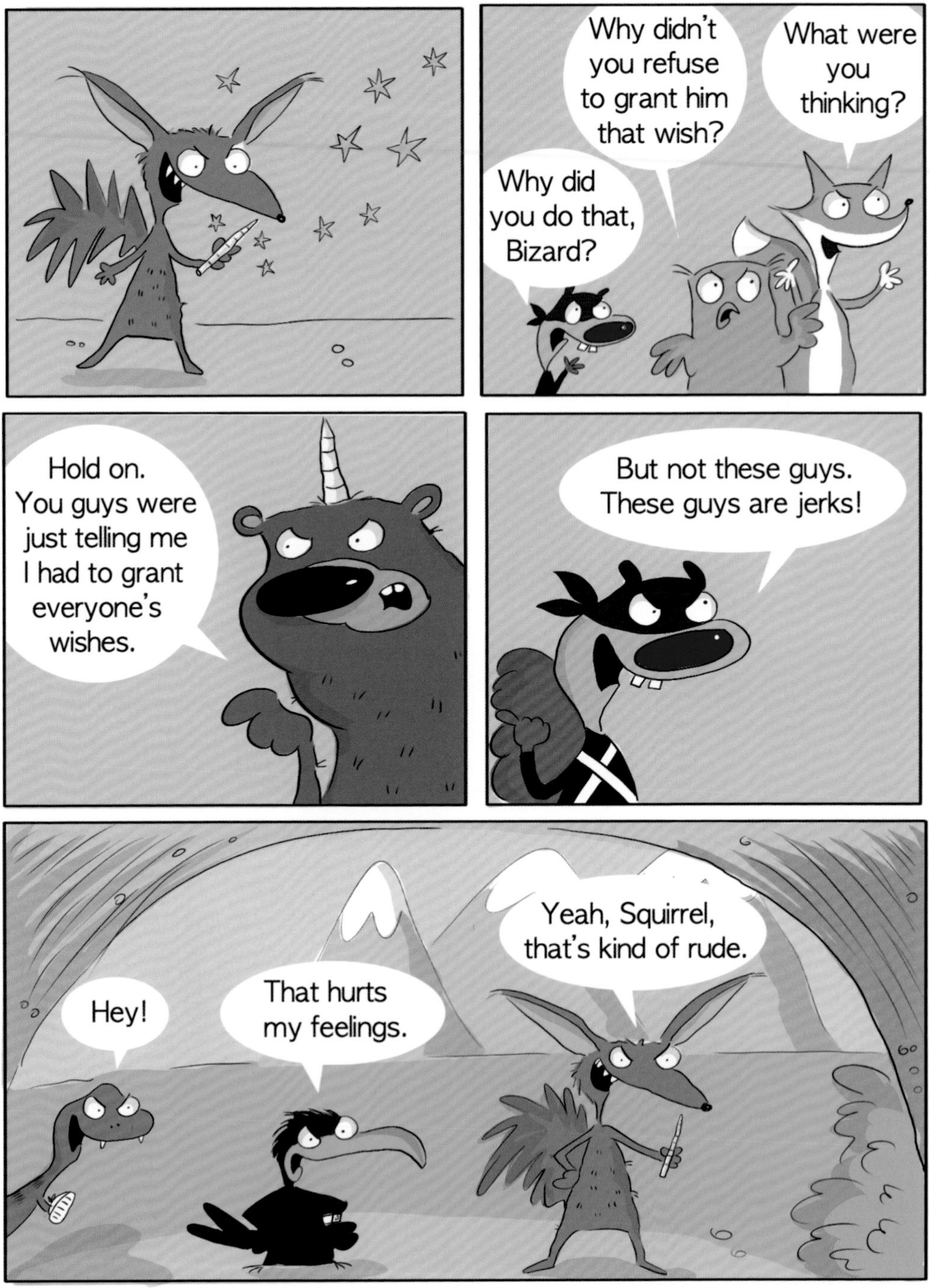

Why did you do that, Bizard?
Why didn't you refuse to grant him that wish?
What were you thinking?
Hold on. You guys were just telling me I had to grant everyone's wishes.
But not these guys. These guys are jerks!
Hey!
That hurts my feelings.
Yeah, Squirrel, that's kind of rude.

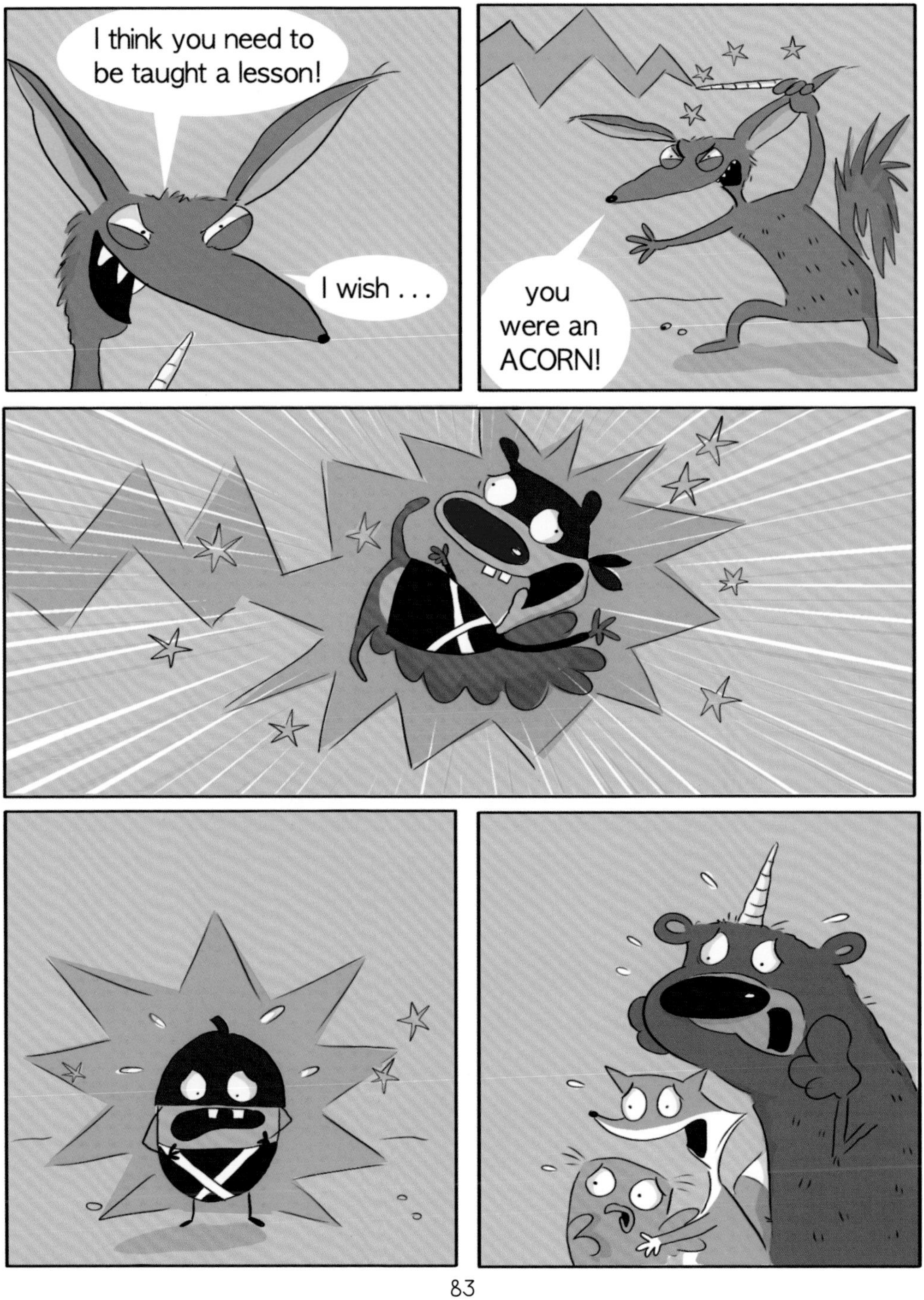
I think you need to be taught a lesson!
I wish . . .
you were an ACORN!

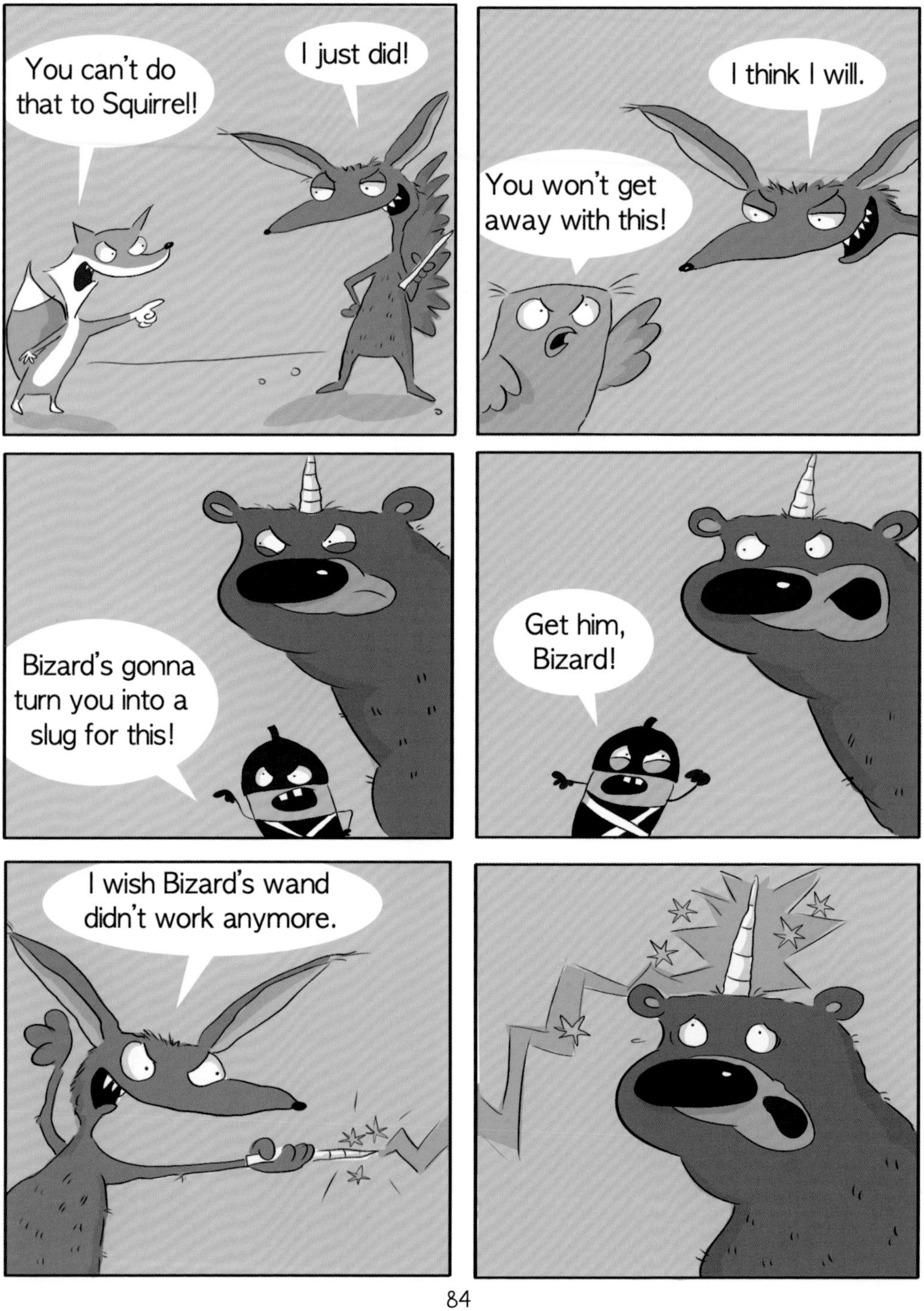
You can't do that to Squirrel!
I just did!
I think I will.
You won't get away with this!
Bizard's gonna turn you into a slug for this!
Get him, Bizard!
I wish Bizard's wand didn't work anymore.

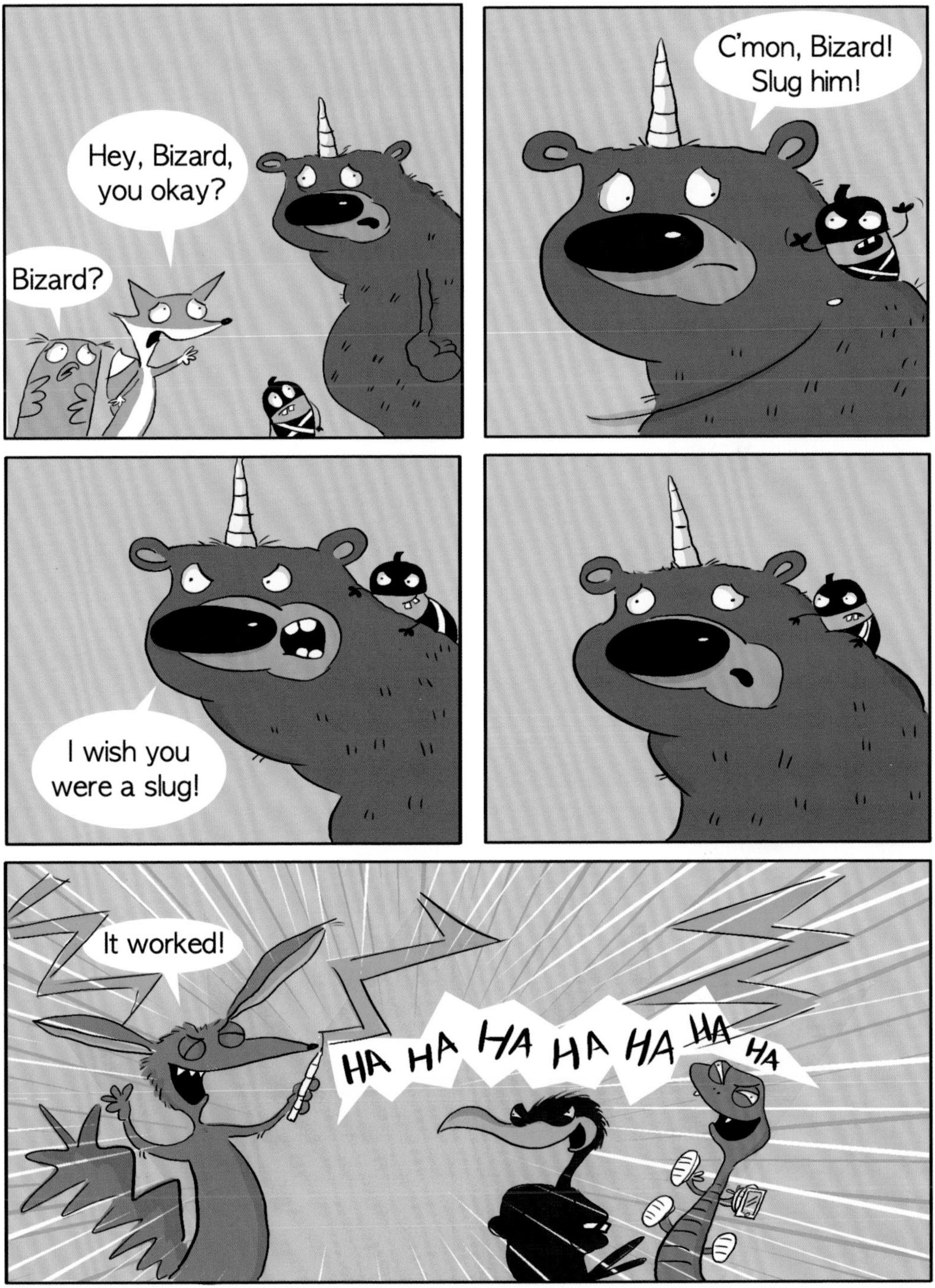
Hey, Bizard, you okay?
Bizard?
C'mon, Bizard! Slug him!
I wish you were a slug!
It worked!
HA HA HA HA HA HA HA

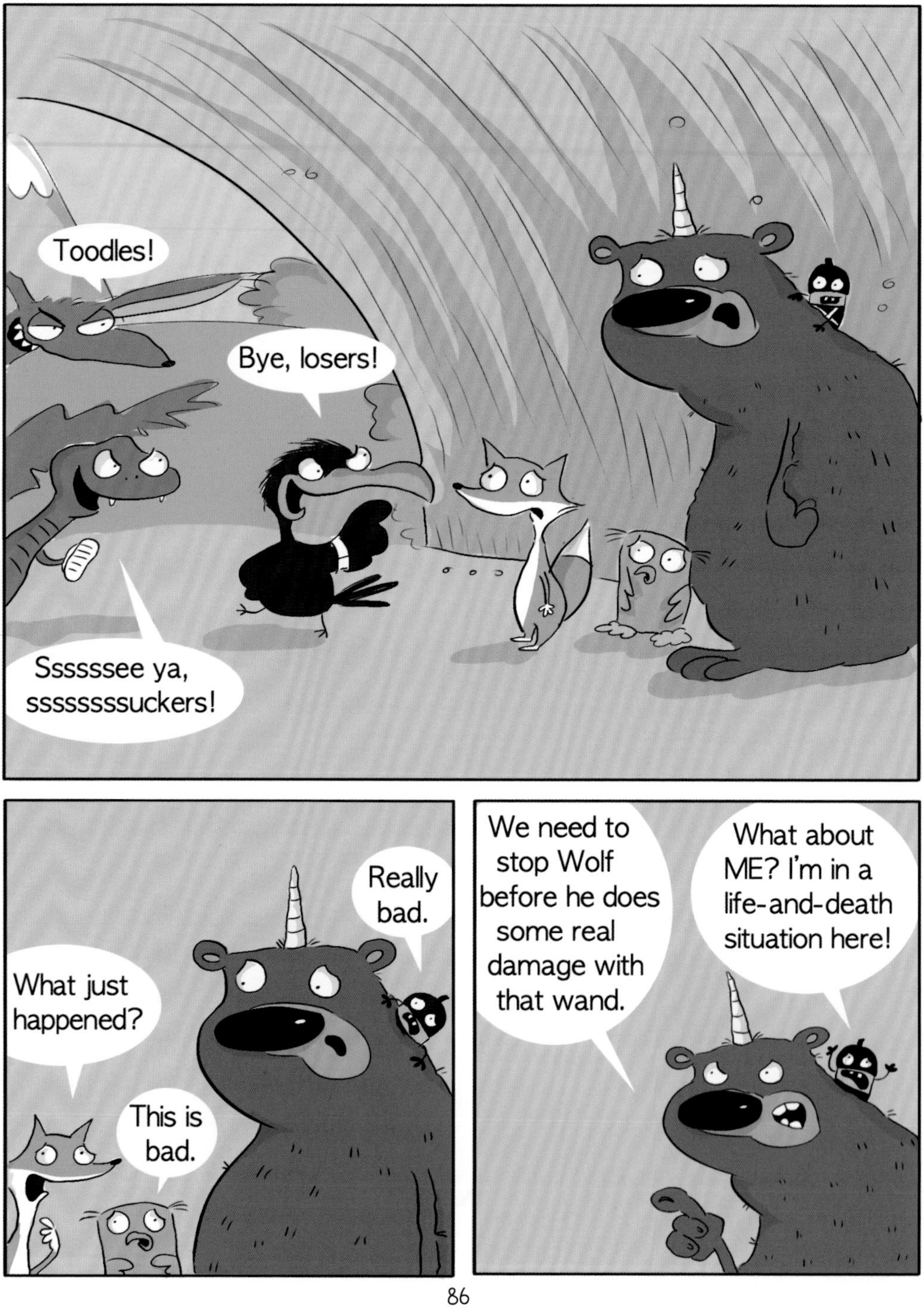
Toodles!
Bye, losers!
Sssssee ya, sssssssuckers!
What just happened?
This is bad.
Really bad.
We need to stop Wolf before he does some real damage with that wand.
What about ME? I'm in a life-and-death situation here!

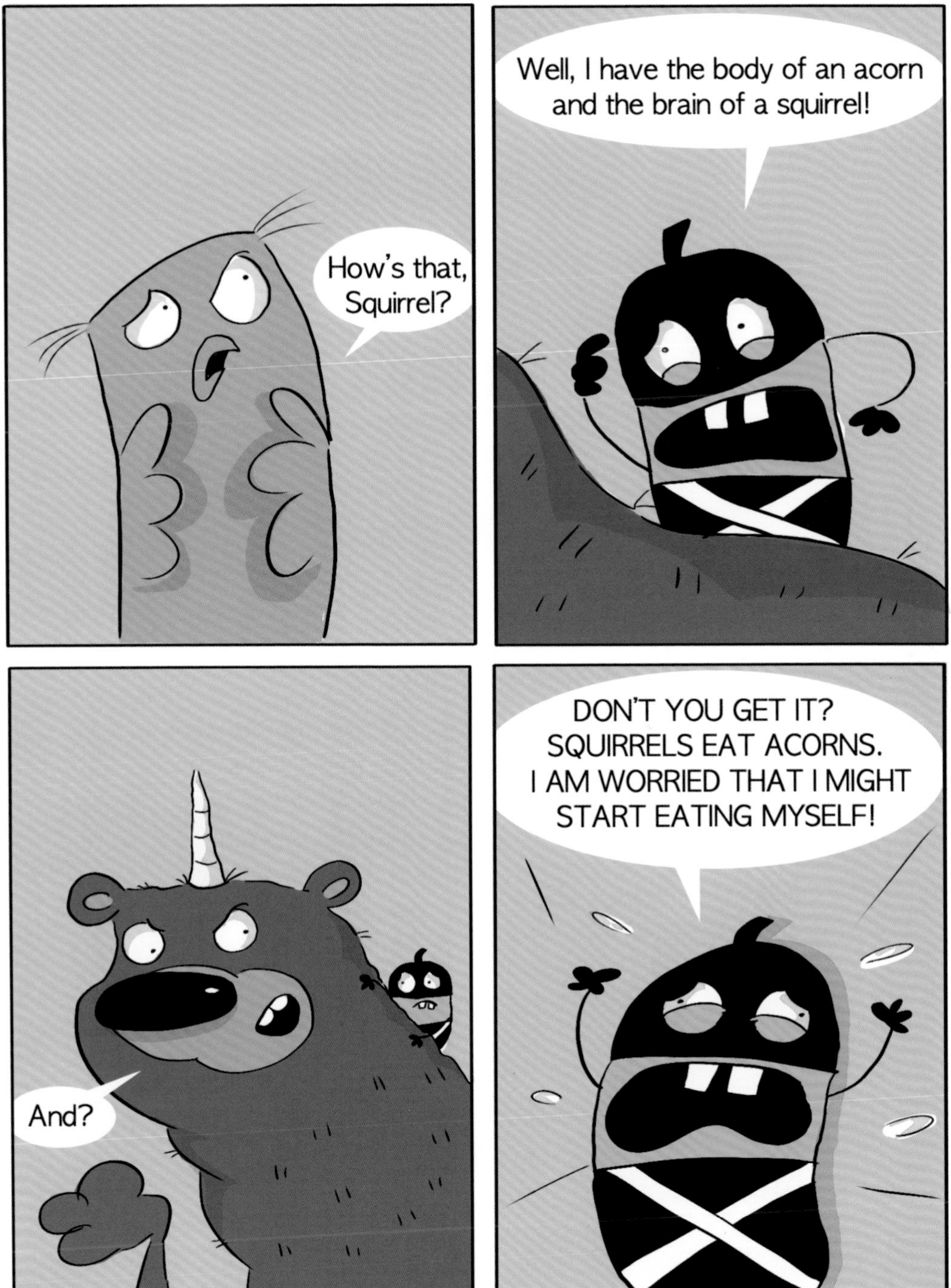
How's that, Squirrel?
Well, I have the body of an acorn and the brain of a squirrel!
And?
DON'T YOU GET IT? SQUIRRELS EAT ACORNS. I AM WORRIED THAT I MIGHT START EATING MYSELF!

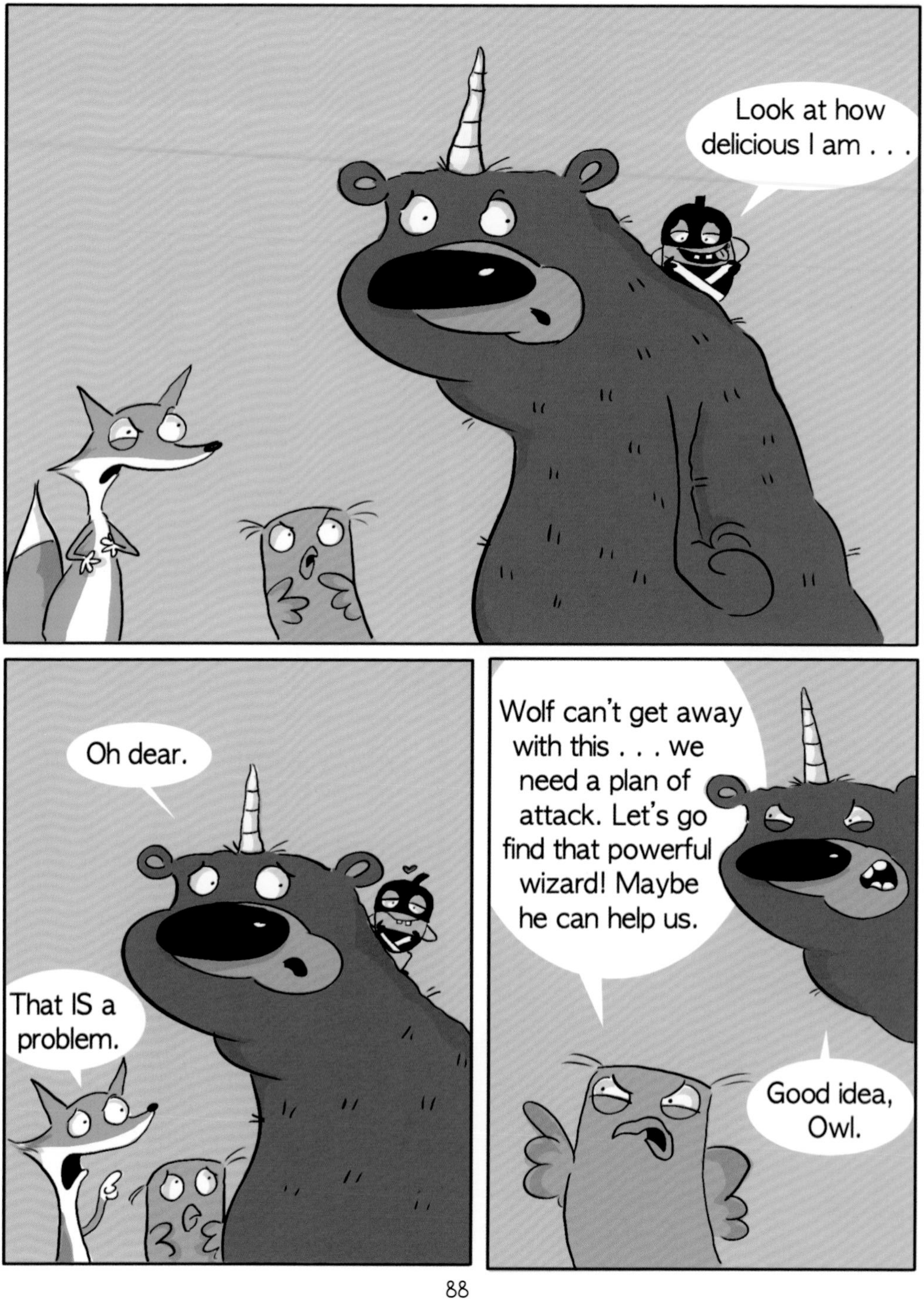

Look at how delicious I am . . .
Oh dear.
That IS a problem.
Wolf can't get away with this . . . we need a plan of attack. Let's go find that powerful wizard! Maybe he can help us.
Good idea, Owl.

CHAPTER 10

IN SEARCH OF THE
POWERFUL WIZARD

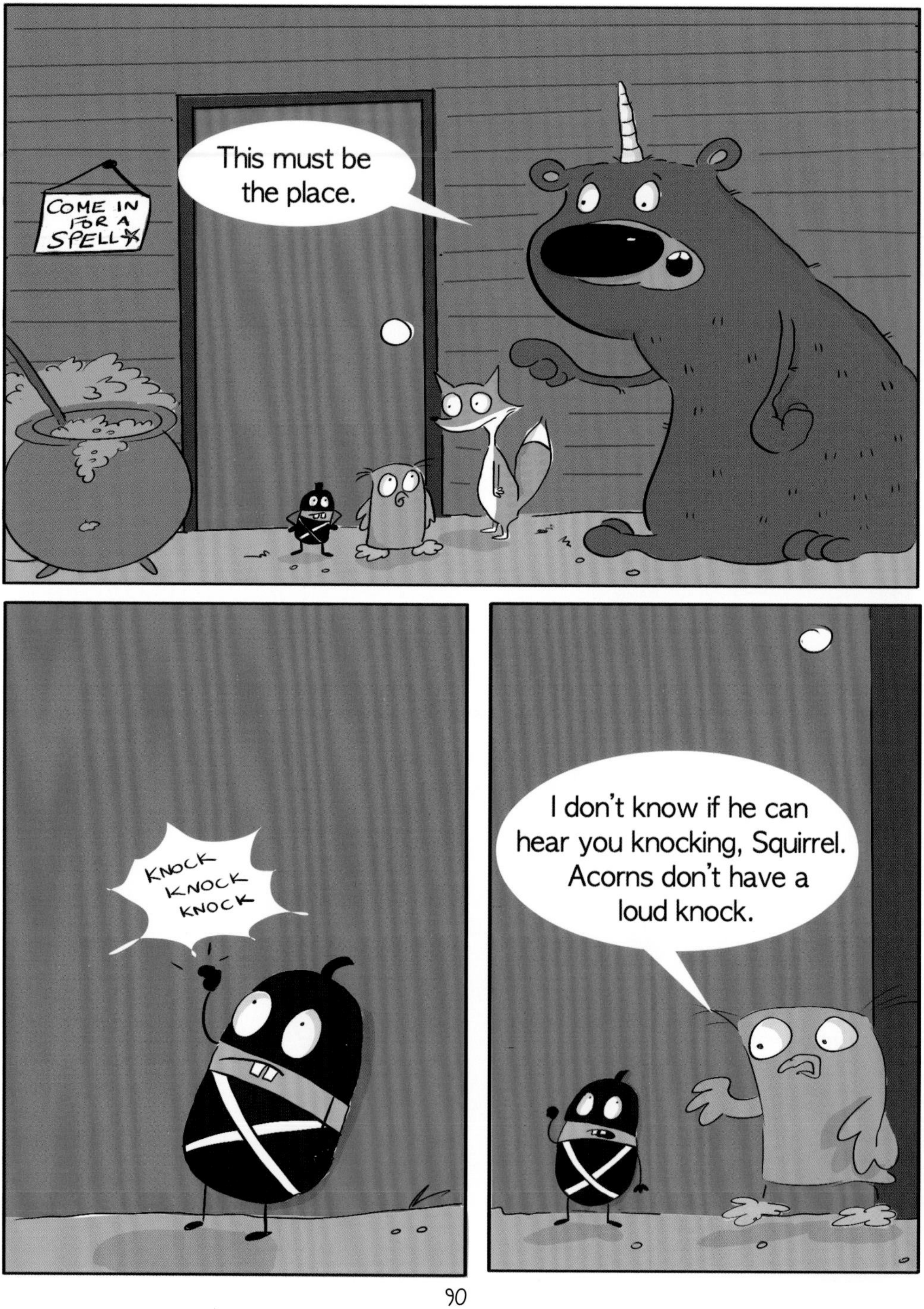
COME IN FOR A SPELL
This must be the place.
KNOCK KNOCK KNOCK
I don't know if he can hear you knocking, Squirrel. Acorns don't have a loud knock.

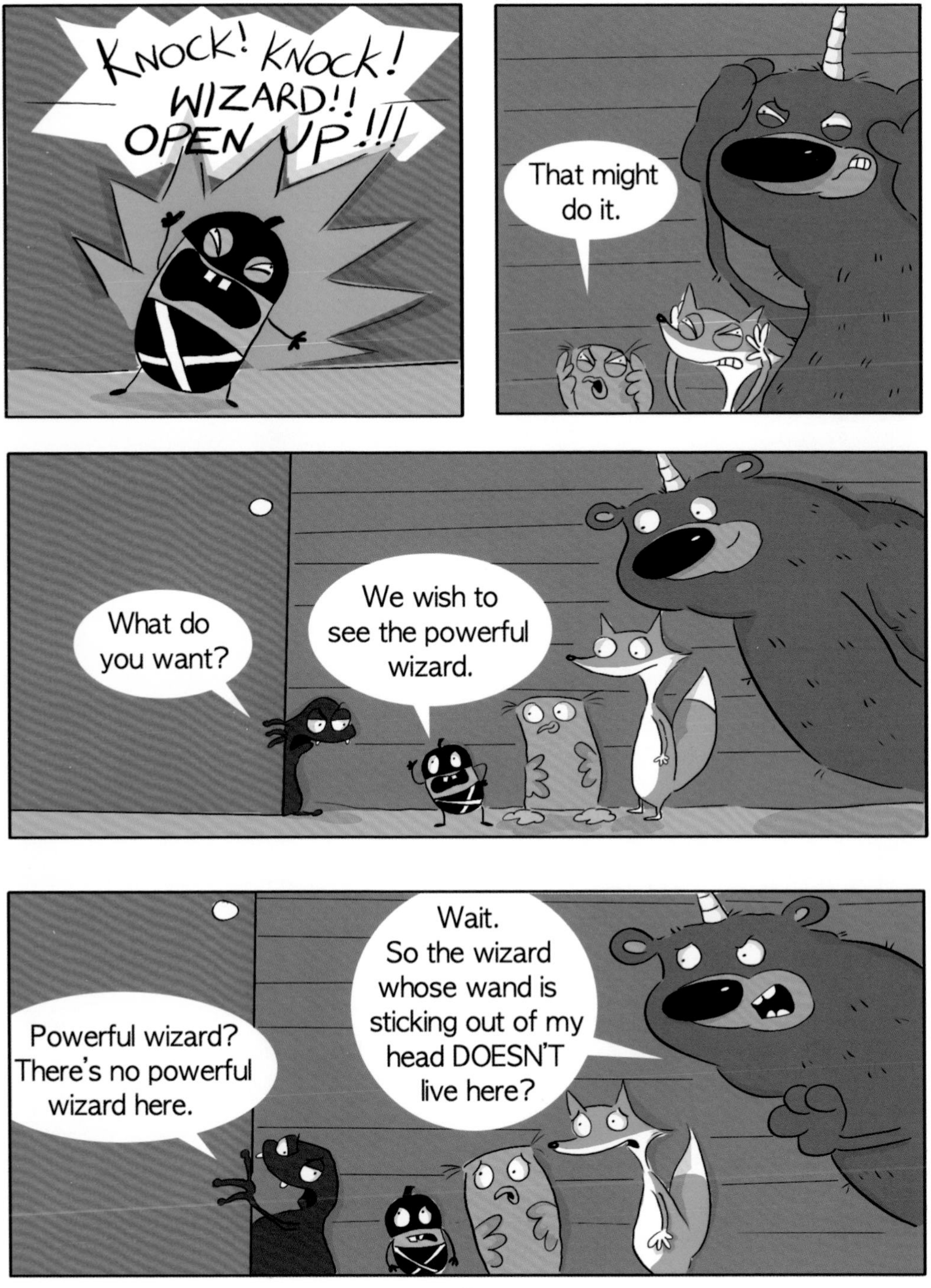
KNOCK! KNOCK! WIZARD!! OPEN UP!!!
That might do it.
What do you want?
We wish to see the powerful wizard.
Powerful wizard? There's no powerful wizard here.
Wait. So the wizard whose wand is sticking out of my head DOESN'T live here?

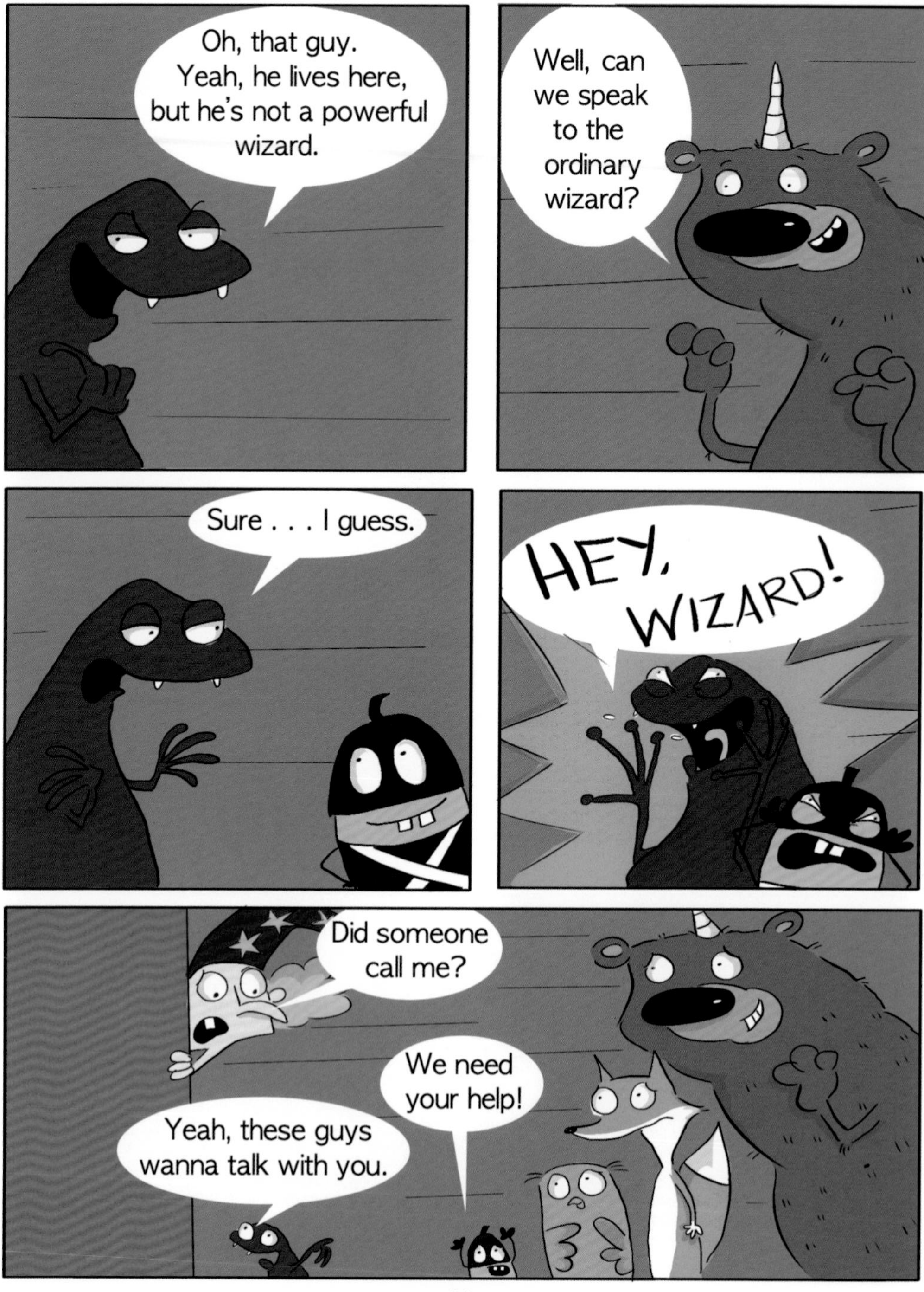

Oh, that guy. Yeah, he lives here, but he's not a powerful wizard.
Well, can we speak to the ordinary wizard?
Sure . . . I guess.
HEY, WIZARD!
Did someone call me?
We need your help!
Yeah, these guys wanna talk with you.

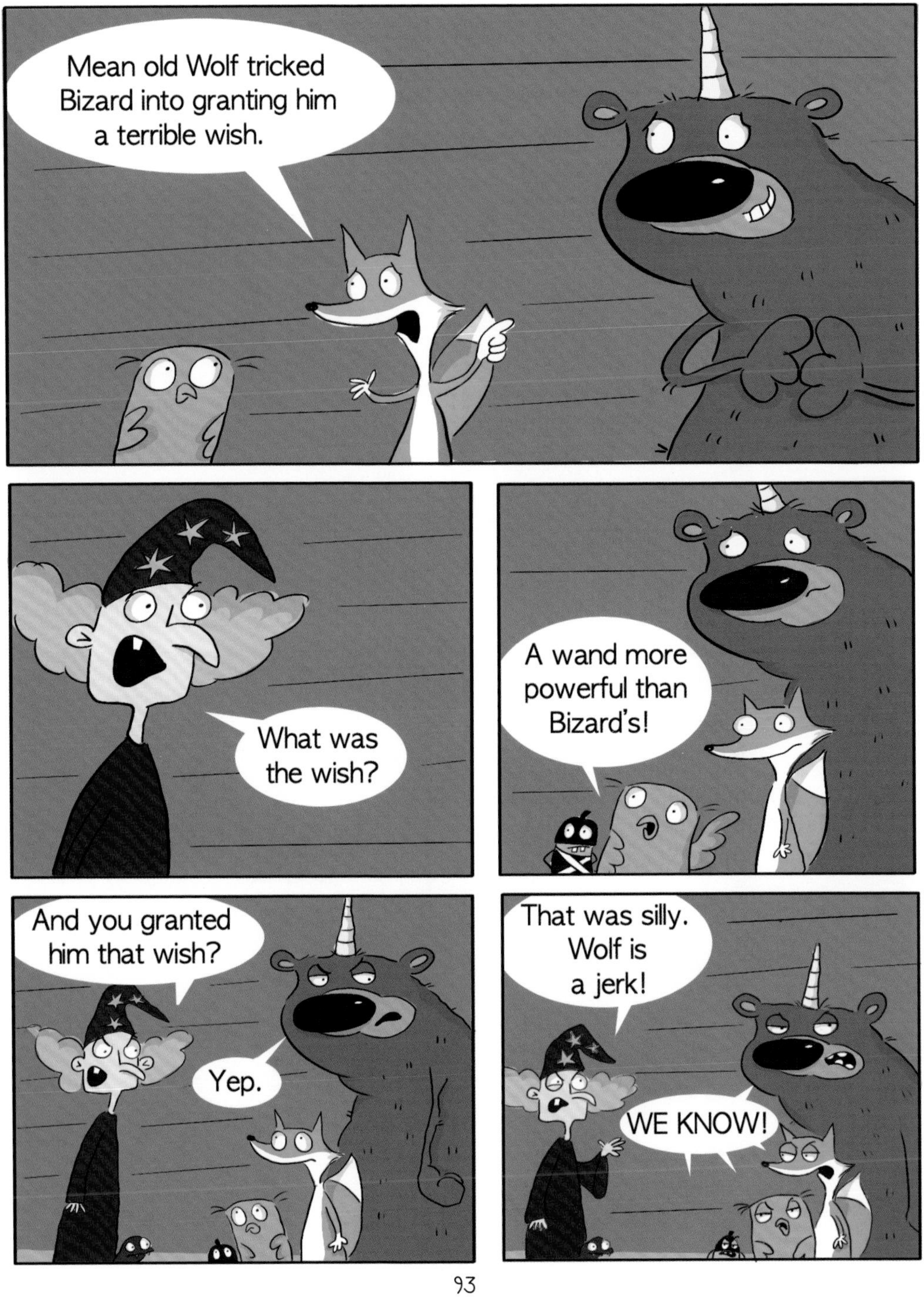
Mean old Wolf tricked Bizard into granting him a terrible wish.
What was the wish?
A wand more powerful than Bizard's!
And you granted him that wish?
Yep.
That was silly. Wolf is a jerk!
WE KNOW!

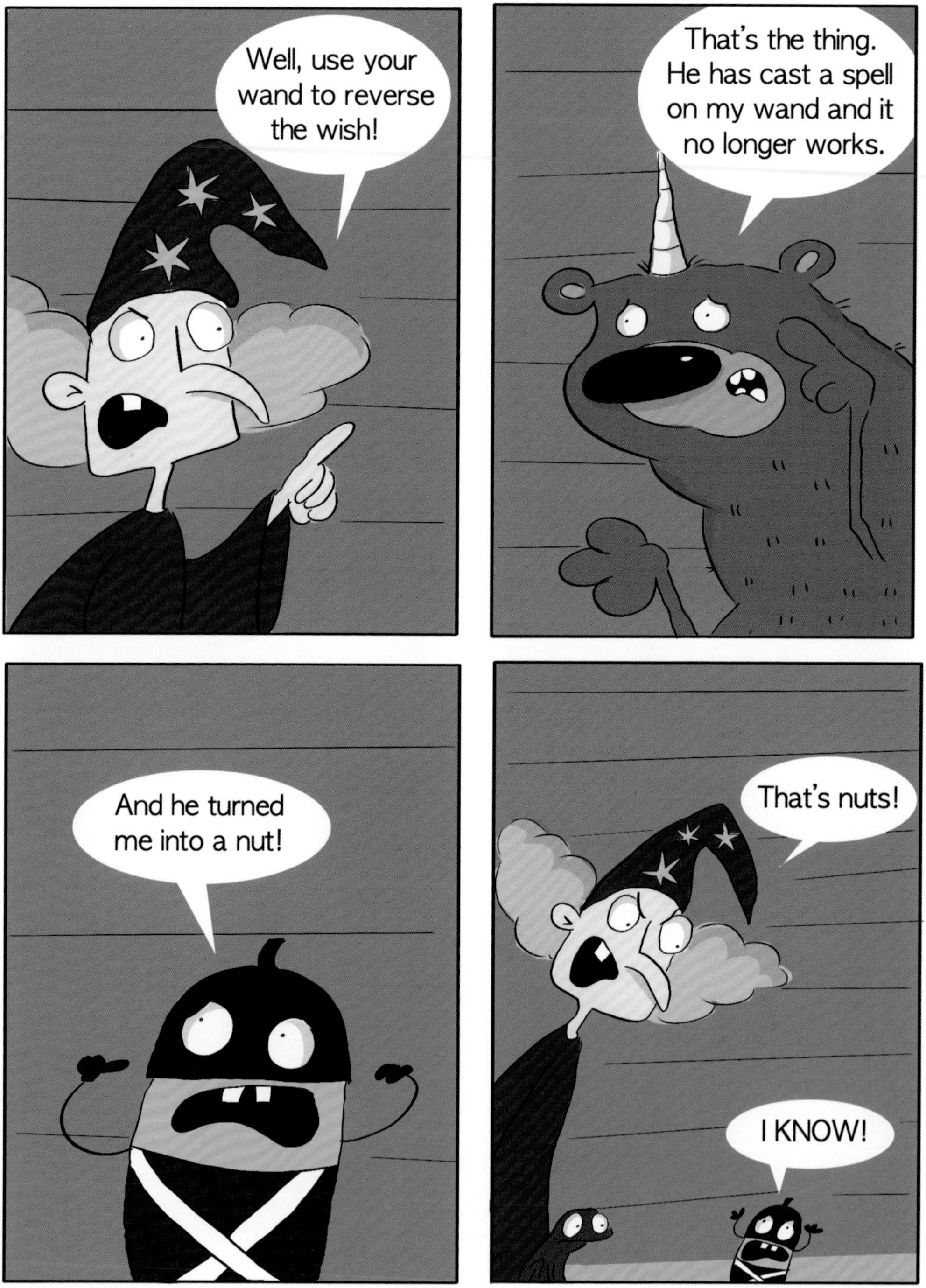
Well, use your wand to reverse the wish!
That's the thing. He has cast a spell on my wand and it no longer works.
And he turned me into a nut!
That's nuts!
I KNOW!

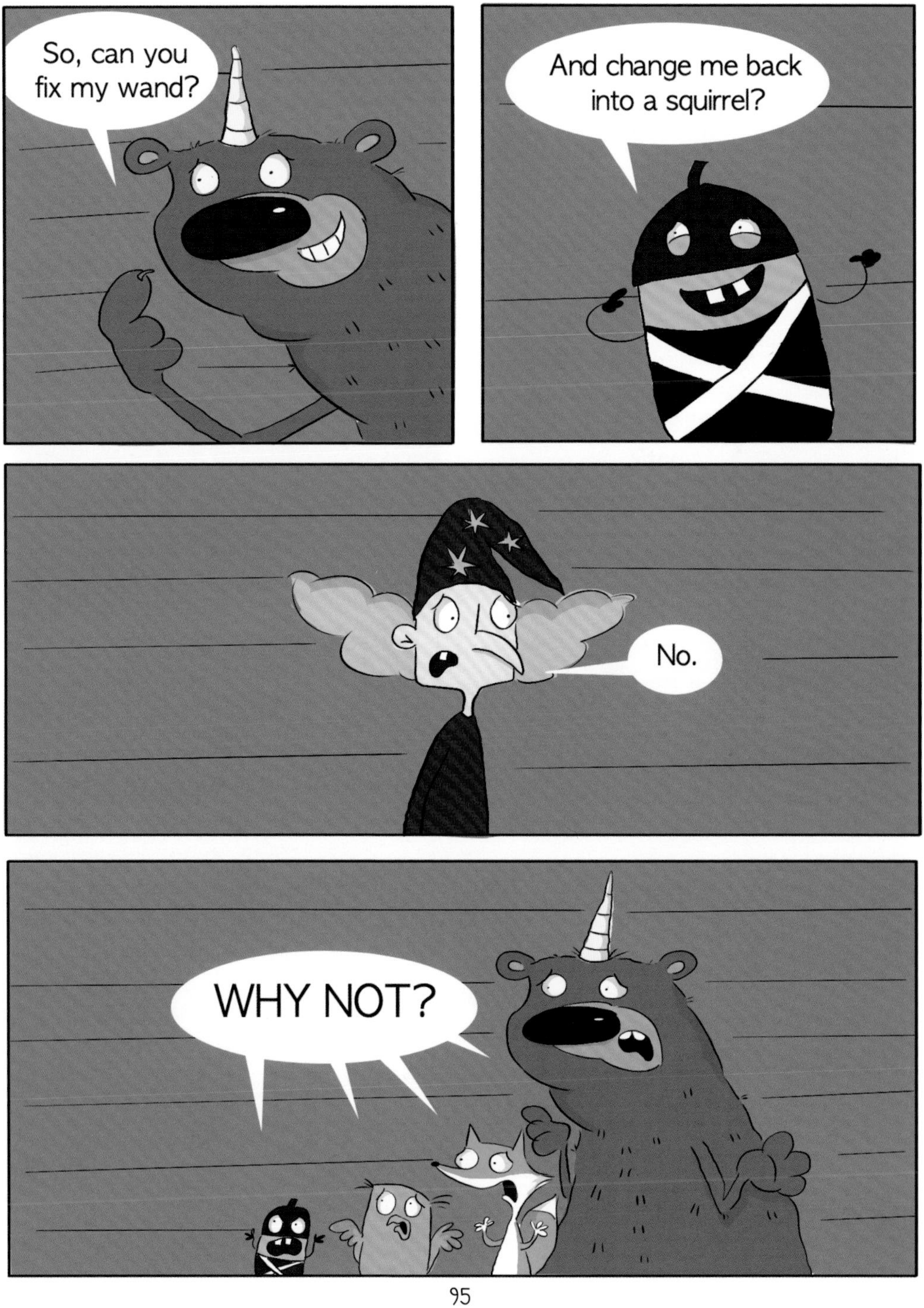
So, can you fix my wand?
And change me back into a squirrel?
No.
WHY NOT?

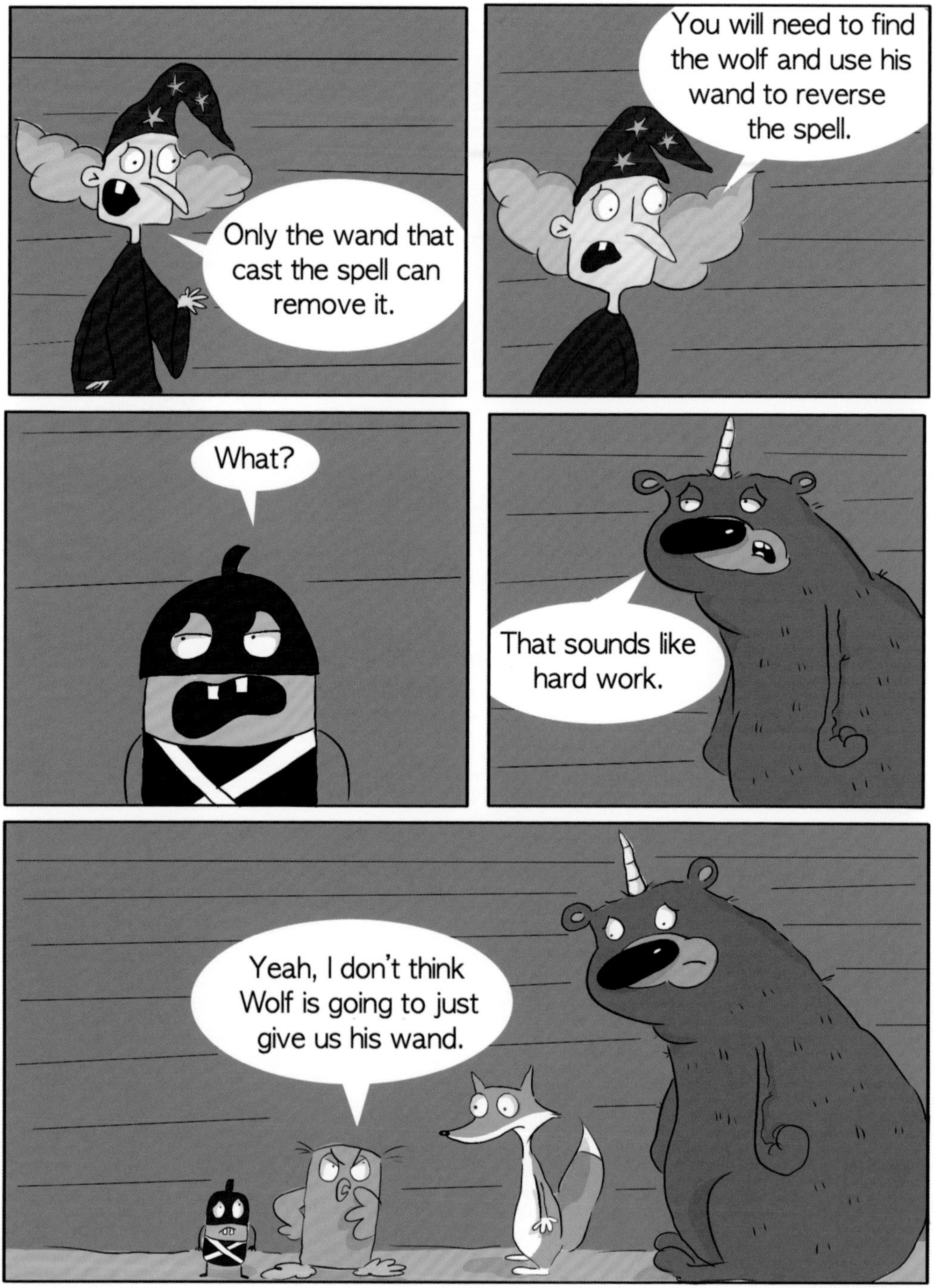
Only the wand that cast the spell can remove it.
You will need to find the wolf and use his wand to reverse the spell.
What?
That sounds like hard work.
Yeah, I don't think Wolf is going to just give us his wand.

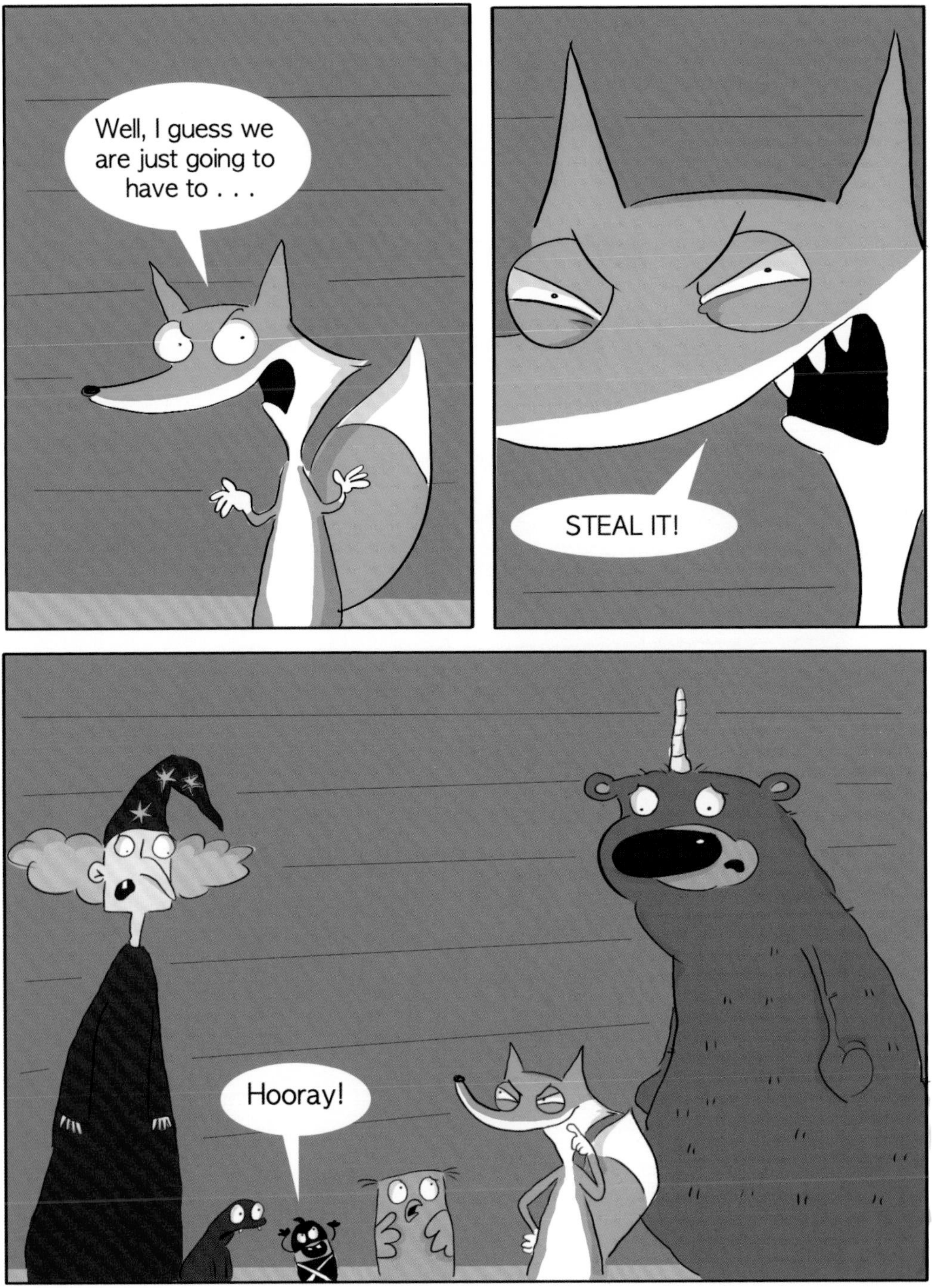
Well, I guess we are just going to have to . . .
STEAL IT!
Hooray!

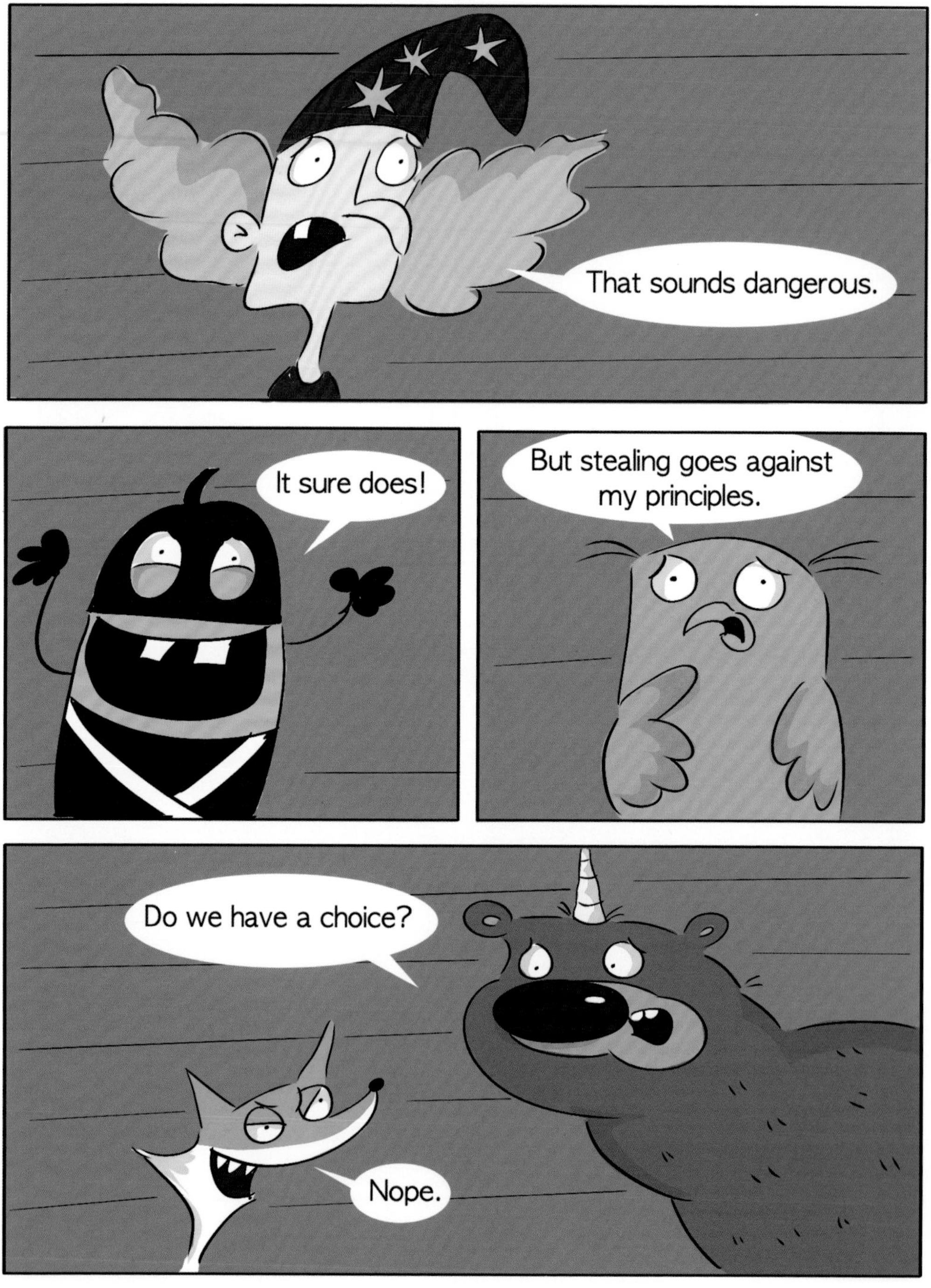
That sounds dangerous.
It sure does!
But stealing goes against my principles.
Do we have a choice?
Nope.

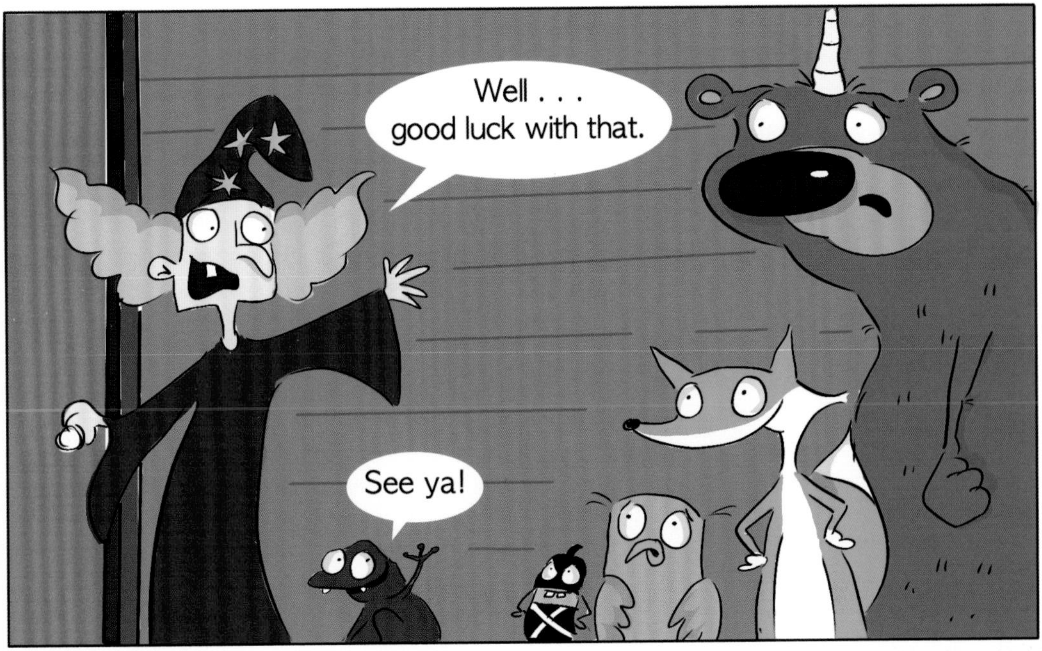
Well . . .
good luck with that.
See ya!

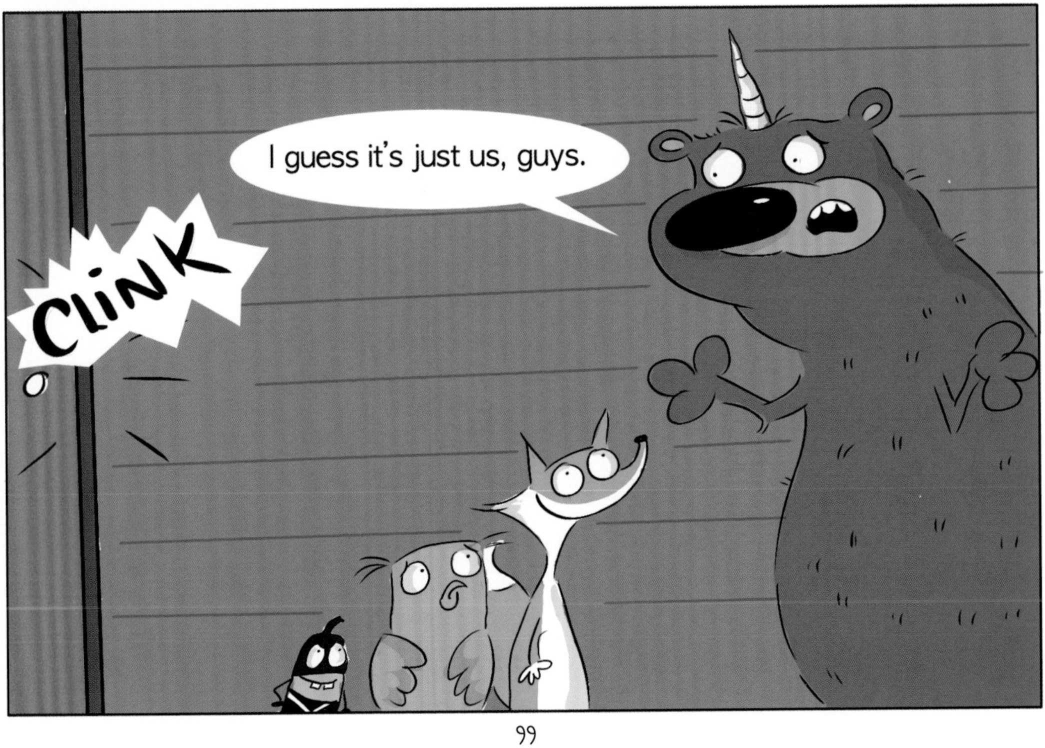
I guess it's just us, guys.
CLINK

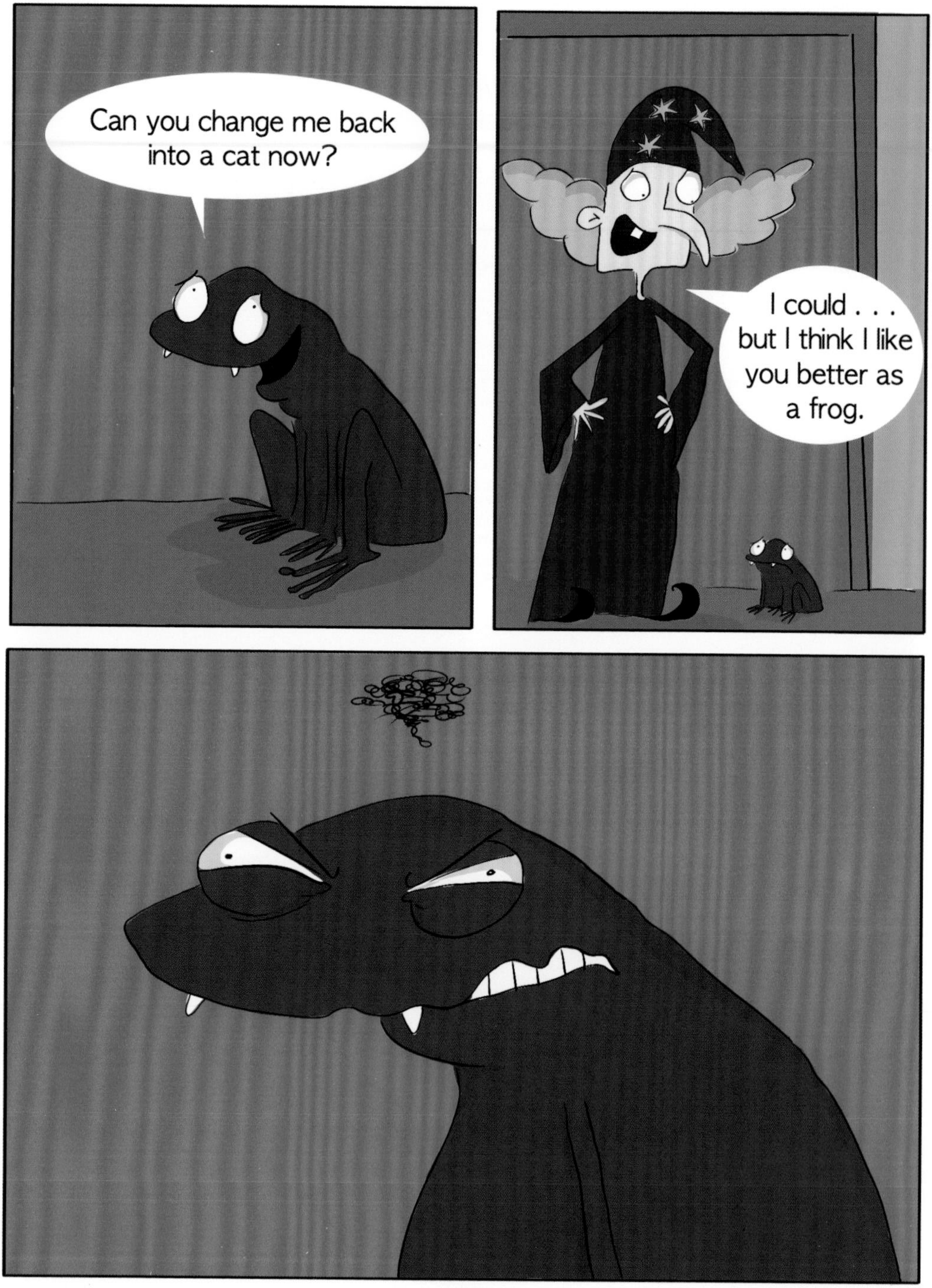
Can you change me back into a cat now?
I could . . . but I think I like you better as a frog.

CHAPTER 11
THE STEALING DILEMMA

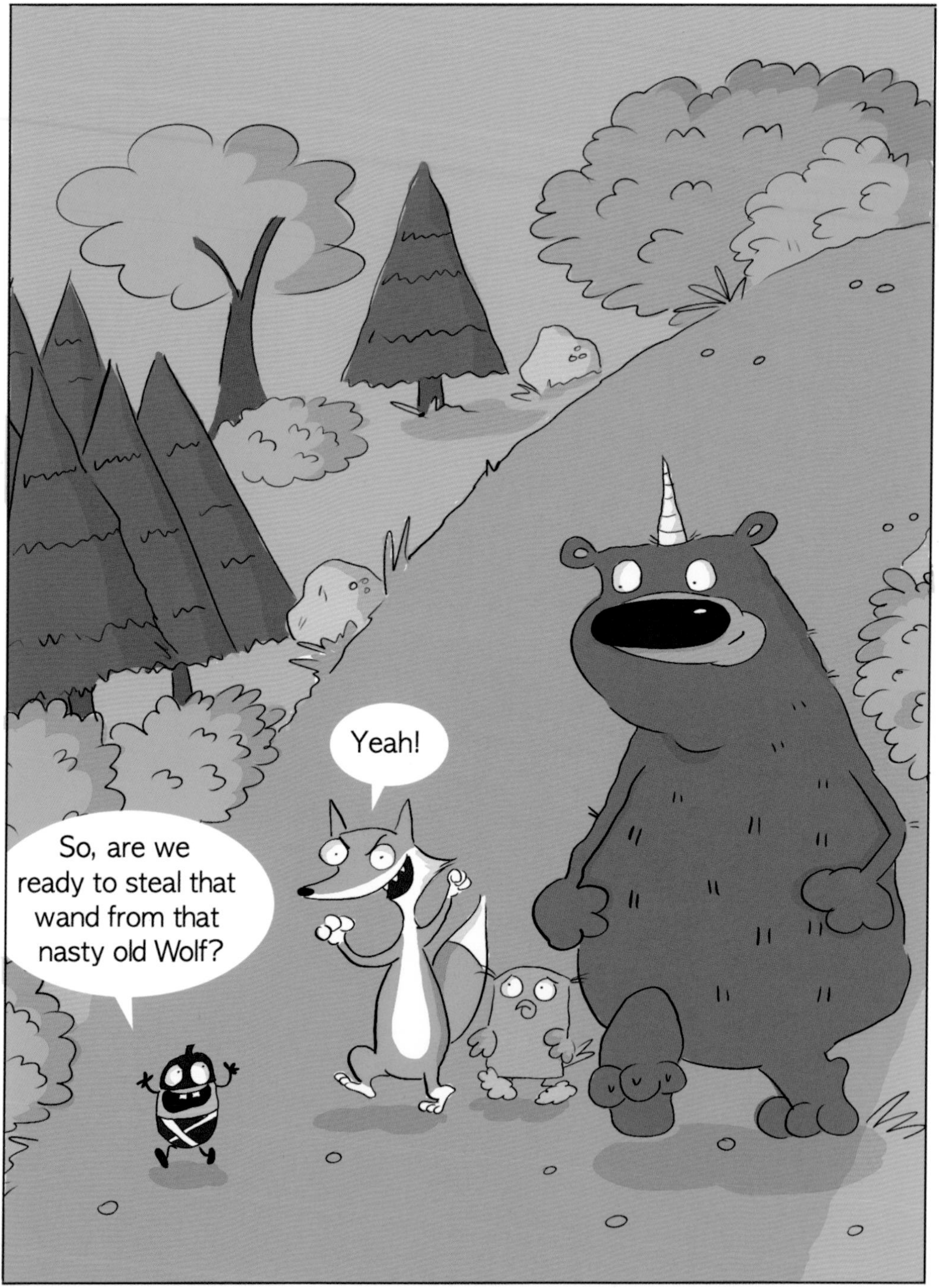
Yeah!
So, are we ready to steal that wand from that nasty old Wolf?

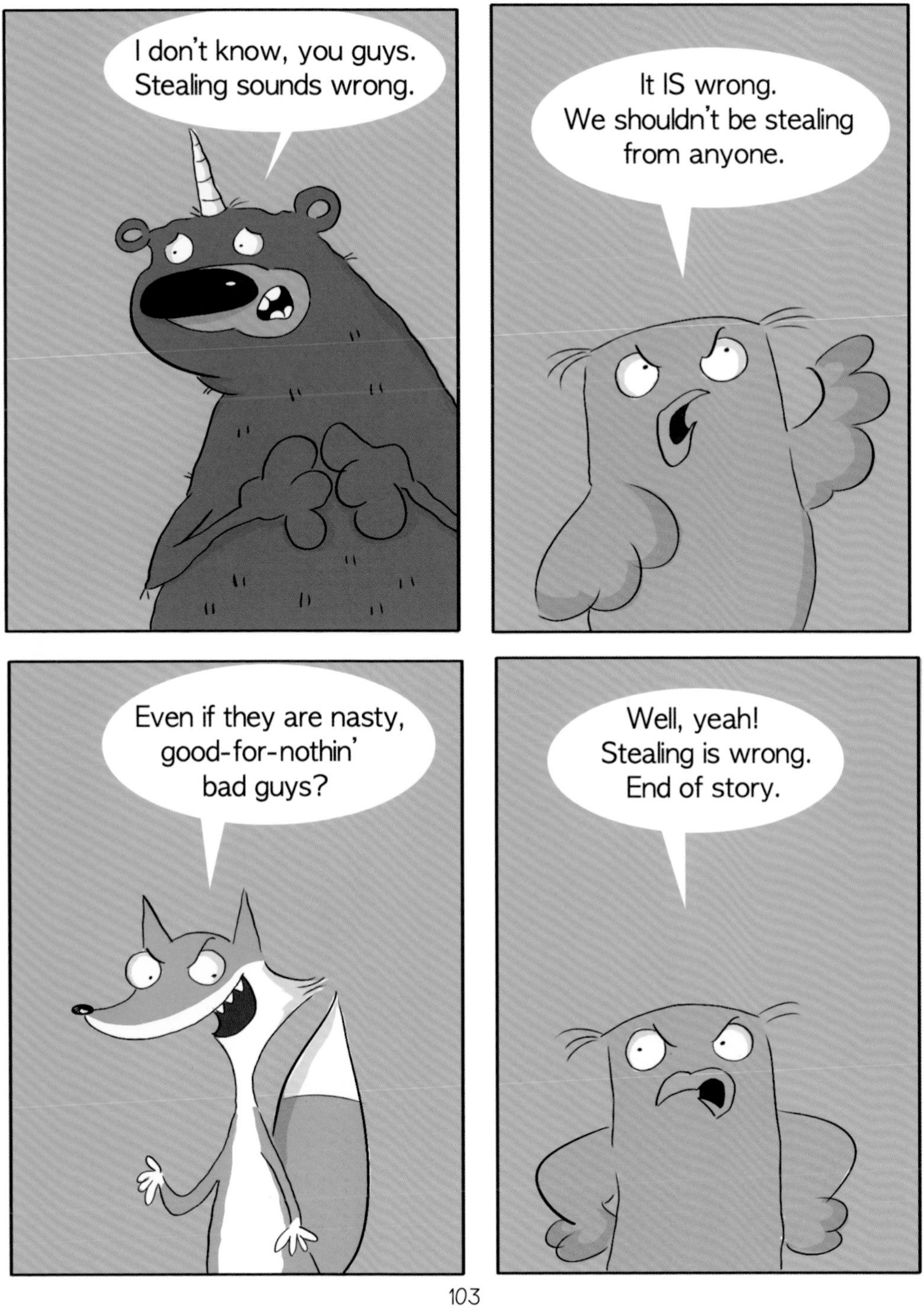
I don't know, you guys. Stealing sounds wrong.
It IS wrong. We shouldn't be stealing from anyone.
Even if they are nasty, good-for-nothin' bad guys?
Well, yeah! Stealing is wrong. End of story.

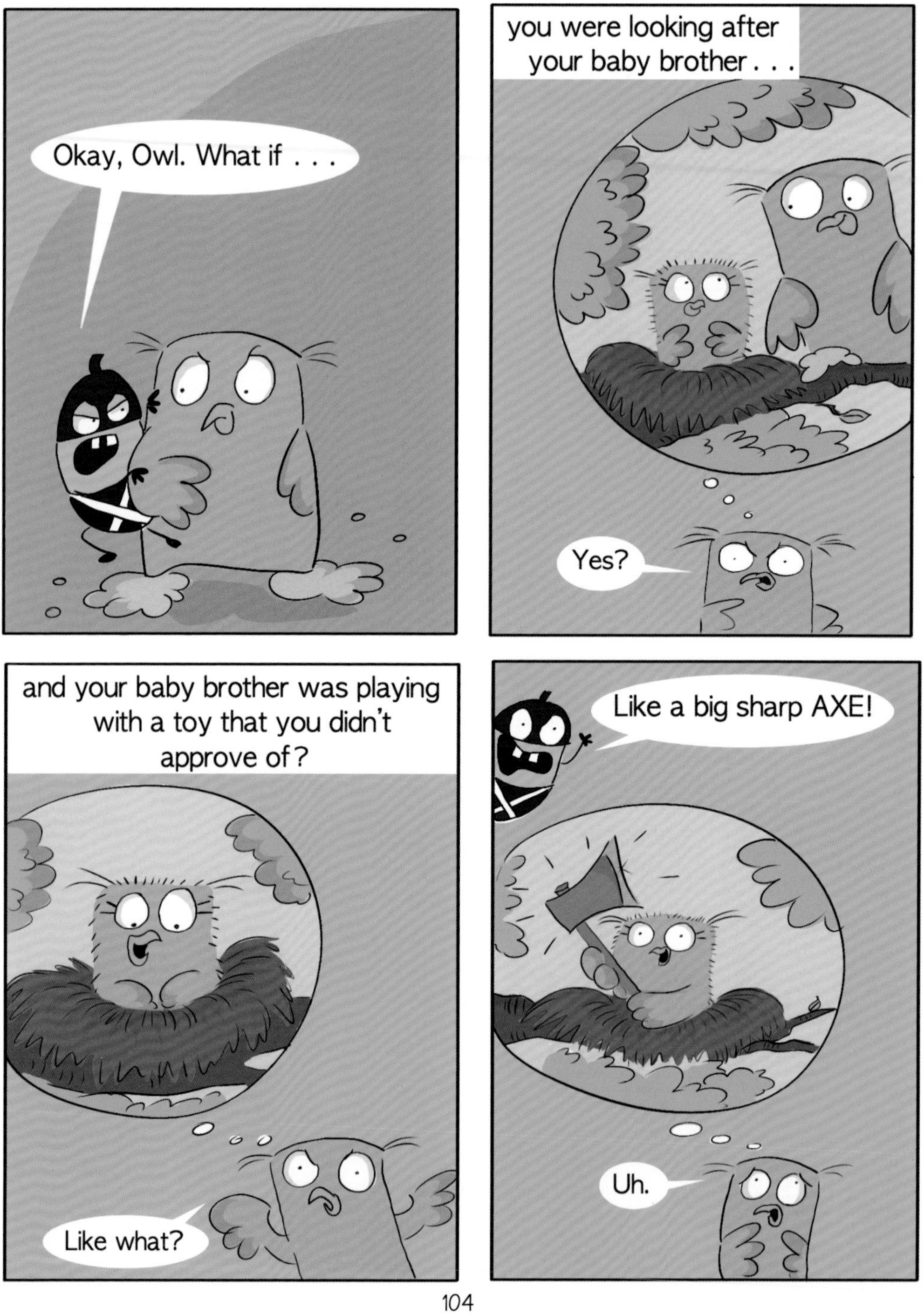

Okay, Owl. What if . . .
you were looking after your baby brother . . .
Yes?
and your baby brother was playing with a toy that you didn't approve of?
Like what?
Like a big sharp AXE!
Uh.

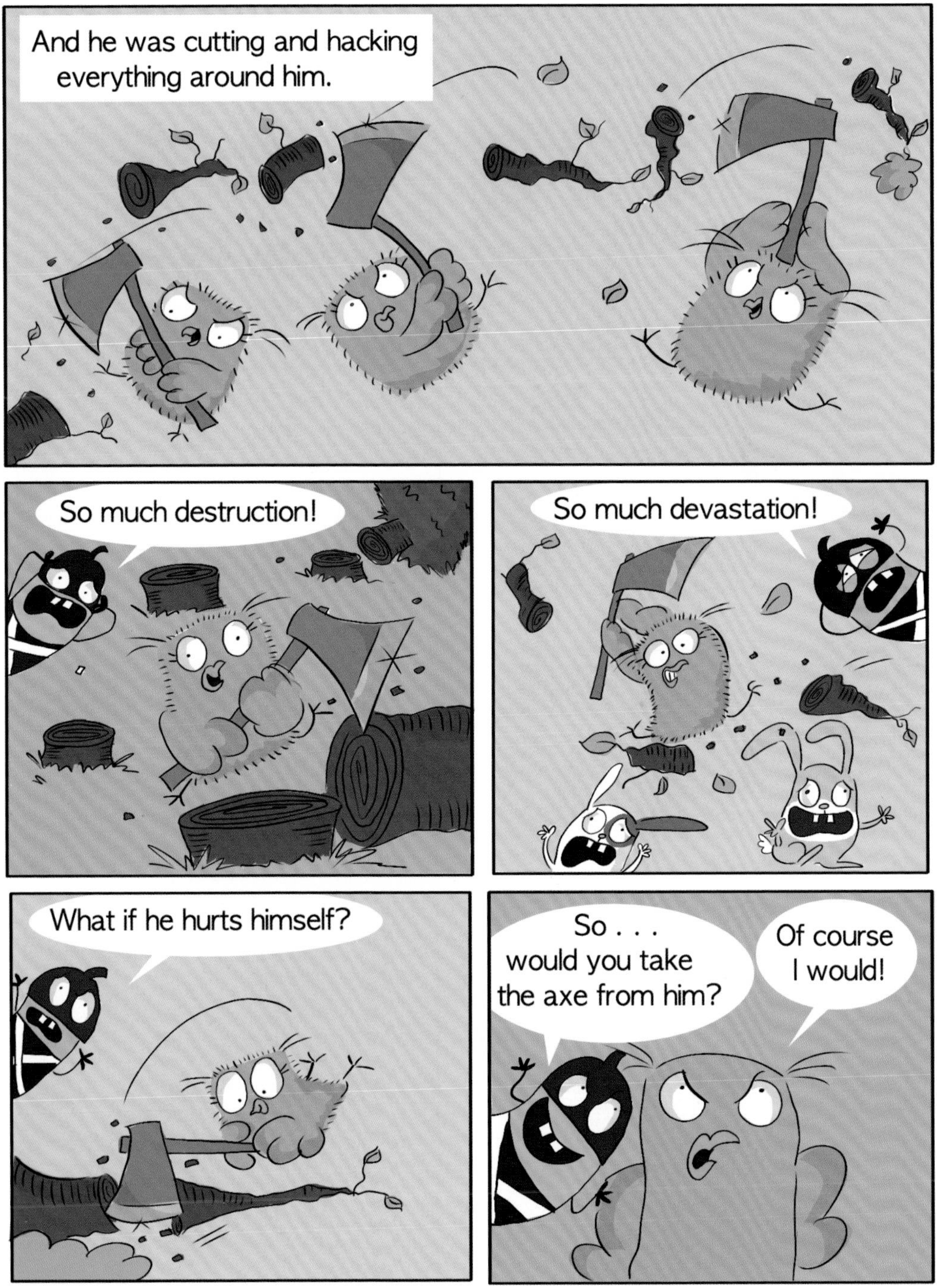
And he was cutting and hacking everything around him.
So much destruction!
So much devastation!
What if he hurts himself?
So . . . would you take the axe from him?
Of course I would!

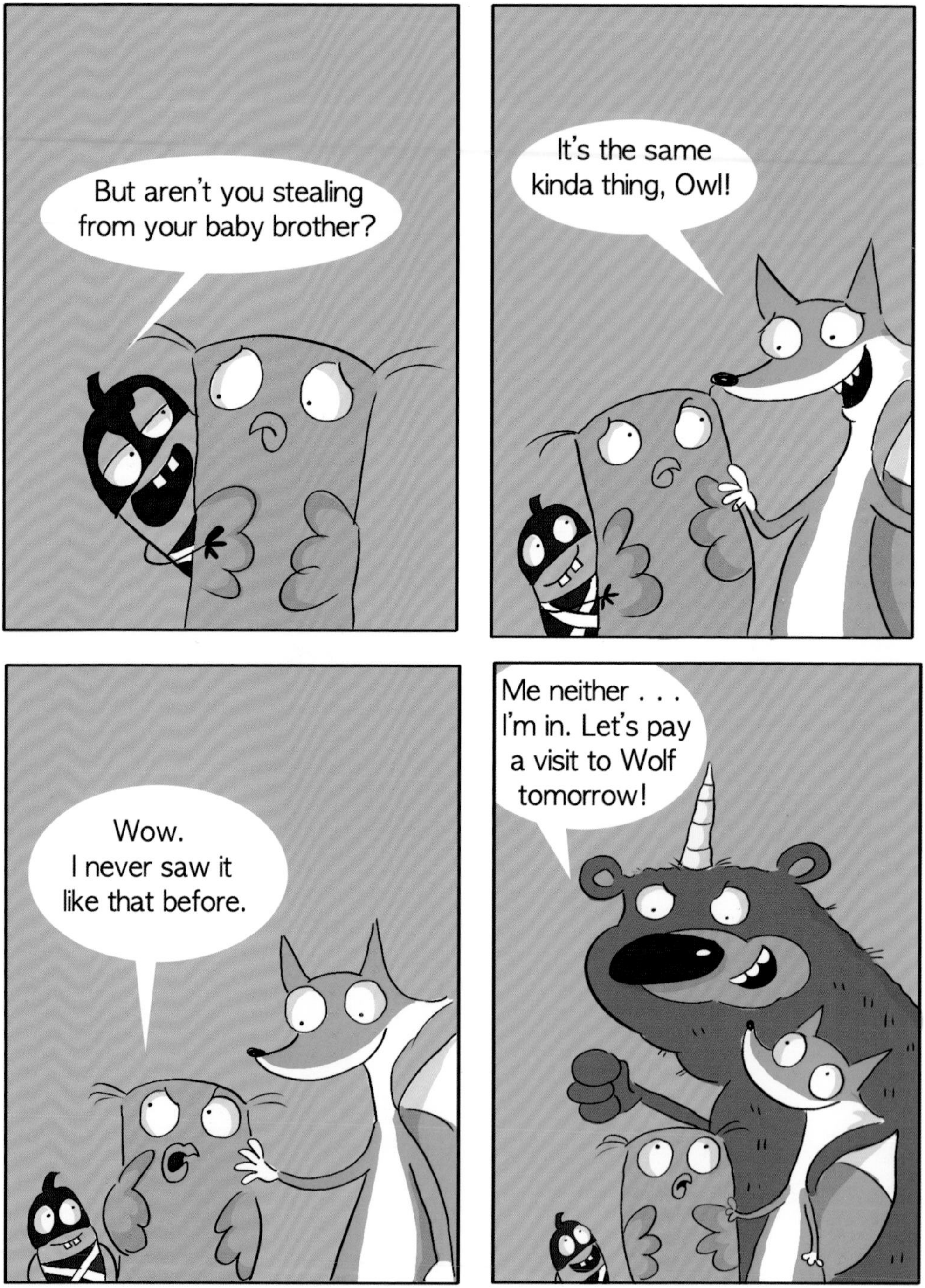
But aren't you stealing from your baby brother?
It's the same kinda thing, Owl!
Wow. I never saw it like that before.
Me neither . . . I'm in. Let's pay a visit to Wolf tomorrow!

CHAPTER 12

MAYHEM IN THE FOREST

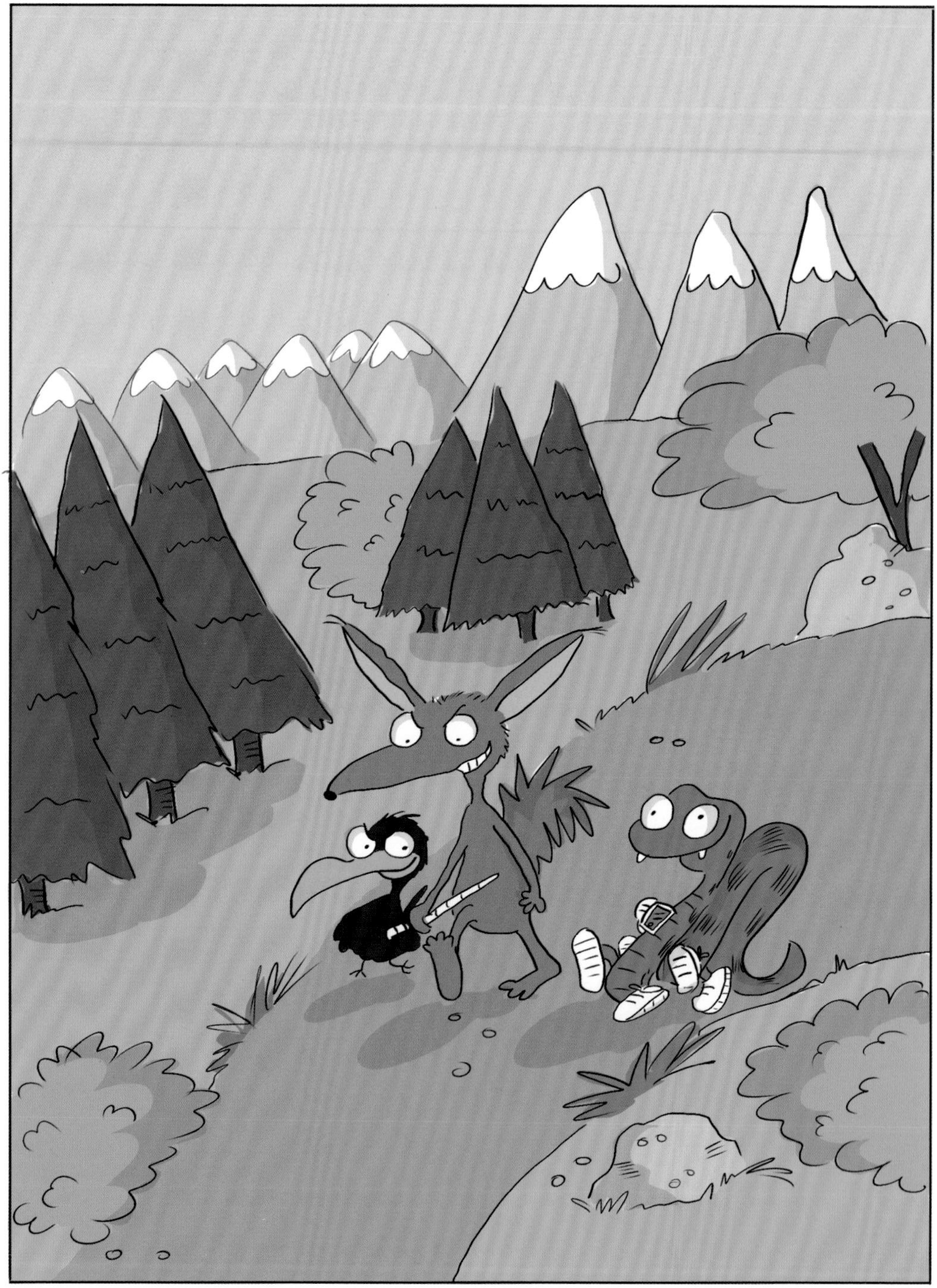

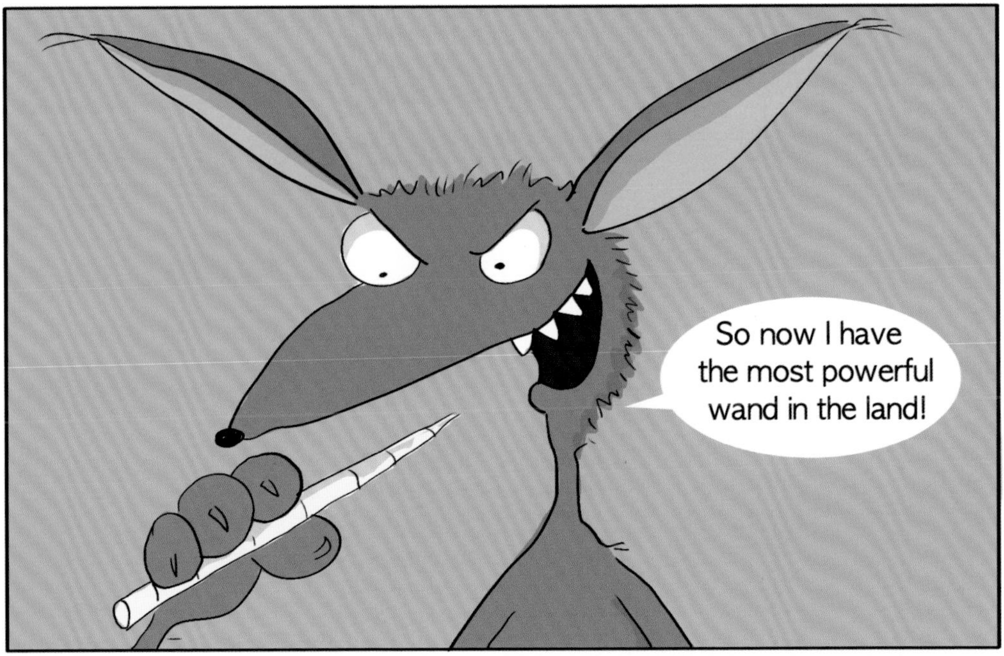
So now I have the most powerful wand in the land!

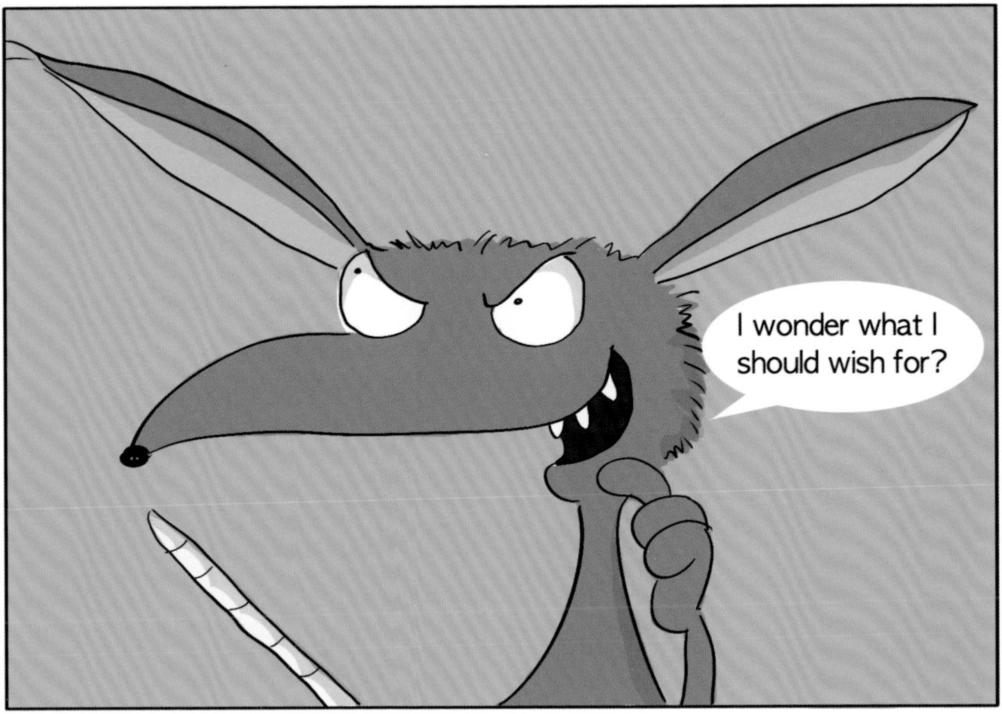
I wonder what I should wish for?

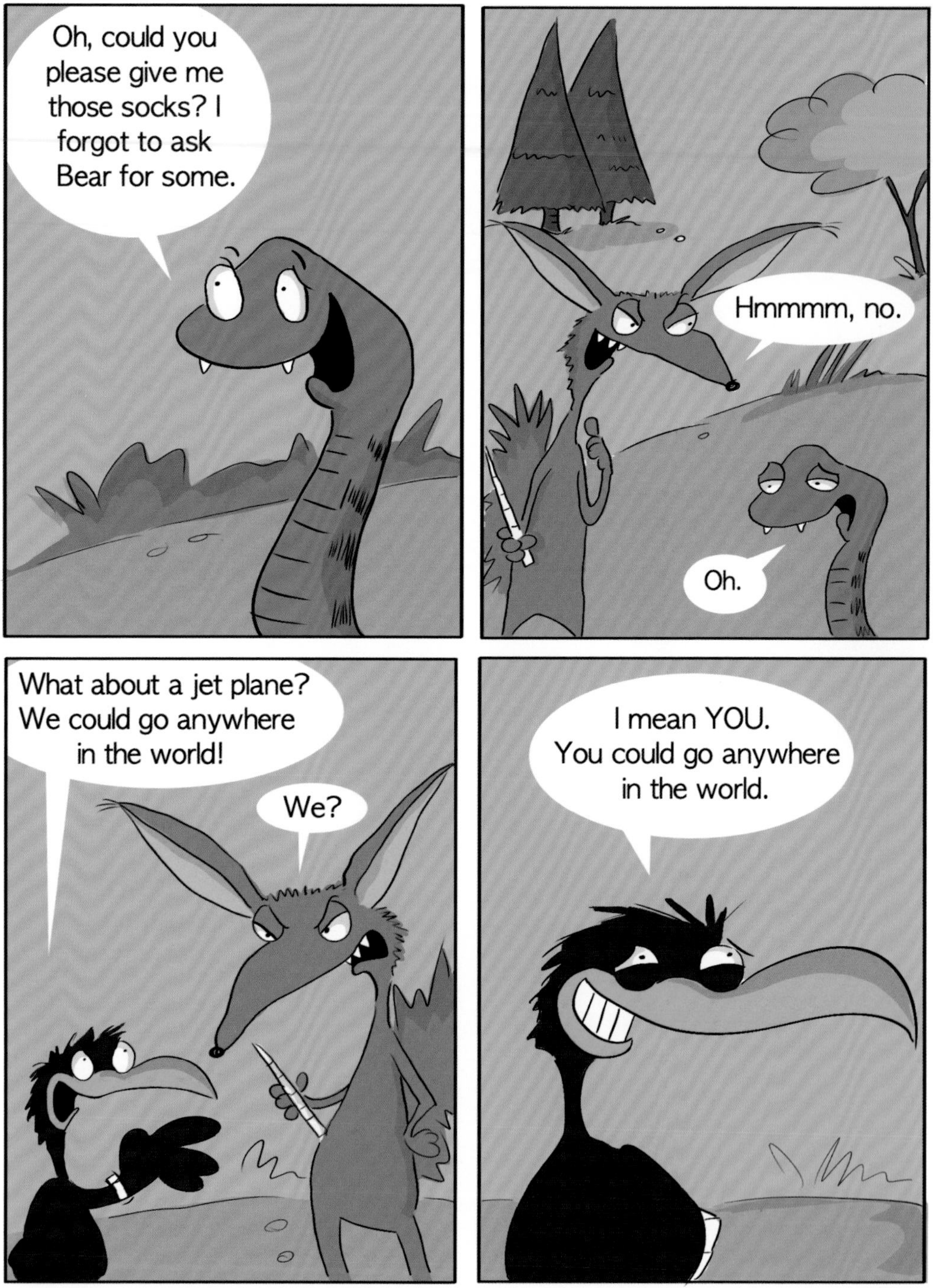
Oh, could you please give me those socks? I forgot to ask Bear for some.
Hmmmm, no.
Oh.
What about a jet plane? We could go anywhere in the world!
We?
I mean YOU. You could go anywhere in the world.

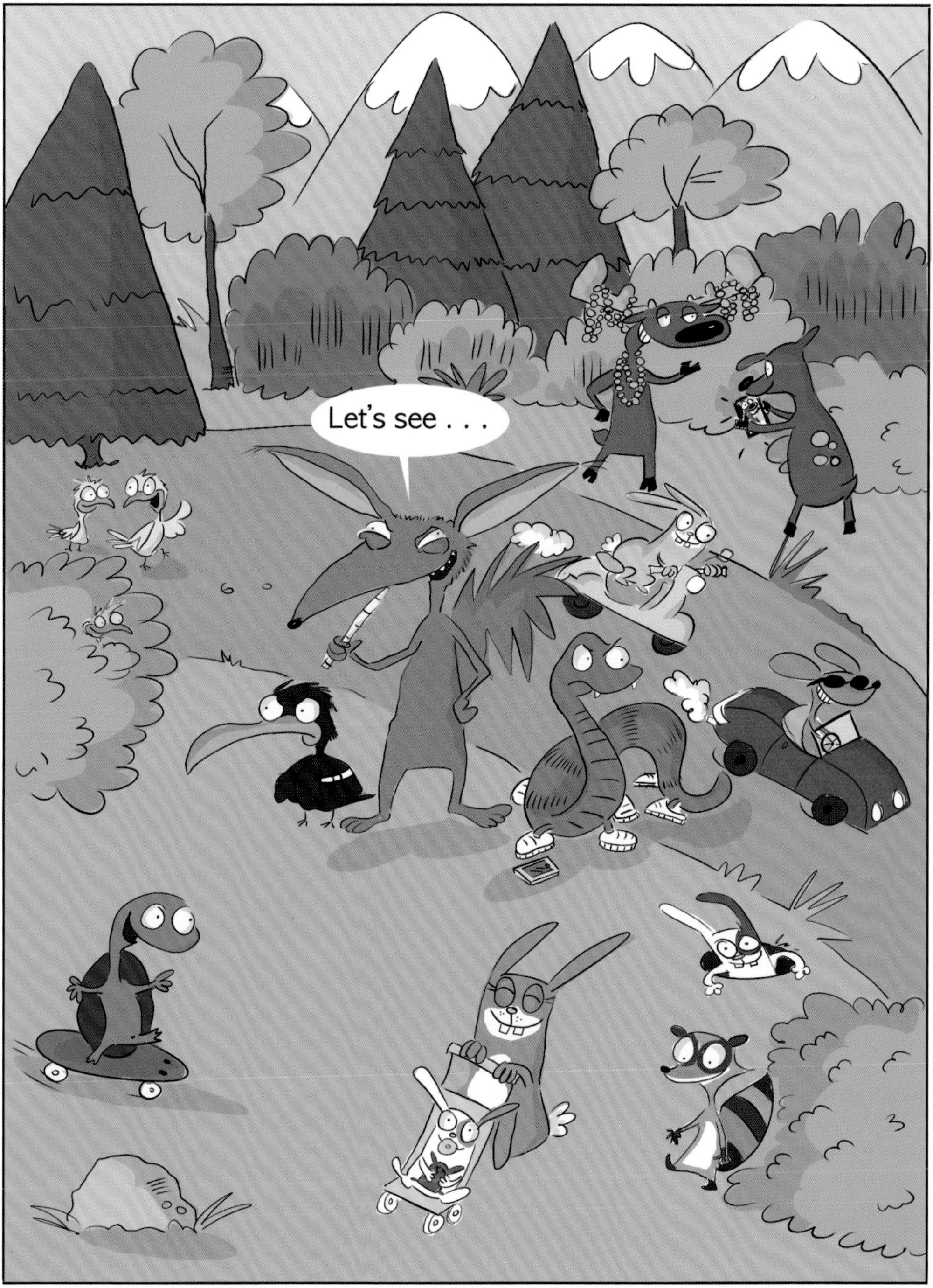
Let's see . . .

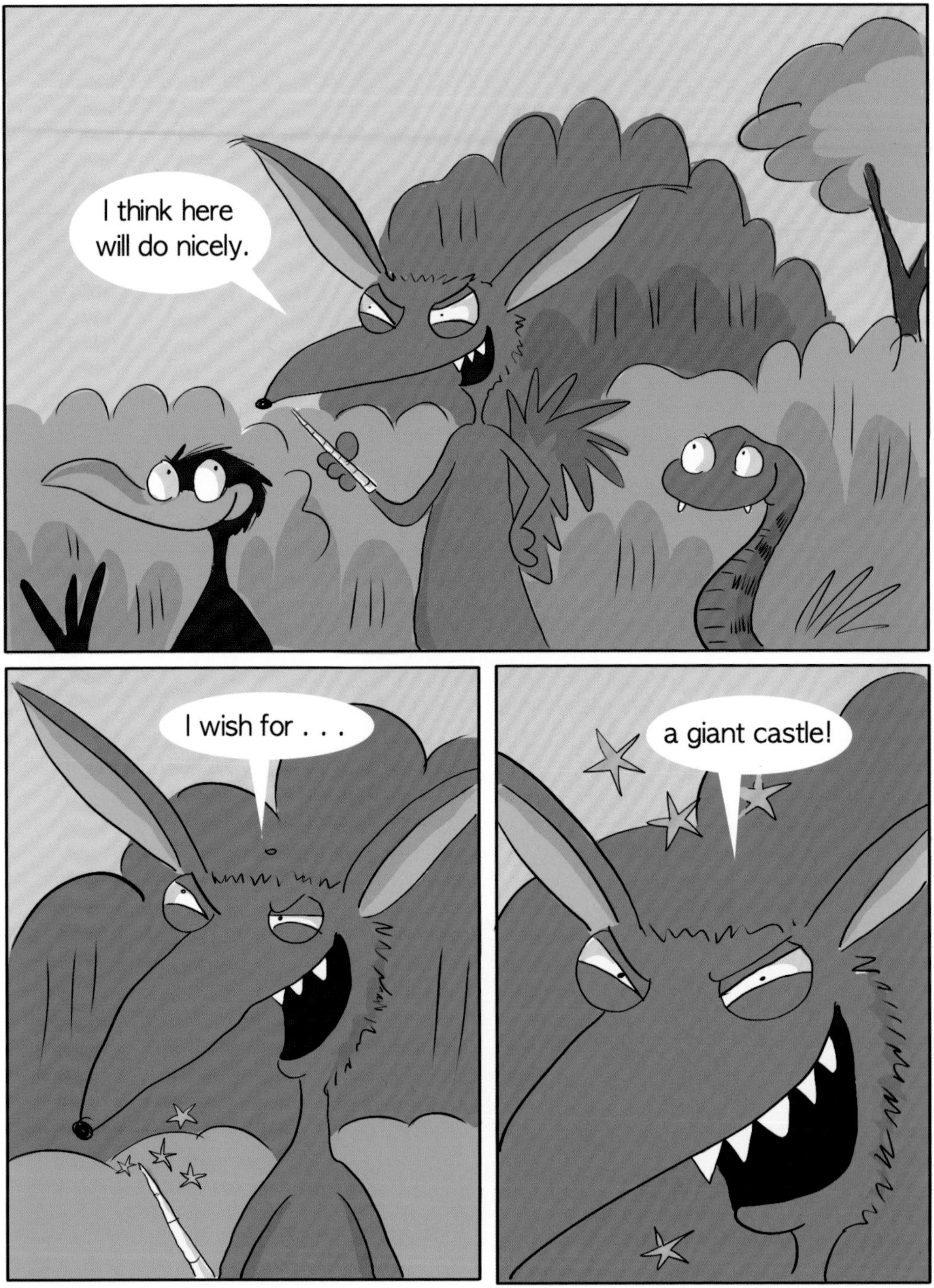
I think here will do nicely.
I wish for . . .
a giant castle!

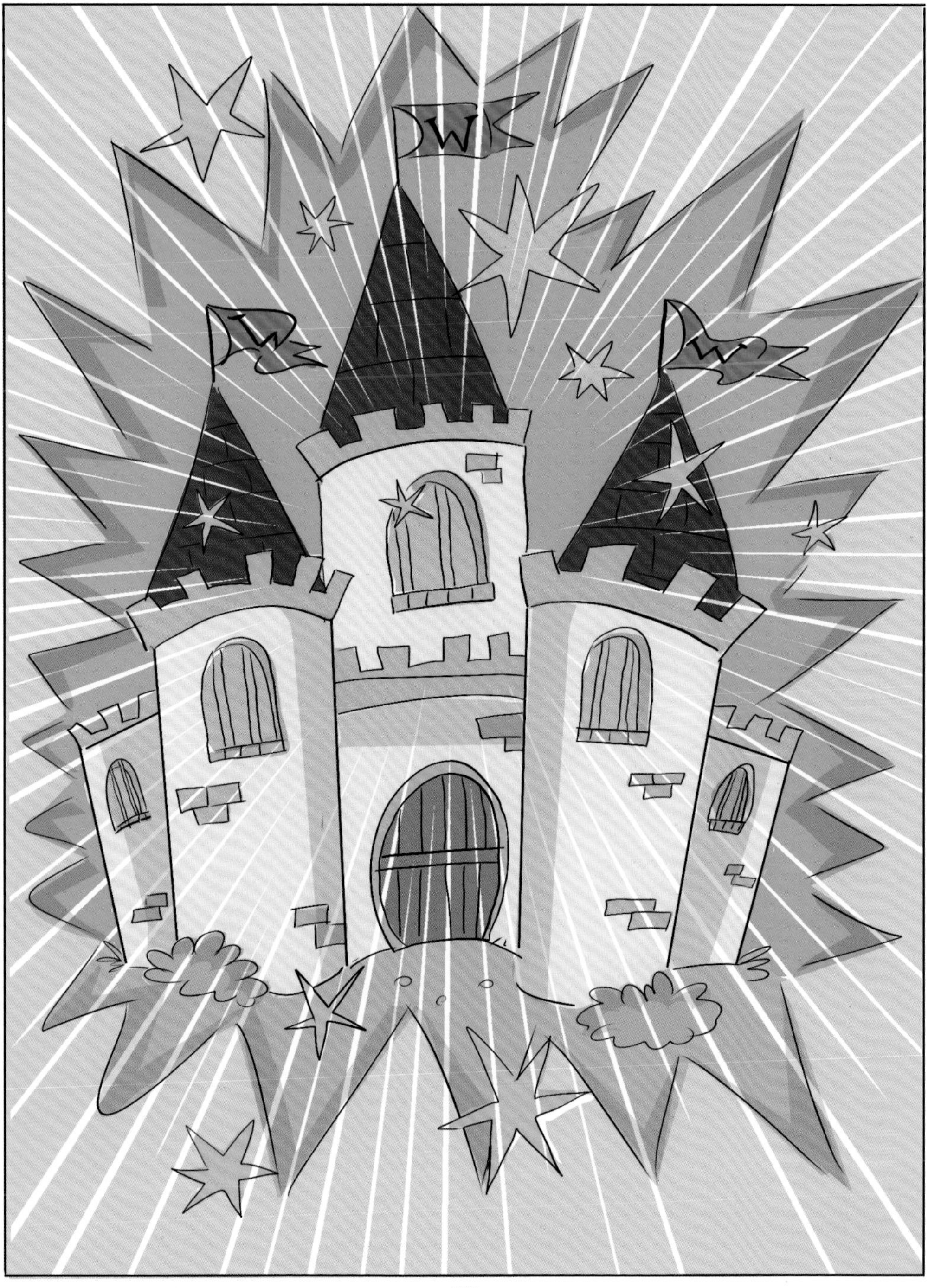
W
W
W

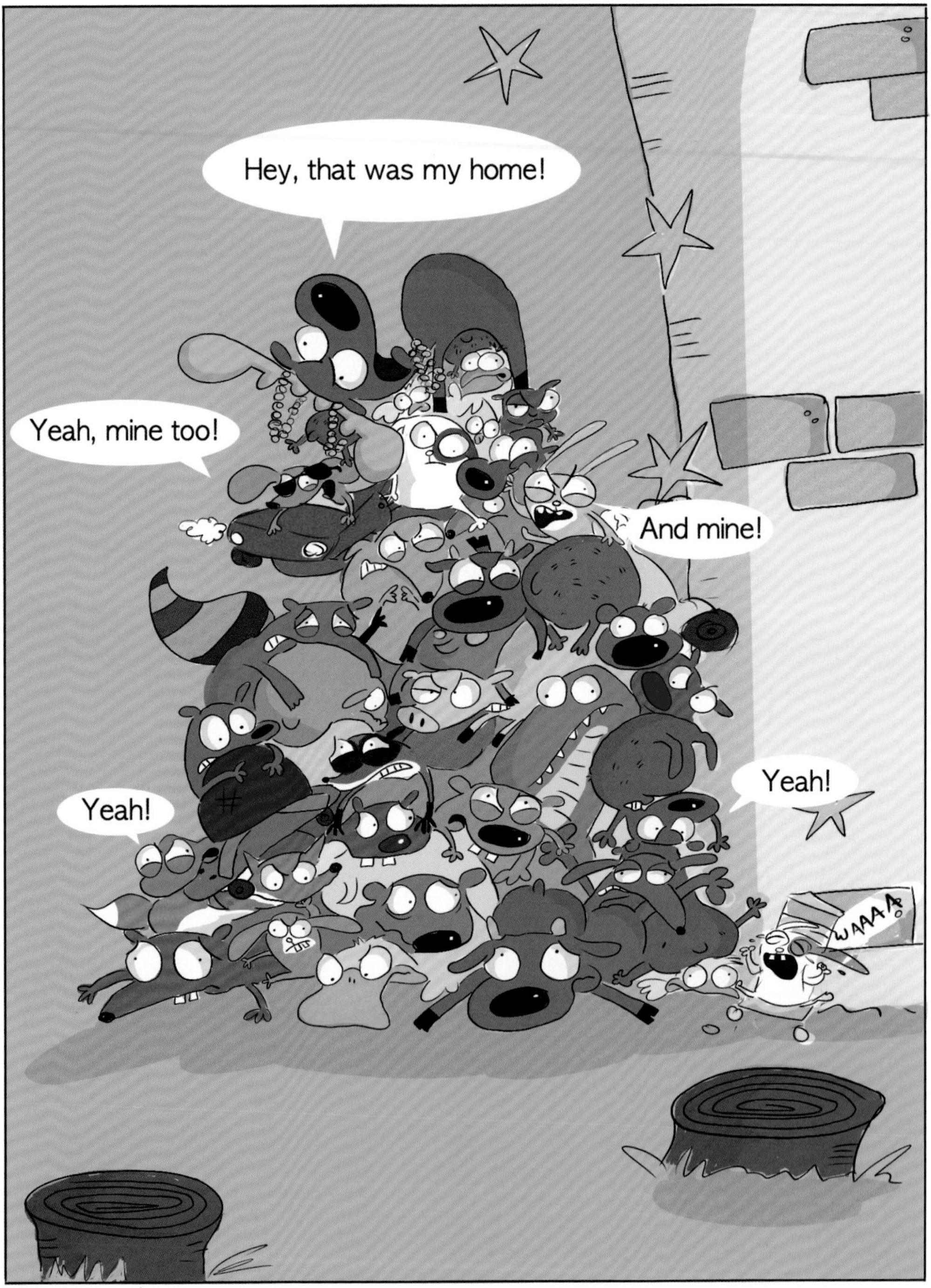
Hey, that was my home!
Yeah, mine too!
And mine!
Yeah!
Yeah!
WAAAA

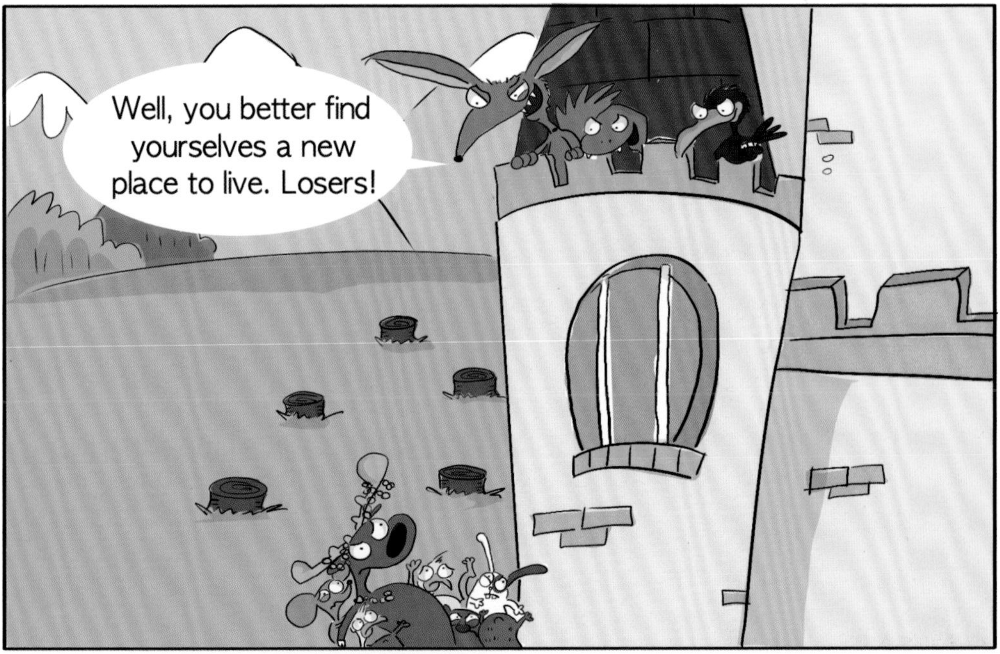
Well, you better find yourselves a new place to live. Losers!

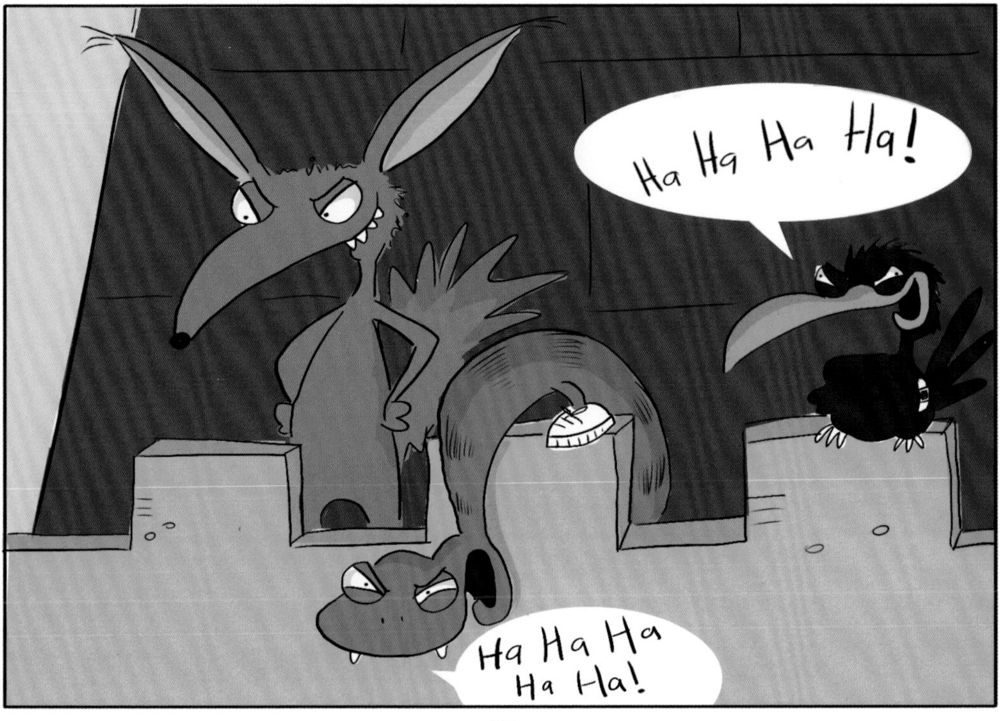
Ha Ha Ha Ha!
Ha Ha Ha Ha Ha!

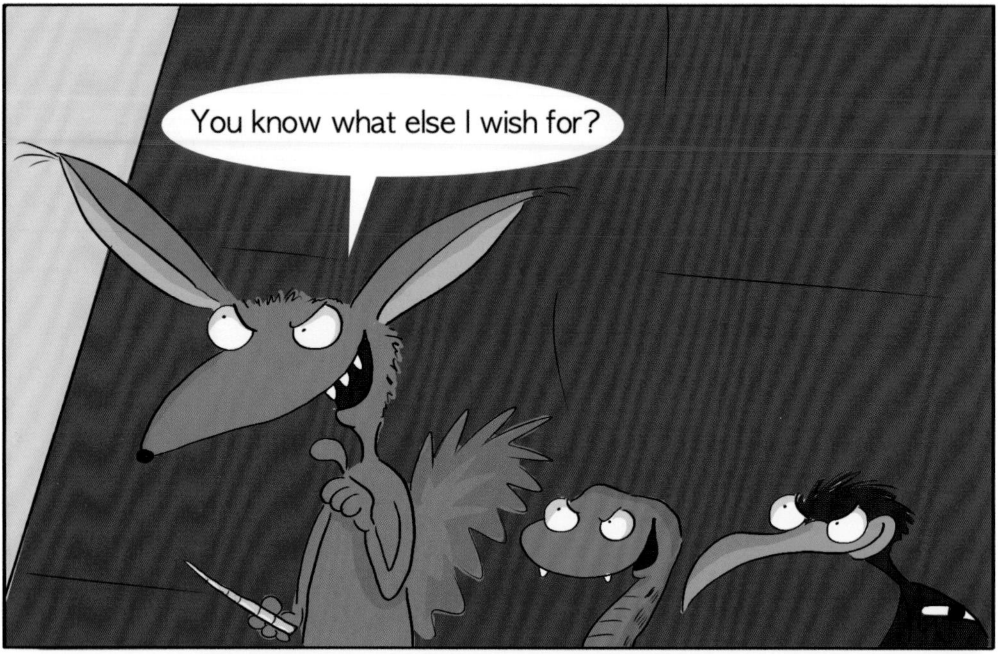
You know what else I wish for?

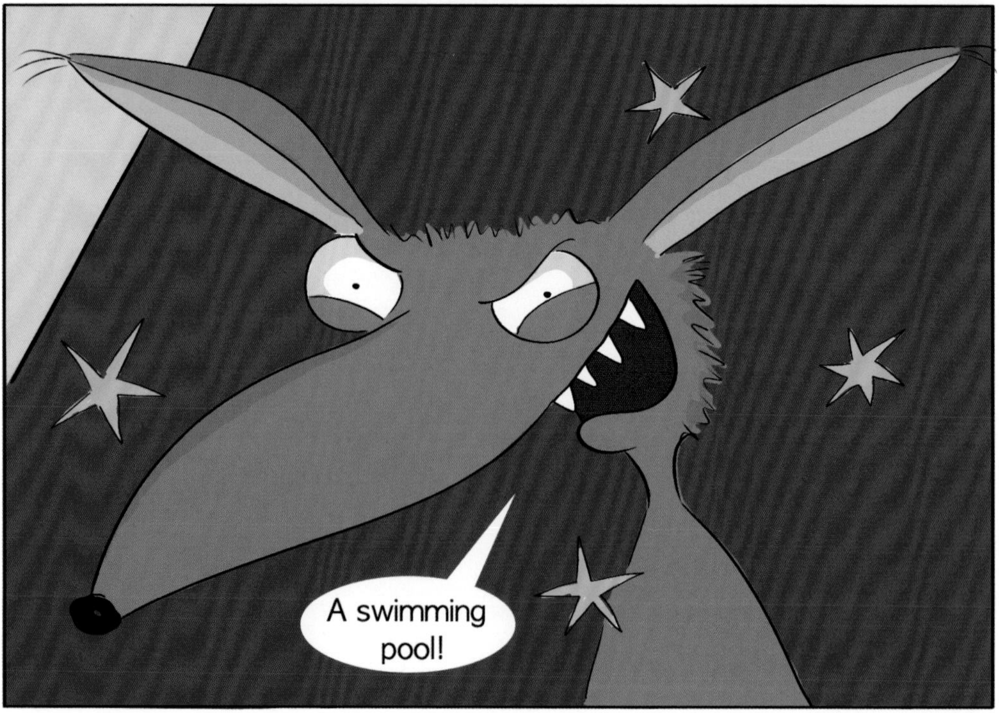
A swimming pool!

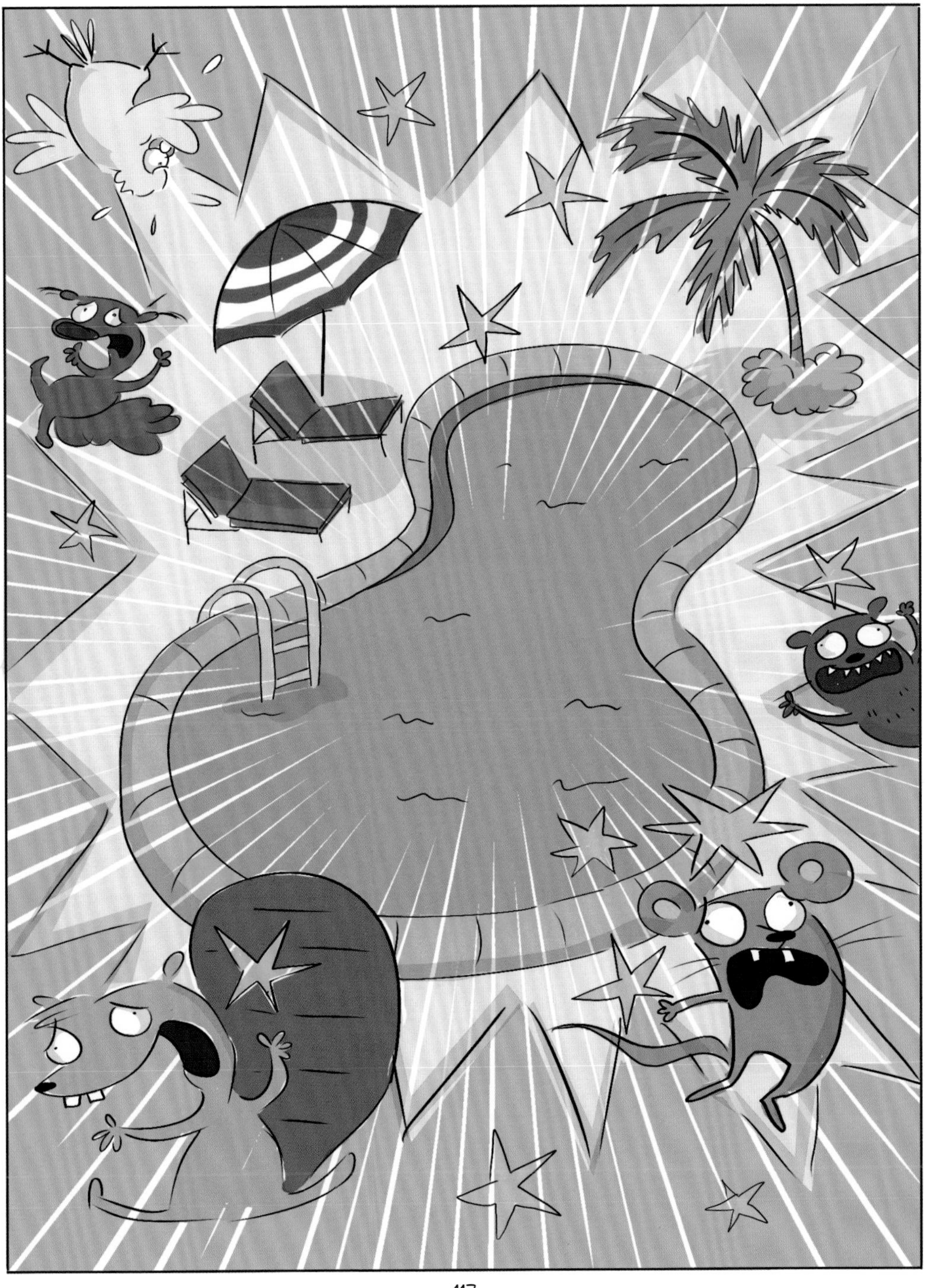

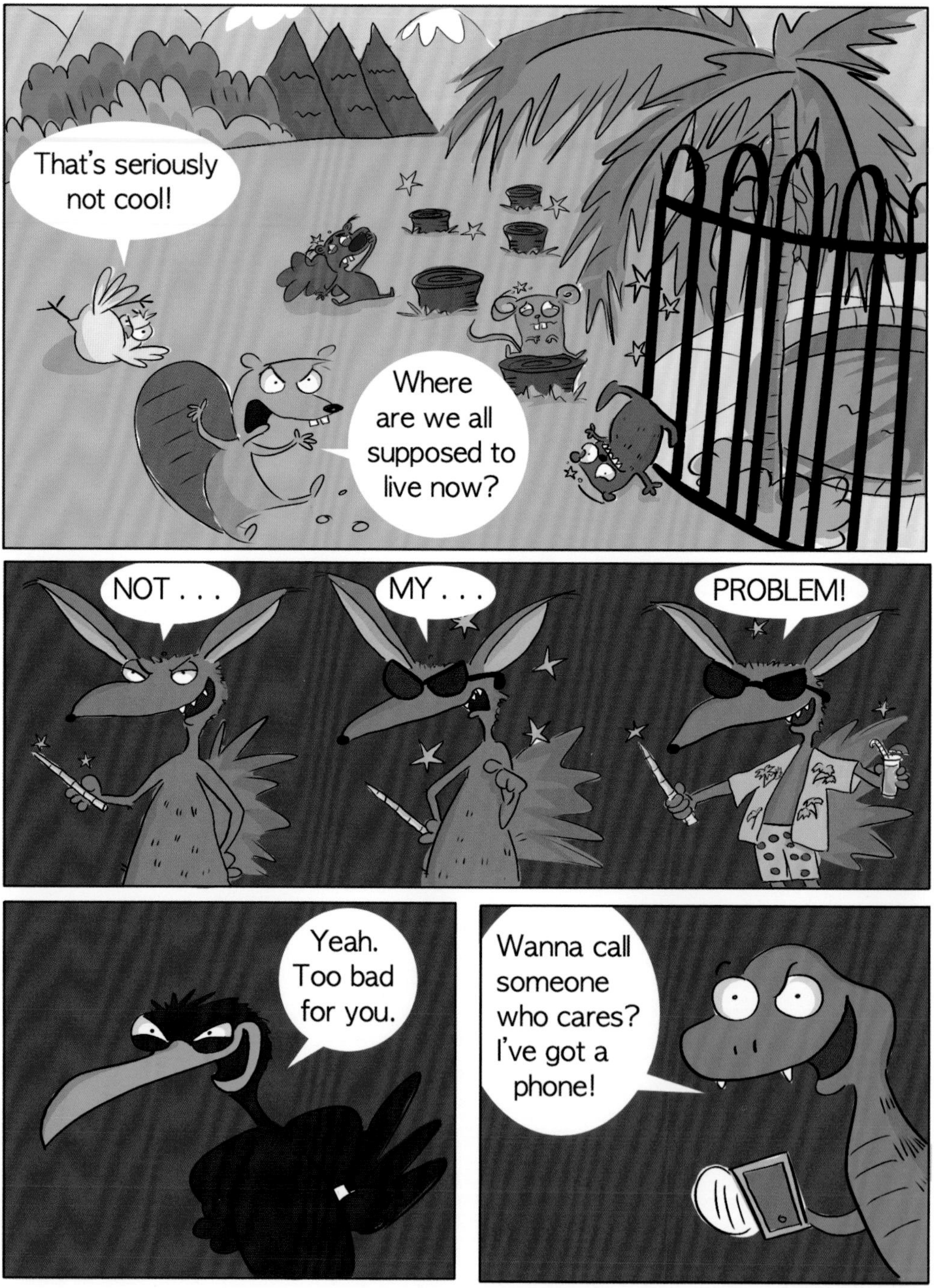
That's seriously not cool!
Where are we all supposed to live now?
NOT . . .
MY . . .
PROBLEM!
Yeah. Too bad for you.
Wanna call someone who cares? I've got a phone!

CHAPTER 13

BIZARD'S BIG PLAN

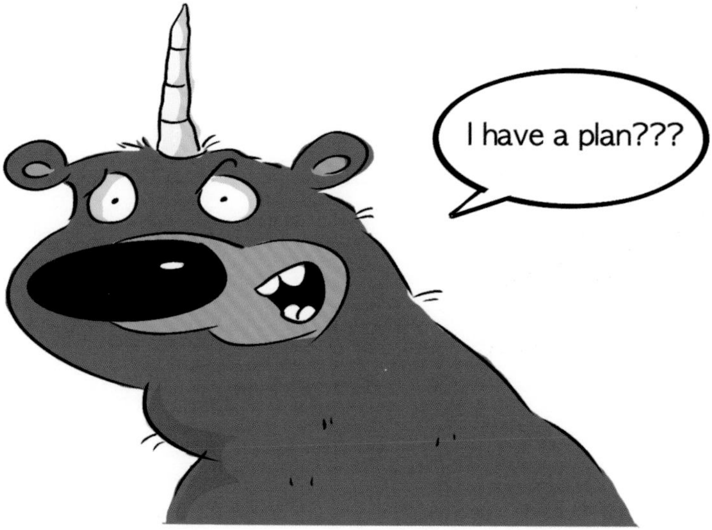
I have a plan???

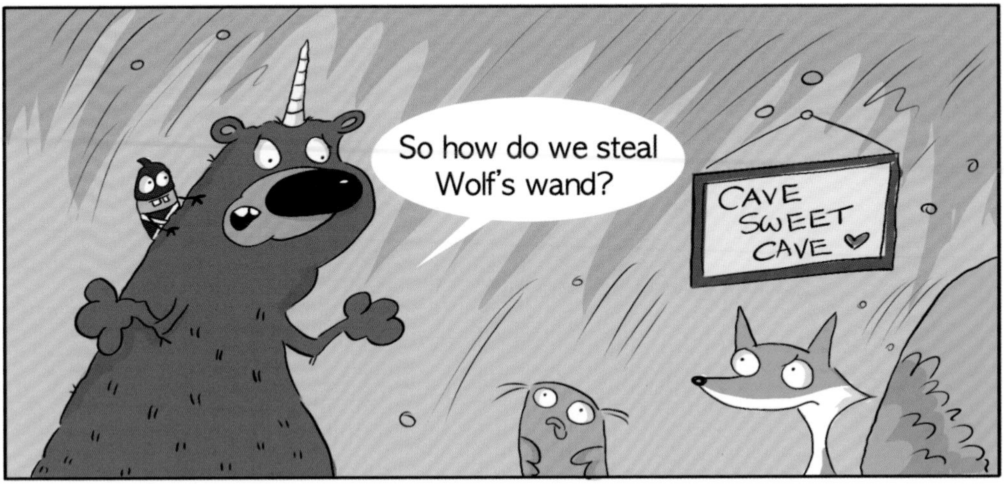
So how do we steal Wolf's wand?
CAVE SWEET CAVE

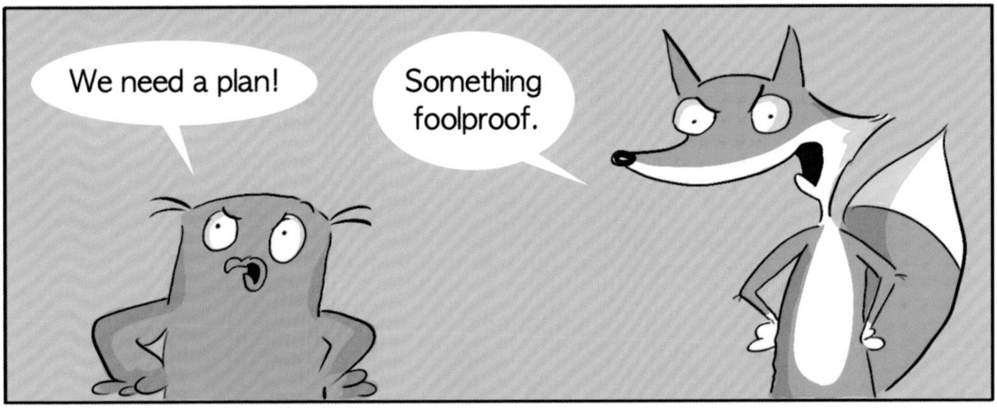
We need a plan!
Something foolproof.

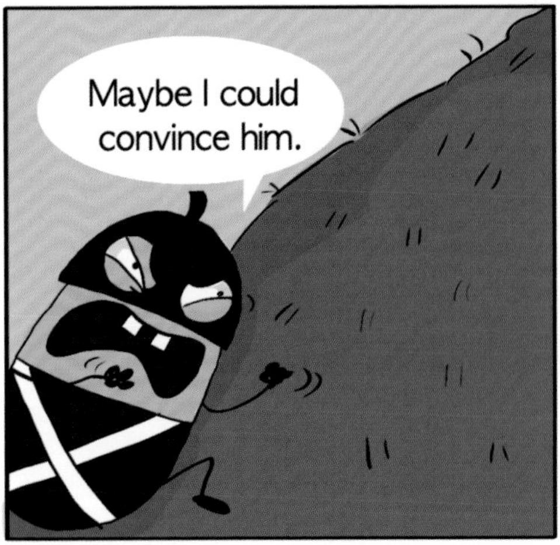
Maybe I could convince him.

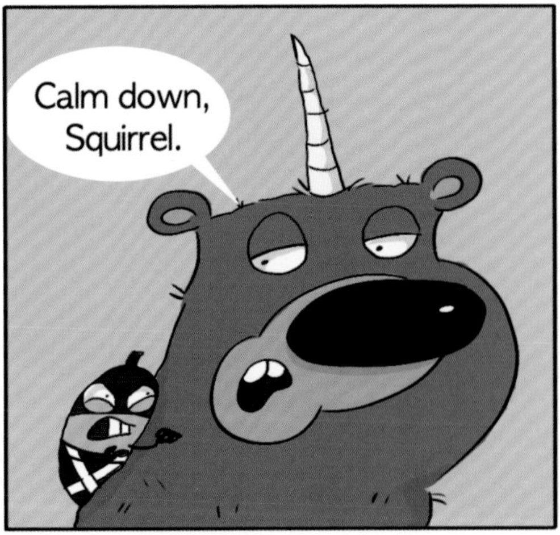
Calm down, Squirrel.

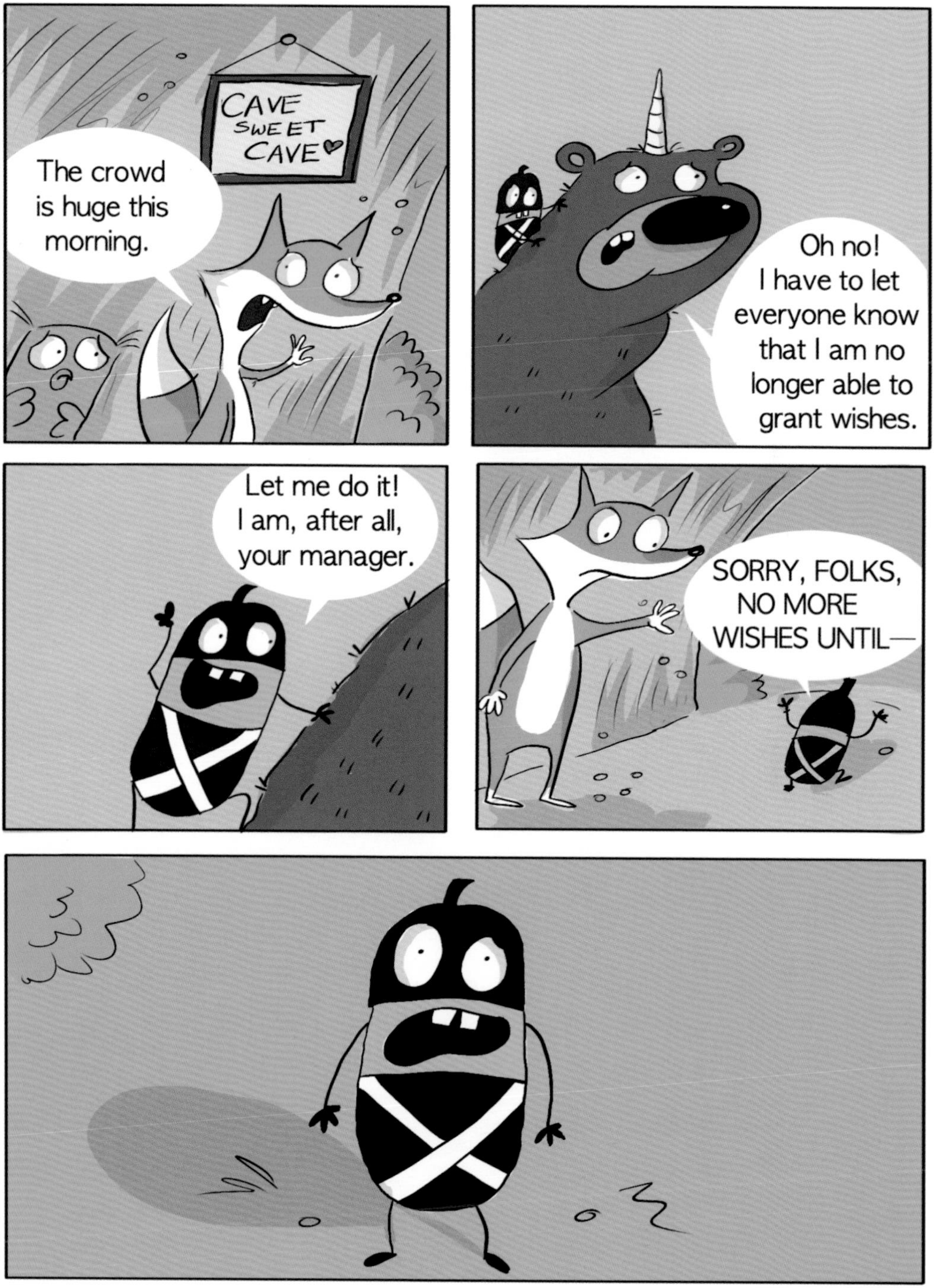
CAVE SWEET CAVE
The crowd is huge this morning.
Oh no! I have to let everyone know that I am no longer able to grant wishes.
Let me do it! I am, after all, your manager.
SORRY, FOLKS, NO MORE WISHES UNTIL—

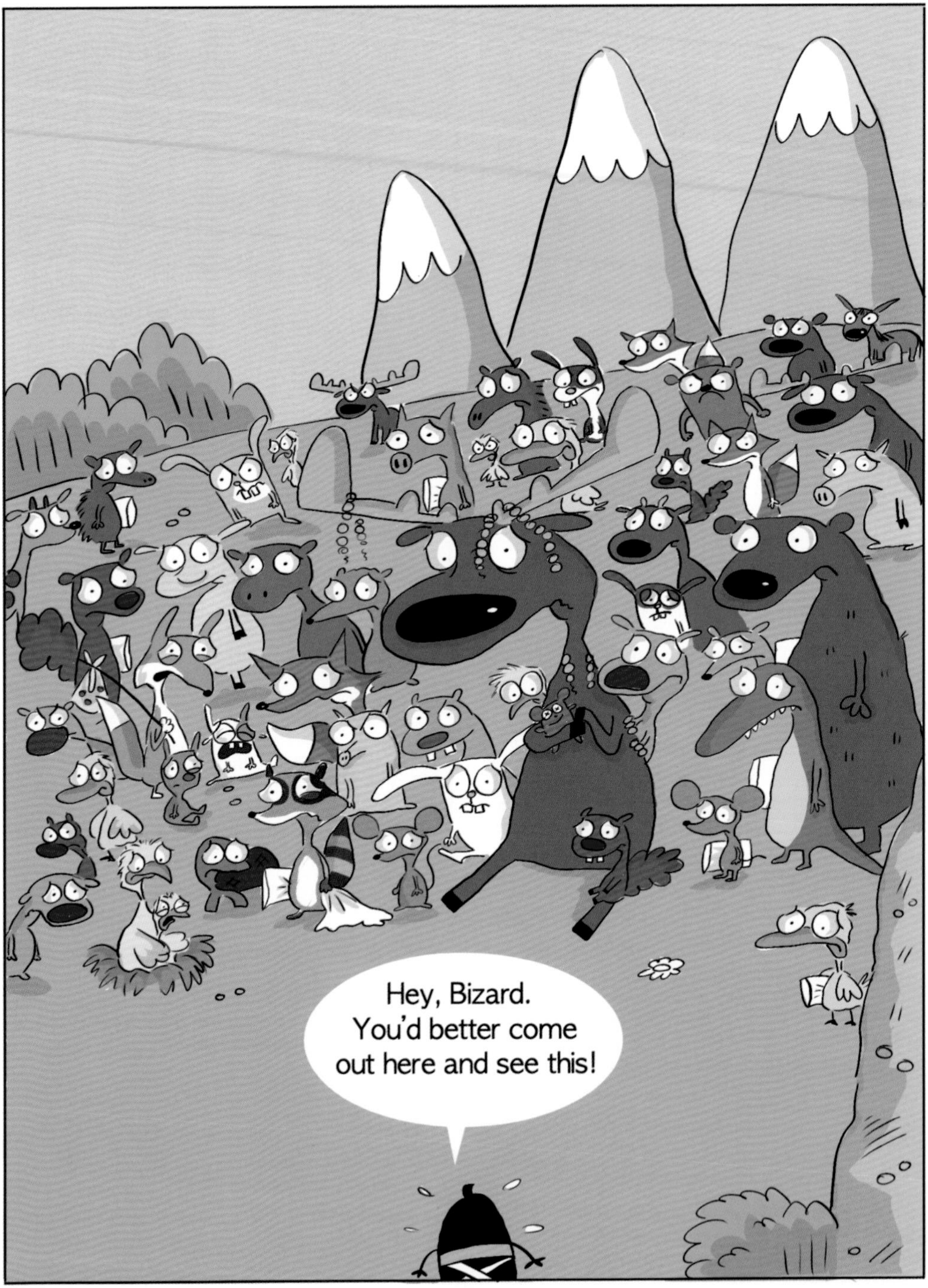
Hey, Bizard. You'd better come out here and see this!

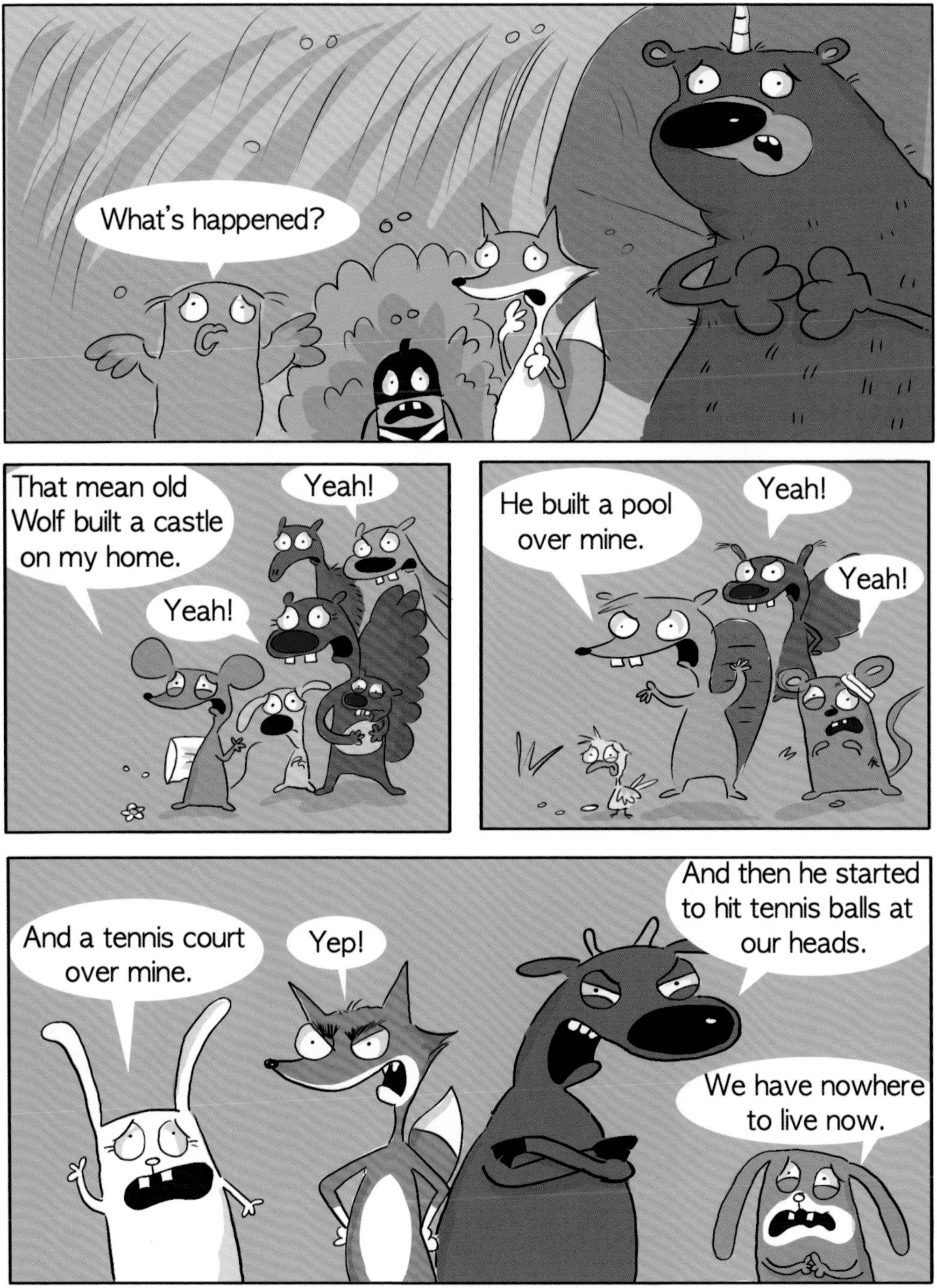
What's happened?
That mean old Wolf built a castle on my home.
Yeah!
Yeah!
He built a pool over mine.
Yeah!
Yeah!
And a tennis court over mine.
Yep!
And then he started to hit tennis balls at our heads.
We have nowhere to live now.

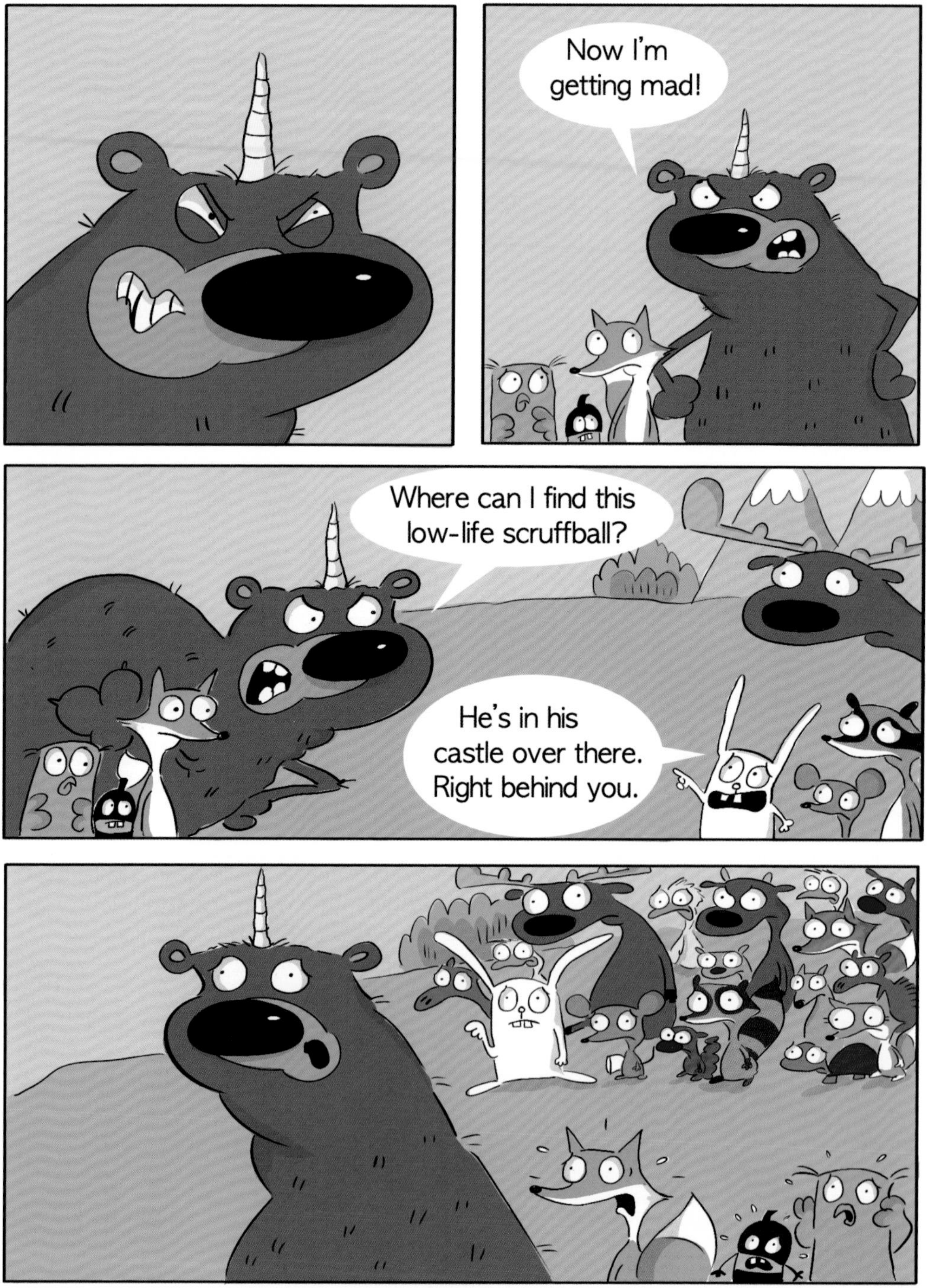
Now I'm getting mad!
Where can I find this low-life scruffball?
He's in his castle over there. Right behind you.

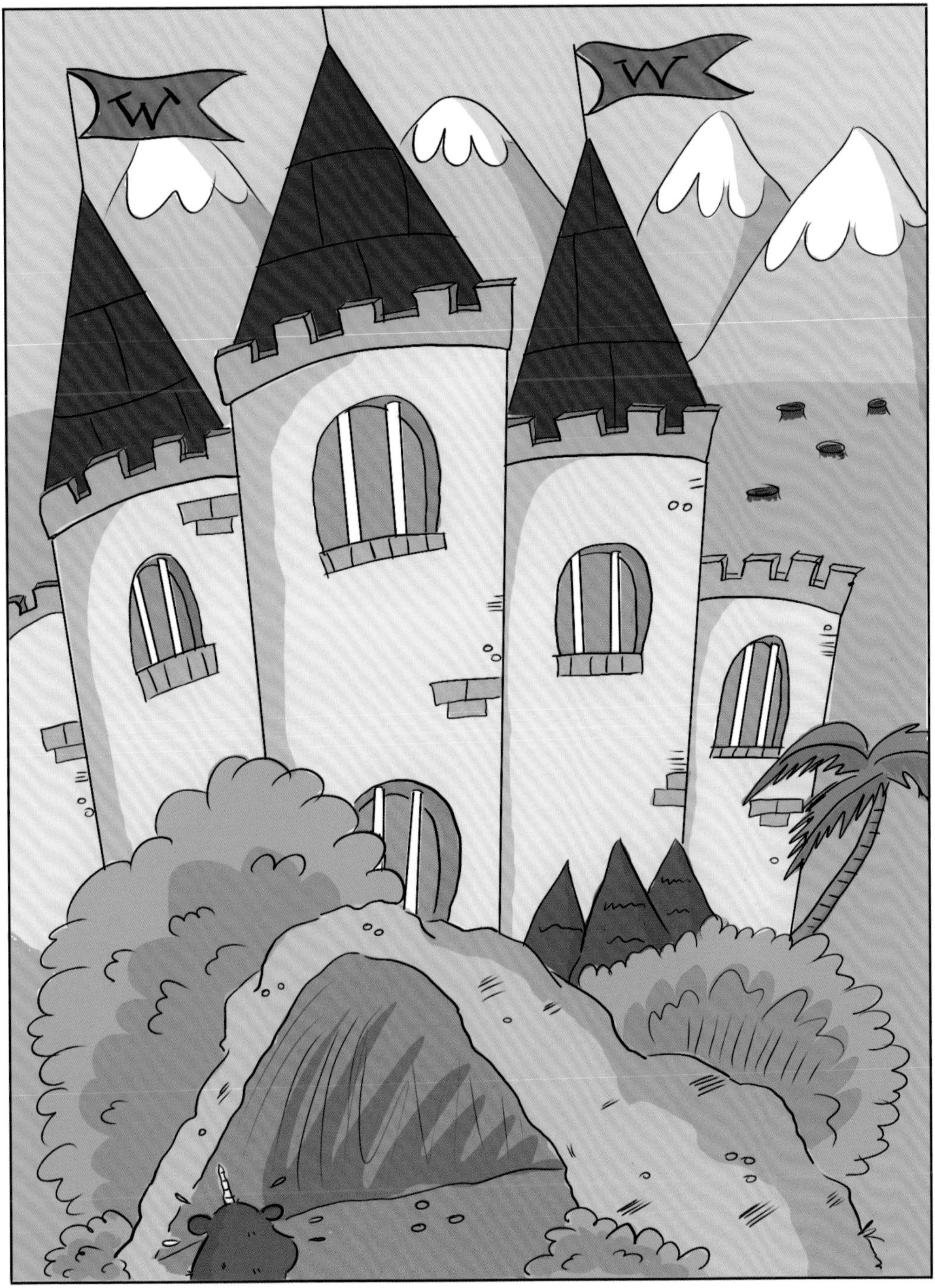
W
W

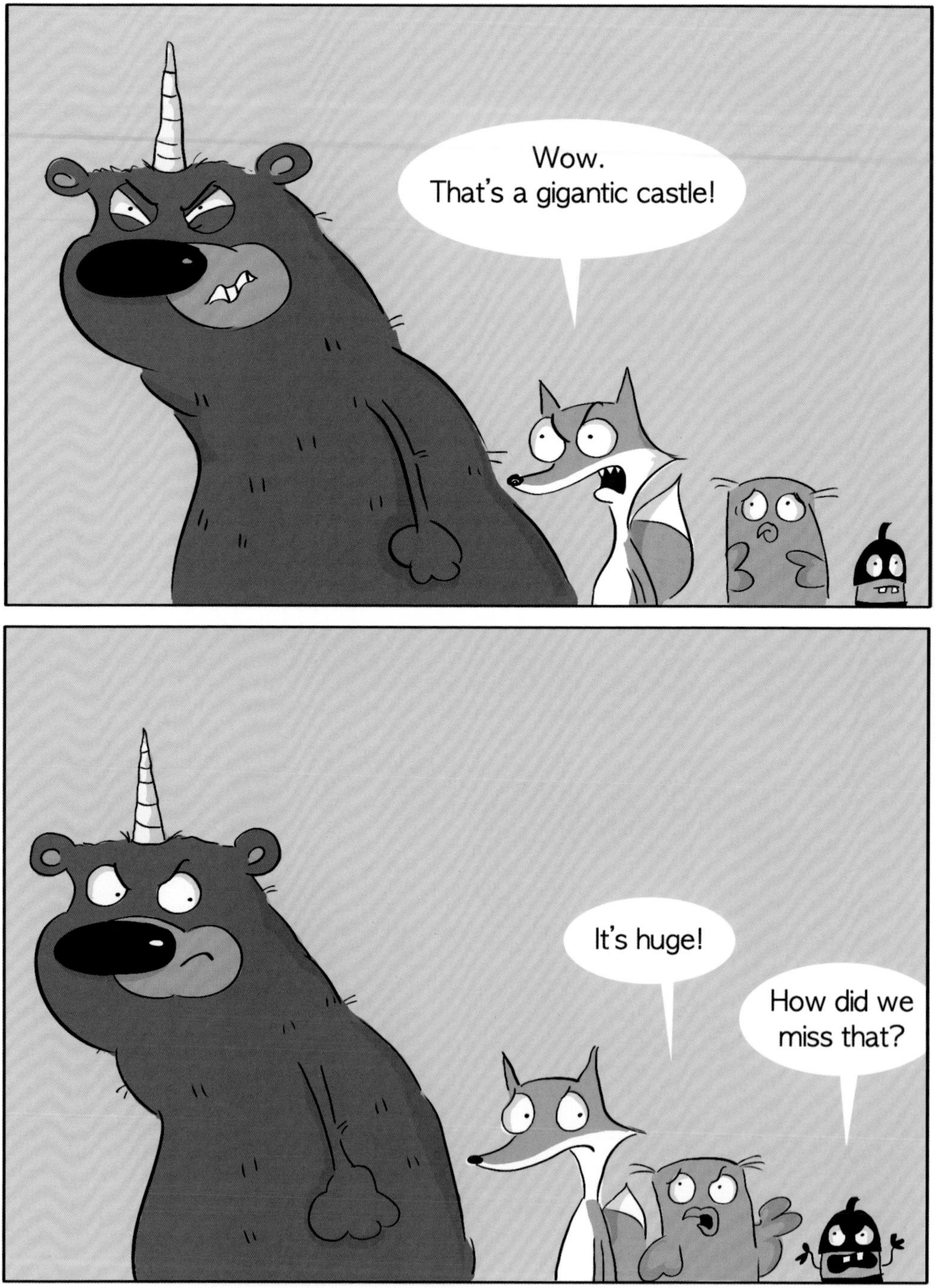
Wow.
That's a gigantic castle!
It's huge!
How did we miss that?

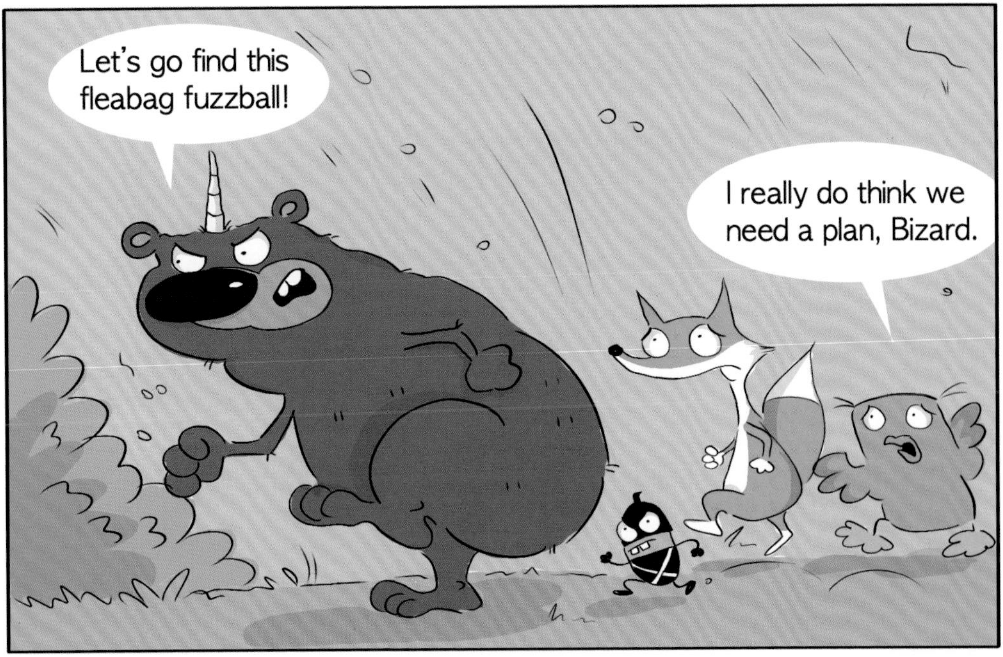
Let's go find this fleabag fuzzball!
I really do think we need a plan, Bizard.

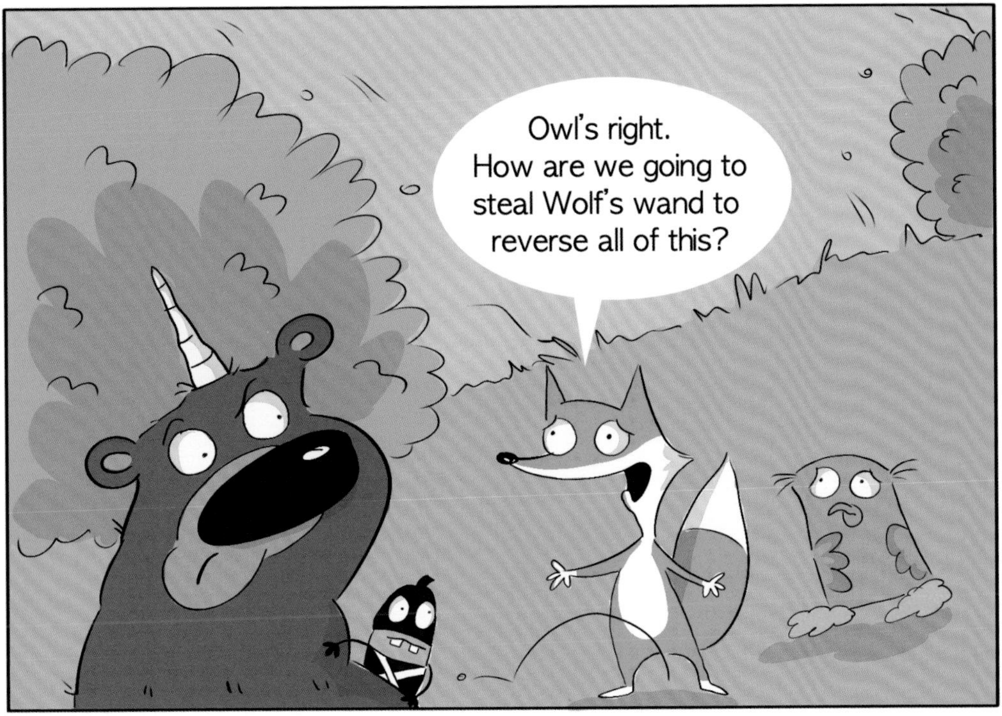
Owl's right. How are we going to steal Wolf's wand to reverse all of this?

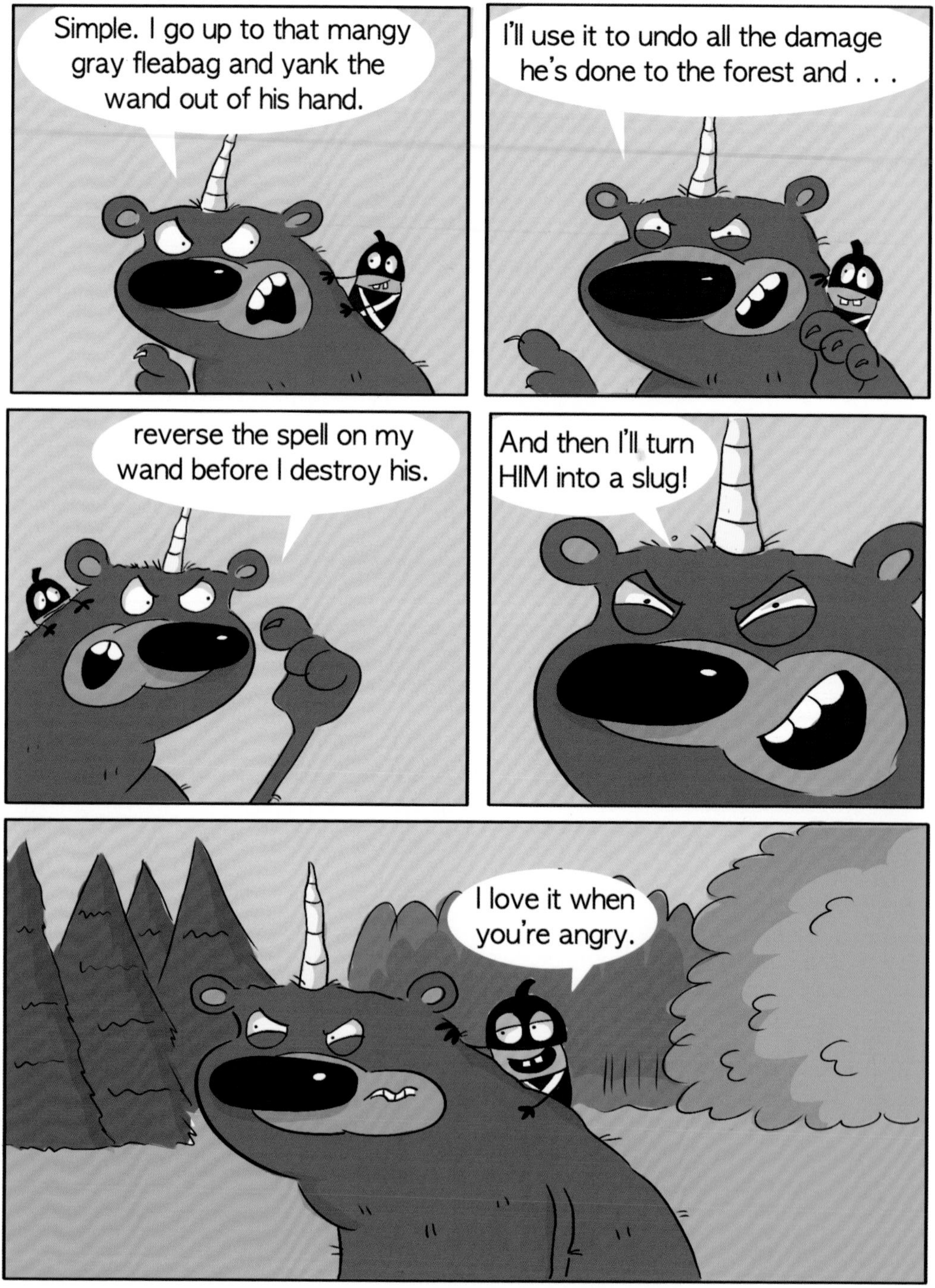
Simple. I go up to that mangy gray fleabag and yank the wand out of his hand.
I'll use it to undo all the damage he's done to the forest and . . .
reverse the spell on my wand before I destroy his.
And then I'll turn HIM into a slug!
I love it when you're angry.

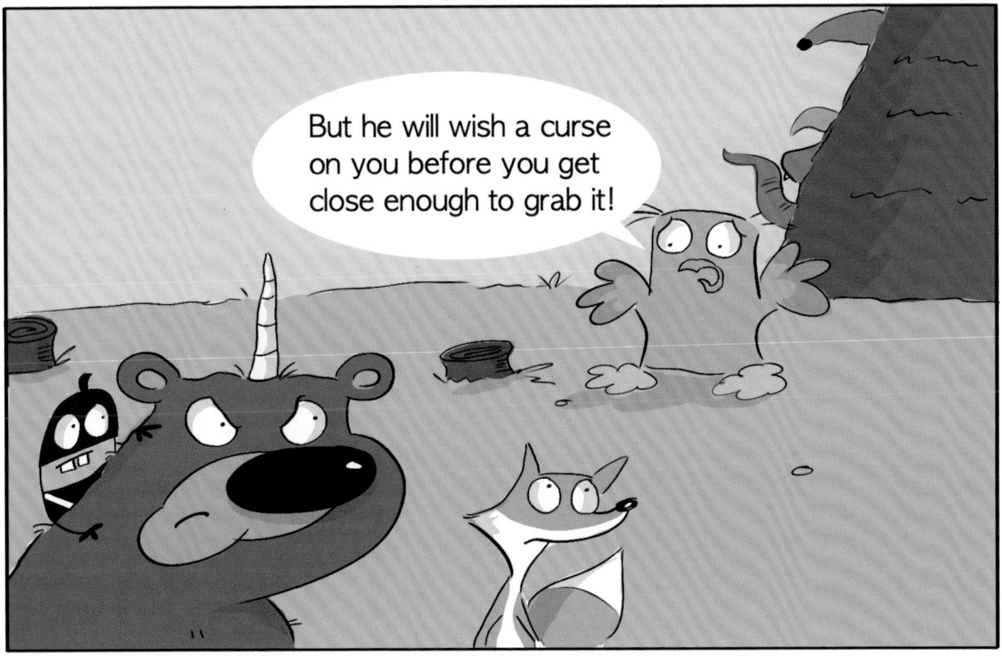
But he will wish a curse on you before you get close enough to grab it!

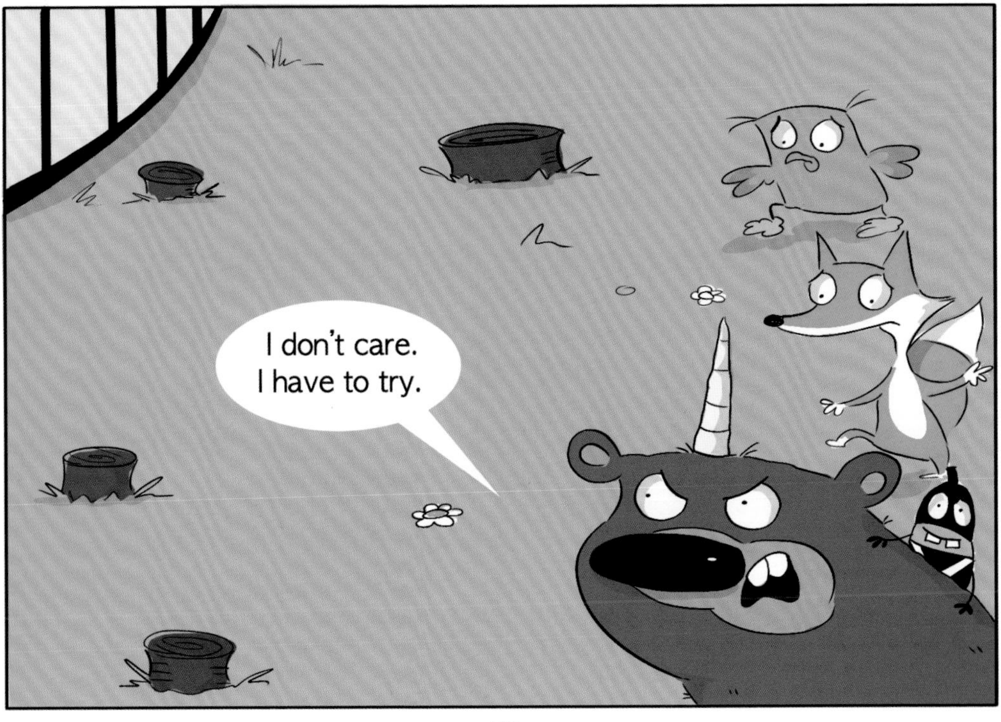
I don't care. I have to try.

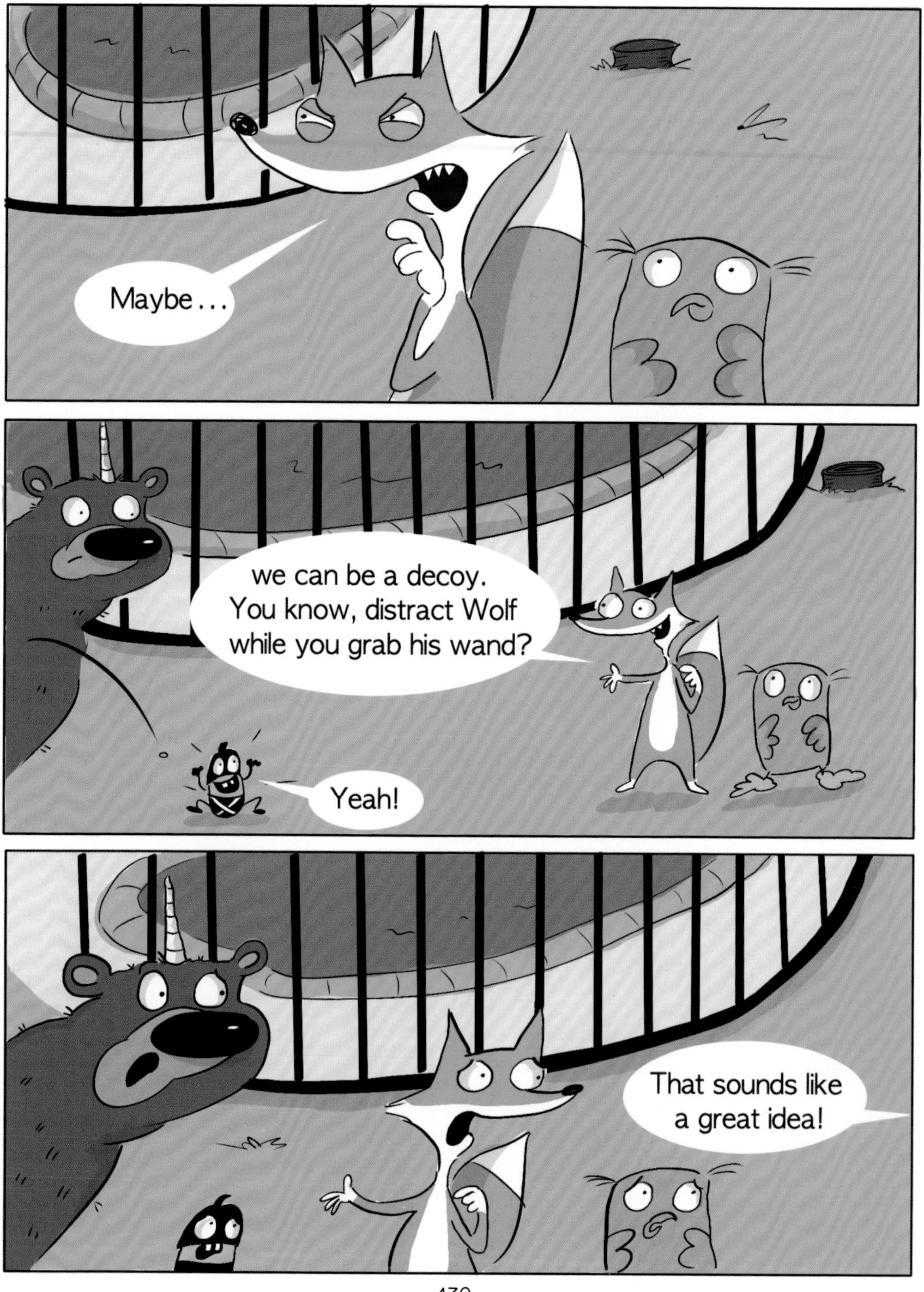
Maybe...
we can be a decoy. You know, distract Wolf while you grab his wand?
Yeah!
That sounds like a great idea!

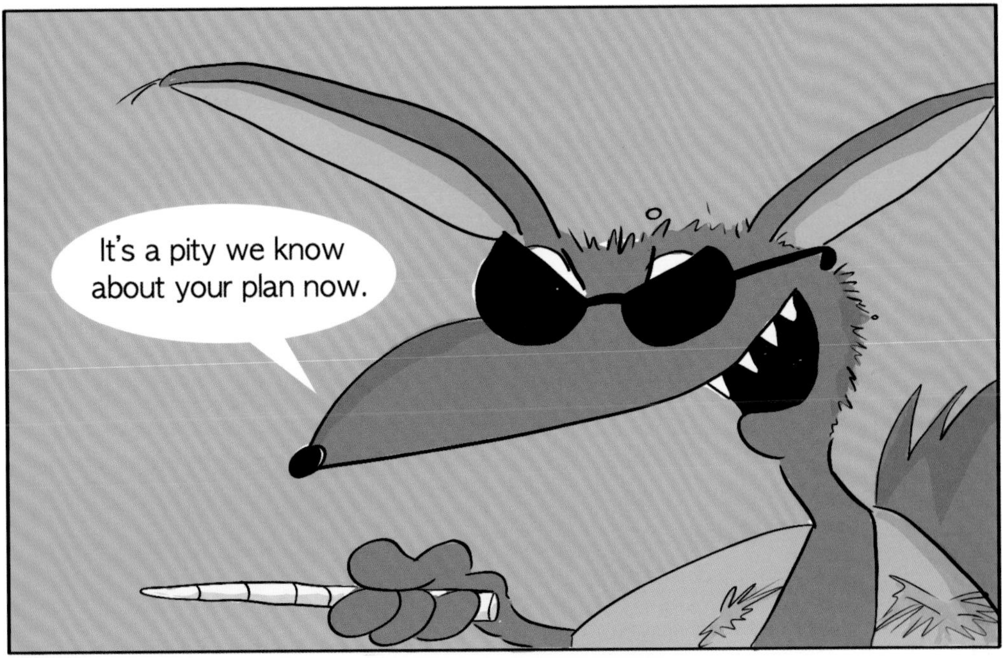
It's a pity we know about your plan now.

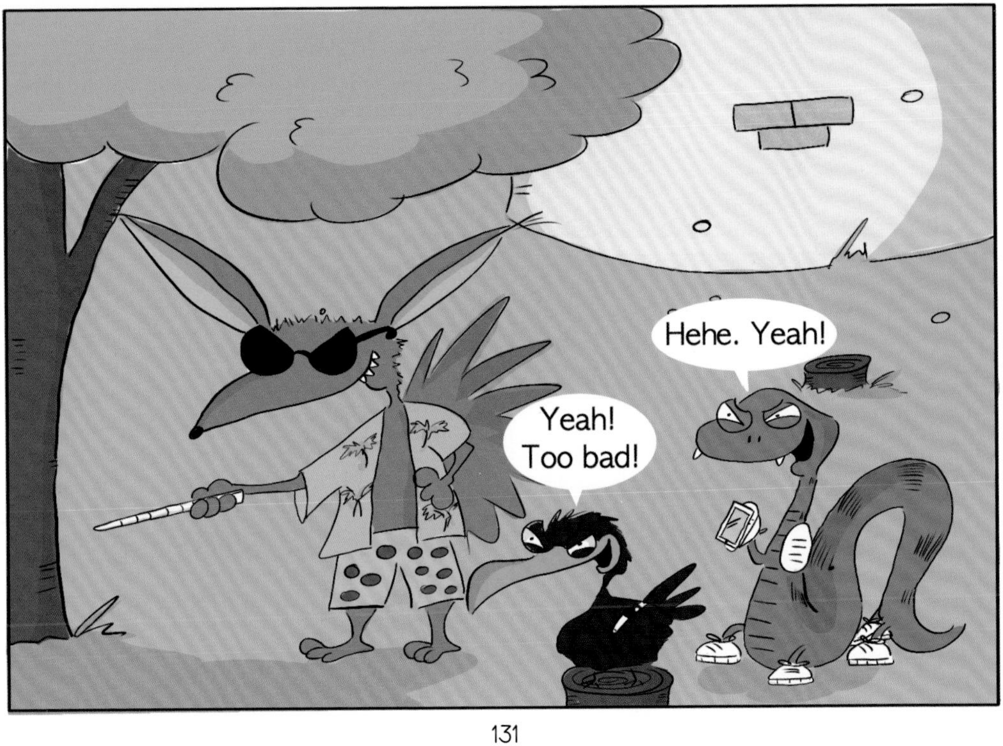
Yeah! Too bad!
Hehe. Yeah!

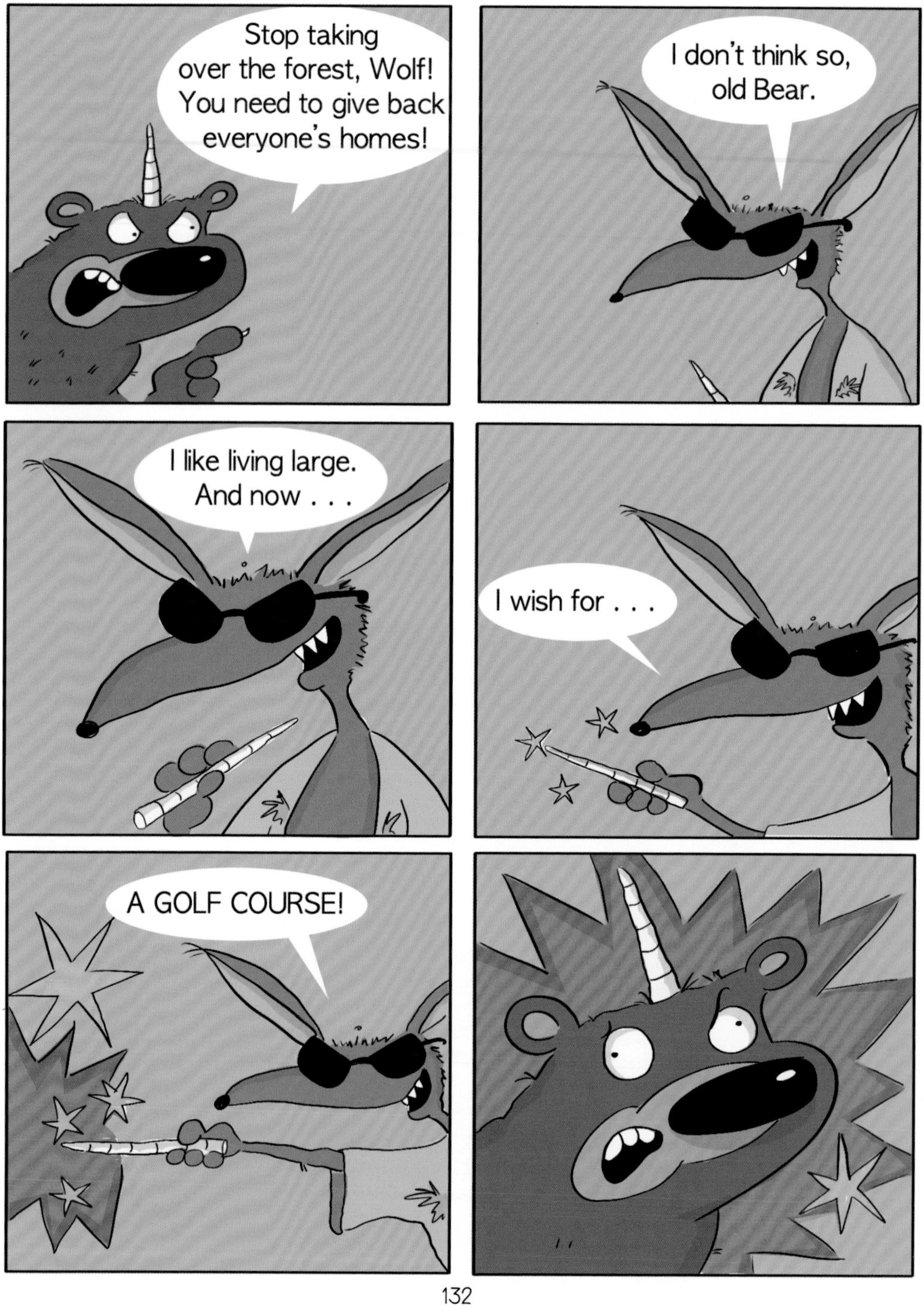
Stop taking over the forest, Wolf! You need to give back everyone's homes!
I don't think so, old Bear.
I like living large. And now . . .
I wish for . . .
A GOLF COURSE!

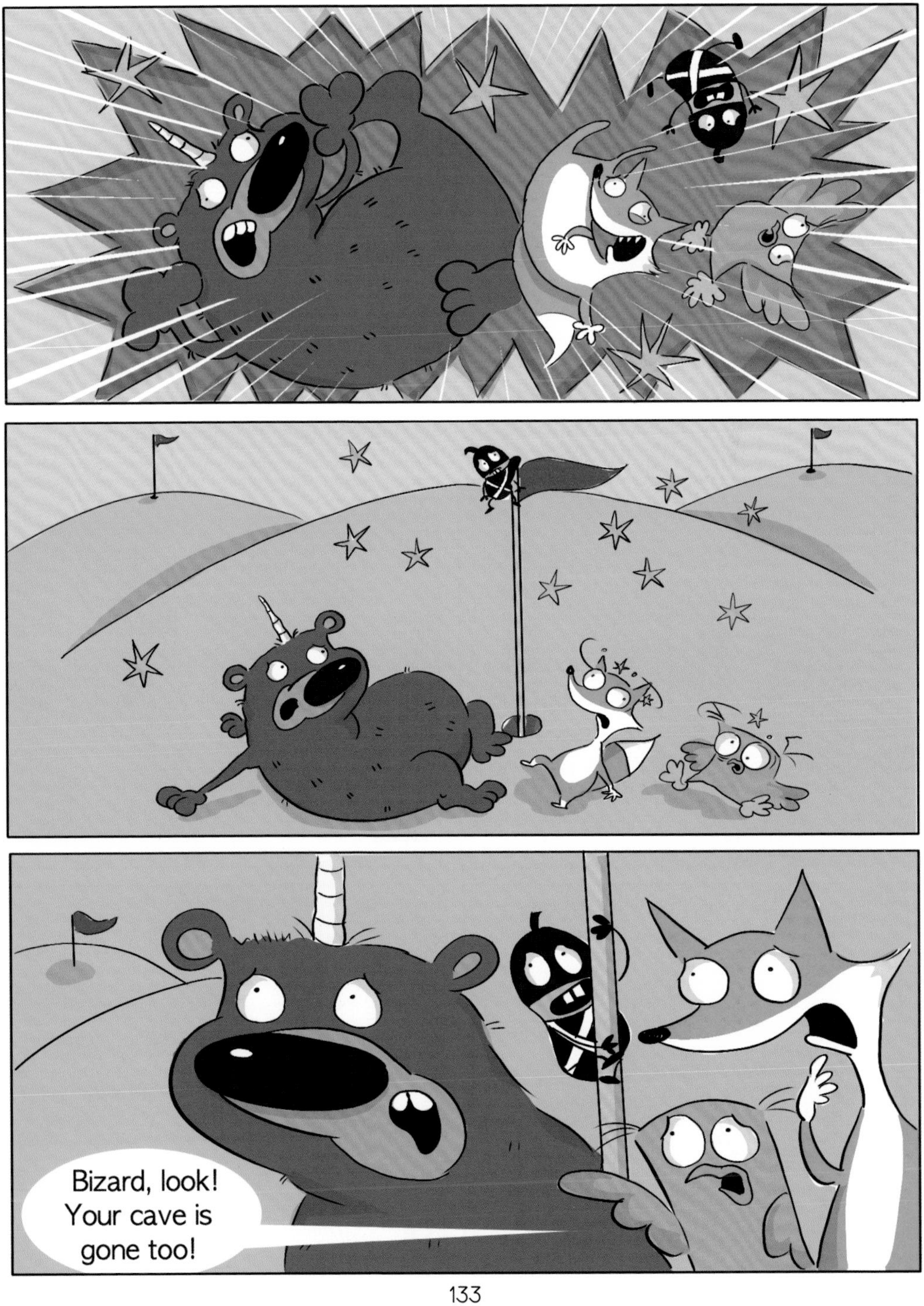
Bizard, look! Your cave is gone too!

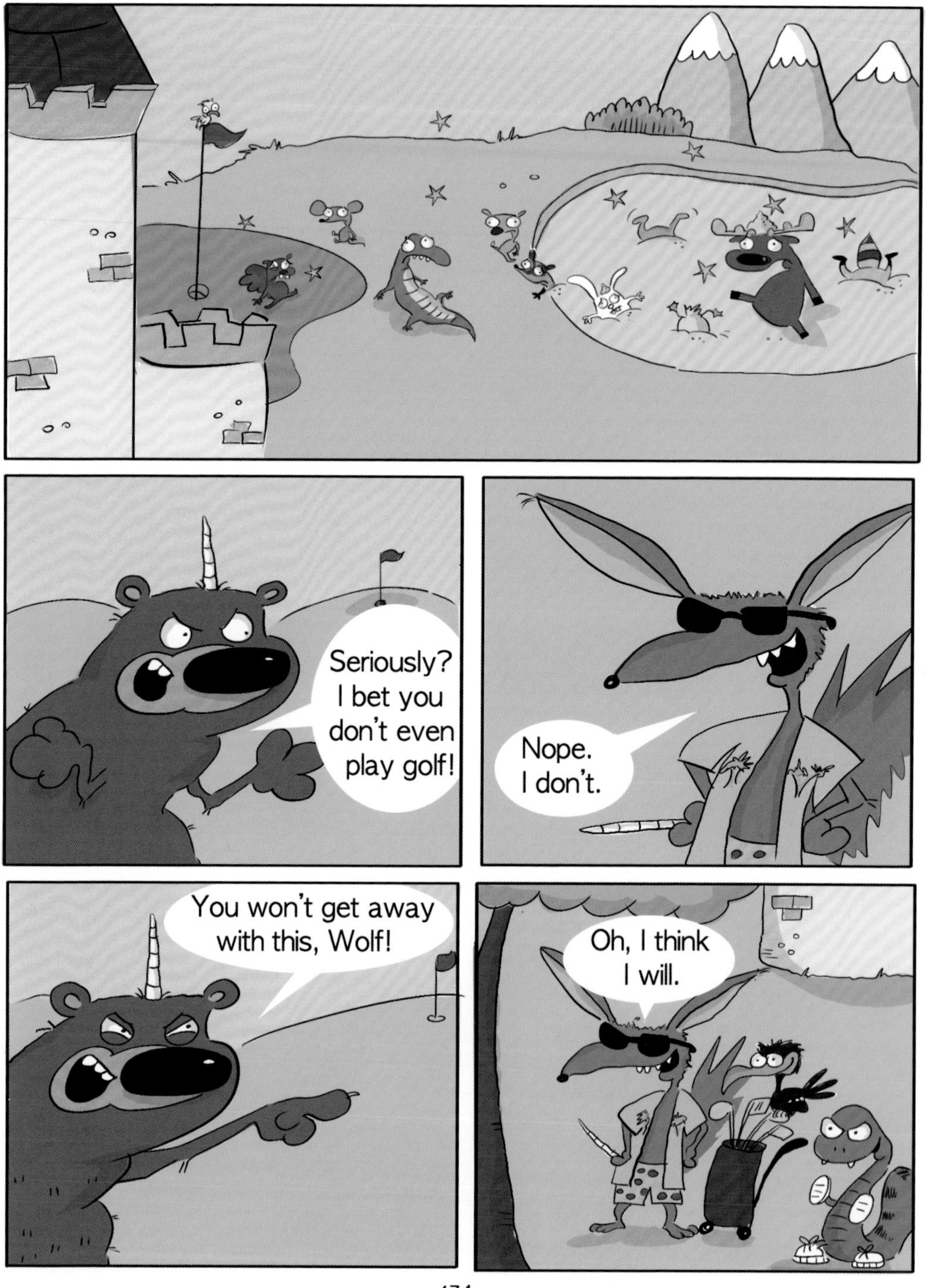
Seriously? I bet you don't even play golf!
Nope. I don't.
You won't get away with this, Wolf!
Oh, I think I will.

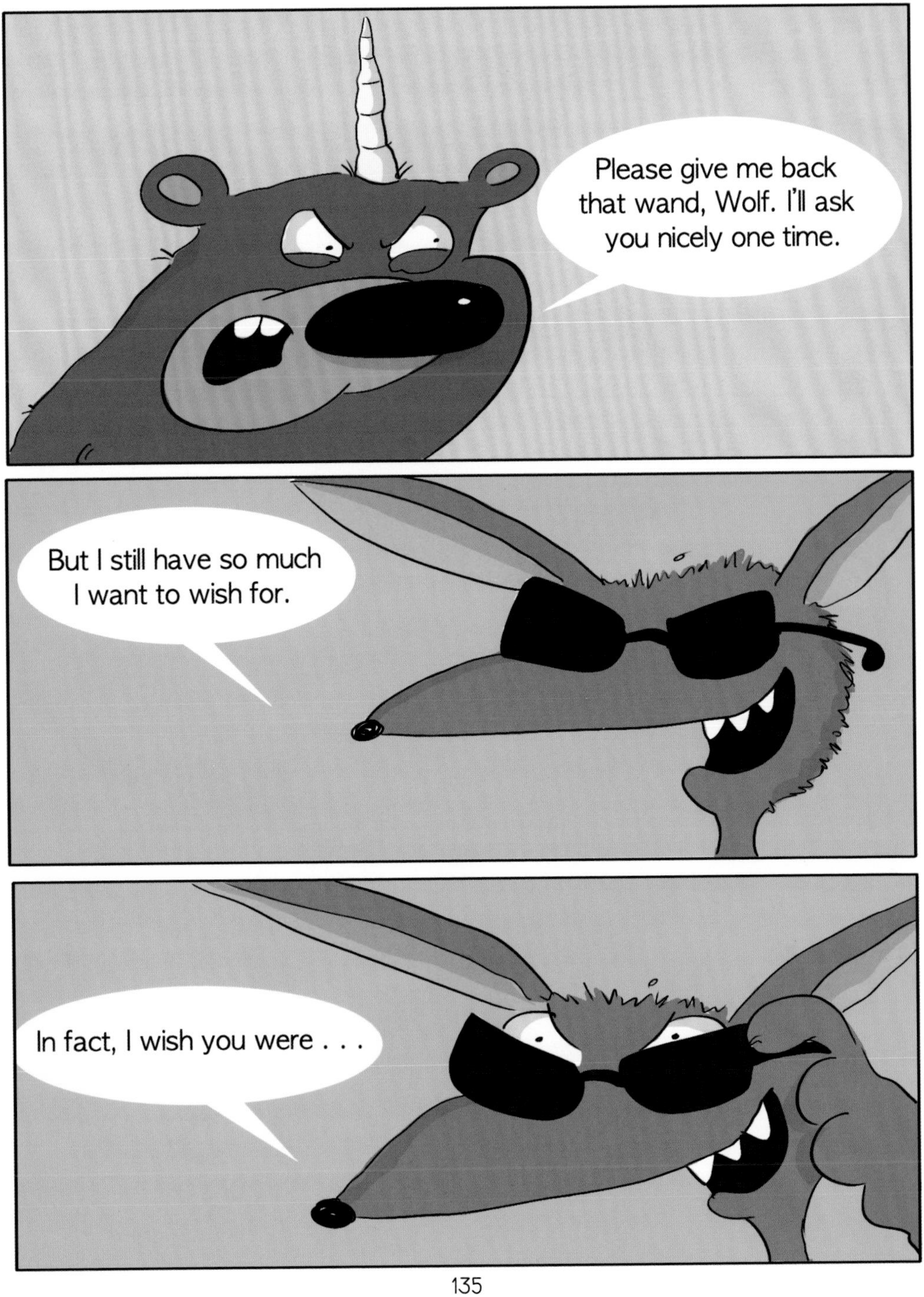
Please give me back that wand, Wolf. I'll ask you nicely one time.
But I still have so much I want to wish for.
In fact, I wish you were . . .

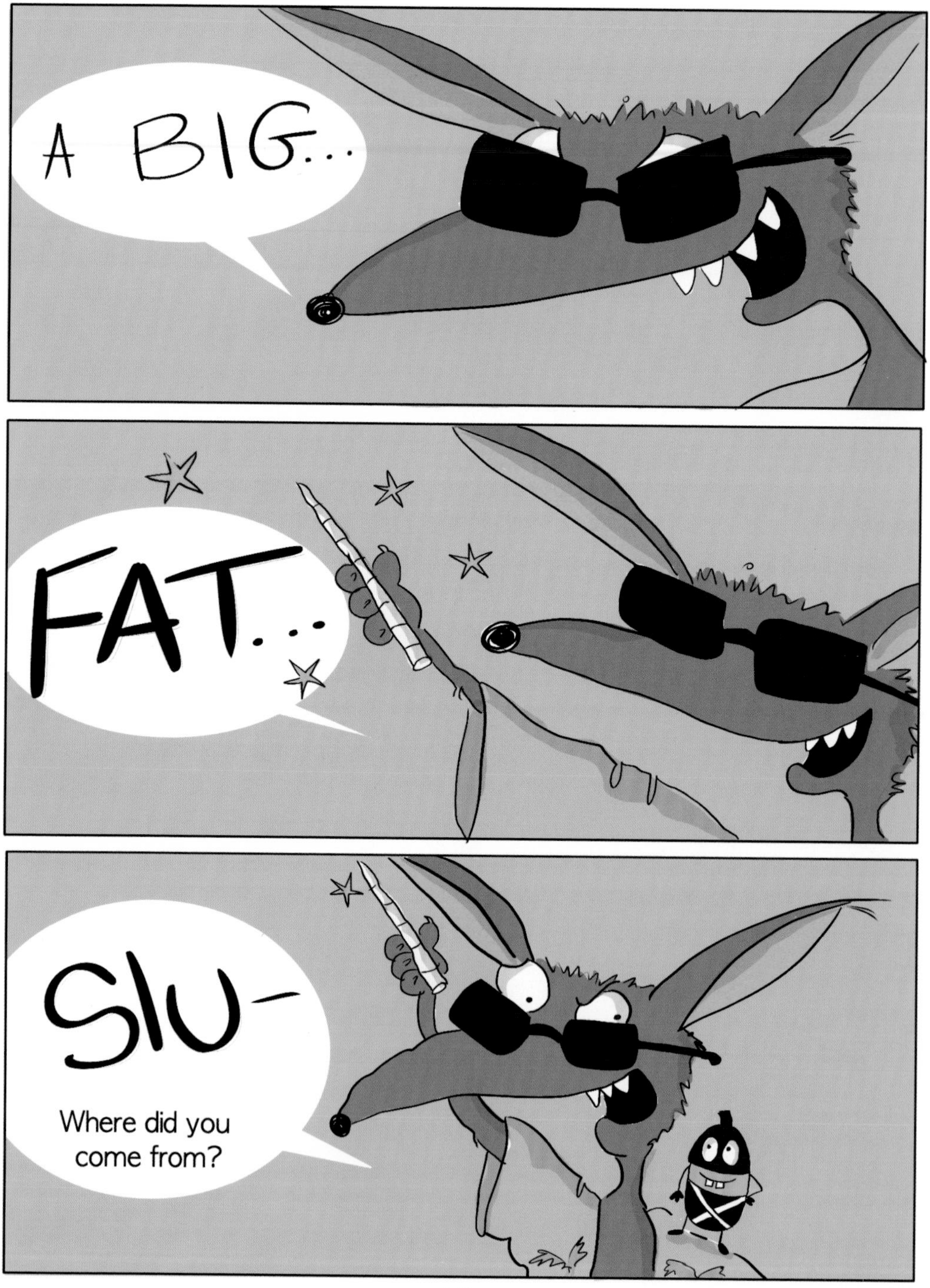
A BIG...
FAT...
Slu-
Where did you come from?

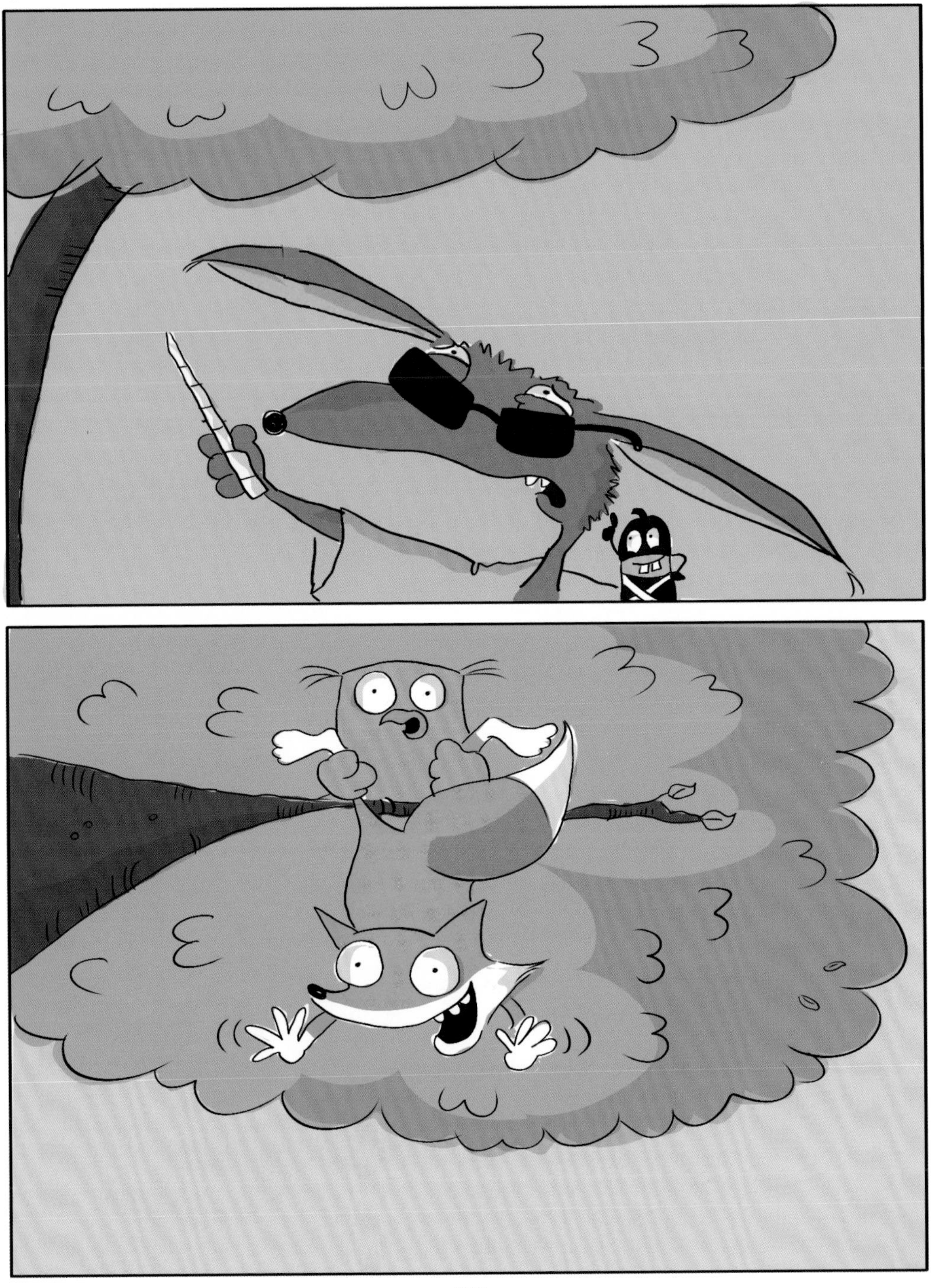

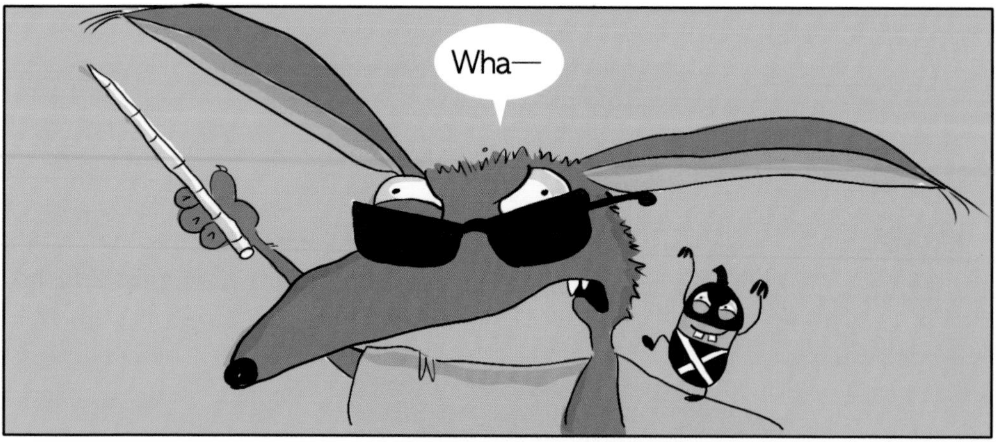
Wha—
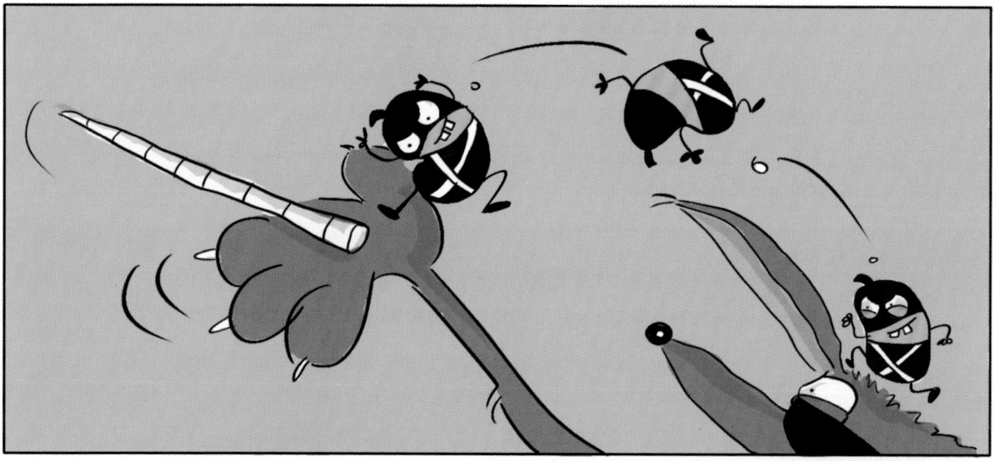
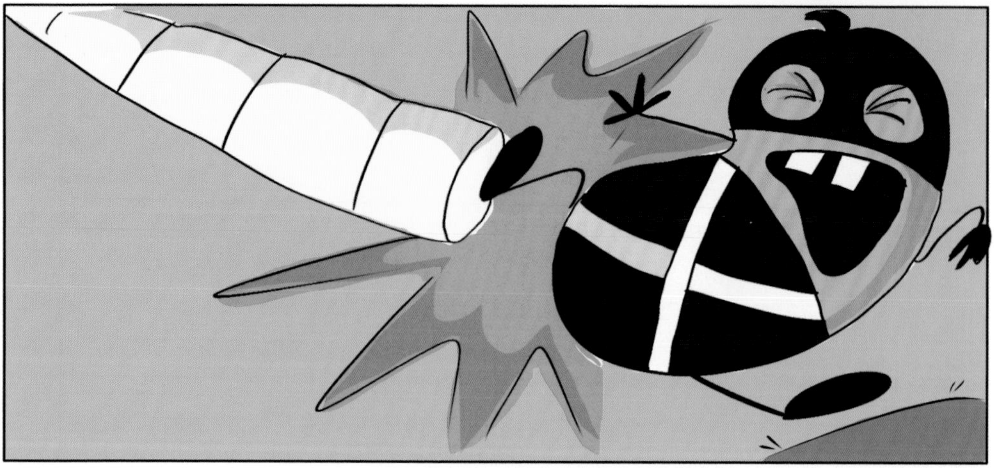

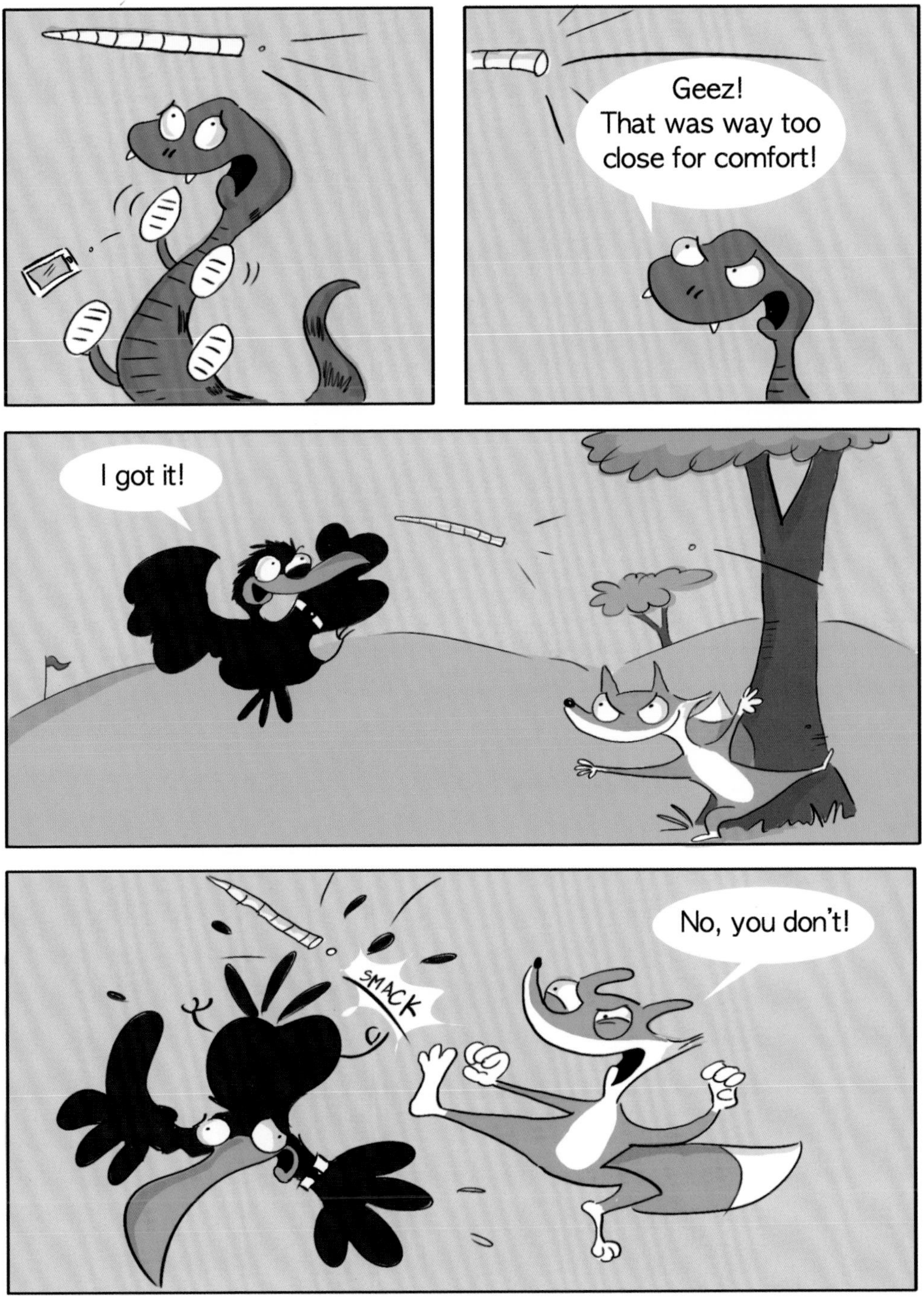
Geez!
That was way too close for comfort!
I got it!
No, you don't!
SMACK

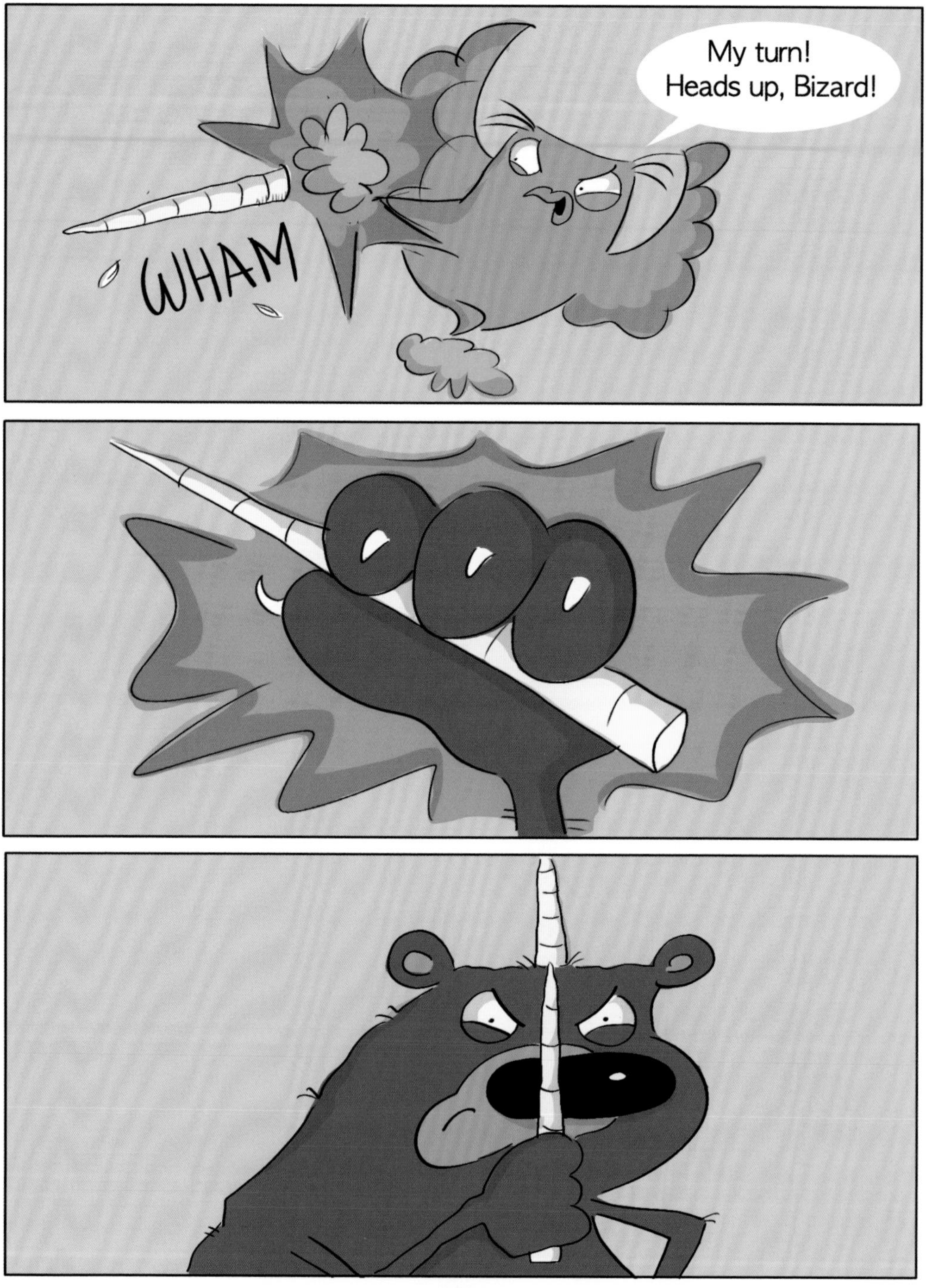
My turn!
Heads up, Bizard!
WHAM

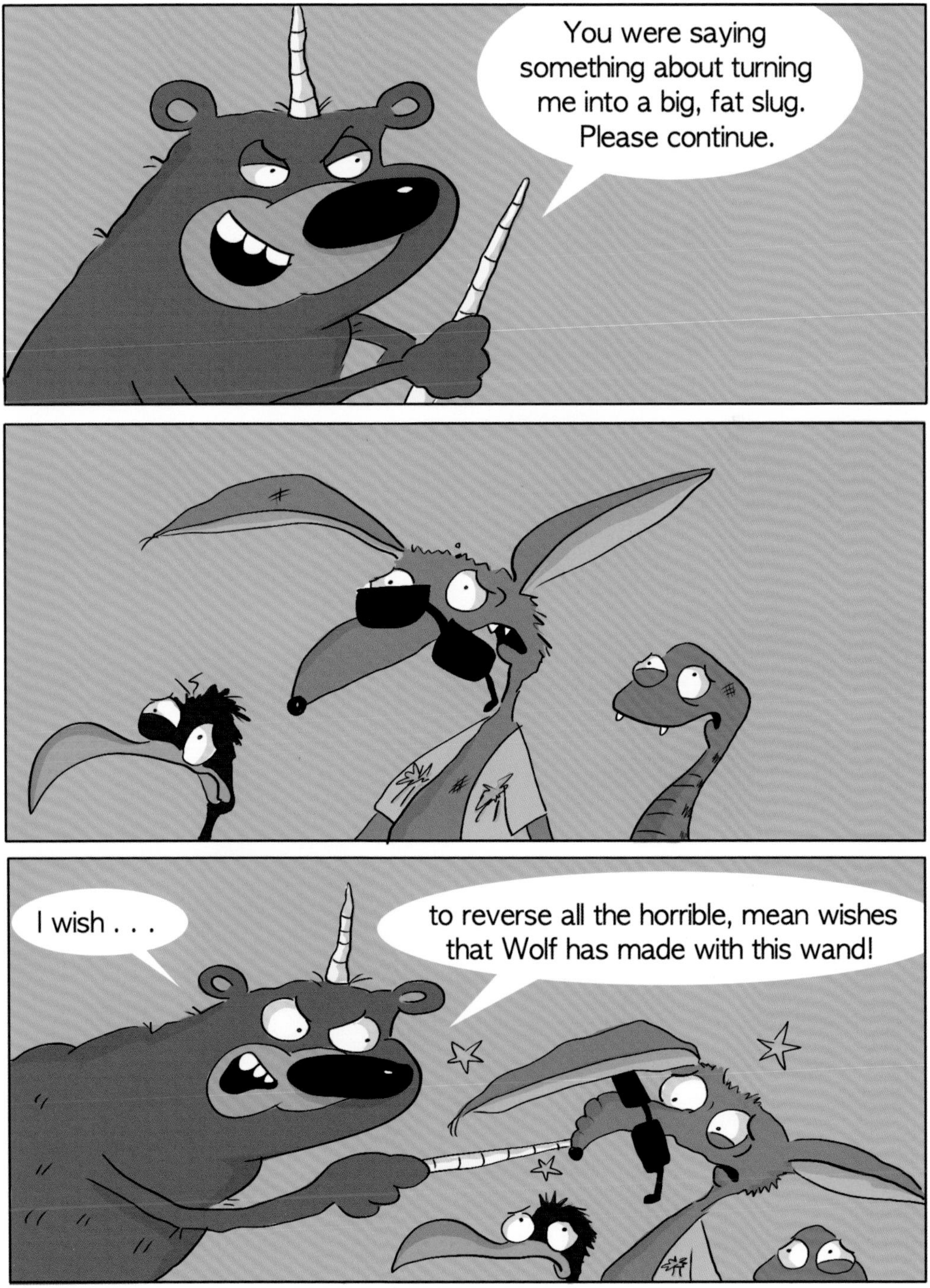
You were saying something about turning me into a big, fat slug. Please continue.
I wish . . .
to reverse all the horrible, mean wishes that Wolf has made with this wand!

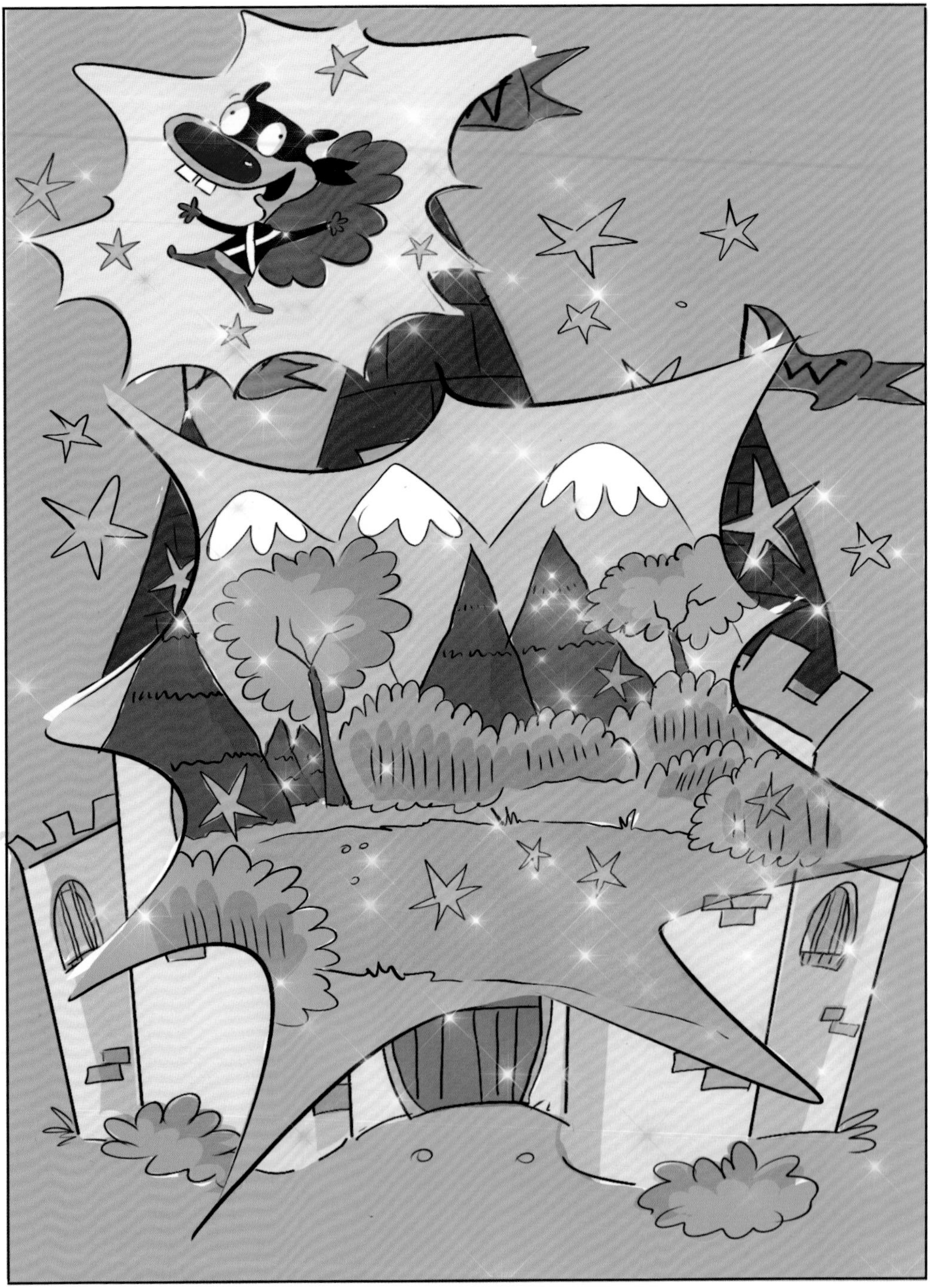

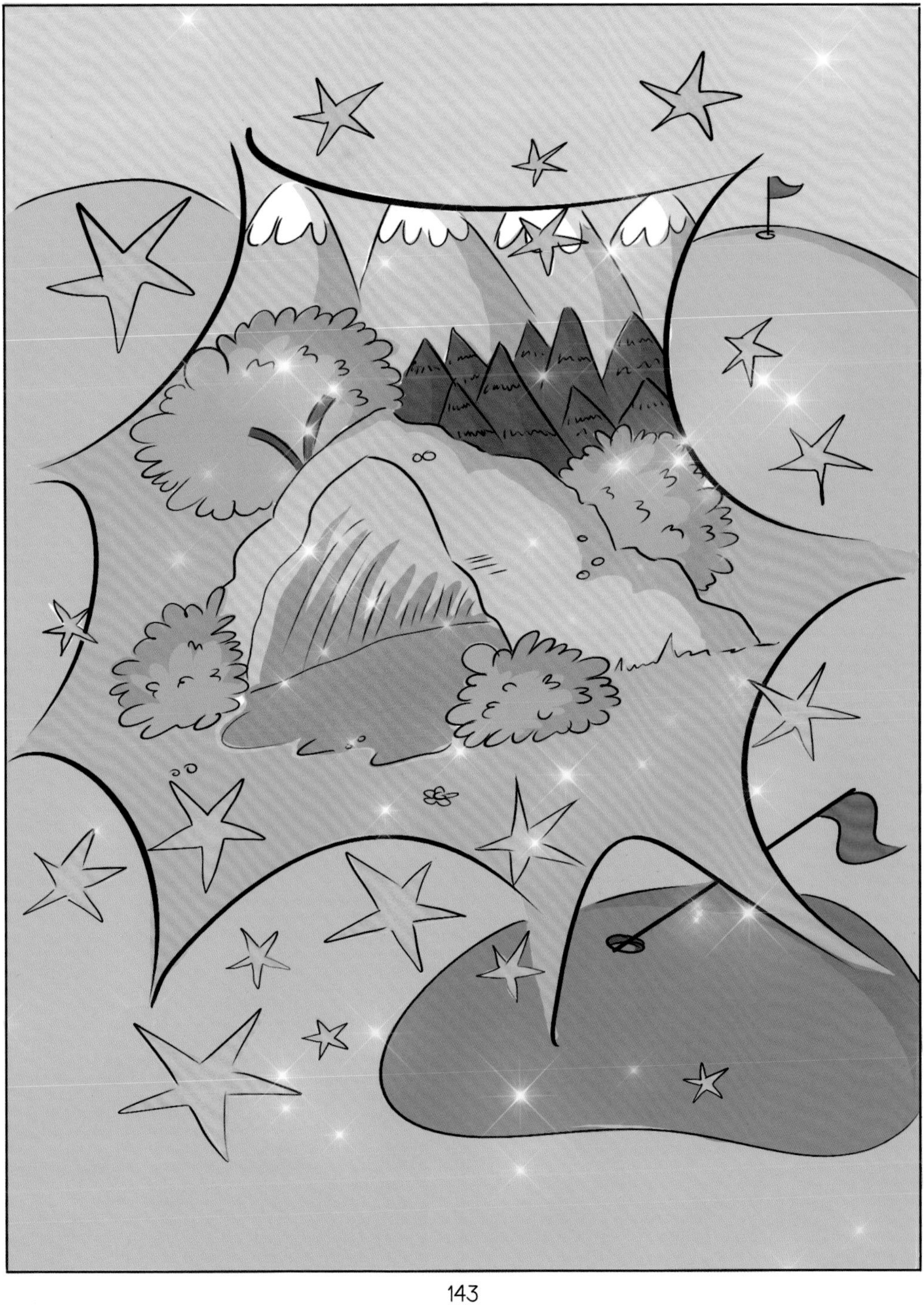

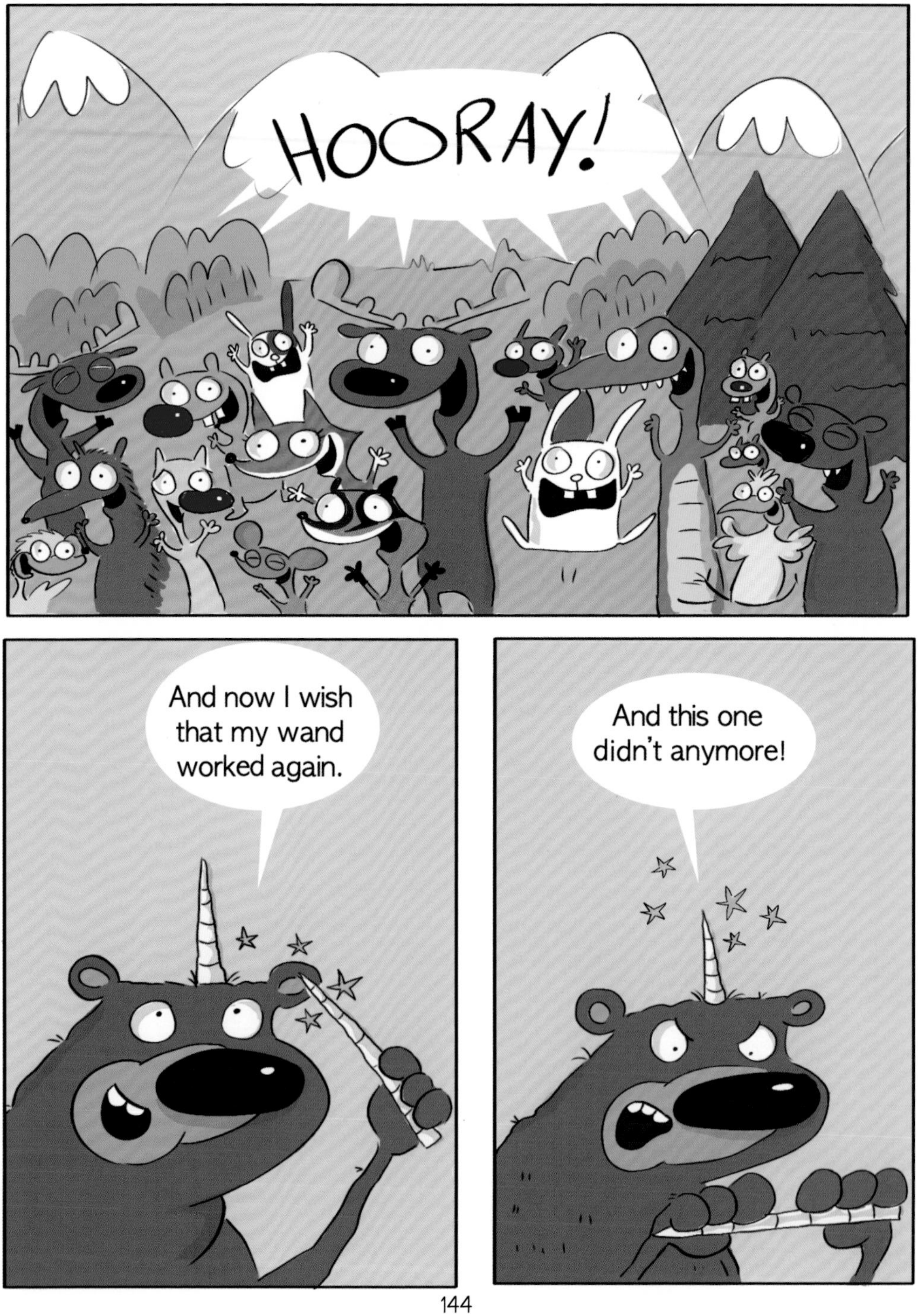
HOORAY!
And now I wish that my wand worked again.
And this one didn't anymore!

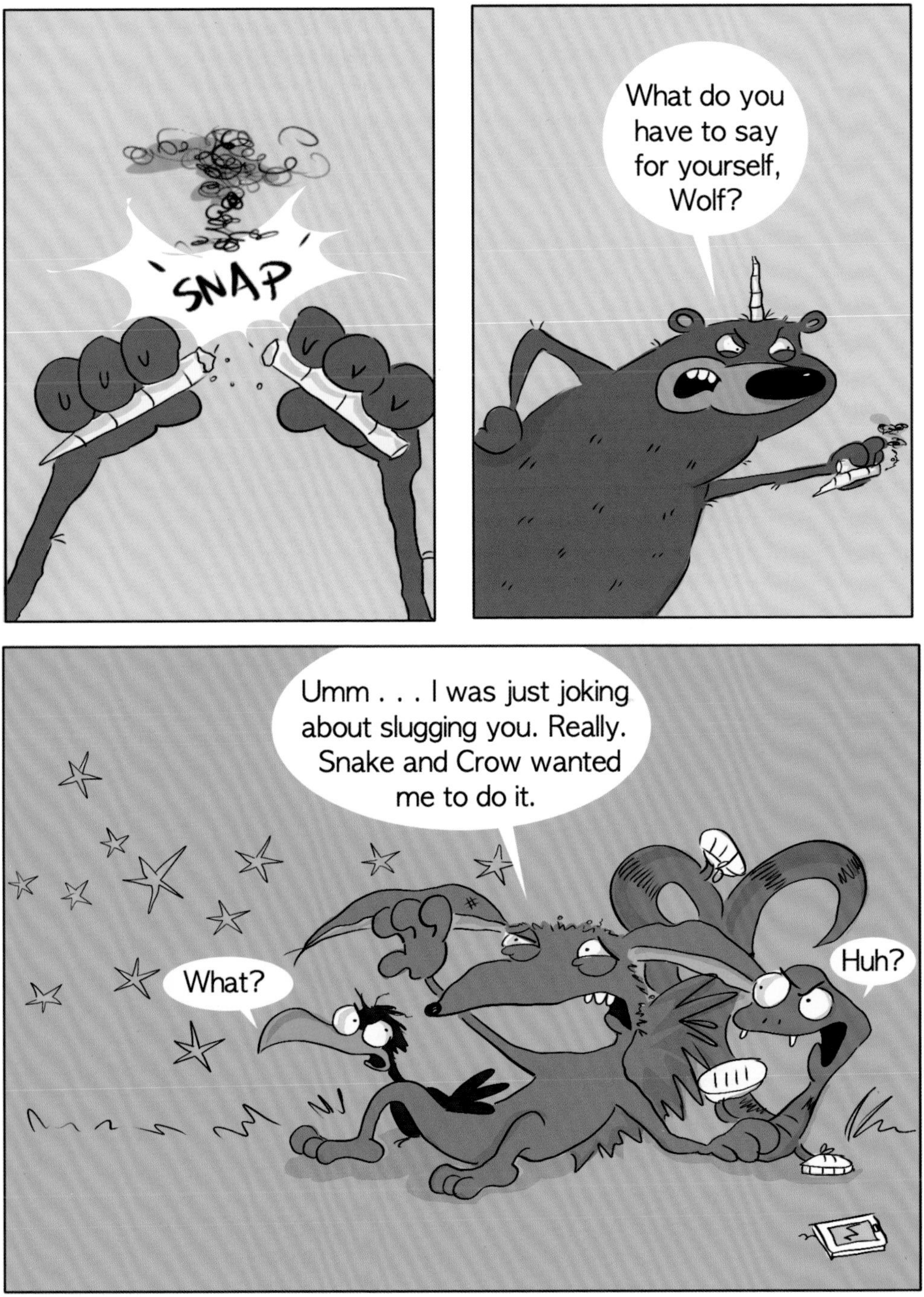
SNAP
What do you have to say for yourself, Wolf?
Umm . . . I was just joking about slugging you. Really. Snake and Crow wanted me to do it.
What?
Huh?

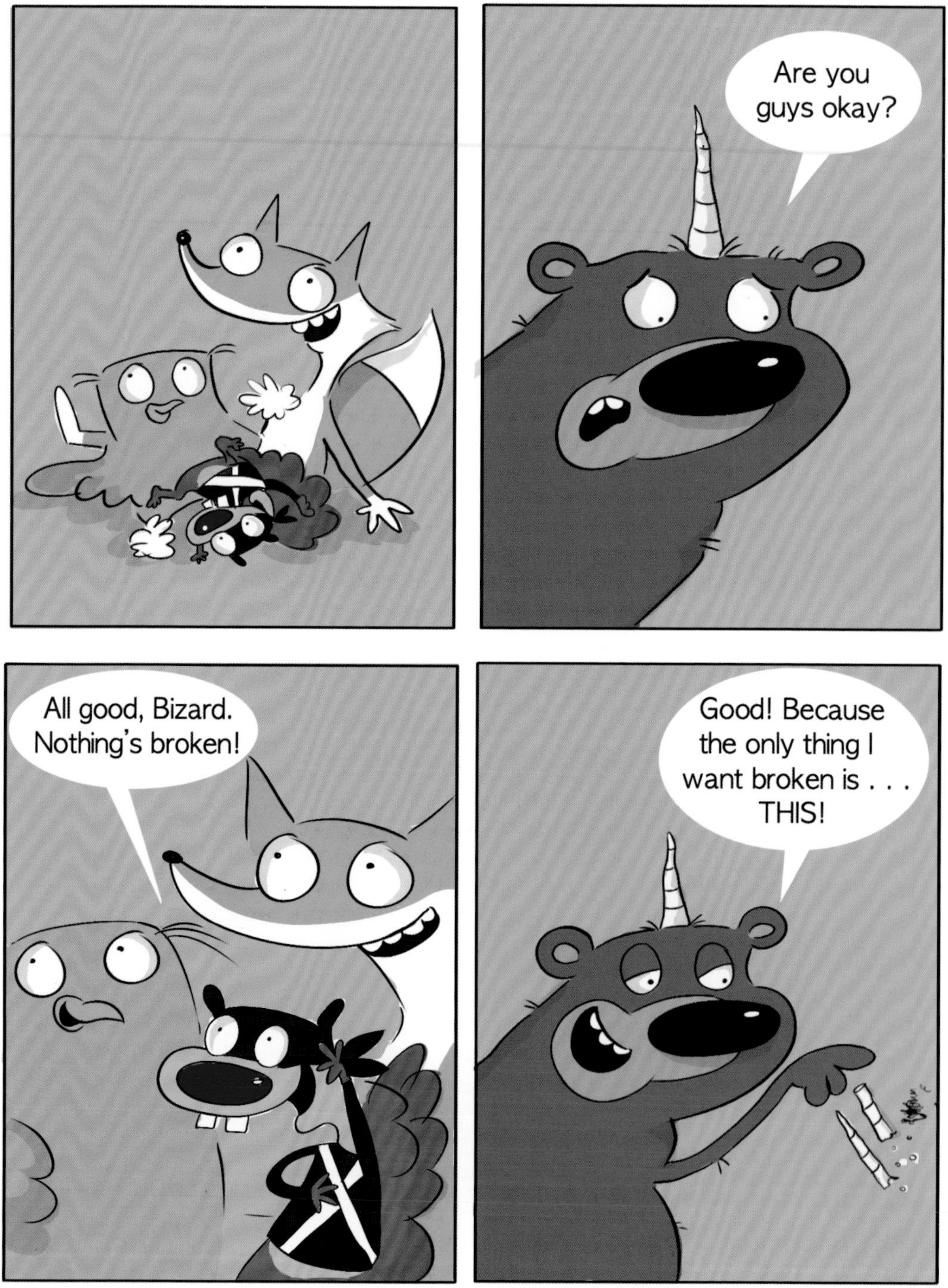
Are you guys okay?
All good, Bizard. Nothing's broken!
Good! Because the only thing I want broken is . . . THIS!

CHAPTER 14
TO SLUG ... OR NOT TO SLUG

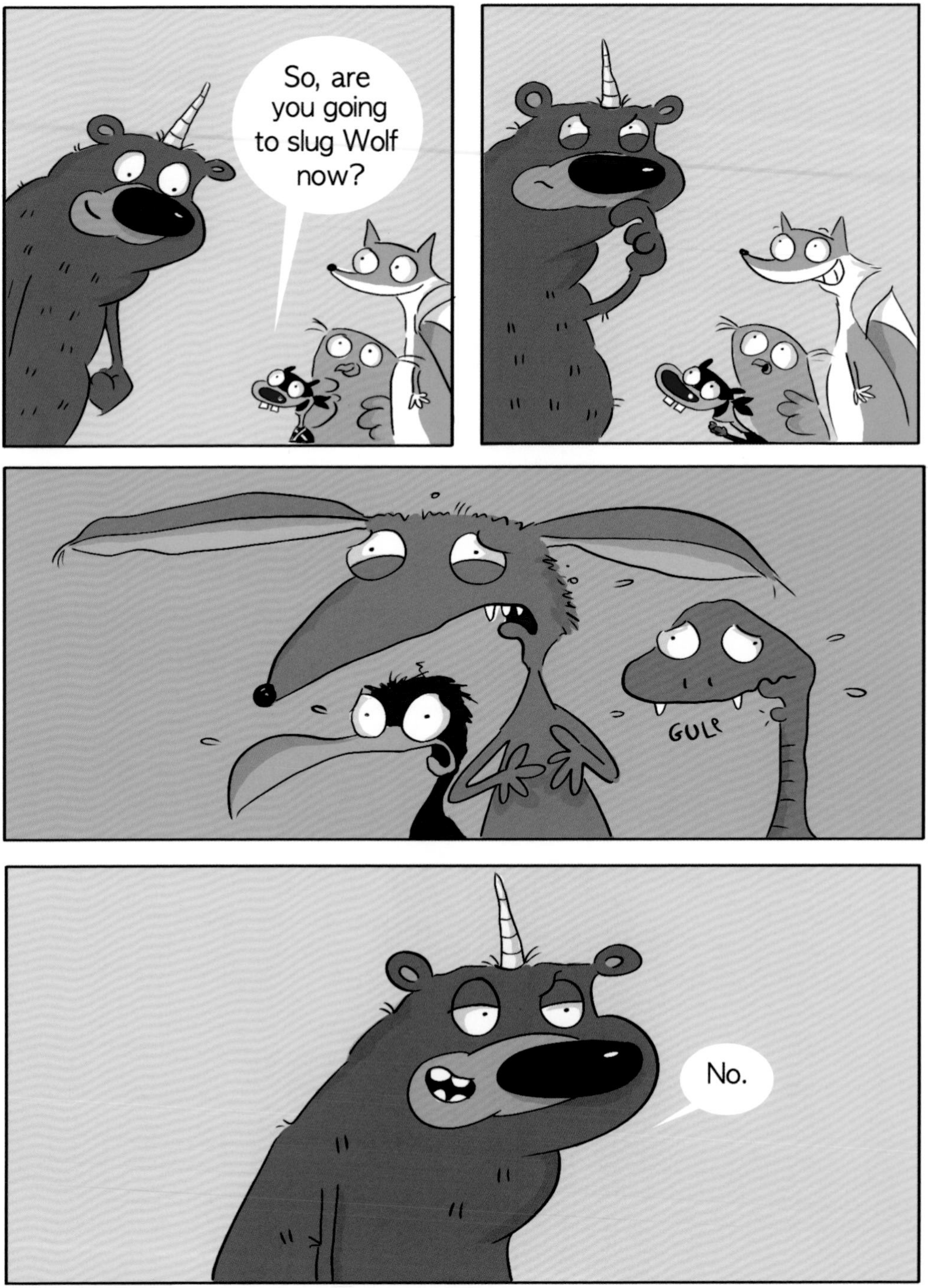
So, are you going to slug Wolf now?
GULP
No.

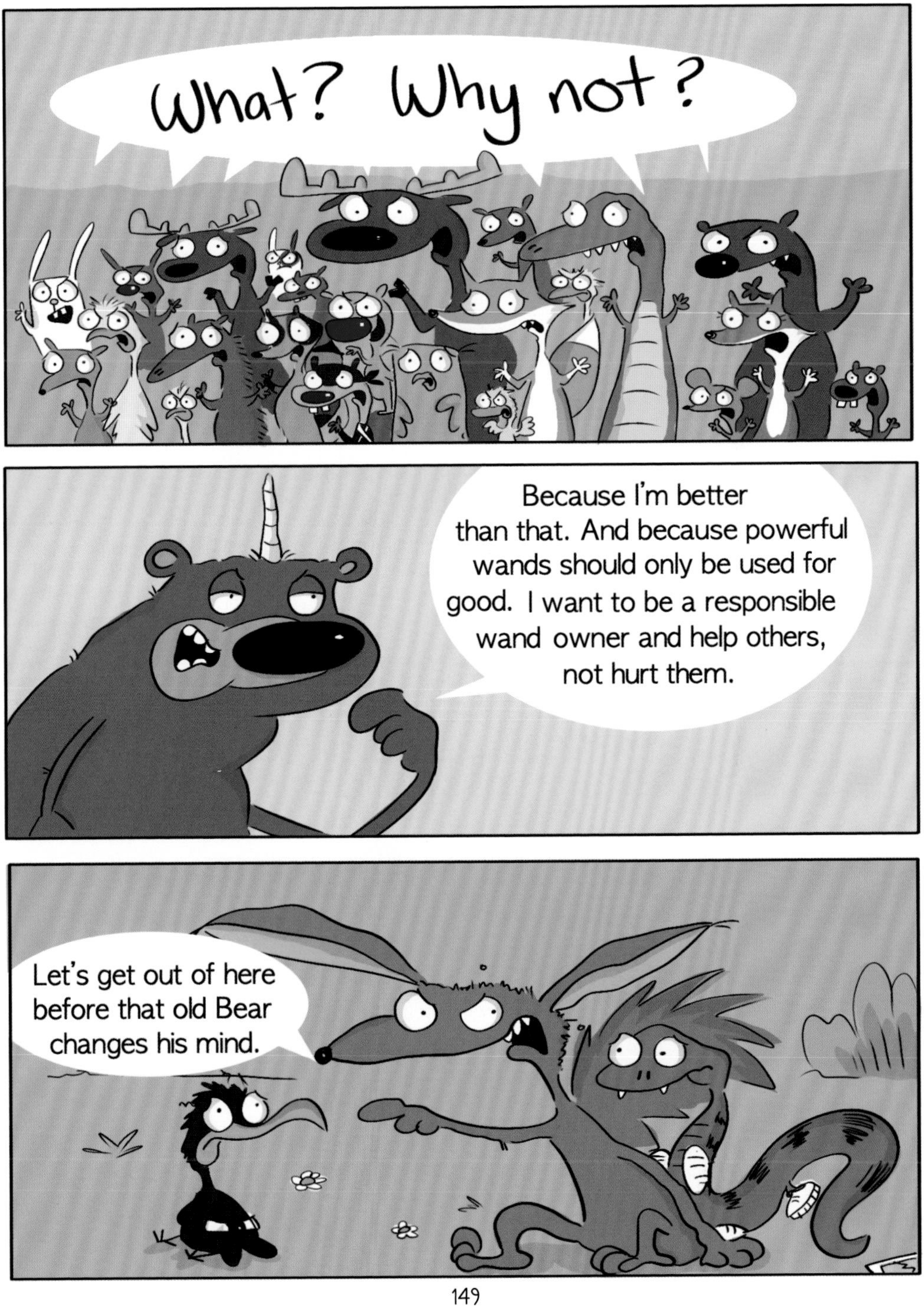
What? Why not?
Because I'm better than that. And because powerful wands should only be used for good. I want to be a responsible wand owner and help others, not hurt them.
Let's get out of here before that old Bear changes his mind.

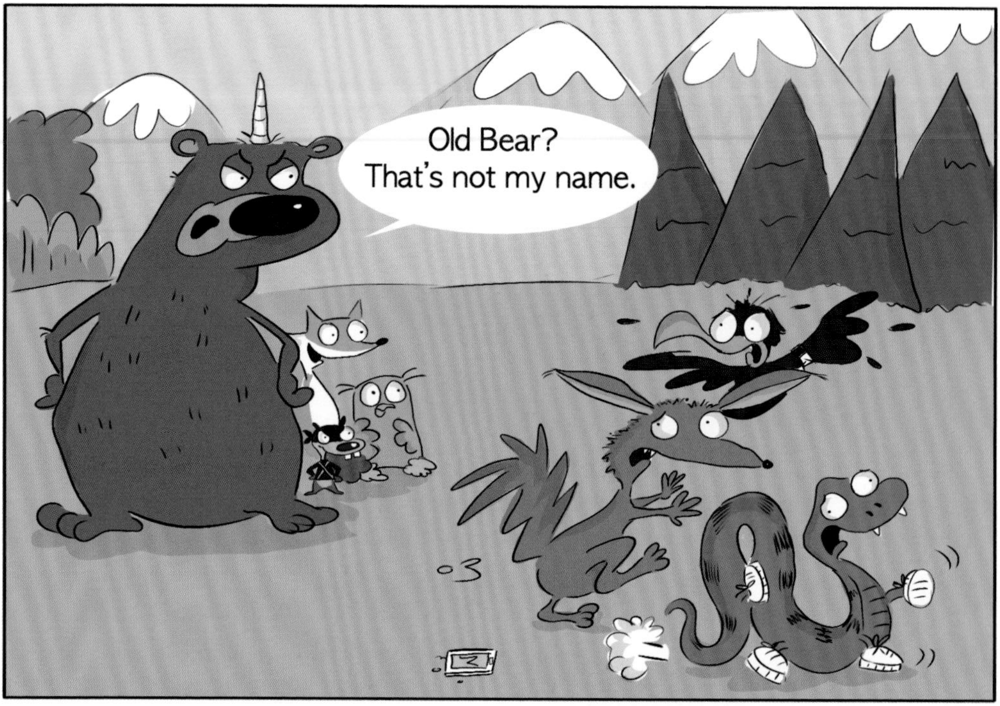
Old Bear? That's not my name.

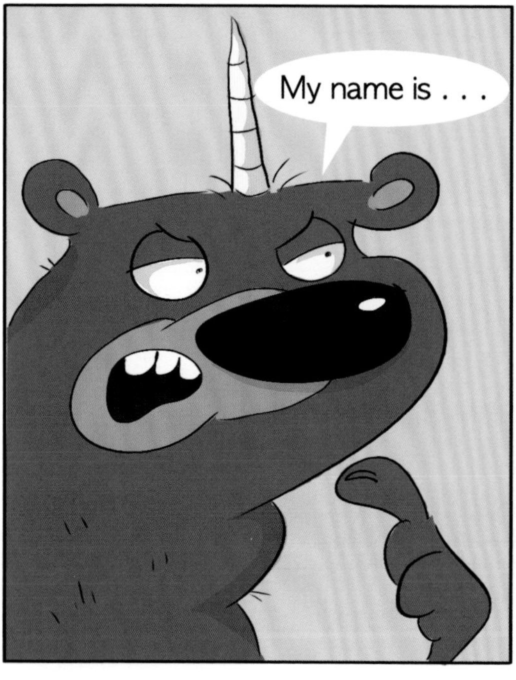
My name is . . .

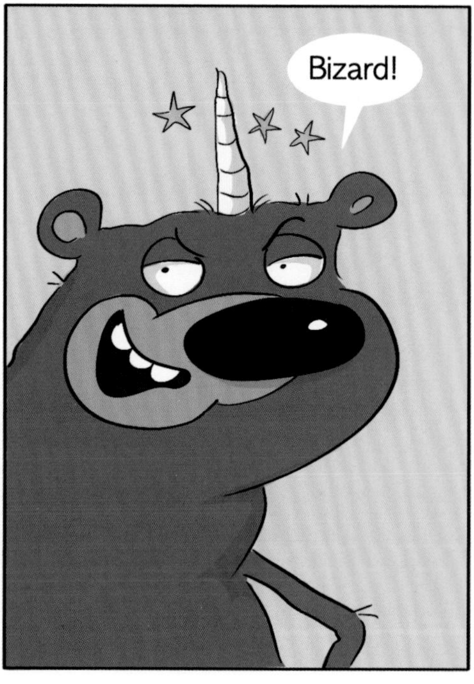
Bizard!

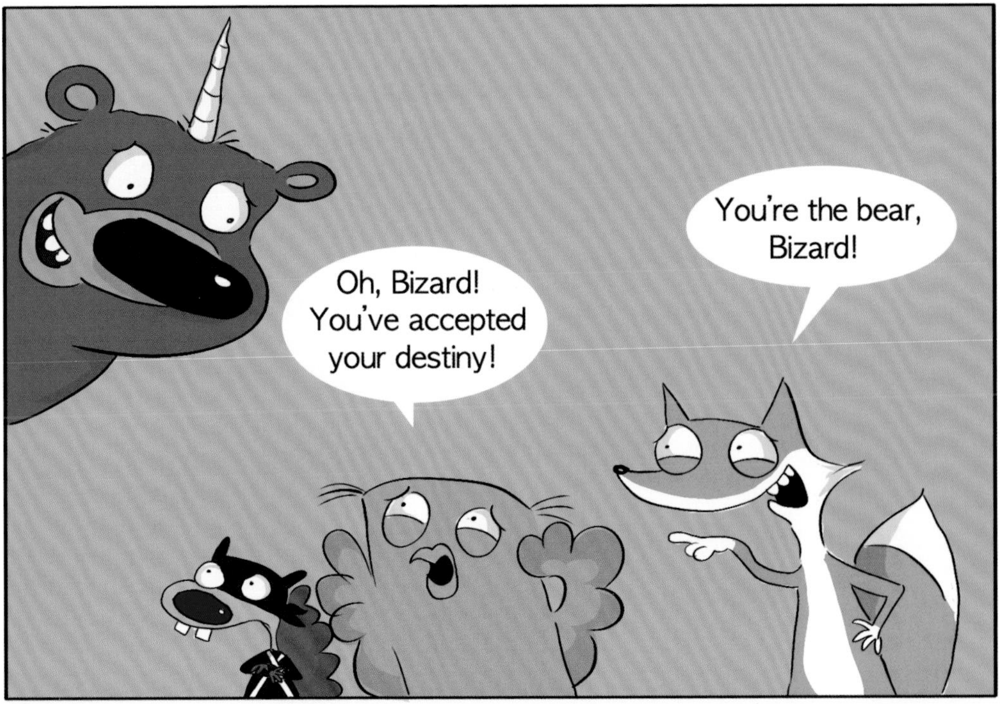
Oh, Bizard! You've accepted your destiny!
You're the bear, Bizard!

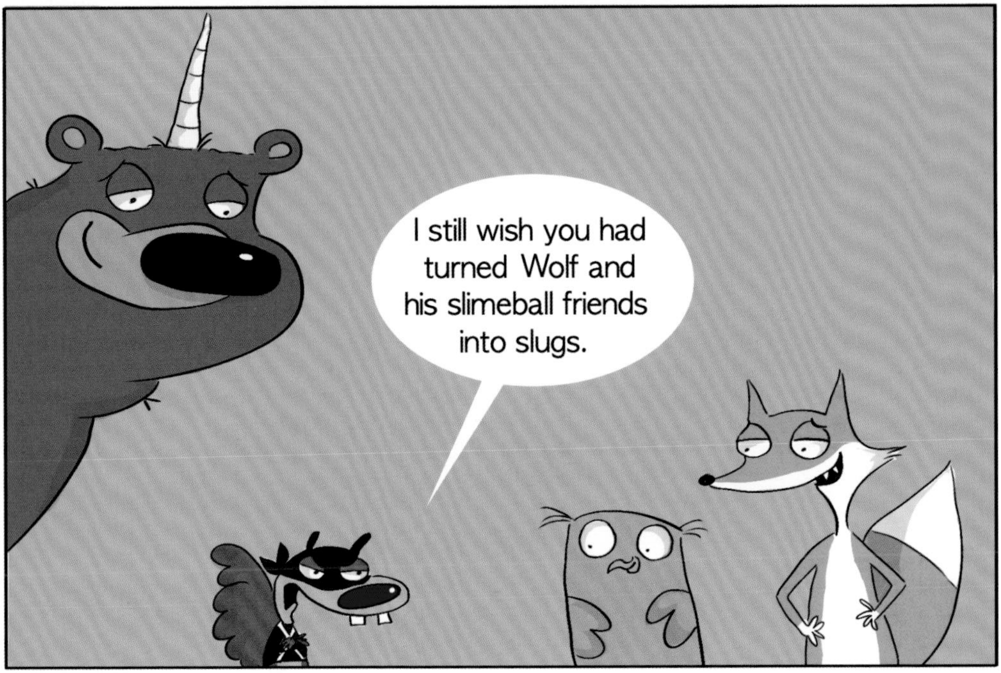
I still wish you had turned Wolf and his slimeball friends into slugs.

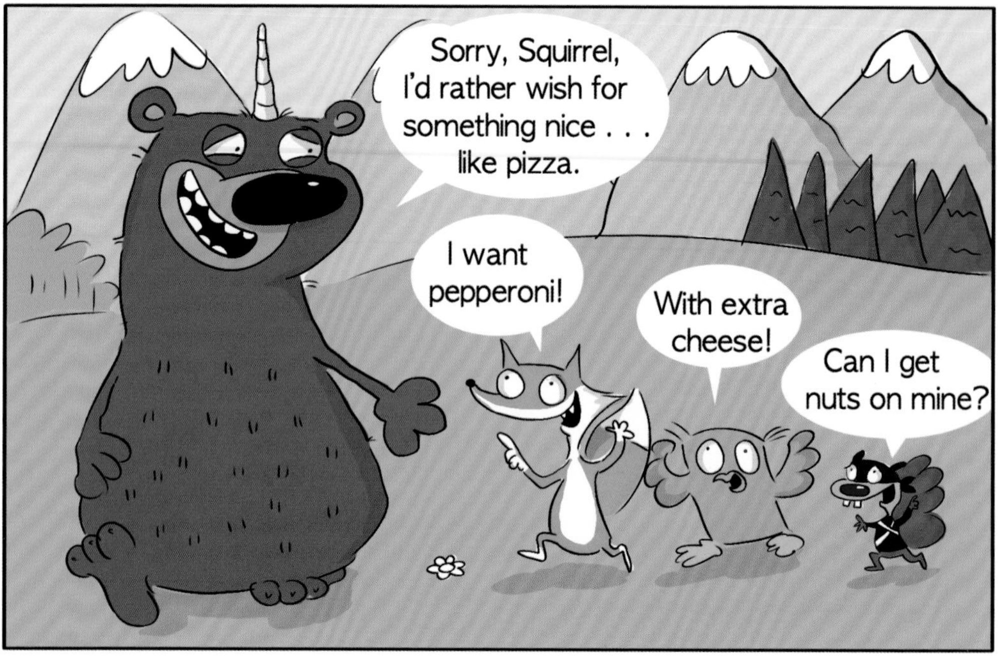
Sorry, Squirrel, I'd rather wish for something nice . . . like pizza.
I want pepperoni!
With extra cheese!
Can I get nuts on mine?

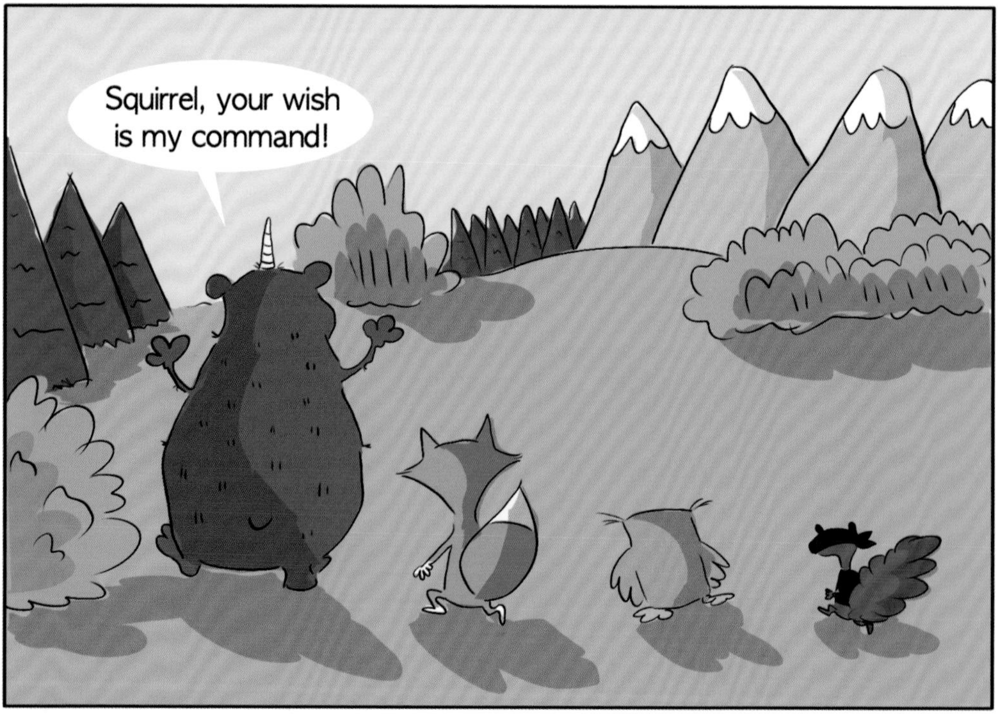
Squirrel, your wish is my command!

DON'T MISS

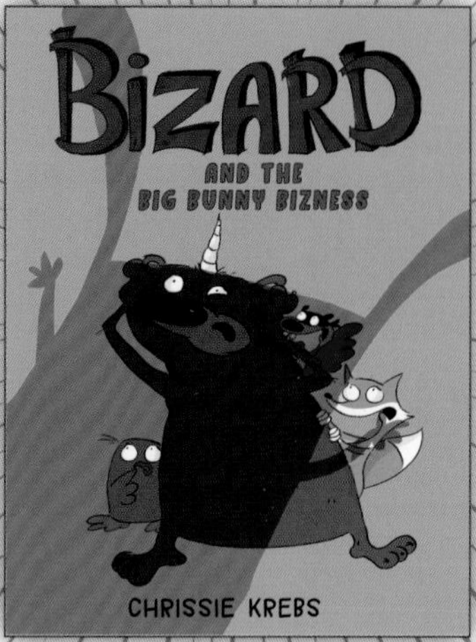
BiZARD
AND THE
BIG BUNNY BIZNESS
CHRISSIE KREBS